SHADOW COMMAND

SHADOW COMMAND

DALE BROWN

wm

WILLIAM MORROW

An Imprint of HarperCollins*Publishers*

SHADOW COMMAND. Copyright © 2008 by Air Battle Force, Inc. All rights reserved. Printed in the United States of America. No part of this book may be used or reproduced in any manner whatsoever without written permission except in the case of brief quotations embodied in critical articles and reviews. For information address HarperCollins Publishers, 10 East 53rd Street, New York, NY 10022.

HarperCollins books may be purchased for educational, business, or sales promotional use. For information please write: Special Markets Department, HarperCollins Publishers, 10 East 53rd Street, New York, NY 10022.

FIRST EDITION

Designed by Renato Stanisic

Library of Congress Cataloging-in-Publication Data has been applied for.

ISBN 978-0-06-117311-0

08 09 10 11 12 WBC/RRD 10 9 8 7 6 5 4 3 2 1

This novel is dedicated to all who make the often difficult decision to do one simple thing: Go For It. When you see it happen, it's more exhilarating than a space launch, and twice as powerful.

CAST OF CHARACTERS

AMERICANS:

JOSEPH GARDNER, President of the United States

KEN T. PHOENIX, Vice President

CONRAD F. CARLYLE, President's National Security Adviser

MILLER H. TURNER, Secretary of Defense

GERALD VISTA, Director of National Intelligence

WALTER KORDUS, White House Chief of Staff

STACY ANNE BARBEAU, senior U.S. senator from Louisiana, Senate majority leader; Colleen Morna, her aide

GENERAL TAYLOR J. BAIN, USMC, chairman of the Joint Chiefs of Staff

GENERAL CHARLES A. HUFFMAN, Air Force chief of staff

AIR FORCE GENERAL BRADFORD CANNON, commander of U.S. Strategic Command (STRATCOM)

ARMY GENERAL KENNETH LEPERS, commander of U.S. Central Command (CENTCOM)

MAJOR GENERAL HAROLD BACKMAN, commander of the Fourteenth Air Force; also commander of Joint Functional Component Command-Space (JFCC-S) of U.S. Strategic Command

LIEUTENANT GENERAL PATRICK McLANAHAN, commander of the High-Technology Aerospace Weapons Center (HAWC), Elliott AFB, Nevada

BRIGADIER GENERAL DAVID LUGER, deputy commander of HAWC

COLONEL MARTIN TEHAMA, incoming commander of HAWC

MAJOR GENERAL REBECCA FURNESS, commander of the First Air Battle Force (air operations), Battle Mountain Air Reserve Base (ARB), Nevada

BRIGADIER GENERAL DAREN MACE, Air Battle Force operations officer, 111th Bomb Wing commander, and EB-1C mission commander

MAJOR WAYNE MACOMBER, deputy commander (ground operations) of the First Air Battle Force, Battle Mountain Air Reserve Base, Nevada

MARINE CORPS MASTER SERGEANT CHRIS WOHL, NCOIC, First Air Battle Force

U.S. ARMY NATIONAL GUARD CAPTAIN CHARLIE TURLOCK, CID pilot

CAPTAIN HUNTER "BOOMER" NOBLE, XR-A9 Black Stallion spacecraft commander, Elliott Air Force Base, Groom Lake

U.S. NAVY LIEUTENANT COMMANDER LISETTE "FRENCHY" MOULAIN, XR-A9 spacecraft commander

U.S. MARINE CORPS MAJOR JIM TERRANOVA, XR-A9 mission commander

ANN PAGE, PH.D., former U.S. senator, astronaut, and space weapon engineer

AIR FORCE MASTER SERGEANT VALERIE "SEEKER" LUKAS, Armstrong Space Station sensor operator

IRANIANS:

GENERAL HESARAK AL-KAN BUZHAZI, leader of the Persian military coup

AZAR ASSIYEH QAGEV, heir presumptive of the Peacock Throne of Persia

LIEUTENANT COLONEL PARVIZ NAJAR and MAJOR MARA SAIDI, Azar Qagev's aides-de-camp

COLONEL MOSTAFA RAHMATI, commander of the Fourth Infantry Brigade, Tehran-Mehrabad Airport

MAJOR QOLOM HADDAD, leader of Buzhazi's personal security team

MASOUD NOSHAHR, Lord High Chancellor of the Qagev royal court and marshal of the court's council of war

AYATOLLAH HASSAN MOHTAZ, supreme leader in exile of the Islamic Republic of Iran

RUSSIANS:

LEONID ZEVITIN, president of the Russian Federation

PETER ORLEV, president's chief of staff

ALEXANDRA HEDROV, minister of foreign affairs

IGOR TRUZNYEV, chief of the Federal Security Bureau

ANATOLI VLASOV, secretary of the Russian security council

MIKHAIL OSTENKOV, minister of national defense

GENERAL KUZMA FURZYENKO, Russian chief of the general staff

GENERAL NIKOLAI OSTANKO, chief of staff of the Russian army

GENERAL ANDREI DARZOV, chief of staff of the Russian air force

WOLFGANG ZYPRIES, German laser engineer working with the Russian air force

WEAPONS AND ACRONYMS

9K89—small Russian surface-to-surface missile

ARB—Air Reserve Base

ATO—air tasking order

BDU-58 Meteor—precision-guided vehicle designed to protect payloads from the heat of re-entry through the atmosphere; can carry approximately 4,000 pounds

CIC—Combat Information Center

coonass—a person of Cajun ethnicity

E-4B—National Airborne Operations Center

E-6B Mercury—U.S. Navy airborne communications and command post aircraft

EB-1D—B-1 Lancer bomber modified as an unmanned long-range supersonic attack plane

ETE—estimated time en route

FAA Part 91—regulations governing private pilots and aircraft

FSB—Russian Federal Security Bureau, follow-on to the KGB

HAWC—High-Technology Aerospace Weapons Center

ICD—implantable cardioverter-defibrillator

Ilyushin—Russian inflight refueling tanker aircraft

MiG—Mikoyan-Gureyvich, Russian military aircraft maker

OSO—offensive systems officer

RQ-4 Global Hawk—high-altitude long-range unmanned reconnaissance aircraft

SAR—synthetic aperture radar; also search and rescue

Skybolt—space-based anti-ballistic missile laser

SPEAR—Self-Protection Electronically Agile Reaction network intrusion defense system

sun-synchronous—an Earth orbit on which a satellite passes over the same spot at the same time of day

Tupolev—twin-engine Russian jet bomber

USAFE—U.S. Air Forces in Europe

VFR—Visual Flight Rules

Vomit Comet—aircraft used to fly parabolic flights to simulate weightlessness

XAGM-279A SkySTREAK (Scramjet Tactical Rapid Employment Attack, or "Streaker")—air-launched hypersonic attack missile, 4,000 pounds, 12 feet long, 24 inches in diameter; uses a solid rocket motor to boost the missile to Mach 3, then switches to a JP-7 jet fuel and compressed atmospheric oxygen scramjet to cruise at Mach 10; inertial and precision GPS navigation; satellite datalink operator mid-course reprogramming; ballistic flight profile max range 600 miles; after accelerating to Mach 10, releases precision-guided warhead with millimeter-wave radar and imaging infrared terminal guidance with auto-target discrimination or satellite datalink remote operator target selection; no warhead; two can be carried aboard EB-1C Vampire bomber in aft bomb bay; four carried internally or four externally by EB-52 Megafortress; four carried internally by B-2 stealth bomber

XR-A9—single-stage to orbit "Black Stallion" spaceplane

REAL-WORLD NEWS EXCERPTS

STRATFOR Morning Intelligence Brief, 18 January 2007—1216 GMT—CHINA, UNITED STATES—U.S. intelligence agencies believe China destroyed the aging Feng Yun 1C polar orbit weather satellite in a successful anti-satellite (ASAT) weapons test Jan. 11, *China Daily* reported Jan. 18, citing an article to appear in the Jan. 22 issue of *Aviation Week & Space Technology*. U.S. intelligence agencies are still attempting to verify the ASAT test, which would signify that China has a major new military capability . . .

. . . The new cloud of debris orbiting the Earth is an indication of things to come should two space-faring nations face off in a conflict. Especially in the case of the United States, space-based assets have become too essential an operational tool to be ignored any longer in times of war.

STRATFOR Daily Intelligence Summary, 3 April 2007—U.S./IRAN: U.S. attacks against Iran would not lead to a decisive military defeat of Tehran and would be a political mistake,

Russia's Chief of the General Staff Gen. Yuri Baluyevsky said. He added that it is possible for the United States to damage Iran's military, but not to win a conflict outright.

STRATFOR INTELLIGENCE BRIEF, 7 SEPTEMBER 2007— Cooperation between the Russian Federal Security Service and Iran's Interior Ministry will enhance Iran's border security, First Deputy Director-General of Russian Federal Security and Border Services Viktor Shlyakhtin said, according to an IRNA report. Shlyakhtin is in Iran to inspect Iranian-Russian projects in areas of Iran's Sistan-Balochistan province that border Afghanistan and Pakistan.

RED OCTOBER: RUSSIA, IRAN, AND IRAQ—STRATFOR Geopolitical Intelligence Report, 17 September 2007—Copyright © Strategic Forecasting Inc.— . . . The Americans need the Russians not to provide fighter aircraft, modern command-and-control systems, or any of the other war-making systems that the Russians have been developing. Above all else, they want the Russians not to provide the Iranians any nuclear-linked technology.

Therefore, it is no accident that the Iranians claimed over the weekend that the Russians told them they would do precisely that.

. . . [Russian president Vladimir] Putin can align with the Iranians and place the United States in a far more complex situation than it otherwise would be in. He could achieve this by supporting Syria, arming militias in Lebanon, or even causing significant problems in Afghanistan, where Russia retains a degree of influence in the North . . .

STRATFOR INTELLIGENCE SUMMARY, 25 OCTOBER 2007, © STRATFOR INC.—During Russian President Vladimir Putin's Oct. 16

visit to Tehran, Iranian Supreme Leader Ayatollah Ali Khamenei asked him to order Russian experts to help Iran figure out how Israel jammed Syrian radars prior to the Sept. 6 air raid, a Stratfor source in Hezbollah said. Iran wants to rectify the problem associated with the failure of Syrian radars because Iran uses similar equipment, the source added.

RUSSIA, IRAN: THE NEXT STEP IN THE DIPLOMATIC TANGO—STRATFOR Global Intelligence Brief, 30 October 2007, © 2007 Stratfor, Inc.— . . . Russia has a fine-tuned strategy of exploiting its Middle Eastern allies' interests for its own political purposes. Iran is the perfect candidate. It is a powerful Islamic state that is locked into a showdown with the United States over its nuclear program and Iraq. Though Washington and Tehran are constantly battling in the public sphere with war rhetoric, they need to deal with each other for the sake of their strategic interests.

Russia, meanwhile, has its own turf war with the United States that involves a range of hot issues, including National Missile Defense, renegotiating Cold War–era treaties, and Western interference in Russia's periphery. By demonstrating that Moscow has some real sway over the Iranians, Russia gains a useful bargaining chip to use in its dealings with the United States . . .

ALTAY OPTICAL-LASER SOURCEBOOK, 28 December 2007—The Scientific Research Institute of Precision Instrument Engineering [of the Russian Federation] has established a branch satellite tracking facility called the Altay Optical-Laser Center (AOLS) near the small Siberian town of Savvushka. The center consists of two sites, one of which is now operational and the other of which is intended to go into operation in or after 2010.

The present site has a laser rangefinder for precision orbit determination, and, for the first time in Russia, a telescope (60 cm aperture) there has been equipped with an adaptive optics system for high-resolution imaging of satellites. The second site will be equipped with a 3.12-meter satellite-imaging telescope generally similar to the one the United States operates in Hawaii.

. . . Successful implementation of the AOLS 3.12-meter system would allow satellites to be imaged with a resolution of 25 cm [9.8 inches] or better out to a range of 1,000 km [621 miles].

SHADOW COMMAND

PROLOGUE

Don't be too timid and squeamish about your actions. All life is an experiment. The more experiments you make the better.

— Ralph Waldo Emerson

Over eastern Siberia

February 2009

"Stand by . . . ready . . . ready . . . begin climb, *now*," the ground controller radioed.

"Acknowledged," the pilot of the Russian Federation's Mikoyan-Gurevich-31BM long-range interceptor responded. He gently eased back on his control stick and began feeding in power. The twin Tumanski R15-BD-300 engines, the most powerful engines ever put on a jet fighter, barked once as the afterburners ignited, then quickly roared to life as the engines' fuel turbopumps caught up with the massive streams of air flooding inside, turning air and fuel into raw power and acceleration.

The pilot's eyes darted back and forth from the power gauges to the heads-up display, which showed two crossed needles with a circle in the middle, similar to an Instrument Landing System. He made gentle, almost imperceptible control inputs to keep the crossed needles centered in the circle. His inputs had to be tiny because the tiniest slip or skid now, with his nose almost forty degrees above the horizon and climbing, could result in a disruption of the smooth airflow into the engine intakes, causing a blowout or compressor stall. The MiG-31, known as "Foxhound" in the West, was not a forgiving machine—it regularly killed sloppy or inattentive crewmembers. Built for speed, it required precise handling at the outer edges of its impressive flight envelope.

"Passing ten thousand meters . . . Mach two point five . . . fifteen thousand . . . forty degrees nose-high . . . airspeed dropping off slightly," the pilot intoned. The MiG-31 was one of the few planes that could accelerate while in a steep climb, but for this test flight they were going to take it higher than its service ceiling of twenty thousand meters, and its performance dropped off significantly then. "Passing twenty K, airspeed below Mach two . . . passing twenty-two K . . . stand by . . . approaching release speed and altitude . . ."

"Keep it centered, Yuri," the MiG's backseater said over intercom. The needles had drifted slightly to the edge of the circle. The circle represented their target tonight, transmitted to them not by the MiG-31's powerful phased-array radar but by a network of space tracking radars around the Russian Federation and fed to them by a nearby data relay aircraft. They would never see their target and would probably never know if their mission was a success or failure.

"It's getting less responsive . . . harder to correct," the pilot breathed. Both crewmembers were wearing space suits and full-face sealed helmets, like astronauts, and as the cabin altitude climbed, the pressure in the suit climbed to compensate, making it harder to move and breathe. "How . . . much . . . longer?"

"Ten seconds . . . nine . . . eight . . ."

"Come on, you old pig, *climb*," the pilot grunted.

"Five seconds . . . missile ready . . . *tree, dva, adeen . . . pazhar*! Launch!"

The MiG-31 was at twenty-five thousand meters above Earth, one thousand kilometers per hour airspeed, with the nose fifty degrees above the horizon, when the ship's computer issued the launch command, and a single large missile was ejected clear of the fighter. Seconds after ejection, the missile's first-stage rocket motor ignited, a tremendous plume of fire erupted from the nozzles, and the missile disappeared from view in the blink of an eye.

Now it was time to fly for himself and not the mission, the pilot reminded himself. He brought back the throttles slowly, carefully, and at the same time started a slight left bank. The bank helped decrease lift and bleed off excessive speed, and would also help bring the nose down without subjecting the crew to negative G-forces. The pressure began to subside, making it a bit easier to breathe—or was it just because their part of the mission was . . . ?

The pilot lost concentration just for a split second, but that was enough. At the moment he let a single degree of sideslip creep in, the fighter flew through the disrupted supersonic air created by the big missile's exhaust tail, and airflow through the left engine was nearly cut off. One engine coughed, sputtered, and then began to scream as fuel continued to pour into the burner cans but the hot exhaust gases were no longer being pushed out.

With one engine running and the other on fire, with not enough air to restart the stalled engine, the MiG-31 launch aircraft was doomed. But the missile it fired performed flawlessly.

Fifteen seconds after the first-stage motor ignited, it separated from the missile and the second-stage motor fired. Speed and altitude climbed quickly. Soon the missile was at five hundred miles above Earth, flying at over three thousand miles per hour, and the second-stage motor separated. Now the third stage remained. High above the atmosphere, it needed no control surfaces to maneuver, instead relying on tiny nitrogen-gas thrusters for maneuvering. A radar in the nose of the third stage activated and began looking at a precise spot in space, and a second later it locked onto its quarry.

The missile didn't have enough speed to begin orbiting the Earth, so as soon as the second stage separated it began its long fall, but it didn't need to orbit: like an atmospheric anti-tank missile, it was falling in a ballistic path toward a computed point in space where its quarry would be in mere seconds. The predicted path, programmed well before launch by ground controllers, was soon verified by on-board targeting computers: the target's orbit had not changed. The intercept was just as planned.

Twenty seconds before impact, the third stage deployed a fifty-yard-wide circular composite net—well above the atmosphere, the net was unaffected by air pressure and stayed round and solid even though traveling several thousand miles an hour. The net was an insurance policy against a near-miss . . . but this time, it didn't need it. With the third stage solidly locked onto the target, and with very little need for hard jarring maneuvering because of the precision of the launch and flight path, the third stage made a direct hit on its intended target.

"Impact, sir," the technician reported. "No telemetry received from the test article."

The commanding general in charge, Russian Air Forces chief of staff Andrei Darzov, nodded. "But what about the flight path? Was it affected by the improper launch parameters?"

The technician looked confused. "Uh . . . no, sir, I do not believe so," he said. "The launch seemed to go perfectly."

"I disagree, Sergeant," Darzov said. He turned to the technician and affixed him with an angry glare. An angry look was bad enough, but Darzov kept his head shaved to best reveal his extensive combat injuries and burns across his head and body, and he looked even more fearsome. "That missile went far off-course, and it may have locked onto an errant satellite by mistake and attacked it."

"Sir?" the technician asked, confused. "The target . . . uh, the American Pathfinder space-based surveillance satellite? That was—"

"Was *that* what we hit, Sergeant?" Darzov asked. "Why, that was not in the flight test plan at all. There has been a horrible mistake, and I will be sure it is investigated fully." His features softened, he smiled, then clasped the technician's shoulder. "Be sure to write in your report that the missile went off-course because of a sideslip in the launch aircraft—I will take care of the rest. And the target was *not* the American SBSS, but our Soyuz target spacecraft inserted into orbit last month. Is that clear, Sergeant?"

CHAPTER ONE

It is better to be violent, if there is violence in our hearts, than to put on the cloak of nonviolence to cover impotence.

— MAHATMA GANDHI

ARMSTRONG SPACE STATION

THAT SAME TIME

"Okay, suckers, c'mon and poke your head out—just a little bit," Captain Hunter "Boomer" Noble muttered. "Don't be afraid—this won't hurt a bit." This was day two of their new patrol, and so far they had squat to show for it except for a persistent headache from watching the sensor monitors for hours at a stretch.

"Hang in there, sir," Air Force Master Sergeant Valerie "Seeker" Lukas said gaily. "You're anticipating, and that negative energy only *keeps* their heads down."

"It's not negative energy, Seeker, whatever *that* is," Boomer said, rubbing his eyes. "It's that TV picture—it's killing me." Hunter rubbed his eyes. They were staring at a wide-screen high-definition image of a suburban section of the southeast side of Tehran, in what

used to be called the Islamic Republic of Iran but was now referred
to by many in the world as the Democratic Republic of Persia. The
image, shot from a telescopic electro-optical camera mounted aboard
a U.S. Air Force RQ-4 Global Hawk unmanned reconnaissance
aircraft orbiting at sixty thousand feet above the city, was fairly
steady, but every shake, no matter how occasional, felt like another
pinch of sand thrown into Boomer's eyes.

The two were not sitting at a console in a normal terrestrial combat control center, but in the main battle management module of
Armstrong Space Station, positioned two hundred and seventy-five
miles above Earth in a forty-seven-degree inclination easterly orbit.
Noble and Lukas were among four additional personnel brought
aboard to run the U.S. Air Force's Air Battle Force monitoring and
command mission over the Democratic Republic of Persia. Although
Boomer was a space veteran with several dozen orbital flights and
even a spacewalk to his credit, floating in zero-G staring at a monitor was not what he joined the Air Force for. "How much longer are
we on station?"

"Just five more hours, sir," Lukas said, smiling and shaking her
head in mock disbelief when Noble groaned at her reply. Seeker was
an eighteen-year U.S. Air Force veteran, but she still looked barely
older than she did the day she enlisted in January 1991 when Operation Desert Storm kicked off, and she loved her profession just as
much now as she did back then. The images of laser- and TV-guided
bombs flying through windows and down ventilator shafts fasci-
nated and excited her, and she started basic training two days after
graduating from high school. She joined every high-tech optronic
sensor school and course she could find, quickly becoming an
all-around expert at remote sensing and targeting systems. "Besides
the power plant, environmental, and electronic systems, the most
important systems in strategic reconnaissance are patience and an
iron butt."

"I'd rather be out there flying myself," Boomer said petulantly,
readjusting himself yet again on his attachment spot on the bulkhead in front of the large monitor. He was a little taller than the av-

erage American astronaut that most of the instruments on the space station were obviously designed for, so he found almost everything on the station just enough of the wrong size, height, or orientation to irk him. Although the twenty-five-year-old test pilot, engineer, and astronaut was a space veteran, most of his time in space had been spent strapped into a nice secure spaceplane seat at the controls, not floating around in zero-G. "All this remote-control stuff is for the birds."

"You calling me a 'bird,' sir?" she asked with mock disapproval.

"I'm not calling anyone anything, Master Sergeant—I'm giving this particular procedure my own personal opinion," Boomer said. He motioned to the screen. "The picture is really good, but it's the radar aiming thingy that's driving me nuts."

"That's the SAR aiming reticle, sir," Seeker said. "It's slaved to the synthetic aperture radar and highlights any large vehicle or device that appears in the sensor field of view that matches our search parameters. If we didn't have it, we'd have to manually scan every vehicle in the city—*that* would really drive you nuts."

"I know what it is, Master Sergeant," Boomer said, "but can't you make it stop darting and flitting and shaking around the screen so much?" The monitor showed a rectangular box that appeared and disappeared frequently in the scene. When it appeared, the box surrounded a vehicle, adjusted its size to match the vehicle, and then if it matched the preprogrammed size parameters, a tone would sound and the camera would zoom in so the humans could see what the computers had found. But it would only stay focused on one vehicle for five seconds before starting the wide-area scan again, so Boomer and Seeker had to almost constantly watch the screen and be prepared to hit the HOLD button to study the image before the computer jumped out again. "It's giving me a damned headache."

"I think it's incredible it's doing what it's doing, sir," Seeker said, "and I'm more than willing to put up with a few jiggles if it helps us spot a—" And at that moment the computer locked onto another vehicle, which had just appeared atop a parking structure beside a cluster of apartment buildings. Seeker slapped the HOLD button a second later.

"Hey, we got one!" she shouted. "It's a Katyusha . . . no, I think it's a Ra'ad rocket! We got them setting up a Ra'ad!"

"You're mine, suckers," Boomer said, instantly forgetting all about his purported headache. He glanced at the monitor, but he was already busy making sure the target coordinates obtained by the Global Hawk were being uploaded properly. The live image was incredibly detailed. They watched as four men carried a large rocket, resembling a large artillery shell with fins, out of the parking garage to the back of a Toyota pickup truck—it must've been very heavy, because it appeared they were having difficulty carrying it. The pickup had a large steel skeletal pedestal mounted in the pickup frame, with a circular cradle atop it. The men rested the rocket on the back of the truck, then two of them hopped up and they began struggling to lift the rocket up to the launcher.

"Don't drop it, boys," Seeker said. "You wouldn't want to spoil our fun, would you?" She turned to Boomer. "How much longer, sir?"

"Target coordinates uploaded," Boomer said. "Counting down now. How long do we have?"

"Once they get it up into the launcher, it could be fired in less than a minute."

Boomer glanced up and watched the monitor. Several children ran up to the truck to watch the terrorists at work—at first they were shooed away, but after a few moments they were allowed to get a closer look. "Looks like 'Career Day' is on in Tehran," he said gloomily.

"Get out of there, kids," Seeker murmured. "It's not safe for you there."

"Not because of us," Boomer said coldly. He hit a transmitter button on his console. "Ripper to Genesis."

"I'm right here, Boomer," responded Lieutenant General Patrick McLanahan, "standing" on the bulkhead behind Boomer and looking over his shoulder. The twenty-one-year Air Force veteran and three-star general was the commanding officer at Elliott Air Force Base, Groom Lake, Nevada, the home of the High-Technology Aer-

ospace Weapons Center, or HAWC. HAWC developed the XR-A9
Black Stallion spaceplane, along with countless other air weapons
and aircraft, but it was leaders like Patrick McLanahan who saw the
capabilities and possibilities of those experimental devices and
brought them to bear in crisis situations where America or her allies
would otherwise suffer tremendous losses or even defeat. Short,
husky but not large, with disarming blue eyes and a quick smile,
Patrick McLanahan did not at all resemble the hard-charging, determined, audacious globe-crossing aerial bombardment expert and
master tactician portrayed by his reputation. Like Boomer and
Seeker, McLanahan was becoming a veteran astronaut—this was
his third trip to Armstrong Space Station in as many months.

"We've got a good one, sir," Boomer said, nodding at his monitor.
"Not a little homemade Qassam or Katyusha this time, either."
Boomer studied the young three-star Air Force general's face carefully, noticing his eyes flicking back and forth across his monitor—not
just looking at the rocket, Boomer thought, but at the kids clustered
around the makeshift terror weapon launcher. "The master sergeant
thinks it's a Ra'ad rocket."

It appeared as if Patrick hadn't heard him, but a few moments
later he nodded excitedly. "I agree, Seeker," he said. "A Hezbollah
weapon, based on a Russian battalion-level battlefield attack missile.
Two-hundred-pound warhead, simple but usually effective baro-
metric fuse, airburst with a backup impact detonation, killing radius
a hundred yards or more, usually loaded up with glass, ball bearings, and pieces of metal along with high explosives to increase the
injury toll. A real terror weapon." He shook his head. "But there are
too many civilians around. Our ROE says no noncombatant casualties and minimal collateral damage. Pick a different target, Boomer,
one with fewer bystanders. There will be plenty of opportunities . . ."

"We don't see many Ra'ad rockets, sir," Seeker said. "That's not a
homemade rocket—that's a military-grade short-range ballistic attack missile."

"I know, Master Sergeant, but our orders are specific and—" At that moment the insurgents shooed the children away again, more forcefully this time, as another insurgent fitted ignition wires to the tail end of the rocket in final preparation for launch. *"Now,"* Patrick snapped. "Take it down."

"Yes, sir," Boomer said enthusiastically. He issued commands on his computer, checked the computer's responses, then nodded. "Here we go . . . missile counting down . . . doors coming open . . . ready . . . ready . . . now, missile away." He checked a countdown timer. "Don't anyone blink, 'cuz this won't take long."

Over the Caspian Sea two hundred and twenty miles north of Tehran, an unmanned EB-1D Vampire bomber opened its combined forward and center bomb bay doors and released a single large missile. The D-model Vampire was a modified U.S. Air Force B-1B strategic bomber, converted by the High-Technology Aerospace Weapons Center to a long-range unmanned flying battleship. It was capable of autonomously flying itself from takeoff to final parking with an inflight-reprogrammable flight plan, or could be flown by satellite remote control like a large multimillion-dollar video game from a laptop computer located almost anywhere.

The missile the Vampire had just released was an even more sophisticated weapon developed by the engineers at HAWC. Its unclassified designator was the XAGM-279A SkySTREAK, but anyone who knew anything about this missile—and there were only a handful of persons on the entire planet who did—called it the "Streaker." It resembled a cross between a bullet and a manta ray, with a pointed carbon-carbon nosecap and bullet-shaped forebody splaying out into a thin, flat fuselage and pointed tail section. After stabilizing itself in the atmosphere, four solid-fuel rocket motors ignited, pushing the weapon to well past Mach 3 and one hundred thousand feet of altitude in just a few seconds.

Within eight seconds the motors had burned out, and a wide, flat oval air intake popped open underneath the missile. Supersonic air was ingested and compressed by the shape of the now-empty rocket motor casings, mixed with jet fuel, and ignited by high-energy pulses of laser energy. The resultant energy propelled the missile to over ten times the speed of sound in just a few more seconds, and the missile ate up the distance between its launch point and its target in no time, climbing to two hundred thousand feet as it raced downrange. The missile burned all of its jet fuel in just a few seconds, and it quickly decelerated and began descending back through the atmosphere. Once the outside skin temperature was within safe limits, the bullet-shaped forebody detached from the spent propulsion section, which automatically blew itself to bits moments later.

Small stabilizer fins popped out of the forebody, and it became a supersonic re-entry vehicle, guiding itself to its target with its on-board navigation computer refined by Global Positioning System signals. Fifteen seconds to impact, the protective nosecap detached, revealing a combination millimeter-wave radar and imaging infrared scanner, and the warhead began uploading video signals via satellite to Boomer and Seeker back in Dreamland. The steering cue in the video image was several yards off, but Seeker used a trackball and rolled the steering rectangle back on the pickup truck, which sent steering correction signals to the warhead.

The video image from the warhead was sharp and clear all the way to impact. Patrick had a brief glimpse of a young man, no more than fifteen or sixteen years old, wearing a mask and carrying an AK-47 assault rifle that looked almost as big as he was, who looked right up at the incoming weapon milliseconds before the image vanished. Patrick knew that the warhead was programmed to explode a tenth of a second before impact, splitting the warhead apart into thousands of small hypervelocity fragments, increasing the killing radius of the weapon out to about forty to fifty yards.

"Direct hit!" Boomer shouted happily. He looked at the control monitor and slapped his hands together. "Total time from detection to impact: forty-eight point nine seconds. Less than a friggin' minute!"

"It's more like a Maverick missile—or a sniper's bullet—only fired from *two hundred miles* away!" Seeker exclaimed. She had switched back to the Global Hawk's image of the target area and zoomed in to take a close look at the Streaker warhead's impact spot. "Pretty good urban weapon effects, sir, exactly what you were hoping for. A really good-sized hole, about fifteen to twenty feet in diameter—looks like the center punched through the concrete parking garage roof into the floor below—but no damage to the nearby buildings that I can see except for a few broken windows. Even a two-hundred-and-fifty-pound Small-Diameter Bomb might have caved in the sides of the building facing the blast."

"With no explosive warhead on the Streaker, there's nothing there to create any collateral damage," Boomer said. "We put just enough shaped explosive charges in the warhead to break it apart milliseconds before impact, and that was both to increase the weapon effect slightly as well as to destroy as much of the evidence as we could. All they should find are tiny pieces of—"

"Oh . . . my . . . God," Seeker breathed. She had zoomed out to survey a little more of the surrounding area. There were clusters of people, perhaps two dozen or so, just outside the apartment complex area lying on the sidewalk and street, with others attending to them, waving frantically for help. "What in hell happened here? Where did those people come from, and why are they lying on the ground like that? Are they from inside the apartment complex . . . ?"

"The Streaker must've set off the Ra'ad rocket's warhead," Boomer said. They all carefully studied the image as Seeker took manual control of the camera and zoomed in. "But what's going on? Those people over there weren't anywhere near the blast, but they're staggering around like they were hit. Was it shrapnel from the Ra'ad warhead? The Streaker doesn't have an explosive payload—it's all kinetic energy. Is the Persian army moving in? What's going . . . ?"

"A chemical weapon cloud," Patrick said.

"*What . . . ?*"

"It looks like some sort of chemical weapon cloud, spreading out from the target area," Patrick said. He pointed to the monitor. "Not more than thirty feet away. Here's a little bit of the cloud . . . see, it's not rising like a cloud from an explosion or from heat, but traveling horizontally, blown around by air currents." He looked closer. "Not twitching . . . it's hard to tell, but it looks like he's rubbing his eyes and face and is having trouble breathing. I'll bet it's a blister agent . . . lewisite or phosgene. Mustard agents would take longer to incapacitate someone, even in high concentrations . . . look, now someone collapsing across the street. Jesus, the warhead must've had several liters of CW in it."

"My God," Seeker gasped. "I've been operating remote sensors for almost twenty years, and I've never seen anyone die from a chemical weapon attack."

"I have a feeling the powers that be aren't going to like this," Patrick said.

"Should we recall the Vampire, sir?"

"Hell no," Patrick said. "We still have three more Streakers on board, and another Vampire loaded and waiting to go at Mosul. Keep on scanning for more insurgents. Congratulations, Boomer. The SkySTREAK worked perfectly. Nail a few more insurgents for us."

"You got it, sir," Boomer said happily.

ARMSTRONG SPACE STATION

A SHORT TIME LATER

Unfortunately, Patrick turned out to be exactly correct. The Global Hawk images were being beamed to several terrestrial locations as well as to Silver Tower, including the Joint Chiefs of Staff Operations Center in Washington, and it was there that he received his first call just moments later: "Genesis, this is Rook." That was from the duty officer at the JCS Operations Center. "Stand by, please." A moment later, the chief of staff of the Air Force, General Charles A. Huffman, appeared on the video teleconference channel, looking a little pale himself but still very angry as well.

Huffman, a tall, dark-haired, and very young man with husky, athletic features—more like a linebacker than a running back, Boomer thought—was typical of the new breed of leaders in the American military. In the five years since the Russian nuclear cruise missile air strike on the continental United States, known as the "American Holocaust," which left several thousand dead, hundreds of thousands injured, several Air Force bases destroyed, and almost all of America's long-range bombers wiped out, the military ranks had filled with eager young men and women wishing to protect their country, and many officers were promoted well below their primary zones and placed into important command positions years before it was ever thought possible. Also, since senior leaders with extensive combat experience were kept in charge of tactical units or major commands, often officers with less direct combat experience were placed in more administrative and training billets—and since the office of the chief of staff was mostly concerned with *equipping* and *training* their forces, not *leading* them into combat, it seemed a good match.

That was true of Huffman as well: Patrick knew he came from the logistics field, a command pilot, wing, and numbered Air Force commander, and former Air Force Materiel Command commander with over fifteen thousand hours flying time in a variety of cargo, transport, and liaison aircraft in two conflicts, and extensive experience in supply, resource management, and test and evaluation. As former head of Materiel Command, Huffman had been notional commander of activities at the top-secret High-Technology Aerospace Weapons Center at Elliott Air Force Base, although that link was mostly administrative and logistical—operationally, the commanders at HAWC reported to the chairman of the Joint Chiefs of Staff or the Secretary of Defense at the Pentagon, the President's National Security Adviser at the White House, or—at least under former President Kevin Martindale—directly to the President himself.

Patrick had never spent any time in logistics, but he knew that logistics officers liked their world as neat, orderly, and organized as possible. Although they learned to expect the unexpected, they very much preferred to *anticipate, predict,* and *manage* the unexpected, and therefore anything unexpected was not welcome. He knew Huffman, however, and he knew that's precisely the way Huffman liked it: *no surprises.* "McLanahan, what in hell happened out there?"

"Calling Genesis, say again, please," Patrick said, trying to remind the general that although the connection was encrypted and as secure as they could make it, it was still a wide-open satellite-based network and prone to eavesdropping.

"We're secure here, McLanahan," Huffman thundered. "What in hell is going on? What happened?"

"We hit an insurgent rocket launcher, and apparently detonated its explosive chemical-weapon warhead, sir."

"What did you hit it with?"

"A XAGM-279 with a kinetic warhead, sir," Patrick responded, using the SkySTREAK's experimental model number instead of its name to confuse any eavesdroppers. "Almost no explosives in it—just enough to fragment the warhead."

"What is a XAGM-279? An experimental precision-guided missile?"

So much for communications security, Patrick thought, shaking his head. It was five years after the American Holocaust and seven

years since 9/11, and many folks had forgotten or abandoned the
tight security measures that had been put in place after those two
devastating attacks. "Yes, sir" was all Patrick said.

"Launched from that unmanned B-1?"

"Yes, sir." Anyone listening to this conversation—and Patrick
didn't delude himself that any number of agencies or units around the
world could've done so easily—could piece together their entire operation by now. "I briefed the staff two days ago on the operation."

"Dammit, McLanahan, you briefed minimal collateral damage,
not dozens of dead women and children lying in the street!" Huffman cried. "That was the only way we could sell your idea to the
President."

"The weapon produced virtually no collateral damage, sir. It was
the chemical warhead on the insurgents' rocket that caused all those
civilian casualties."

"Do you believe anyone is gong to care about that one bit?" Huffman said. "This is a major fuckup, McLanahan. The press is going
to have a field day with this." Patrick remained silent. *"Well?"*

"I don't feel it's my task force's or my responsibility to worry
about what the enemy's weapons do to the civilian population, sir,"
Patrick said. "Our job is to hunt for insurgents firing rockets into
population centers in Tehran and destroy them."

"The Qagev members inside the Turkmeni insurgent network
and Buzhazi's spies inside Mohtaz's security staff briefed us that the
insurgents could use weapons of mass destruction at any time,
McLanahan," Huffman said. Patrick suppressed another irritated
breath: Huffman had just revealed two highly classified intelligence
sources—if anyone was eavesdropping, those sources were dead
meat in just a matter of days, perhaps hours. "You should have adjusted tactics accordingly."

"Tactics *were* adjusted, sir—I was ordered to reduce the number
of bombers on station from three to one," Patrick responded—*by
you,* he added to himself. "But we don't have enough coverage of the
city to effectively deal with the number of launchers being reported.
I recommend we launch two more bombers so we can hunt down

more launchers before the insurgents actually start firing live chemical warhead munitions into the city."

"Are you crazy, McLanahan?" Huffman retorted. "The President will probably order the entire program shut down because of this! The *last* thing he will do is put more bombers up there. As it is, we'll spend a week defending ourselves from being accused of releasing those chemical warheads. You will recall your aircraft immediately, then prepare to debrief the JCS and likely the entire national security staff. I want a full report on the incident on my desk in one hour. Understood?"

"Yes, sir."

"And after the briefing is complete, get your ass off that damned space station," Huffman said. "I don't know why my predecessor allowed you to go up there, but you've got no business traipsing up to that floating pile of tubes every time you feel like it. I need you down *here*—if for no other reason than to have you personally answer to the national command authority regarding another lapse in judgment."

"Yes, sir," Patrick replied, but the transmission had already been ended by the time he spoke. He terminated the videoconference link, thought for a moment, then spoke, "McLanahan to Mace."

Another window popped open on the opposite lower corner of Boomer's large multifunction screen, and he saw the image of Brigadier General Daren Mace, the operations officer and second-in-command of the Air Battle Force attack wing at Battle Mountain Air Reserve Base in northern Nevada. The air wing at Battle Mountain was the home base and central control facility for the unmanned long-range bombers, although commanders at HAWC could also issue instructions to the bombers as well.

"Yes, General?" Mace responded. Older than Patrick by just a few years, Daren Mace was a veteran B-1B Lancer strategic bomber OSO, or offensive systems officer, and bomb wing commander. His expertise on the B-1's attack systems and capabilities led him to be chosen to head the Air Battle Force's long-range supersonic attack fleet.

"Recall the damned Vampires," Patrick ordered tonelessly.

"But sir, we've still got three more Streakers on board the Vampire, and it's got at least two more hours' endurance before it has to head back to Batman Air Base in Turkey," Boomer interjected. "Intel briefed us that—"

"The operational test was successful, Boomer—that's what we needed to find out," Patrick said, rubbing his temples. He shook his head resignedly. "Recall the Vampire now, General Mace," he said quietly, his head lowered, his voice sounding utterly exhausted.

"Yes, sir," the veteran bomber navigator responded. He entered keyboard instructions on his computer console. "The Vampire's on the way back to Batman Air Base in Turkey, sir, ETE forty-five minutes. What about the follow-on sorties?"

"Hold them in their hangars until I give the word," Patrick replied.

"And what about our shadow, sir?" Daren asked.

Patrick looked at another monitor. Yep, it was still there: a Russian MiG-29 Fulcrum jet fighter, one of several that had been hanging near the bomber since it started its patrol, always within one or two miles of the Vampire, not making any threatening moves but certainly able to attack at any second. It certainly had a front-row seat for the SkySTREAK launch. The Vampire bomber had taken several photographs of the fighter with its high-resolution digital camera so detailed that they could practically read the pilot's name stenciled on the front of his flight suit.

"If it locks onto the Vampire, shoot it down immediately," Patrick said. "Otherwise we'll let it—"

And at that moment they heard a computer-synthesized voice announce, *"Warning, warning, missile launch! SPEAR system activated!"*

Patrick shook his head and sighed audibly. "The game's afoot, crew," he said. "The battle begins today, and it has little to do with Persia." He turned to the computer screen of the command center at Battle Mountain. "Shut that bastard down, Daren," Patrick radioed.

"He's down, sir," Daren said.

As soon as the Vampire bomber detected the missile launch, its newest and most powerful self-defense system activated: the

ALQ-293 SPEAR, or Self-Protection Electronically Agile Reaction system. Large sections of the composite skin of the EB-1D Vampire had been redesigned to act as an electronically scalable antenna that could transmit and receive many different electromagnetic signals, including radar, laser, radio, and even computer data code.

As soon as the MiG's radar was detected, the SPEAR system immediately classified the radar, examined its software, and devised a method to not just jam its frequency but to interface with the radar's digital controls themselves. As soon as the missile launch was detected, SPEAR sent commands to the MiG's fire control system to send a command to the missile to switch immediately to infrared seeker mode, then shut down the digital guidance uplink from the fighter. The missiles automatically deactivated their on-board radars and activated its infrared seeker, but they were too far away from the Vampire bomber to lock on using its heat-seeking sensor, and the missiles harmlessly plummeted to the Caspian Sea without acquiring a target.

But SPEAR wasn't done. After defeating the missiles, SPEAR sent digital instructions to the MiG-29 via the fire control system to start shutting down aircraft systems controlled by computer. One by one, the navigation, engine controls, flight controls, and communications all turned themselves off.

In the blink of an eye, the pilot found himself sitting in a completely silent and dark glider, as if he were sitting on the ramp back at his home base.

To his credit, the veteran pilot didn't panic and eject—he was not out of control, not yet, but just . . . well, *turned off.* There was only one thing to do: turn all switches off to reset the computers, then turn everything back on, and hope he could get his stricken jet running again before he crashed into the Caspian Sea. He flipped his checklist to the BEFORE POWER ON pages and started shutting every system in the plane off. His last image out his canopy was watching the big American B-1 bomber bank sharply left, as if giving the Russian a farewell wing-wag, and fly off toward the northwest, speeding quickly out of sight.

No one in the Russian air force had ever run a series of checklists faster than he. He had descended from forty-two thousand feet all the way down to four thousand feet above the Caspian Sea before he was able to get his jet shut down, turned back on, and the engines started again. Thankfully, whatever evil spirits had entered his MiG-29 were no longer present.

For a brief instant the Russian MiG pilot considered pursuing the American bomber completely radar-silent and putting a load of cannon shells into his tail—he was going to be blamed for almost crashing his plane anyway, so why not go out in a blaze of glory?—but after briefly considering it, he decided that was a foolish notion. He didn't know what caused the mysterious shutdown—was it an American weapon of some kind, or a glitch in his own plane? Besides, the American bomber was not launching any more missiles that could be "mistaken" for an attack against him. This was not a war between the Americans and the Russians . . .

. . . although he felt it certainly could blossom into one at any moment.

"Let's put together a debrief, then get ready to head back to HAWC, Boomer," Patrick said after they were assured that the EB-1C Vampire bomber was safely on its way back to Batman Air Base in Turkey. His voice sounded very tired, and his facial expression appeared even more so. "Good job. The system seems to be working fine. We've proven we can control unmanned aircraft from Silver Tower. That should get us some sustainment funding for another year at least."

"General, it wasn't your fault that the damned insurgents had a bunch of kids around when the SkySTREAK attacked, or that they loaded up that Ra'ad missile with poison gas," Hunter Noble responded, looking worriedly at Master Sergeant Lukas.

"I know, Boomer," Patrick said, "but it still doesn't make watching innocent men, women, and children die like that any easier."

"Sir, we're on station, the Vampire is loaded, the SkySTREAKs are running cool, and no doubt there are more of those Ra'ads out there with poison gas warheads," Boomer said. "I think we should stay and—"

"I hear you, Boomer, but we've validated the system—that was the mission objective," Patrick said.

"Our other objective was to try to control multiple bombers and multiple engagements," Boomer reminded him. "We had enough trouble getting authorization and funding to fly *this* mission—getting approval for another mission to do what we could have done on this flight will be even more difficult."

"I know, I know," Patrick said wearily. "I'll ask, Boomer, but I'm not counting on it. We've got to analyze the data, prepare a summary report, and brief the chief. Let's get to it."

"But sir—"

"Meet you back here in ten, Boomer," Patrick said finally, detaching himself from his anchor position and floating his way toward the sleeping module.

"Looks like he took that one hard," Seeker said after the general had left the control module. Boomer didn't respond. "It kind of shook me up too. Is the general feeling okay?"

"He had a rough trip up here," Boomer said. "Every push into orbit has been hard on him, but he keeps on flying up here. The last push took a lot out of him, I think. He probably shouldn't be making these trips anymore."

"It could be watching those people getting killed like that," Seeker said. "I've seen the aftereffects of a guided missile attack plenty of times, but somehow a biochem weapon attack is . . . different, you know? More violent." She looked at Boomer curiously, unable to read his rather flat expression. "Did it shake you up too, Boomer?"

"Well . . ." And then he shook his head and added, "No, it didn't, Seeker. All I want to do now is hunt down *more* bad guys. I don't understand why the general wanted to wrap this up so soon."

"You heard the chief, sir," Seeker said. "The general wanted to send the other two bombers."

"I know, I know." Boomer looked around the module. "The

things we can do on board this station are amazing, Sergeant, really amazing—we should be allowed to do them. We need to convince the powers that be that we can turn the Air Force on its ear. We can't do that if we pull our planes out when a little kid ten thousand miles away gets caught in the crossfire. Can't believe the general got all misty-eyed like that."

Master Sergeant Lukas looked at Boomer sternly. "Do you mind if I say something, sir?" she finally asked.

"Go right ahead, Seeker . . . or is it 'Master Sergeant' now?"

"I haven't been working at HAWC that long—not as long as you," Lukas said, ignoring the sarcastic remark, "and I don't know General McLanahan that well, but the guy is a friggin' hero in my book. He's spent almost twenty years laying his ass on the line fighting battles all over the world. He's been kicked out of the Air Force twice, but he came back because he's dedicated to his country and the service."

"Hey, I'm not bad-mouthing the guy—"

"The 'guy' you're referring to, sir, is a three-star general in the U.S. Air Force and commands the largest and most highly classified aerospace research facility in the U.S. armed forces," Lukas interrupted hotly. "General McLanahan is nothing short of a *legend*. He's been shot up, shot down, blown up, beat up, ridiculed, busted, demoted, and called every name in the book. He's lost his wife, a close friend, and dozens of crewmembers under his command. You, sir, on the other hand, have been in the force now . . . seven years? Eight? You're a talented engineer and a skillful pilot and astronaut—"

"But?"

"—but you're not in the general's league, sir—far, far from it," Lukas went on. "You don't have the experience and haven't shown the same level of commitment and dedication as the general. You're not qualified to pass judgment on the general—in fact, in my opinion, sir, you haven't earned the right to be talking about him the way you are."

"Like you're talking to *me* now?"

"Write me up if you want, sir, but I don't appreciate you second-guessing the general like that," Lukas said flatly. She logged herself off from her console and detached herself from the bulkhead with a perturbed jerk and a loud *riip!* of Velcro. "I'll help you download the sensor data and prepare your debrief for the general, and then I'll be happy to help you prepare the Black Stallion for undocking . . . so you can go home as soon as possible, *sir.*" She said the word "sir" more like the word "cur," and that jab wasn't lost on Boomer.

With Seeker's exasperated and irate help—not to mention they didn't do very much chatting as they worked—Boomer was indeed done quickly. He uploaded his data and findings to the general. "Thanks, Boomer," McLanahan radioed back. "We're scheduled to do the videoconference in about ninety minutes. I found out the Joint Chiefs chairman and National Security Adviser are going to sit in. Kick back for a while and get some rest."

"I'm fine, sir," Boomer responded. "I'll go hide out in Skybolt, get my e-mail, and check in on my girlfriends."

" 'Girlfriends' . . . plural?"

"I don't know—we'll see what the e-mails say," Boomer said. "None of them like me disappearing for days and weeks, and I certainly can't tell them I've been blasting terrorists to hell from space."

"They probably wouldn't believe you if you *did* tell them."

"The ladies I hang out with don't know a space station from a gas station—and that's the way I like it," Boomer admitted. "They don't know, or care, what I do for a living. All they want is attention and a good time on the town, and if they don't get it, they split."

"Sounds lonely."

"That's why I always like to have more than one on the hook, sir," Boomer said.

"Could be fireworks if they ever run into each other, eh?"

"We hook up together all the time, sir," Boomer said. "No brag, just fact. Like I said, all they want is attention, and they get even more attention if folks see them arm in arm with another hot babe. Besides, if there's ever any conversation—"

"Wait, wait, I know this one, Boomer: 'If there's any conversation, *you* don't have to get involved,' " Patrick interjected with a laugh. "Okay, go say hi to your girlfriends, and don't tell me how many you got waiting for you to get back. Meet me in the command module in sixty minutes so we can rehearse our dog and pony show."

"Yes, sir," Boomer replied. Before McLanahan clicked off, he asked, "Uh, General?"

"Go ahead."

"I'm sorry if I got out of line earlier."

"I expect you to give me your professional opinion and point of view anytime, Boomer, especially on a mission," Patrick said. "If you were out of line, I wouldn't hesitate to let you know."

"It got me pretty steamed, watching those bastards setting up a rocket with a damned chemical warhead on it. All I wanted to do was blast a few more."

"I hear you. But it's more important we get this program off and running. We both know we're going to catch some flak for what happened in Tehran—shooting more missiles wouldn't have helped us."

"Maybe offing a few more terrorists would compel them to keep their heads down and hide in their ratholes for a few days more."

"We have some incredible weapons at our disposal, Boomer—let's not let the power go to our heads," Patrick said patiently. "It was an operational test, not an actual mission. I know the temptation to play Zeus with a few SkySTREAK missiles is powerful, but that's not what we're here for. Meet back here in sixty."

"Yes, sir," he responded. Just before the general logged off, Boomer remarked to himself that the general looked even wearier than any other time since embarking on this sortie to the space station—maybe the combination of witnessing the chemical weapon release and the monthly trips into space were starting to get to him. Boomer was half his age, and sometimes the stress of the trips, especially the recent quick-turn, high-G re-entry profiles, and multiple sorties they had been flying, wore him down fast.

Boomer floated back to the crew quarters module, retrieved his wireless headphones and video goggles, and floated to the Skybolt laser module at the "bottom" of the station. Skybolt was the station's most powerful and so most controversial piece of technology, a multi-gigawatt free-electron laser powerful enough to shoot through

Earth's atmosphere and melt steel in seconds. Tied to Silver Tower's radars and other sensors, Skybolt could attack targets as small as an automobile and burn through the top armor of all but the most modern main battle tanks. Classified as a "weapon of mass destruction" by all of America's adversaries, the United Nations had been calling for the weapon's deactivation for many years, and only America's veto power in the Security Council kept it alive.

Ann Page, Skybolt's designer, operator, and chief advocate, was on Earth preparing to testify to Congress on why funding for the weapon should be continued, and Boomer knew that very few others on the station ever went near the thing—Skybolt was powered by an MHDG, or magnetohydrodynamic generator, which used two small nuclear reactors to rapidly shoot a slug of molten metal back and forth through a magnetic field to produce the enormous amount of power required by the laser, and no amount of shielding and assurances by Ann could assuage anyone's fears—so he often went into the module to get some peace and quiet. The Skybolt module was about a fourth of the size of the main modules on the station, so it was relatively cramped inside, and it was crammed with pipes, wire conduits, and a myriad of computers and other components, but the gentle hum of the MHDG drive's circulating pumps and the excellent computers and communications gear there made it Boomer's favorite place to get away from the others for a while.

Boomer connected his headphones and video goggles to the module's computers, logged in, and began downloading e-mail. Even though the headphones and goggles were a pain, there was precious little privacy on Silver Tower, even in the huge modules, so the only semblance of privacy had to come down to the space between one's ears. Everyone assumed that if personnel from the super-secret High-Technology Aerospace Weapons Center were on board the space station that all incoming and outgoing transmissions of any kind were being recorded and monitored, so "privacy" was a vacuous idea at best.

It was a good thing he had bothered to put on the gear, because the video e-mails from his girlfriends were definitely not for public viewing. Chloe's video was typical: "Boomer, where the hell are you?" it began, with Chloe sitting in front of her videophone photo-graphing herself. "I'm getting tired of you disappearing like this. Nobody at your unit would tell me a goddamned thing. That sergeant that answers the phone should be booted out of the service, the fag." Chloe called any man who didn't immediately hit on her a "fag," believing being gay was the only reason that any normal male wouldn't want to screw her right away.

She paused for a moment, her features softening a bit, and Boomer knew the show was about to begin: "You'd better not be with that blond spiky-haired bitch, Tammy or Teresa or whatever the hell her name is. You're over at her place, aren't you, or you two have jetted off to Mexico or Hawaii, haven't you? You two just fucked and you're checking mail while she takes a shower, right?" Chloe set the videophone down on her desk, unbuttoned her blouse, and slipped her large, firm breasts out from under her brassiere. "Let me just remind you what you're missing here, Boomer." She put a finger sensuously in her mouth, then circled her nipples with it. "Get your ass back here and stop screwing around with those skanky bottle-blond hos." She smiled seductively, then hung up.

"Crazy bitch," Boomer muttered as he continued to scroll through the messages, but resolved to look her up as soon as he got back. After previewing more messages he stopped and immediately entered the code to access the satellite Internet server. Another benefit of the new American space initiative, of which Armstrong Space Station was the hub, was the coming availability of almost universal Internet access via a constellation of over a hundred low-Earth-orbit satellites that provided global low-speed Internet access, plus ten geostationary satellites that provided high-speed broadband Internet access to most of the Northern Hemisphere.

"No IP address, no extensions, no open active server identification code—this has got to be a call from outer space," came the reply from Jon Masters a few moments later after establishing a videophone connection to the designated secure address. Jon Masters was the vice president of a small high-tech research and development company called Sky Masters Inc. that designed and licensed many different

emerging aerospace technologies, from microsatellites to space boosters. Masters, a multidegree, multidoctorate scientist and engineer regarded as one of the world's most innovative aerospace designers and
thinkers, had formed his company at the ripe old age of twenty-five,
and he still looked and acted the part of the geeky, eccentric, and flip-
pant child prodigy. "Thanks for returning my call, Boomer."

"No problem, Jon."

"How are things up there?"

"Fine. Good."

"I know you can't talk about it on a satellite server, even if it is
encrypted. Just wanted to be sure you're okay."

"Thanks. I'm fine."

There was a slight pause; then: "You sound a little down, my
friend."

"No."

"Okay." Another pause. "So. What do you think of my offer?"

"It's extremely generous, Jon," Boomer said. "I'm not sure if I
deserve it."

"I wouldn't offer it if I didn't think you did."

"And I get to work on whatever I want?"

"Well, we hope we can entice you to help out on other projects,"
Masters said, "but I want you to do what you do best: think outside
the box and come up with fresh, innovative, and kick-ass designs. I
don't try to game or anticipate the aerospace market, Boomer—I try
to *shape* it. That's what I want you to do. You won't answer to anyone else but me, and you get to pick your team, your protocols, your
design approach, and your timelines—within reason, of course. You
knock my socks off with your ideas, and I'll back you all the way."

"And this estimated budget figure for my lab . . . ?"

"Yes?"

"Is this for real, Jon?"

"That's just the *starting* point, Boomer—that's the *minimum,*"
Masters chuckled. "You want that in writing, just say so, but I'm
guaranteeing you that you'll have a generous budget to build the
team to research and evaluate your designs."

"Even so, it's not enough for the entire division. I'll need—"

"You don't understand, Boomer," Masters interjected excitedly. "That money is just for *you* and your team, not split up between everyone in your division, existing projects, or specific company-mandated programs or technology."

"You're kidding!"

"I'm serious as a heart attack, brother," Masters said. "And it's not for stuff like company-wide expenses, compliance mandates, or security, but for your team- and project-specific costs. I believe in giving our top engineers the tools they need to do their job."

"I can't believe it. I've never even heard of that kind of money being invested by a small company like this."

"Believe it, Boomer," Masters said. "We may be small, but we've got investors and a board of directors who think big and expect big things to happen."

"Investors? A board of directors . . . ?"

"We all answer to someone, Boomer," Masters said. "I ran my company by myself with a handpicked board of directors, which was okay until the projects got smaller and the money got tight. There were a lot of investors out there who wanted to be part of what we were doing here, but no one wants to dump hundreds of millions of dollars into a one-man show. We're public, and I'm not president anymore, but everyone knows I'm the guy who makes the magic."

"I don't know . . ."

"You don't worry about the board, Boomer. You report to me. Be advised, I'm going to make you work for every dime. I'm going to expect big things from you, and I'll be putting bugs in your ear about what I know or discover about government requests for proposals, but like I said, I don't want you waiting around for some weenie in the Pentagon to tell us what they might want—I want *us* to tell *them* what *they* want. So, what do you say? Are you in?"

"I'm thinking about it, Jon."

"Okay. No problem. I know your commitments to the Air Force are up in eight months, correct?" Boomer guessed that Jon Masters knew to the *day* when his educational commitments to the Air Force for pilot training were up. "I guarantee they'll offer you a regular commission before that, along with a big fat bonus. They might try to stop-loss you, claiming you're in a critical specialty, but we'll deal with that when and if we have to. I have enough contracts with the Air Force, and enough buddies in the Pentagon, to put a little pressure on them to respect your decisions. After all, you're not getting out to go work for the airlines or be a consultant or lobbyist—you'll be working for the company that builds *them* the next generation of hardware."

"That sounds good."

"You bet it does, Boomer," Jon Masters said. "Don't worry about a thing. One more thing, buddy. I know I'm older than you, probably old enough to be your dad if I started real early, so I get to give you a little heads-up."

"What's that, Jon?"

"I know trying to tell you to take it easy, be safe, and maybe don't fly so many missions is like trying to tell my golden retriever to stay out of the lake, but I wouldn't want to have the company's future vice president of R&D become a shooting star, so take it easy, okay?"

"Vice president?"

"Oh, did I say that out loud?" Masters deadpanned. "You weren't supposed to hear that. Forget I said that. Forget the board was considering it but didn't want me to reveal that. Gotta go before I tell you about the other thing the board was kicking around . . . oops, almost did it again. Later, Boomer."

OFFICE OF THE PRESIDENT, THE KREMLIN, MOSCOW, RUSSIAN FEDERATION

A SHORT TIME LATER

The room was loudly called to attention as Russian Federation president Leonid Zevitin quickly strode into the conference room, followed by his chief of staff Peter Orlev, the secretary of the security council, Anatoli Vlasov; the minister of foreign affairs, Alexandra Hedrov; and the chief of the Federal Security Bureau, Igor Truznyev. "Take seats," Zevitin ordered, and the officers already in the room—General Kuzma Furzyenko, the chief of staff; General Nikolai Ostanko, chief of staff of the army; and General Andrei Darzov, the chief of staff of the air force—shuffled to their chairs. "So. I gave the command for our fighter to attack the unmanned American bomber if it fired a missile, and since we're meeting like this so quickly, I assume it did, and we did. What happened?"

"The American B-1 bomber successfully launched a missile from over the Caspian Sea that reportedly destroyed a Hezbollah squad preparing to launch a rocket from an apartment complex in southeast Tehran," General Darzov replied. "The missile made a direct hit on the launch squad's location, killing the entire crew . . ." He paused, then added, "including our Special Forces adviser. The bomber then—"

"Hold on, General, hold on a sec," Zevitin said impatiently, holding up a hand. "They launched a missile from *over* the Caspian Sea? You mean a cruise missile, and not a laser-guided bomb or TV-guided missile?" Many of those around the table narrowed their eyes, not because they disliked Zevitin's tone or question but because they were unaccustomed to someone with such a distinct Western accent at a classified meeting in the Kremlin.

Leonid Zevitin, one of Russia's youngest leaders since the fall of the czars, was born outside St. Petersburg but was educated and had spent most of his life in Europe and the United States, and so had almost no Russian accent unless he wanted or needed one, such as when speaking before Russian citizens at a political rally. Frequently seen all over the world with starlets and royalty, Zevitin came from the world of international banking and finance, not from politics or the military. After decades of old, stodgy political bosses or bureau-cratic henchmen as president, the election of Leonid Zevitin was seen by most Russians as a breath of fresh air.

But behind the secretive walls of the Kremlin, he was something altogether different than just expensive silk suits, impeccable hair, jet-setter style, and a million-dollar smile—he was the puppet mas-ter in the grand old Russian tradition, every bit as cold, calculating, and devoid of any warm personality traits as the worst of his prede-cessors. Because he had no political, *apparatchik*, military, or intelli-gence background, no one knew how Zevitin thought, what he desired, or who his allies or captains in government were—his henchmen could be anyone, anywhere. That kept most of the Krem-lin off-guard, suspicious, tight-lipped, and at least overtly loyal.

"No, sir—the missile went faster than Mach four, which is the fastest speed our fighter's radar can track a target. I would describe it as a very high-speed guided rocket."

"I assume, then, that you compared the time of launch and the time of impact and came up with a number?"

"Yes, sir." His eyes looked pained—no one could tell whether it was because the general was afraid of telling the president the bad news, or because he was being lectured to by this foreign-sounding young playboy.

"But you don't believe the number you computed," Zevitin said for the air force chief of staff. "Obviously this weapon was some-thing we did not expect. What was the speed, General?"

"Average speed, Mach five point seven."

"Almost *six times the speed of sound*?" That news rocked every member of the security staff back in their chairs. "And that was the *average* speed, which means the *top* speed was Mach . . . ten? *The Americans have an attack missile that can fly at Mach ten?* Why didn't we know of this?"

"We know now, sir," General Furzyenko said. "The Americans made the mistake of using their new toy with one of our fighters on his wingtip."

"Obviously they were not concerned enough about our fighter to cancel their patrol or their attack," Zevitin offered.

"It was what the Americans call an 'operational test,' sir," air force chief of staff General Andrei Darzov said. A short, battle-worn air force bomber pilot, Darzov preferred his head shaved bald because he knew how it intimidated a lot of people, especially politicians and bureaucrats. He had visible burn scars on the left side of his neck and on his left hand, and the fourth and fifth fingers of his left hand were missing, all a result of injuries sustained in the bombing of Engels Air Base, Russia's main bomber base, several years earlier, when he served as Forces of Long-Range Aviation division commander.

Darzov had wanted nothing short of bloody payback for the utter devastation wreaked on his headquarters during the sneak attack on Engels, and swore revenge on the American air commander who had planned and executed it . . . Lieutenant General Patrick McLanahan.

Under former military chief of staff turned president Anatoliy Gryzlov, who wanted revenge on the United States as badly as Darzov, he soon got his opportunity. Andrei Darzov was the architect of the plan just a year later to modify Russia's long-range Tu-95 Bear, Tu-26 Backfire, and Tu-160 Blackjack bombers with aerial refueling probes to allow them the range to attack the United States. It was an audacious, ambitious plan that succeeded in destroying most of the United States' long-range bombers and the control centers for over half of their land-based intercontinental ballistic nuclear-tipped missiles. The devastating assault killed over thirty thousand people and injured or sickened thousands more, and soon became known as the "American Holocaust."

But Darzov hadn't heard the last of his archenemy, Patrick McLanahan. When McLanahan's counterattack destroyed almost an equivalent number of Russia's most powerful silo-based and mobile intercontinental ballistic missiles, someone had to take the blame—other than the then-president of Russia, General Gryzlov, who had been killed during an American air strike on his Ryazan underground command center—and Darzov was it. He was blamed for making the decision to stage all of the Ilyushin-78 and Tupolev-16 tanker aircraft at one isolated air base in Siberia, Yakutsk, and for not providing enough security there, which allowed McLanahan and his Air Battle Force to take over the base and use the enormous amount of fuel stored there to be used by McLanahan's bombers to hunt down and destroy Russia's land-based nuclear deterrent force.

Darzov was demoted to one-star general and sent to Yakutsk to oversee the cleanup and eventual closing of that once-vital Siberian base—because in an attempt to destroy McLanahan's bombers on the ground, Gryzlov had ordered Yakutsk attacked by low-yield nuclear weapons. While only four of the dozens of nuclear warheads penetrated McLanahan's anti-missile shield around the base, and they were all high-altitude airbursts designed to minimize radioactive fallout, most of the base had been severely damaged, and the heart of it had been flattened and rendered uninhabitable. There was much speculation that the general staff hoped Darzov would become sick from the lingering radioactivity so they would be spared the chore of eliminating the popular, intelligent young general officer.

But not only did Darzov not die, he didn't stay long in virtual exile in Siberia. Health-wise, Darzov and his loyal senior staff members survived by using the radioactivity decontamination equipment left behind by the Americans when they evacuated their personnel from Yakutsk. Career- and prestige-wise, he survived by not giving in to despair when it seemed like the entire world was against him.

With the financial and moral support of a young investment banker named Leonid Zevitin, Darzov rebuilt the base and soon made it operational again instead of preparing it for demolition and abandonment. The move revitalized Russia's Siberian oil and gas industry, which relied on the base for much-needed support and supply, and the government raked in enormous amounts of revenue from Siberian oil, most sold to Japan and China through new pipelines. The young base commander garnered the attention

and gratitude of Russia's wealthiest and most successful investment banker, Leonid Zevitin. Thanks to Zevitin's sponsorship,
Darzov was brought back to Moscow, promoted to four-star general, and eventually picked as chief of staff of the air forces by
newly elected president Zevitin.

"The Americans have tipped their hand and revealed a new hypersonic air-to-ground weapon," Furzyenko said. "It shows how
overconfident they are, and that will be their weakness. Not only
that, but they wasted a multimillion-dollar missile destroying a truck
and homemade rocket worth a few dollars."

"Seems to me they have every right to be overconfident,
General—they can quickly and accurately destroy any target from
two hundred miles away as easy as a child plinking a can with a .22
rifle from twenty meters away," Zevitin said. Many of the generals
knitted their eyebrows, as much in confusion at some of Zevitin's
Western terms as in struggling to understand his heavily accented
Russian. "Plus, they did it right before our eyes, knowing we'd be
watching and measuring the weapon's performance. It was a dem-
onstration for our benefit, as well as a very effective terror weapon
against the Islamists." Zevitin turned to Darzov. "What happened
to the fighter that was shadowing the B-1 bomber, Andrei?"

"The pilot landed safely but with most of his plane's electronic
equipment completely disabled," the air force chief of staff responded.

"How? Their terahertz weapon again?"

"Possibly, but the American so-called T-Ray weapon is a suba-
tomic wide-area weapon that destroys electronic circuits at ranges
exceeding six hundred kilometers," Darzov replied. "No other stations reported any disruption. The pilot reported that as soon as he
launched his missiles his fighter . . . simply shut itself down."

"You mean, the missile shut itself down."

"No, sir. The entire *airplane* shut itself down, as if the pilot had
turned everything off all at once."

"How is that possible?"

"The terahertz weapon may have been able to do it," Darzov

said. "We will not know until we look at the fighter computer's error logs. But my guess would be that McLanahan has deployed his 'netrusion' system on the Dreamland bombers, and possibly all of his aircraft and spacecraft."

" 'Netrusion'? What's that?"

"The ability to 'hack' into an opponent's computer systems through any sensor or antenna that receives digital signals," Darzov explained. "We do not completely understand the process, but the bombers can transmit a signal that is picked up and processed like any other digital instruction or message. The enemy signal can be false radar targets, confusing coded messages, flight control inputs, or even electronic commands to aircraft systems . . ."

"Such as a shutdown order," Zevitin said. He shook his head. "He conceivably could have commanded the MiG to fly straight down or around in circles—luckily he only ordered it to shut down. Must be nice to be so rich that you can build such wonderful toys to load up on your planes." He nodded. "Looks like your old friend is still in the game, eh, General?"

"Yes, sir," Darzov said. "Patrick McLanahan." He smiled. "I will welcome a chance to take him on again and repay him for imprisoning my men and women, taking my base, and stealing my fuel. However, from what I understand, he may not be around much longer. The new administration does not like him at all."

"If McLanahan had any political savvy, he'd have resigned the moment the new president took the oath of office," Zevitin said. "Obviously that has not happened. Either McLanahan is more dedicated—or dumber—than we thought, or Gardner isn't going to fire him, which means he might not be the buffoon we think he is." He looked at the generals around him. "Forget about McLanahan and his high-tech toys that never get built—he's the best they've got, but he's only one man, and he's squirreled away in that awful desert base in Nevada instead of in the White House now, which means no one has the opportunity to listen to him anymore." To Truznyev, chief of the Federal Security Bureau, successor organization to the KGB, he asked, "What about your 'adviser' in Iran? Did you get him out?"

"What was left of him, yes, sir," the FSB chief replied.

"Good. The last thing we need is some enterprising American or Persian investigator finding Russian clothing or weapons mixed in with a lot of Iranian body parts."

"He was replaced with another agent," Truznyev said. He turned angrily to Alexandra Hedrov, the foreign minister. "Giving those Hezbollah bastards weapons like the 9K89 is a waste of time and money, and hurt us in the long run. We should stop supplying them with such advanced missiles and let them go back to firing home-made Katyushas and mortars at the Persian collaborators."

"You agreed to General Furzyenko's recommendation to send the 'Hornet' missile to Iran, Director," Zevitin pointed out.

"I agreed that the Hornet missile should be used to attack Persian army and air force bases with high-explosive and mine-laying warheads, sir," Truznyev said, "not to just fire them indiscriminately into the city. The launch point was at the very edge of the rocket's maximum range to hit the Doshan Tappeh air base, which was the target they told us they were going to strike. The Hezbollah crew also reportedly dragged their feet launching the missile—they even let children come around and watch the launch. This has been reported many times."

"We will obviously have to instruct the insurgents to adjust tactics now that we know about this new American weapon," General Darzov said.

"Will you also instruct them not to put their own homemade poison brews in the warhead?" Truznyev asked.

"What are you talking about, Director?"

"The Hezbollah insurgents loaded the Hornet missile's warhead up with some sort of chemical weapon concoction, similar to mustard gas but much more effective," the FSB chief said perturbedly. "The gas killed a dozen people on the street and injured several dozen others."

"They cooked up their own mustard gas?"

"I do not know where the hell they got it, sir—Iran has a lot of chemical munitions, so maybe they stole it or had it secretly stored away," Truznyev said. "The stuff went off when the American missile hit. But the point is, they violated our directives and attacked an unauthorized target with an unauthorized warhead. There are only a few truck-launched missiles that have the fusing necessary to carry out a chemical weapon attack—it will not be hard for the Americans to discover we supplied the Iranians with the Hornet missiles."

"Get Mohtaz on the phone, *now*," Zevitin ordered. Chief of staff Orlev was on the phone in an instant.

"Now that the Pasdaran has brought in foreign fighters from all over the world to join this damned *jihad* against Buzhazi's coup," Truznyev said, "I do not think the clerics have very tight control over their forces." The Ayatollah Hassan Mohtaz, the former Iranian national defense adviser—and the most senior member of the former Iranian government to survive Buzhazi's bloody purge of Islamists—had been proclaimed president-in-exile, and he called upon all the Muslims of the world to come to Iran and fight against the new military-monarchist government. The anti-Persia insurgency grew quickly, spurred on by tens of thousands of Shi'a Muslim fighters from all over the world who answered the *fatwa* against Buzhazi. Many of the insurgents had been trained by Iran's Revolutionary Guards Corps, the Pasdaran, so their fighting effectiveness was even greater. Within days after Mohtaz's call to arms went out, most of the cities of the new Persia were embroiled in bitter fighting.

But part of the chaos in Persia was due to the fact that the coup leader, General Hesarak al-Kan Buzhazi, inexplicably refused to form a new government. Buzhazi, the past chief of staff and former commander of the paramilitary Internal Defense Forces that battled the Revolutionary Guards Corps, had led a stunningly successful coup, killing most of Iran's theocratic rulers and sending the rest fleeing to neighboring Turkmenistan. It had been assumed that Buzhazi, together with former chief of staff Hoseyn Yassini, the officers of the regular armed forces, and supporters of one of Iran's past royal families, the Qagevs, would take control of the capital city of Tehran and form a government. A name had even been chosen—the Democratic Republic of Persia, indicating a clear direction the people wanted to take—and the country was now referred to by its historic name, "Persia," instead of the name "Iran," which was the name decreed to be used by Reza Shah Pahlavi in 1935. Only supporters of the theocracy still used the name "Iran."

"But I do not think we should stop arming the insurgents," General Darzov said. "Every successful attack against the Persians will weaken them. We need patience."

"And every time the *jihadis* launch another missile into the city and kill innocent women and children, the insurgency suffers the same fate—it gets weakened, as does Russia, General," foreign minister Alexandra Hedrov said. Tall, dark-haired, and as alluring as any woman in the senior echelons of Russian government could be, Alexandra Hedrov was the highest-ranking woman to ever serve in the Kremlin. Like Zevitin, she came from an international finance background, but as a lifelong resident of Moscow and a married mother of two, she didn't have the jet-setting reputation of her superior. Serious and sharp and without extensive political connections, Hedrov was widely considered the brains behind the presidency. "We look even worse if we are seen supporting baby-killers."

She turned to Zevitin. "Mohtaz has got to find a way to tone down the *jihadis*, Mr. President, without relieving the pressure on Buzhazi and Qagev to give up and evacuate the country. We cannot be seen supporting mass murder and instability—that makes us look unstable ourselves. If Mohtaz continues on this path, the only recourse we have is to support Buzhazi."

"Buzhazi?" Zevitin asked, confused. "Why support Buzhazi? He turned to the Americans for help."

"That was our fault—he acted out of desperation, and we were not there for him when he needed us, so he turned to McLanahan," Hedrov explained. "But Washington inexplicably has not thrown its support behind Buzhazi, and this creates an opportunity for Russia. We secretly support Mohtaz because Russia benefits from the instability in the region with higher oil prices and greatly increased arms sales. But if we end up backing a loser, we should reverse course and support whom I believe will be the eventual winner: Buzhazi."

"I disagree, Minister," Darzov said. "Buzhazi is not strong enough to destroy Mohtaz."

"Then I suggest you get out of your airplanes and laboratories and take a look at the world as it really is, General," Hedrov said. "Here is the real question, Mr. President: Whom do you *want* to win, Buzhazi or Mohtaz? That is who we should be supporting. We support Mohtaz because the chaos in the Middle East keeps America from meddling in our affairs in our own spheres of influence. But is a theocratic Iran a better choice for Russia? We know Buzhazi. You and I have both met with him; we supported him for many years, before, during, and after his removal as chief of staff. We still supply each other with intelligence information, although he is keeping information about the American presence in Iran closely guarded and more expensive to obtain. Maybe it is time to increase the level of contact with him."

The phone vibrated beside Orlev, and he picked it up and moments later put it on hold. "Mohtaz on the line, sir."

"Where is he?"

"Iranian embassy in Ashkhabad, Turkmenistan," Orlev replied, anticipating the question.

"Good." When the Ayatollah Mohtaz and his advisers fled Iran, he unexpectedly holed up in the Russian embassy in Ashkhabad, demanding protection from Buzhazi's forces and the so-called monarchist death squads. That created a lot of curiosity and questions from most of the rest of the world. It was well known that Moscow was an ally of Iran, but would they go so far as to protect the old regime? What if elections were held and the theocrats were voted out? Would the clerics and Islamists become an albatross around Russia's neck?

As a concession to the rest of the world, Zevitin had Mohtaz leave the embassy, but quietly guaranteed his safety with Russian FSB units stationed in and around the Iranian compound. At first he thought the Islamist wouldn't leave the embassy—or, worse, threaten to expose Russia's involvement in Iran if he was forced out—but thankfully things didn't reach that stage. He knew Mohtaz could always produce that card in the future, and he needed to decide what to do if he tried to play it.

Zevitin picked up his phone. "President Mohtaz, this is Leonid Zevitin."

"Please stand by for His Excellency, sir," a heavily Persian-accented voice said in Russian. Zevitin rolled his eyes impatiently. It was always a game with weak men like Mohtaz, he thought—it was always so damned important to try to gain the smallest advantage by making the other party wait, even over something as simple as a phone call.

A few moments later, the voice of a young translator said, "The Imam Mohtaz is on the line. Identify yourself please."

"Mr. President, this is Leonid Zevitin calling. I hope you are well."

"Praise be to God for his mercy, it is so."

No attempt to return pleasantries, Zevitin noted—again, typical of Mohtaz. "I wanted to discuss the recent air attack by the Americans in Tehran against a suspected Hezbollah rocket launcher."

"I know nothing of this."

"Mr. President, I warned you against allowing the insurgents to arm the rockets with weapons of mass destruction," Zevitin said. "We specifically chose the Hornet rocket because it is in use all over the world and would be harder to trace back to Russia. The only rocket force known to have the technology to put chemical warheads on them was Russia."

"I know no details of what the freedom fighters do in their struggle against the crusaders, nonbelievers, and Zionists," the translator said. "All I know is that God will reward all who have answered the call of holy retribution. They will earn a place at His right hand."

"Mr. President, I urge you to keep your forces in check," Zevitin said. "Armed resistance to foreign occupation is acceptable to all nations, even with unguided rockets against suspected sympathizers, but using poison gas is not. Your insurgency risks a popular backlash if—"

Zevitin could hear Mohtaz shouting in the background even be-

fore the translator finished speaking, and then the flustered young
man had to scramble to keep up with the Iranian cleric's sudden ti-
rade: "This is not an insurgency, damn your eyes," the translator
said in a much calmer voice than Mohtaz's. "Proud Iranians and
their brothers are taking back the nation that has been illegally and
immorally taken from us. That is not an insurgency—it is a holy
war of freedom against oppression. And in such a struggle, all weapons and all tactics are justified in the eyes of God." And the connection was broken.

"Fucking bastard," Zevitin swore—not realizing until it was too
late that he had done so in English—as he slammed the receiver
down.

"Why bother with that insane zealot, sir?" foreign affairs minister Hedrov asked. "The man is crazy. He cares for nothing else but
retaking power—he does not care how many innocent people he
must kill to do it. He is bringing in foreign *jihadis* from all over the
world, and most of them are crazier than *he* is."

"Do you think I care about Mohtaz or anyone in that damned
country, Minister?" Zevitin asked heatedly. "For the time being, it is
better for Russia with Mohtaz alive and stirring up the Islamists,
calling for them to go to Iran and fight. I hope that country tears itself apart, which is almost a certainty if the insurgency grows."

"I wish Buzhazi had called on *us* rather than McLanahan when
he wanted support for his insurgency—Mohtaz and that monarchist
bitch Qagev would be dead by now, and Buzhazi would be firmly in
command, with us at his side," Hedrov said, casting a disapproving
glare at Federal Security Bureau chief Truznyev. "We should have
recruited him the moment he surfaced in the Iranian People's Mili-
tia."

"Buzhazi was completely off our radar screens, Minister,"
Truznyev said dismissively. "He was disgraced and all but con-
demned to die. Iran had drifted into the Chinese sphere of influence . . ."

"We sold them plenty of weapons."

"After oil prices rose, yes—they bought Chinese crap because it was cheaper," Truznyev said. "But then we found many of those weapons in the hands of Chechen separatists and drug runners within our own borders in short order. China stopped their support for Iran long ago because they support Islamists in Xinjiang and East Turkestan—Chinese Islamic insurgents were fighting government troops *with their own damned weapons*! The theocrats in Iran are completely out of control. They do not deserve our support."

"All right, all right," Zevitin said wearily, shaking his hand at his advisers. "These endless arguments are getting us nowhere." To Truznyev, he said, "Igor, get me all the data on that American hypersonic missile you can get your hands on, and get it fast. I don't need to know how to counter it—yet. I need enough information so that I can make Gardner *believe* that I know *all* about it. I want to argue that it's a threat to world peace, regional stability, the arms balance, blah, blah, blah. Same with their damned Armstrong Space Station. And I'd like an update on *all* the new American military technology. I'm tired of hearing about it *after* we encounter it in the field."

"*Argue* with the Americans, eh, Mr. President?" chief of the general staff Furzyenko asked sarcastically. "Perhaps we can go in front of the Security Council and argue that the sunlight reflecting off their station's radar arrays keeps us up at night."

"I don't need snide remarks from you today, General—I need results," Zevitin said acidly. "The Americans are settled in Iraq, and they may have gained a foothold in Iran if Buzhazi and the Qagev successfully forms a government friendly to the West. Along with American bases in central Asia, the Baltics, and eastern Europe, Iran adds yet another section of fence with which to pen us in. Now they have this damned space station, which passes over Russia ten times a day! Russia is virtually surrounded—" And at that, Zevitin slapped his hand down hard on the table. "—and that is *completely unacceptable*!" He looked each of his advisers in the eye, his gaze pausing momentarily on Truznyev and Darzov before sitting back in his seat and irritably running a hand over his forehead.

"That hypersonic missile surprised us all, sir," Truznyev said.

"Bullshit," Zevitin retorted. "They need to test-fire the thing, don't they? They can't do that in an underground laboratory. Why can't we be observing their missile tests? We know exactly where their high-speed instrumented test ranges are for hypersonic missile development—we should be all over those sites."

"Good espionage costs money, Mr. President. Why spy for the Russians when the Israelis and Chinese can offer ten times the price?"

"Then perhaps it's time to cut some salaries and expensive retirement benefits of our so-called leaders and put the money back into getting quality intelligence data," Zevitin said acidly. "Back when Russian oil was only a few dollars a barrel, Russia once had hundreds of spies deep inside every nook and cranny of American weapons development—we once had almost unfettered access to Dreamland, their most highly classified facility. And what places we didn't infiltrate ourselves, we were able to buy information from hundreds more, including Americans. The FSB's and military intelligence's task is to get that information, and since Gryzlov's administration we haven't done a damned thing but whine and moan about being surrounded and possibly attacked again by the Americans." He paused again, then looked at the armed forces chief of staff. "Give us a status report on *Fanar*, General Furzyenko."

"One unit fully operational, sir," the chief of staff replied. "The mobile anti-satellite laser system proved very successful in downing one of the American spaceplanes over Iran."

"*What?*" chief of staff Orlev exclaimed. "Then, what the Americans said was true? One of their spaceplanes *was* downed by us?"

Zevitin nodded to Furzyenko as he pulled a cigarette from his desk drawer and lit up, wordlessly giving him permission to explain. "The *Fanar* project is a top-secret mobile anti-satellite laser system, Mr. Orlev," the military chief of staff explained. "It is based on the Kavaznya anti-satellite laser system developed in the 1980s, but greatly modified, enhanced, and improved."

"Kavaznya was a massive facility powered by a nuclear reactor, if I remember correctly," Orlev observed. He was only in high school when he learned about it—at the time the government had said there was an accident and the plant had been shut down for safety upgrades. It was only when he assumed his post as chief of staff that he learned that Kavaznya had actually been bombed by a single American B-52 Stratofortress bomber, a highly modified experimental "test-bed" model known as the "Megafortress"—crewed by none other than Patrick McLanahan, who was then just an Air Force captain and crew bombardier. The name *McLanahan* had popped up many times in relation to dozens of events around the world in the two decades since that attack, to the point that Darzov and even Zevitin seemed obsessed with the man, his high-tech machines, and his schemes. "How can such a system be mobile?"

"Twenty years of research and engineering, billions of rubles, and a lot of espionage—*good* espionage, not like today," Zevitin said. "Continue, General."

"Yes, sir," Furzyenko said. "*Fanar*'s design is based on the Israeli Tactical High-Energy Laser program and the American airborne laser program, which puts a chemical laser on a large aircraft such as a Boeing 747 or B-52 bomber. It is capable of destroying a ballistic missile at ranges as far as five hundred kilometers. It is not as powerful as Kavaznya was, but it is portable, easily transported and maintained, is durable and reliable, extremely accurate, and if locked onto target long enough, can destroy even heavily shielded spacecraft hundreds of kilometers in space . . . like the Americans' new Black Stallion spaceplane."

Orlev's mouth dropped. "Then the rumors are true?" Zevitin smiled, nodded, then took another deep drag of his cigarette. "But we denied we had anything to do with the loss of the American spaceplane! The Americans must realize we have such a weapon!"

"And thus the game begins," Zevitin said, smiling as he finished the last of his cigarette. He ground the butt into the ashtray as if demonstrating what he intended to do to anyone who dared oppose him. "We'll see who is willing to play, and who is not. Continue, General."

"Yes, sir. The system can be disguised as a standard twelve-meter tractor-trailer rig and can be driven almost anywhere and mixed in with normal commercial traffic. It can be set up and readied to fire in less than an hour, can fire about a dozen bursts on one refueling, depending on how long the laser is firing at one target—and, most importantly, it can be broken down and moved within minutes after firing."

"Only a dozen bursts? That does not sound like very many engagements."

"We can bring along more fuel, of course," Furzyenko said, "but *Fanar* was never designed to counter large numbers of spacecraft or aircraft. The system can only fire for up to thirty seconds at a time due to heat, and one load of fuel can fire the laser for approximately sixty seconds total. The next barrage can be fired thirty to forty minutes later after refueling, depending on if the fuel comes from the fire vehicle or a separate support vehicle. Most spacecraft in low-Earth orbit would be well beyond the horizon before another barrage, so we decided it would be best not to try to fire too many barrages at once.

"In addition, everything else in the convoy increases in size as well—security, provisions, spare parts, power generators—so we decided to limit the extra laser fuel to one truck. With one command and fire vehicle, one power and control vehicle, one refueling and supply vehicle, and one support and crew vehicle, it can still travel anonymously enough on open highways anywhere without drawing attention. We brought it back to Moscow for additional tests and upgrades. That will take some time to accomplish."

"I think you've had enough time, General," Zevitin said. "The Americans need to see how vulnerable their precious space station and spaceplanes can be. I want that system up and running *now*."

"If I had more engineers and more money, sir, I could finish the three that are in the construction pipeline within a year," Furzyenko said. He glanced at General Darzov. "But there seems to be a lot of attention being paid to General Darzov's *Molnija* project, and I'm afraid our resources are being unduly diverted."

"Darzov has made some good arguments for *Molnija*, General Furzyenko," Zevitin said.

"I'm afraid I do not know what *Molnija* is, Mr. President," Alexandra Hedrov said. "I assume it's not a fine watch maker. Is this a new secret weapon program?"

Zevitin nodded to Andrei Darzov, who stood and began: "*Molnija* is an air-launched anti-satellite weapon, Madam Minister. It is a prototype weapon only, a combination of the Kh-90 hypersonic cruise missile reprogrammed for extreme high-altitude flight with a combination of rocket-ramjet-rocket propulsion to allow it to fly up to five hundred kilometers above Earth. The system was first developed by the Americans in the 1980s; we had a similar system but canceled it many years ago. The technology has improved greatly since then."

"*Molnija* is a big step backward," Furzyenko said. "The laser system has proven its worth. Air-launched anti-satellite weapons were rejected years ago because it was unreliable and too easily detected."

"With respect, sir, I disagree," Darzov said. Furzyenko turned to glare at his subordinate, but it was difficult to stare at the man's rather disturbing wounds, and he was forced to look away. "The problem with a fixed anti-satellite weapon, as was found with the Kavaznya anti-satellite laser, is that it is too easy to attack it, even with numerous and sophisticated anti-aircraft weapon systems protecting it. Even the mobile laser system we developed is vulnerable to attack since it takes so much support and takes so long to set up, fuel, and aim. We saw how quickly the Americans were able to attack the laser site in Iran—luckily, we had time to move the real system and construct a decoy in its place. *Molnija* can be carried to many air bases in the target's path and can attack from multiple angles.

"A single *Molnija* missile is carried aloft by a MiG-29 fighter or Tupolev-16 light bomber, or two missiles can be carried by a Tupolev-95 or Tupolev-160 heavy bomber," Darzov went on. "The launch aircraft are maneuvered into position by ground-based or airborne radars and then the missiles are released. *Molnija* uses a solid rocket motor to boost it to supersonic speed, where it then uses a ramjet engine to accelerate to eight times the speed of sound and climb to target altitude. Once in range of the target, it uses its on-board sensors to track the target and ignites its third-stage rocket motor to begin the intercept. It uses precision thrusters to get within range, then detonates a high-explosive fragmentary warhead. We can also place a nuclear or X-ray laser warhead on the weapon, depending on the size of the target."

"X-ray laser? What is that?"

"An X-ray laser is a device that collects and focuses X-rays from a small nuclear explosion and produces extremely powerful long-range energy beams that can penetrate even heavily shielded spacecraft as far as two hundred kilometers away," Darzov said. "It is designed to disable spacecraft by scrambling its electronics and guidance systems."

"Using nuclear weapons in space will create problems in the international community, General," Hedrov pointed out.

"The Americans have had a nuclear reactor flying over Russia for decades, and no one seemed to notice, Alexandra," Zevitin said bitterly. "The X-ray laser is just one option—we'll use it only if it's deemed absolutely necessary."

"The nuclear reactor on board the American space station is just for generating power, sir," Hedrov pointed out. "Yes, the laser has been used as an offensive weapon, but the reactor is thought of differently . . ."

"It is still an atomic device," Zevitin argued, "which is expressly prohibited by treaty—a treaty the Americans casually ignore!"

"I am in agreement with you, sir," Hedrov said, "but after the air attacks against the United States using nuclear weapons by President Gryzlov—"

"Yes, yes, I know . . . America gets a pass, and the world waits in fear to see what Russia will do next," Zevitin said, the frustration thick in his voice. "I'm sick of the double standard." He shook his

head, then turned to General Darzov again. "What is the status of
the anti-satellite missile program, General? Can we deploy the system or not?"

"Additional underground tests with the prototype *Molnija* unit
were highly successful," Darzov went on. "The technicians and engineers want more tests done, but I believe it is ready for battle now,
sir. We can make improvements, upgrades, and enhancements for
years and make it better, but I think it is ready as is, and I recommend deployment immediately."

"Excuse me, sir," Furzyenko interjected, looking at Minister of
National Defense Ostenkov in confusion, "but General Darzov isn't
in charge of *Molnija*. It's a secret project that is still being overseen by
my research and development bureau."

"Not anymore, General," Zevitin said. "I have tasked General
Darzov to develop strategies for dealing with the American space
station and spaceplanes. He will report to me and Minister Ostenkov
directly."

Furzyenko's mouth opened and closed in confusion, then hardened in sheer anger. "This is an outrage, sir!" he blurted out. "This
is an insult! The chief of staff is responsible for organizing, training,
and equipping the armed forces, and I should have been informed
of this!"

"You are being informed now, General," Zevitin said. "*Fanar* and
Molnija belong to Darzov. He will keep me informed of his actions
and will make recommendations to the national security bureau,
but he takes his orders only from me. The farther outside your chain
of command he operates, the better." Zevitin smiled and nodded
knowingly. "A little lesson we've learned from our friend General
Patrick Shane McLanahan over the years, yes?"

"I believe the man is obsessive, compulsive, paranoid, and probably schizophrenic, sir," Darzov said, "but he is also courageous and
intelligent—two traits I admire. His unit is extremely effective because it operates with speed and daring with small numbers of
highly motivated and energetic forces in command of the latest technological innovations. McLanahan also seems to completely disre-

gard most regulations, normal conventions, and chains of command, and acts precipitously, perhaps even recklessly. Some say he is crazy. All I know is, he gets the job done."

"As long as you don't go off the deep end yourself," Zevitin warned.

"Unfortunately I agree with Minister Hedrov, sir: nuclear weapons in space will not be seen as a defensive weapon by the world community," Minister of National Defense Ostenkov said.

"The world community looks the other way and shuts its eyes and ears while the Americans orbit a nuclear reactor over their heads and fill the skies with satellites and spaceplanes—I really don't give a shit about their opinions," Zevitin said angrily. "The Americans can't be allowed to freely go in and out of space as they please. Our mobile ground-based laser got one and almost got another of their spaceplanes—we almost took out their entire active fleet. If we can bring down whatever they have left, we can cripple their military space program and possibly give us a chance to catch up again." He glared at Ostenkov. "Your job is to support the development and fielding of *Fanar* and *Molnija,* Ostenkov, not tell me what *you* think the world will say. Understood?"

"Yes, sir," Ostenkov said. "The anti-satellite missile is ready for operational testing. It could be the most feared weapon in our arsenal since the Kh-90 hypersonic cruise missile which Gryzlov used successfully to attack the United States. It can be deployed quickly and easily anywhere in the world, faster than a spacecraft can be launched or repositioned in an orbit. We can transport *Molnija* anywhere and run only a small risk of discovery until it's fired."

"And then what?" Orlev asked. "The Americans will retaliate with everything they have. You know they consider space part of their sovereign territory."

"That's why we need to employ *Fanar* and *Molnija* carefully—very, very carefully," Zevitin said. "Their usefulness as weapons depend more on quietly degrading the Americans' space assets, not trying to outright destroy them. If it's possible to make it look like their space station, spaceplanes, and satellites are unreliable or wasteful, the Americans will shut them down on their own. This is not an attack plan or a cat-and-mouse game—it's a game of irritation, of quiet degradation and growing uncertainty. I want to bug the shit out of the Americans."

" 'Bug the shit,' sir?" Orlev asked. "What does this mean?"

"It means attack the Americans with mosquito bites, not swords," Zevitin said in Russian this time, not realizing until just then that in his excitement he had switched to English again. "Americans have no tolerance for failure. If it doesn't work, they'll scrap it and replace it with something better, even if the malfunction is no fault of theirs. Not only will they scrap something that doesn't work, but they'll blame the failure on everyone else, waste billions of dollars indicting someone to take the blame, then spend billions more to try to come up with a solution that is oftentimes inferior to the first." He smiled, then added, "And the key to this working is President Joseph Gardner."

"Naturally, sir—he is the President of the United States," Orlev remarked, confused.

"I'm not talking about the office, but of the man himself," Zevitin said. "He may be the commander-in-chief of the most powerful military force in the world, but the thing he is *not* in command of is the most important path to success: control of *himself*." He looked at the advisers around him and saw mostly blank expressions. "Thank you, all, thank you, that's all for now," he said dismissively, reaching for another cigarette.

Chief of Staff Orlev and Minister of Foreign Affairs Hedrov remained behind; Orlev didn't even try to suggest to Hedrov that he and the president be allowed to talk privately. "Sir, my impression, one that I share, is that the staff is confused about your intentions," Orlev said pointedly. "Half of them see you surrendering power to the Americans; the others think you are ready to start a war with them."

"Good . . . that's good," Zevitin said, taking a deep drag of his cigarette, then exhaling noisily. "If my advisers leave my office guessing—especially in opposite directions—they don't have an opportunity to formulate a counterstrategy. Besides, if *they're* confused, the Americans certainly *should* be as well." Orlev looked worried. "Peter, we can't yet beat the Americans in a military confrontation—we'd bankrupt this country trying. But we have lots of opportunities to stand in opposition to them and deny them a victory. Gardner is the weak link. He needs to be niggled. Irritate him enough and he'll turn on even his most trusted advisers and loyal countrymen." Zevitin thought for a moment, then added, "He needs to be irritated right now. The attack on our fighter . . . he needs to know how angry we are that they downed our fighter with a low-yield nuclear device."

"But . . . the fighter was not *downed*," Orlev reminded him, "and the general said the weapon was not a nuclear T-Ray weapon, but a—"

"For God's sake, Peter, we're not going to tell the Americans what we *know,* but what we *believe,*" Zevitin said, irritation in his voice but a smile on his face. "My reports state that they shot down our fighter with a T-Ray nuclear device, without provocation. That is an act of war. Get Gardner on the phone immediately."

"Should Minister Hedrov make contact and—?"

"No, I will make the protest directly with Gardner," Zevitin said. Orlev nodded and picked up the phone on Zevitin's desk. "Not the regular phone, Peter. Use the 'hot line.' Voice and data both." The emergency "hot line" between Washington and Moscow had been upgraded after the conflicts of 2004 to allow voice, data, and video communications between the two capitals, as well as teletype and facsimile, and also allowed for more satellite circuits that gave the leaders easier access to one another. "Minister Hedrov, you will file a formal complaint with the United Nations Security Council and the American State Department as well. And I want every media outlet on the planet given a report of the incident immediately."

Orlev made the call to the foreign ministry first, then contacted the Kremlin signal officer to open the "hot line" for the president. "Sir, this could backfire," Orlev warned as he waited for the connection. "Our pilot certainly initiated the attack by firing on the American bomber—"

"But only after the bomber launched their hypersonic missile," Zevitin said. "That missile could've been headed anywhere. The Americans were clearly the aggressors. The pilot was fully justified in firing his missiles. It turns out he was correct, because the missile the Americans fired into Tehran carried a chemical warhead."

"But—"

"The first reports may be proved inaccurate, Peter," Zevitin said, "but that doesn't mean we can't protest this incident *now*. I believe Gardner will act first and *then* check out the facts. You wait and see."

Alexandra Hedrov looked at Zevitin silently for a long moment; then: "What is this all about, Leonid? Do you just want to harass Gardner? What for? He is not worth the effort. He will more likely self-destruct without you constantly . . . how did you say, 'niggled' him. And certainly you cannot want Russia to align with and support the Iranians. As I said before, they are just as likely to turn on us after they retake their country."

"This has absolutely nothing to do with Iran, Alexandra, and everything to do with Russia," Zevitin said. "Russia will not be encircled and isolated any longer. Gryzlov was a megalomaniac, sure, but because of his insane ideas Russia was feared once more. But in their absolute fear, or pity, the world began to give the United States all it wanted, and that was to encircle and try to squash Russia again. I will not allow that to happen."

"But how will deploying these anti-spacecraft weapons accomplish this?"

"You don't understand, Alexandra—threatening war against the Americans will only serve to increase their resolve," Zevitin explained. "Even a spineless fop like Gardner will fight if his back is forced against the wall—at the very least, he'll turn his junkyard dog McLanahan loose on us, as much as he resents his power and determination.

"No, we must make the Americans themselves believe they are weak, that they must cooperate and negotiate with Russia to avoid war and disaster," Zevitin went on. "Gardner's hatred—and fear—of McLanahan is the key. To make himself look like the brave leader he can never be, I'm hoping Gardner will sacrifice his greatest general, dismantle his most advanced weapon systems, and retreat from important alliances and defensive commitments, all on the altar of international cooperation and world peace."

"But why? To what end, Mr. President? Why risk war with the Americans like this?"

"Because I won't stand to see Russia encircled," Zevitin said sharply. "Just look at a damned map, Minister! Every former Warsaw Pact country is a member of the North Atlantic Treaty Organization; almost every former Soviet republic has a NATO or American base of some kind on it."

Zevitin went to light up another cigarette, but threw them across his desk in blind anger. "We are wealthy beyond the dreams of our fathers, Alexandra, and yet we can't *spit* without the Americans complaining, measuring, analyzing, or intercepting it," he cried. "If I wake up and see that damned space station shooting across the sky—*my Russian sky!*—once more, I am going to scream! And if I see another youngster on the streets of Moscow watching an American TV show or listening to Western music because he or she has free Internet access courtesy of the American domination of space, I will kill someone! No more! *No more!* Russia will not be encircled, and we will not be smothered into submission by their space toys!

"I want Russian skies cleared of American spacecraft, and I want our airwaves cleansed of American transmissions, and I don't care if I have to start a war in Iran, Turkmenistan, Europe, *or in space* to do it!"

Aboard Armstrong Space Station

A short time later

"Stud Zero-Seven is ready to depart, sir," Master Sergeant Lukas reported.

"Thanks, Master Sergeant," Patrick McLanahan responded. He flipped a switch on his console: "Have a good trip home, Boomer. Let me know how the module release experiments and new re-entry procedure works."

"Will do, sir," Hunter Noble responded. "Feels weird not having you on board flying the jet."

"At least you get to pilot it this time, right?"

"I had to arm-wrestle Frenchy for it, and it was close—but yes, I won," Boomer said. He got an exasperated glance in his rear-cockpit camera from U.S. Navy Lieutenant Commander Lisette "Frenchy" Moulain, an experienced F/A-18 Hornet combat pilot and NASA space shuttle mission commander and pilot. She had recently qualified to be spacecraft commander of the XR-A9 Black Stallion spaceplane and was always looking for another chance to pilot the bird, but none of her arguments worked this time on Boomer. When Patrick flew to and from the station—which was quite often recently—he usually picked Boomer to be his back-seater.

Minutes later the Black Stallion detached from the docking bay aboard Armstrong Space Station, and Boomer carefully maneuvered the craft away from the station. When they were far enough away, he maneuvered into retrorocket firing position, flying tailfirst. "Countdown checklists complete, we're in the final automatic count-down hold," he announced over intercom. "We're about six hundred miles to touchdown. Ready for this one, Frenchy?"

"I've already reported my checklists are complete, Captain," Moulain responded.

Boomer rolled his eyes in mock exasperation. "Frenchy, when we get back home, we need to sit down at a nice bar somewhere on the Strip, have an expensive champagne drink, and talk about your attitude—toward me, toward the service, toward life."

"Captain, you know very well that I'm engaged, I don't drink, and I love my work and my life," Moulain said in that same grinding hair-pulling monotone that Boomer absolutely hated. "I might also add, if you haven't realized it by now, that I hate that call-sign, and I don't particularly care for *you,* so even if I was unattached, drank alcohol, and you were the last man on earth with the biggest cock and longest tongue this side of Vegas, I wouldn't be seen dead in a bar or anywhere else with you."

"Ouch, Frenchy. That's harsh."

"I think you're an outstanding spacecraft commander and engineer and a competent test pilot," she added, "but I find you a disgrace to the uniform and I often wonder why you are still at Dreamland and still a member of the United States Air Force. I think your skill as an engineer seems to overshadow the partying, hanging out at casinos, and the constant stream of women in and out of your life—mostly *out*—and frankly I resent that."

"Don't hold back, Commander. Tell me how you *really* feel."

"Now when I report 'checklist complete,' Captain, as you fully well know, that indicates that my station is squared away, that I have examined and checked everything I can in your station and the rest of the craft and found it optimal, and that I am prepared for the next evolution."

"Oooh. I love it when you talk Navy talk. 'Squared away' and 'evolution' sound so nautical. Kinda kinky too, coming from a woman."

"You know, Captain, I put up with your nonsense because you're Air Force and this is an Air Force unit, and I know Air Force officers always act casually around each other, even if there's a great difference in rank," Moulain pointed out. "You're also the spacecraft commander, which puts you in charge despite the fact that I outrank you. So I'm going to ignore your sexist remarks during this mission.

But it certainly doesn't change my opinion of you as a person and as an Air Force officer—in fact, it verifies it."

"Sorry. I didn't catch all that. I was busy sticking pencils in my ears to keep from listening to you."

"Can we follow the test flight plan and just do this, Captain, without all the male macho bullshit nonsense? We're already thirty seconds past the planned commencement time."

"All right, all right, Frenchy," Boomer said. "I was just trying to act like we're part of a crew and not serving on separate decks of a ship in the nineteenth-century Navy. Pardon me for trying." He pressed a control stud on his flight control stick. "Get me out of this, Stud Seven. Begin powered descent."

"Commencing powered descent, stop powered descent . . ." When the computer did not receive a countermanding order, it began: *"Commencing deorbit burn in three, two, one, now."* The Laser Pulse Detonation Rocket System engines, or LPDRS, pronounced "leopards," activated and went to full power. Burning JP-7 jet fuel and hydrogen peroxide oxidizer with other chemicals and superheated pulses from lasers to increase the specific impulse, the Black Stallion's four LPDRS engines produced twice as much thrust as all of the engines aboard the space shuttle orbiters combined.

As the spacecraft slowed, it began to descend. Normally at a certain velocity Boomer would shut down the main engines and then turn the spacecraft using its thrusters to a forward-flying nose-high attitude and prepare for "entry interface," or the first encounter with the atmosphere, and then use aerobraking—scraping the shielded underside against the atmosphere—to slow down for landing. This time, however, Boomer kept it flying tailfirst and the LPDRS engines running at full power.

Most spacecraft could not do this for long because they didn't carry enough fuel, but the Black Stallion spaceplane was different: because it refueled while on Armstrong Space Station, it had as much fuel as it would have when blasting *into* orbit, which meant it could keep its engines running for much longer periods during re-entry. Although aerobraking was much more fuel-efficient, it had its own set of hazards—namely, the intense heat of friction that built up on the underside of the spacecraft—so the crew was trying a different re-entry method.

As the Black Stallion slowed even more, the descent angle got steeper, until it seemed as if they were pointed straight up. The flight and engine control computers adjusted power to maintain a steady 3-G deceleration force. "I hate to ask," Boomer grunted through the G-forces pressing his body back into his seat, "but how are you doing back there, Frenchy? Still optimal?"

"In the green, Captain," Frenchy responded, forcing her breath through constricted throat muscles in order to keep her abdominal muscles tight, which increased blood pressure in her head. "All systems in the green, station check complete."

"A very squared-away report, thank you, M. Moulain," Boomer said. "I'm optimal up here too."

Passing through Mach 5, or five times the speed of sound, and just before reaching the atmosphere at approximately sixty miles' altitude, Boomer said, "Ready to initiate payload separation." His voice was much more serious now because this was a much more critical phase of the mission.

"Roger, payload separation coming up . . . program initiated," Moulain responded. The cargo bay doors on top of the Black Stallion's fuselage opened, and powerful thrusters pushed a BDU-58 container out of the bay. The BDU-58 "Meteor" container was designed to protect up to four thousand pounds of payload as it descended through the atmosphere. Once through the atmosphere the Meteor could glide up to three hundred miles to a landing spot, or release its payload before impacting the ground.

This mission was designed to show that the Black Stallion spaceplanes could quickly and accurately insert a long-duration reconnaissance aircraft anywhere on planet Earth. The Meteor would release a single AQ-11 Night Owl unmanned reconnaissance aircraft about thirty thousand feet altitude near the Iran-Afghanistan border. For the next month, the Night Owl would monitor the area with imaging infrared and millimeter-wave radars for signs of

Muslim insurgents crossing the border, or Iranian Revolutionary Guards Corps or al-Quds convoys smuggling in weapons or supplies from neighboring countries.

After the Meteor container was away, Boomer and Frenchy continued their powered descent. The atmosphere made the spaceplane slow down much more quickly, and soon the LPDRS engines were throttling back to maintain the maximum 3-G deceleration. "Hull temperatures well within the green," Moulain reported. "I sure like these powered descents."

Boomer fought off the G-forces, reached out, and patted the top of the instrument panel. "Good spaceship, nice spaceship," he cooed lovingly. "She likes these powered descents too—all that heat on the belly is not nice, is it, sweetie? Did I tell you, Frenchy, that those 'leopards' engines were *my* idea?"

"Only about a million times, Captain."

"Oh yeah."

"Air pressure on the surface is up to green . . . computers are securing the reaction control system," Moulain reported. "Mission-adaptive control surfaces are in test mode . . . tests complete, MAW system responding to computer commands." The MAW, or Mission Adaptive Wing, system was a series of tiny actuators on the fuselage that in essence turned the entire body of the spaceplane into a lift or drag device—computers shaped the skin as needed to maneuver, climb or descend, make the craft slipperier, or slow down quickly. Even flying backward, the MAW system allowed complete control over the spaceplane. With the atmospheric controls active, Boomer took control of the Black Stallion himself, turned so they were flying forward like a normal aircraft, then hand-flew the ship through a series of steep, high angle-of-attack turns to help bleed off more speed while keeping the descent rate and hull temperatures under control.

At the same time, he was maneuvering to get into position for landing. This landing was going to be a bit trickier than most, because their landing spot was in southeast Turkey at a joint Turkey-NATO military base at a city named Batman. Batman Air

Base was a Special Operations Joint Task Force base during the 1991 Gulf War, with American Army Special Forces and Air Force pararescue troops running clandestine missions throughout Iraq. It was returned to Turkish civil control after the war. In a bid for greater cooperation and better relations with its fellow Muslim nations in the Middle East, Turkey forbade NATO offensive military operations to be staged from Batman, but America had convinced the Turks to allow reconnaissance and some strike aircraft to fly from Batman to hunt down and destroy insurgents in Iran. It was now one of the most vital forward air bases for American and NATO forces in the Middle East, eastern Europe, and central Asia.

"Passing sixty thousand feet, atmospheric pressure in the green, ready to secure the 'leopards,'" Moulain said. Boomer chuckled—securing the "leopards" and transitioning to air-breathing turbojet mode was done automatically, as were most operations on the space-plane, but Moulain always tried to pre-guess when the computer would initiate the procedure. Cute, yes—but she was generally correct, too. Sure enough, the computer notified him that the LPDRS engines were secure. "We're still in 'manual' mode, Captain," Moulain reminded him. "The system won't restart the engines automatically."

"You're really on top of this stuff, aren't you, Frenchy?" Boomer quipped.

"That's my job, Captain."

"You're never going to call me 'Boomer,' are you?"

"Unlikely, Captain."

"You don't know what you're missing, Frenchy."

"I'll survive. Ready for restart."

Part of her allure was definitely the chase. Maybe she was all businesslike in bed too—but that was going to have to wait for a time when they weren't seated in tandem. "Unspiking the engines, turbojets coming alive." They had enough oxygen in the atmosphere now to stop using hydrogen peroxide to burn jet fuel, so Boomer reopened the movable spikes in the engine inlets and initiated the engine start sequence. In moments the turbojets were idling and ready to fly. Their route of flight was taking them over central Europe and Ukraine, and now they were over the Black Sea, heading southeast toward Turkey. Along with keeping hull temperatures low, the powered descent procedures allowed them to descend out of orbit much quicker—they could come down from two hundred miles' altitude into initial approach position, called the "high gate," in less than a thousand miles, where a normal aerobraking descent might take almost five thousand miles.

Below sixty thousand feet they were in Class A positive control airspace, so now they had to follow all normal air traffic control procedures. The computer had already entered the proper frequency in the number one UHF radio: "Ankara Center, this is Stud Seven, due regard, one hundred twenty miles northwest of Ankara, passing flight level five-four-zero, requesting activation of our flight plan. We will be MARSA with Chevron Four-One."

"Stud Seven, Ankara Center, remain outside Turkish Air Defense Identification Zone until radar identified, squawk one-four-one-seven normal." Boomer read back all the instructions.

At that moment, on their secondary encrypted radio, they heard: "Stud Seven, Chevron Four-One on Blue Two."

Boomer had Frenchy monitor the air traffic control frequency, then switched to the secondary radio: "Four-One, this is Stud Seven." They performed a challenge-and-response code exchange to verify each other's identity, even though they were on an encrypted channel. "We launched out of Batman because we heard from Ankara ATC that they are not letting any aircraft cross their ADIZ, even ones with established flight plans. We don't know what's going on, but usually it's because an unidentified aircraft or vessel drifted into their airspace or waters, or some Kurds fired some mortars across the border, and they shut everything down until they sort it out. We're coming up on rendezvous point 'Fishtail.' Suggest we do a point-parallel there, then head out to MK."

"Thank you for staying heads-up, Four-One," Boomer said, the relief obvious in his voice. Using the powered descent profile grossly depleted their fuel reserves—they were almost bingo fuel right now, and by the time they reached the initial approach fix at Batman Air Base they'd be in an emergency fuel status, and they would have no fuel to go anywhere else. Their closest alternate landing site was Mihail Kogălniceanu Airport near Constanţa, Romania, or simply "MK" for short, the first U.S. military base established in a former Warsaw Pact country.

With the two aircraft linked via the secure transceiver, their multi-function displays showed them each other's position, the track they had to follow to rendezvous, and the turnpoints they'd need to get into position. The Black Stallion reached the Air Refueling Initial Point fifteen minutes early, four hundred knots too fast, and thirty thousand feet too high, so Boomer started a series of high-bank turns to bleed off the excess airspeed. "I love it—boring holes in the sky, flying around in the fastest manned aircraft on the planet."

"Odin to Stud Seven," Boomer heard on his encrypted satellite transceiver.

"It's God on GUARD," he quipped. "Go ahead, Odin."

"You're cleared to proceed to MK," Patrick McLanahan said from Armstrong Space Station. He was monitoring the spaceplane's progress from the command module. "Crews are standing by to secure the Black Stallion."

"Do I have to have someone back home looking over my shoulder from now on?" he asked.

"That's affirmative, Boomer," Patrick responded. "Get used to it."

"Roger that."

"Any idea why Ankara wasn't letting anyone in, sir?"

"This is Genesis. Still negative," David Luger chimed in. "We're still checking."

Eventually the Black Stallion was able to slow down and descend to get into proper position, five hundred feet below and a half mile behind the tanker. "Stud Seven is established, checklist complete, got you in sight, ready," Boomer reported.

"Roger, Seven, this is Chevron Four-One," the boom operator in the tanker's tail pod responded. "I read you loud and clear, how me."

"Loud and clear."

"Roger that. I have a visual on you too." On intercom, he said, "Boom's lowering to contact position, crew," and he motored the refueling book into position, its own steerable fly-by-wire wings stabilizing it in the big tanker's slipstream. Back on the radio: "Seven is cleared to precontact position, Four-One is ready."

"Seven's moving up," Boomer said. He opened the slipway doors atop the fuselage behind the cockpit, then smoothly maneuvered the spaceplane to the precontact position: aligned with the tanker's centerline, the top of the windscreen on the center seam of the director light panel. The immense belly of the converted Boeing 777 filled the windscreen. "Seven's in precontact position, stabilized and ready, JP-7 only this time," he said.

"Copy precontact and ready, JP-7 only, cleared to contact position, Four-One ready," the boom operator said. He extended the nozzle and set the "maneuver" light blinking, the signal for the receiver to move into position. Boomer barely had to move the controls because the plane was so light—almost as if just by thought, he carefully maneuvered the Black Stallion forward and up. When the maneuver light turned steady, Boomer held his position, again as if by thought only, and the boom operator slid the nozzle into the receptacle. "Contact, Four-One."

"Seven has contact and shows fuel flow," Boomer acknowledged. "You're a very welcome sight, boys."

"We're a Cabernet crew, sir," the tanker pilot said.

It took the KC-77 ten minutes to transfer thirty thousand pounds of jet fuel to the Black Stallion. "Let's start heading west, Four-One," Boomer said. "We're starting to get too close to Krasnodar." Krasnodar on the east coast of the Black Sea was the location of a major Russian air base, and although they were well outside theirs or anyone else's airspace, it was best not to fly around such areas unannounced. Along with their big air defense radar and numerous long-range surface-to-air missile batteries, Krasnodar was one of the largest fighter bases in the entire world, with no less than three full air defense fighter wings based there, including one with the Mikoyan-Gurevich MiG-29 "Fulcrum," considered one of the best interceptors in the world.

Even four years after the American retaliatory attacks in Russia, nerves were still frayed throughout the entire region, and operators were on a hair trigger to scramble fighters and activate air defense systems. Luckily, there were no signs of any air defense activity behind them. "Right turn is best."

"Coming right to two-seven-zero," the tanker's pilot said. Boomer expertly banked behind the modified Boeing 777 aircraft as they started to turn south, maintaining contact in the turn.

They had just rolled out on the new heading when the tanker's boom operator said, "Well well, folks, looks like we have a visitor. Seven, your three o'clock, real damned close."

"What is it, Frenchy?" Boomer asked, concentrating on staying in the refueling envelope.

"Oh shit . . . it's a Russian MiG-29," Moulain said nervously, "three o'clock, less than a half mile, right on our wingtip."

"See if he has a wingman," Boomer said. "Russkies don't fly around single-ship too often."

Moulain scanned the sky, trying to stay calm, straining to look as far back as she could. "Got him," she said moments later. "Seven o'clock, about a mile." The one at three o'clock slid closer, riveting her attention. In her fifteen-year Navy career she had never seen a MiG-29 except the ones in service in Germany, and that was on a static display, not inflight. It could've been a fixed-wing clone of the F-14 Tomcat Navy carrier fighter, with broad wings, beefy fuselage, and a large nose for its big fire control radar. This one was in green, light blue, and gray camouflage stripes, with the big white, blue, and red flag of Russia on the vertical stabilizer—and she could clearly see one long-range and two short-range air-to-air missiles hanging off the MiG's left wing. "He's loaded for bear, that's for sure," she said nervously. "What are we going to do?"

"I'm going to finish getting my gas," Boomer said, "and then we're going to proceed to landing at MK. This is international airspace; sightseeing is allowed. Let Genesis and Odin know what's out there."

Boomer could hear Frenchy on the number two radio talking to someone, but she stopped a moment later: "That prick at three o'clock's moving closer," she said nervously.

"How are we doing on gas?"

"Three-quarters full."

"We got enough to get to MK with reserves?"

"Plenty."

"I want to top 'em off just in case. How close is the MiG now?"

"He's right on our right wingtip," Frenchy said. "You going to do a disconnect, Captain?"

"Nah. I'm showing him how it's done. No doubt he wants a glimpse of the future too." But the little game wasn't over. The MiG-29 kept on coming closer until shortly Boomer could hear his engine roar and vibration outside his cockpit canopy. "Okay, now he's starting to piss me off. How are we on gas?"

"Almost full."

"Where's the wingman?"

Moulain began to shift in her seat so she could turn all the way around to her left again . . . but soon found she didn't have to, because the second MiG had zoomed forward and was now sitting right off the tanker pilot's left cockpit window, close enough for his engine exhaust and jet wash to shake the tanker's left wing, barely noticeably at first but soon more violently as the MiG slid closer.

"Seven, this is Four-One. It's getting hard to keep it under control. What do you say?"

"Bastard," Boomer muttered. "Time to call it quits." On the radio he responded, "Four-One, let's do a disconnect and—"

But at that moment the second MiG to the left of the tanker's cockpit stroked its afterburners, its exhausts just yards away from the tanker's left wing's leading edge, causing the wing to shove first violently downward, then upward, causing the tanker to roll right. *"Breakaway, breakaway, breakaway!"* the boom operator shouted on the radio. Boomer immediately chopped the throttles, hit the voice command button, and spoke, "Speed brakes seventy!" The Mission Adaptive Wing system immediately commanded a maximum drag setting, creating thousands of little speed brakes all over the spaceplane's surface and allowing it to sink quickly . . .

. . . and it wasn't a moment too soon, because the tanker pilot, struggling with his plane's controls and at the same time jamming on full military power and a thirty-degree climb angle when he heard the "breakaway" call, had overcorrected and was now violently rolling to his left, in the grip of a full power-on stall and on the verge of a tail-low spin. Boomer could swear he was going to be face-to-face with the boom operator as he saw the tanker's tail swing lower and lower toward him. "C'mon, Chevron, recover, dammit, *recover . . . !"*

The KC-77 tanker seemed to be doing a pirouette on the tip of the still-extended refueling boom, rolling left and right as if clawing the sky for a handhold, its wings fluttering like a giant osprey in a climb, except the tanker wasn't climbing but was getting ready to roll over and spin out of control at any second. Just when Boomer thought it was going to roll over on its back and dive uncontrollably into the Black Sea, it stopped its death's oscillations, the left wing stayed down, and the nose started to creep toward the horizon. As the nose dipped below the horizon, the right wing slowly, agonizingly started to come down. When the tanker disappeared from view, it was almost wings-level, steeply nose-low but quickly regaining its lost airspeed.

"Chevron, you guys okay?" Boomer radioed.

A few moments later he heard a high, squeaky, hoarse male voice say, "I got it, I got it, holy shit, I got it . . . Seven, this is Four-One, we're okay. Man oh man, I thought we were goners. We're at twelve thousand feet. We're okay. One engine flamed out, but we're restarting now."

Boomer scanned the sky and saw the two MiG-29s joined up far above him, heading east. He could almost hear them laughing over their radios on the little scare they put into the Americans. *"You motherfuckers!"* he shouted into his oxygen visor, and he shoved the throttles forward to max afterburner.

"Noble! What are you doing?" Moulain shouted when she had gotten her breath back after the sudden G-force shove to her chest. But it was soon obvious what he was doing—he was flying right for the middle of the MiG formation. By the time she could cry out, they had blasted past the two MiGs, passing less than a hundred yards above them, traveling more than seven hundred miles an hour! "Jesus, Noble, are you *insane?*"

Boomer pitched the Black Stallion into a steep sixty-degree climb, still accelerating. "We're going to see if they like scrapping with the other alley cats or if they just pick on the big fat tabbies," he said. The threat warning receiver blared—the MiGs had been running radar-silent until now, which is how they were able to sneak up on their formation so easily, but now they had their big N-019 radar on and searching. Boomer leveled off at forty thousand feet, pulled the throttles back to military power, and switched his multifunction display to the threat depiction, which gave him his best picture of the situation. "Keep an eye on my fuel and let me know when we're getting close to bingo fuel on MK, Frenchy."

"Stud, this is Odin," Patrick McLanahan radioed from Armstrong Space Station. "We just picked up the threat warning. You've got two MiGs behind you! Where are you going?"

"I'm going to drag these guys east as much as possible so they'll stay away from the tanker," Boomer said, "and I'm going to teach them a lesson about screwing with a Black Stallion and especially its tanker."

"Do you know what you're doing, Boomer?" Patrick asked.

"I'm hoping these guys will take a shot at me, General," Boomer said, "and then I'm *really* going to water their eyes. Any other questions, sir?"

There was a slight pause, during which time Moulain was positive the general would be swearing a blue streak and literally bouncing off the ceiling of the command module in pure anger at Noble's adolescent stunt. To her shock, she heard McLanahan reply: "Negative, Boomer. Just try not to scratch the paint."

"Fifteen minutes to bingo fuel at this rate and course, SC," Moulain reported. "Stop this shit and turn us around!"

"Five more minutes and we'll do a U-turn, Frenchy," Boomer said, then muttered, "C'mon, you chickenshits, shoot already. We're right dead in your sights and we're not jamming—take the—"

At that instant the two "bat-wing" symbols on the threat warning display depicting the MiG's search radars started to blink. *"Warning, warning, missile alert, six o'clock, twenty-three miles, MiG-29K . . ."* followed moments later by: *"Warning, warning, missile launch, missile launch, AA-12!"*

"Here we go, Frenchy—hold on to your bloomers," Boomer said. He jammed the throttles to max afterburner, then spoke, "Leopards online."

"Leopards online, stop leopards . . . leopards activated," the computer responded, and both crewmembers were shoved back into their seats when the full force of the Laser Pulse Detonation Rocket System engines fired up in full turbojet mode—with the throttles already in full afterburner, rather than moving them up gradually, they got almost full turbojet power in just a few seconds. The airspeed jumped from just below Mach 1 to Mach 2, then 3, then 4 in the blink of an eye. He then started a steep climb, then kept the pitch input in until they were headed straight up, passive fifty, then sixty thousand feet.

"Missiles . . . still . . . tracking," Moulain grunted through the nearly seven Gs. "Still . . . closing . . ."

"I'm almost . . . done . . . with these bozos, Frenchy," Boomer grunted back. He pulled the power back at Mach 4 and kept pulling on the control stick until they were inverted. He rolled upright, his nose now aimed down almost directly vertical, then glanced at the threat display. As he hoped, the two MiGs were still transmitting radar energy, searching for him—the AA-12 missile, a copy of the American AIM-120 Advanced Medium-Range Air-to-Air Missile, was homing in using its own on-board radar.

"Wondering where I went, boys? You'll find out in a sec." Boomer aimed the Black Stallion at a point in space where he thought the MiGs would be in the next heartbeat or two—at his relative speed, the MiGs appeared to be hovering in space, although the threat display said they were flying at almost twice the speed of sound. Just as he caught a glimpse of the black dots below him, he rolled left until he was knifing right between the two Russian jets. He had no idea if he had judged the turn correctly, but it was too late to worry now . . .

The MiGs were nothing more than imperceptible blurs as he flew directly between them, missing the closest by just fifty yards. As soon as he passed them he pulled the throttles to idle, deactivated the LPDRS engines to conserve fuel, used the MAW system to assist the spaceplane to level off without breaking itself into pieces—at their current rate of speed they would hit the Black Sea in just eight seconds without the Mission Adaptive Wing technology—and started a tight left turn just in case the AA-12 missiles were still tracking . . .

. . . but he didn't have to worry about the missiles, because moments later they caught a glimpse of a large flash of light above them, then another. He rolled upright, let the G-forces subside, and scanned the sky. All they could see were two black clouds above them. "Payback's a bitch, huh, comrades?" Boomer said as he headed westbound once again.

They had to chase down the tanker again and refuel because they had reached emergency fuel status in just a couple minutes with the LPDRS engines activated. The tanker crew was jubilant, but Moulain was even more quiet and businesslike than usual—she said nothing else except required call-outs. "You guys okay, Four-One?" Boomer asked.

"We got our dentures loosened big-time," the tanker pilot said, "but it's better than the alternative. Thanks, Stud."

"You can thank us by giving us a little more gas so we can make it to MK."

"As long as we have enough to make it to the nearest runway, you can have the rest," the tanker pilot said. "And don't even think about buying any drinks for any other gas-passer anywhere on the planet—your money's no good with us anymore. Thanks again, Stud Seven."

Less than an hour later the two aircraft made their approach and landing at Constanța-Mikhail Kogălniceanu Airport in Romania. The airport was located fifteen miles from Constanța and nine miles from the city's famed Mamaia Beach on the Black Sea, so it was rarely affected by the freezing fog that shrouded the coastal city in winter. The U.S. Air Force had built an aircraft parking ramp, hangars, and maintenance and security facilities on the northeast side of the airfield, as well as upgraded the airport's control tower, radar and communications facilities, and civil airport terminal. Along with NATO and European Union membership, the investments made in Romania by the United States had quickly turned this area known before only for its busy seaport and historic sites into a major international business, technology, and tourist destination.

The two aircraft were escorted to the security area by a small convoy of armored Humvees and parked together in the largest hangar. There was a lot of hugging and handshakes between the crews as they deplaned. They debriefed their mission together and then separately, with promises to meet up for dinner and drinks later in Constanța.

Noble and Moulain's mission debriefing took considerably longer than the tanker crew's. It took nine grueling hours to debrief the maintenance and intelligence crews, Patrick McLanahan on Armstrong Space Station, Dave Luger at Dreamland, and get their usual post-flight physical exams. When they were finally released, they cleared Romanian customs at the civil airport, then took a shuttle bus to the Best Western Savoy Hotel in Constanța, where the U.S. military contracted for transient lodging.

The Black Sea coast was not busy at all in winter, so except for a few airline crews from Romania, Germany, and Austria and some surprised businessmen unaccustomed to seeing much partying in Constanța in winter, the Americans had the bar to themselves. The tanker crew had already been partying hard and was buying drinks for anyone who wore wings, especially the foreign female flight attendants. Boomer was ready as well, but to his surprise he saw Lisette heading for the elevator to her room. He extricated himself from the arms of two beautiful blond flight attendants, with promises he'd be right back, and hurried to follow her.

He barely squeezed himself past the closing elevator doors. "Hey, Frenchy, turning in so soon? The party's just getting started, and we haven't had dinner yet."

"I'm beat. I'm done for the day."

He looked at her with concern. "You haven't said much since our little run-in with the Russkies," he said. "I'm a little—"

Suddenly Moulain whirled toward him and smacked him across the jaw with a closed right fist. It wasn't that hard a blow, but it was still a fist—he was smarting, but mostly from the surprise. "Hey, what'd you do that for?"

"You *bastard*! You *prick*!" she shouted. "You could've gotten us both killed today out there!"

Boomer rubbed his jaw, still looking at her with concern; then he nodded and said, "Yeah, I could have. But no one pushes around my tanker." He smiled, then added, "Besides, you gotta admit, Frenchy, that it was one helluva ride."

Moulain looked as if she was going to punch him again, and he was determined to let her do it if it made her feel better . . . but to his surprise, she rushed forward in the elevator, threw her arms around his neck, smothered him with a kiss, and pressed herself against him, pinning him against the wall.

"You're damned right, Boomer, it *was* one helluva ride," she breathed. "I've flown jets off of carriers in two wars and been shot at dozens of times, and I have *never* been so turned on as I was today!"

"Jeez, Moulain . . ."

"Frenchy. Call me Frenchy, dammit," she ordered, then silenced him with another kiss. She didn't let him up for air for a long time.

"You were so quiet on the way back and in debriefing, I was afraid you were going into some kind of shell-shocked fugue state, Frenchy," Boomer said as Moulain started kissing his neck. "You sure have a funny way of showing your excitement."

"I was so excited, so turned on, so friggin' *aroused* that I was embarrassed to show it," Moulain said in between kisses, her hands quickly finding their way south of his waist. "I mean, two fighter pilots *died,* but I was so jacked up I thought I was going to come in my damned flight suit!"

"Dang, Frenchy, this is one strange side of you that I never—"

"Shut up, Boomer, just shut up," she said as the elevator slowed on their floor. She had him practically unzipped and unbuttoned by then. "Just take me to my room and fuck my brains out."

"But what about your fiancé and your—?"

"Boomer, I said, shut the hell up and fuck me, and do not stop until it's morning," Moulain said as the elevator doors slid open. "I'll explain it to . . . to . . . oh hell, whatever his name is, in the morning. Remember, Captain, I outrank you, so that's an order, mister!" It was obvious that issuing orders was just as much of a turn-on for her as flying the hypersonic spaceplane.

CHAPTER TWO

*One likes people much better when they're battered
down by a prodigious siege of misfortune than when
they triumph.*

— VIRGINIA WOOLF

ARMSTRONG SPACE STATION

THE NEXT MORNING

The command module was the center of activity aboard Armstrong
Space Station, and it was here that Patrick McLanahan attended the
video teleconference with select members of President Gardner's
national security staff: Conrad F. Carlyle, the President's National
Security Adviser; Gerald Vista, the Director of Central Intelligence,
who had remained in his post from the Martindale administration;
Marine Corps General Taylor J. Bain, chairman of the Joint Chiefs
of Staff; Charles A. Huffman, Air Force chief of staff; and Air
Force General Bradford Cannon, commander of U.S. Strategic
Command and—until the details could be worked out by Congress
and the Pentagon—the theater commander of all U.S. space operations and responsible for training, equipping, and directing all space

combat missions. Hunter Noble—a little bleary-eyed after not very much sleep, both because of the time difference and because of Lisa Moulain—was linked in to the teleconference via satellite from the command post at Constanţa Air Base.

Patrick and Master Sergeant Valerie Lukas were floating in front of the wide-screen high-definition teleconference monitor, secured by Velcro sneakers to the bulkhead of the command module. Patrick kept his hair buzz-cut short, but Lukas's longer hair floated free on either side of her headset's crossband, giving her a weird wolverine-like appearance. "Armstrong Space Station is online and secure, sir," Patrick announced. "This is Lieutenant General Patrick McLanahan, commander, High-Technology Aerospace Weapons Center, Elliott Air Force Base, Nevada. With me is U.S. Air Force Master Sergeant Valerie Lukas, noncommissioned officer in charge of this station and the sensor operator on duty at the time of the attack in Tehran. Joining us via satellite link from Constanţa, Romania, is Air Force Captain Hunter Noble, chief of manned spaceflight operations and hypersonic weapon development, High-Technology Aerospace Weapons Center. He was the officer in charge of the attack mission over Tehran and the designer of the SkySTREAK missile that was used in the attack. He returned to Earth yesterday after completing a reconnaissance aircraft insertion mission over eastern Iran, which we will brief you on later."

"Thank you, General," General Taylor Bain said from the "Gold Room," also known as the "Tank," the Joint Chiefs of Staff conference center on the second floor of the Pentagon. As was the case of most officers in the post–American Holocaust United States, Bain was young for a four-star Marine Corps officer, with dark brown hair trimmed "high and tight," a ready smile, and warm gray eyes that exuded trust and determined sincerity. "Welcome, everyone. I believe you know everyone here. Joining us from the White House is National Security Adviser Conrad Carlyle; and from Langley, the Director of Intelligence, Gerald Vista.

"I first want to say that I'm pleased and frankly more than a little amazed to be talking to you, General McLanahan, aboard a facility that just a few short years ago was considered little more than a Cold War relic at best and a floating money pit at worst," Bain went on. "But now we're considering putting hundreds of billions of dollars into the next five budgets to create a space force centered on that very same weapon system. I'm convinced we're seeing the beginning of a new direction and future for the American armed forces. Captain Noble, I've been briefed on your incident yesterday, and although we need to discuss your judgment skills I'm impressed with how you handled yourself, your crew, your fellow airmen, and your craft. I believe it was yet another example of the amazing capabilities being developed, and the future path we're on looks incredible indeed. But we've got a long way to go before we take that journey, and the events of the past few days will be critical.

"First, we're going to get a briefing from General McLanahan on Armstrong Space Station and his operational tests recently run, and Captain Noble's incident over the Black Sea. We'll discuss a few other matters, and then my staff will prepare our recommendations to SECDEF and the national security staff. I'm sure it will be a long uphill fight, both in the Pentagon and up on Capitol Hill. But regardless of what ensues, Patrick, I'd like to say 'job well done' to you and your fellow airmen—or should I say, fellow 'astronauts.' Please proceed."

"Yes, sir," Patrick began. "On behalf of everyone aboard Armstrong Space Station and our support crews at Battle Mountain Air Reserve Base, Elliott Air Force Base, and Peterson Air Force Base in Colorado, thank you for your kind words and continuing support."

Patrick touched a button that presented photographs and drawings in a separate window to the videoconference audience as he continued: "A brief overview first: Armstrong Space Station was constructed in the late 1980s and early 1990s. It is the military version of the much smaller NASA Skylab space station, built of spent Saturn-I and Saturn-IV rocket fuel tanks joined together on a central keel structure. Four such tanks, each with over thirty thousand cubic feet of space available inside, form the main part of the station. Over the years other modules had been attached to the keel for specialized missions or experiments, along with larger solar panels for increased power generation for the expanding station. We can house as many as twenty-five astronauts on the facility for as long as a month without resupply.

"The station hosts several advanced American military systems, including the first space-based ultra-high-resolution radar, improved space-based global infrared sensors, advanced space-based global communications and high-speed computer networking, and the first space-based anti-missile laser system, code-named 'Skybolt,' designed to shoot down intercontinental ballistic missiles from space. The station's space-based radar is a sophisticated radar system that scans the entire planet once a day and can detect and identify objects as small as a motorcycle, even underground or underwater.

"The destruction of our strategic command and control systems and ballistic missile defense sites by the Russian Federation's air attacks against the United States highlight the need for a capable, secure, and modern base of operations to conduct a wide spectrum of vital defense activities, and Armstrong Space Station is that facility," Patrick continued. "The station is now the central data collection and dissemination hub of a network of satellites in high- and low-Earth orbits linked together to form a global reconnaissance and communications system, continuously feeding a wide array of information to military and government users around the world in real time. The station and its supporting reconnaissance satellites can track and identify targets on the surface, in the sky, on or under water, underground, or in space, and it could direct manned and unmanned defenders against them, like a space-based multifunction combat control system.

"The state-of-the-art systems aboard Armstrong Space Station give it other important capabilities that complement its primary military function," Patrick went on. "In case of war or natural disaster, the station can serve as an alternate national military op-erations center, similar to the Air Force's E-4B or Navy's E-6B Mercury airborne command posts, and can communicate with bal-listic missile submarines even while deeply submerged. It can tie into radio and television airwaves and the Internet worldwide to broadcast information to the public; act as a nationwide air, mari-time, or ground traffic control center; or serve as the central coordi-nation facility for the Federal Emergency Management Agency. The station supports the International Space Station, acts as a space rescue and repair service, supports numerous scientific research and education programs, and is, I believe, the inspiration for a general reawakening to the exploration of outer space for young people around the world.

"Currently, Armstrong Space Station hosts twelve systems opera-tors, technicians, and officers, set up very much like the combat crew aboard an airborne command post or sensor operators aboard a ra-dar aircraft. Additional crews are brought aboard as necessary to run specialized missions—the station has accommodations for an-other dozen personnel, and can be expanded quickly and easily by attaching additional modules brought aloft by the shuttle, the SR-79 Black Stallion spaceplane, the Orion crew expeditionary vehicle, or remotely piloted launch vehicles—"

"Excuse me, General," National Security Adviser Carlyle inter-jected, "but how is it possible to bring additional modules up to the station on a spaceplane or remotely piloted vehicles?"

"The fastest and easiest way is to use inflatable modules, Mr. Carlyle," Patrick responded.

" *'Inflatable'*? You mean, not rigid, like a balloon?"

"Like a balloon, only a very high-tech balloon. The technology is based on NASA's 'Transhab' experiments of ten years ago, when inflatable modules were suggested for the International Space Sta-tion. The walls of our models are primarily made of electro-reactive material that is flexible like cloth until a current is applied and it's struck, when it hardens into a material that resists impact a thou-sand times better than steel or Kevlar; this material is backed up with other non-electro-reactive materials that are still many times stronger than steel or Kevlar. Inflatable structures give just enough to absorb energy from impact without damage—you can't ding the walls of these things.

"The stuff is lightweight and easily packed for launch, then easily and remotely inflated in just a few hours. We've already lofted small inflatable modules on the spaceplanes and Orion, and the technology is sound. We haven't lofted a full crew-sized module yet, but that's in the works. Future space stations and perhaps even habitation modules on the Moon or Mars will probably be inflatable." Carlyle didn't look convinced at all, and neither did several other attendees, but he offered no other comments.

Patrick took a sip of water from a squeeze bottle Velcroed to the bulkhead and was amused to find a line of nervous sweat on his upper lip. How many briefings, he thought, had he given during his over two decades of military service? *None,* he reminded himself wryly, from space before! Briefing four-star generals was nerve-racking enough, but doing it while flying at over seventeen thousand miles an hour over two hundred miles above Earth made it even more challenging.

"Armstrong Space Station is the ultimate expression of taking the 'high ground' and is, I believe, the centerpiece of America's stated goal of maintaining access and control of space," Patrick went on. "It and the Black Stallion spaceplanes constitute the foundation of what I call the U.S. Space Defense Command, an integrated joint services command that manages all space-based offensive and defensive assets and supports terrestrial theater commanders with reliable, high-speed communications, intelligence, reconnaissance, attack, and transportation services from space. Our mission will be to—"

"That's very interesting, General McLanahan," National Security Adviser Carlyle interjected with a wry and rather bemused expression, "and as interesting as the idea was when you first proposed it last year, that sort of organization is still many years down the road—we don't have time to bring back Buck Rogers right now.

Can we move on to a discussion of the Iran operations, General Bain?"

"Of course, Mr. Adviser. General McLanahan?"

"Yes, sir," Patrick said expressionlessly—he was quite accustomed to being tuned out, interrupted, and ignored whenever he brought up his idea of the U.S. Space Defense Command. "Along with all of the other advanced technological capabilities of this station, my staff has recently added another: the ability to control remotely piloted tactical aircraft *and their weapons* from space. We demonstrated the capability of controlling an unmanned supersonic EB-1C Vampire bomber completely from this station throughout all phases of flight, including several aerial refuelings and hypersonic precision-guided weapon deployment, in real time and with complete man-in-the-loop control. Our communications and networking abilities are entirely and quickly scalable and expandable, and I envision the capability of controlling entire air task forces of potentially hundreds of un-manned combat aircraft, from small reconnaissance micro-UAVs to giant cruise missile haulers, right from Armstrong—securely, safely, and virtually unassailable."

Patrick stuck his briefing notes on the bulkhead. "I hope all of you have received my after-action report on the employment of the XAGM-279 SkySTREAK hypersonic precision-guided cruise mis-sile in Tehran," he said. "The attack was a complete success. The operational test was terminated due to the unintended and unfor-tunate casualties caused by detonation of an apparent chemical weapon warhead on the target rocket. The casualties were caused by the unexpected detonation of the chemical weapon warhead on the insurgent attacker's rocket, not by the SkySTREAK missile, and therefore—"

"And as I stated in my comments on McLanahan's report," Air Force chief of staff General Charles Huffman interjected, "I believe the SkySTREAK weapon was not the appropriate weapon to use and could negatively impact our efforts to de-escalate the conflict in Iran and bring about a negotiated settlement between the warring parties. Iran was not the right place to test that weapon, and it appears to me that General McLanahan skewed his proposal and the weapon's potential effects in order to dramatize his system. Firing SkySTREAK on his restricted ranges in Nevada wouldn't have had such a 'wow' factor as watching one slam into an insurgent pickup truck. Unfortunately, his magic show resulted in the deaths of dozens of innocent civilians, including women and children, by poison gas."

Joint Chiefs chairman Bain shook his head, then looked straight ahead at his videoconference camera. "General McLanahan?" His brow furrowed as he looked at Patrick's image on the videoconference screen: Patrick was taking another deep sip from a squeeze bottle, and seemed to have some difficulty re-Velcroing the bottle to the bulkhead. "Care to respond?"

Patrick nodded, placing a hand up to his mouth to corral an errant drop of water. "Sorry, sir. Even simple tasks like drinking water take a little extra concentration up here. Almost everything requires a conscious effort."

"Understood, Patrick. I've ridden the 'Vomit Comet' a couple times so I know what zero-G can do to someone, but it's nothing like *living* the experience 24/7." The 'Vomit Comet' was a modified C-135 cargo plane flown on a roller-coaster-like flight path that allowed several seconds of weightlessness for the occupants during its steep descent. "Any comment on General Huffman's report?"

"I didn't think it was necessary for me to respond with a strong denial, sir," Patrick said, "but to make myself perfectly clear: General Huffman's analysis is dead wrong. I assembled the SkySTREAK operational test exactly as delineated in the general's air tasking order: a precision-guided aerial standoff attack force to support Persian anti-insurgent operations with minimal collateral casualties or damage. We didn't stray outside the ATO one iota.

"I'd like to point out a few other things as well, if I may, sir." He didn't wait for permission to continue: "SkySTREAK was approved by the general's operations staff, along with eight other task forces and units that are operating over Tehran and other cities in Free

Persia. So far SkySTREAK has been the only unit to successfully engage *any* insurgents, even though all the other units have access to the Global Hawk's sensor imagery, Armstrong Space Station's automated surveillance system, and even to SkySTREAK's sensor downlinks. In short, sir, SkySTREAK is *working*."

"And the civilian casualties?"

"A result of the detonation of the insurgent warhead, sir—it wasn't caused by SkySTREAK."

"It *was* caused by your missile, McLanahan," Huffman interjected. "You were briefed about the possibility of the insurgents using weapons of mass destruction in Tehran and directed to withhold and request enhanced analysis of the target before engaging. You failed to do that, which resulted in unnecessary civilian casualties."

"As I see it, sir, we *limited* the casualty count by taking out that Ra'ad rocket before the insurgents had a chance to launch it."

"Be that as it may, McLanahan, you failed to follow my directives," Huffman said. "The technology's not at fault here. But because of your error in judgment, the whole program might be shut down."

"I'm not quite ready to shut anything down yet, Charlie," General Bain said. "My staff and I have reviewed the report submitted by General McLanahan and your response, with a special emphasis on the issue of collateral civilian casualties. My intelligence directorate looked at all spectrums of the Global Hawk surveillance video and the space station's own network of sensors. Everyone has concluded that it *would* have been possible to determine with certainty that the rocket indeed carried a chemical warhead, and that nearby innocent civilians were at risk if the rocket was hit and the warhead detonated and activated." Huffman smiled and nodded confidently . . .

. . . until Bain glared at the Air Force chief of staff, held up a hand, and continued: ". . . *if* General McLanahan had the time to study freeze-frame hi-res imagery for at least ninety seconds, sitting at a desk at Langley, Beale, or Lackland Air Force Bases instead of falling around planet Earth traveling at seventeen thousand five hundred miles per hour, or if he had taken the time to consult with expert analysts on the ground; and *if* he wasn't a three-star general officer and an Air Force tactical officer and air weapons expert and wasn't *expected* to make command decisions such as this. However, if he had taken the time to ask or had decided not to attack, we feel that the loss of life would've been far greater if the rocket had dispersed its deadly payload as designed.

"The civilian loss of life is regrettable and is something we wish to avoid at all costs, but in this case we feel General McLanahan made a proper decision in line with his rules of engagement and is not responsible for the loss of life. Therefore, the command staff will not convene an investigation board on the matter, unless other evidence is brought forward, and considers the case closed. General McLanahan is free to continue his patrols over Iran as directed and as originally planned with the extra patrols added back into the package, and the joint staff recommends to the National Command Authority that he be allowed to do so.

"On a personal note, I wish to commend General McLanahan and his crews for a job well done," Bain added. "I have no idea what the difficulties of working and living in space could be like, but I imagine the stress levels to be enormous and the operating conditions to be challenging to say the least. You and your people are doing a great job in tough circumstances."

"Thank you, sir."

"This concludes my portion of the video teleconference. Mr. Carlyle, any remarks or questions?" Patrick looked at the image of the National Security Adviser, but he was busy talking on the telephone. "Well, it looks like Mr. Carlyle is already busy on another matter, so we'll log off. Thank you, every—"

"Hold on a minute, General Bain," Conrad Carlyle interjected. "Stand by." Carlyle shifted his seat sideways, the camera zoomed back, widening the view to three seats at the conference table in the White House . . . and a moment later, the President of the United States, Joseph Gardner, took his place with Carlyle, along with

White House chief of staff Walter Kordus, a tall but rather slight man who seemed to wear a perpetual scowl.

Cameras—any kind of camera, even relatively lo-res videoconference ones—loved Joseph Gardner. Dark-haired, thin, and square-jawed, he possessed that strange, almost mystical appearance that defied any efforts by anyone to classify him by ethnicity—at the very same time he looked Italian, Iberian, Black Irish, Latin American, even round-eyed Asian—and therefore he appealed to all of them. He exuded immense self-confidence from every pore, and seemed to project authority like laser beams through his dark green eyes. After just a couple years of his two terms in the U.S. Senate, everyone knew he was destined for bigger and better things.

Being from the state of Florida and coming from a long line of Navy veterans, Gardner had always been a big advocate of a strong navy. Nominated for Secretary of the Navy by then-President Kevin Martindale in his first term, Gardner pushed hard for a grand expansion of the Navy, not just in its traditional maritime roles but in a lot of nontraditional ones as well, such as nuclear warfighting, space, tactical aviation, and ballistic missile defense. Just as the Army was America's primary ground fighting service, he argued, with the Marine Corps as a support service, the Navy should be the leader in maritime warfare and tactical aviation, with the Air Force as its support service. His rather radical "out-of-the-box" ideas had many skeptics but nonetheless got a lot of attention and favorable support from Congress and the American people . . .

. . . even before the utter devastation of the American Holocaust, in which Russian long-range bombers armed with nuclear-tipped cruise missiles decimated all but a handful of America's intercontinental ballistic missiles and strategic nuclear-capable long-range bombers. In just a few hours, the U.S. Navy suddenly became the one and only service able to project American military power around the globe, and at the same time virtually the sole keeper of America's nuclear deterrent forces, which were seen as absolutely vital for the very survival of the United States of America in its weakened condition.

Joseph Gardner, the "engineer of the American twenty-first century Navy," was suddenly regarded as a true visionary and the nation's savior. In Martindale's second term of office, Gardner was nominated and unanimously confirmed as Secretary of Defense, and he was universally acknowledged as the de facto Vice President and National Security Adviser rolled into one. His popularity soared, and there were few around the world who doubted he would become the next President of the United States.

"Greetings, gents," Gardner said after positioning himself just so before the videoconference camera. "Thought I'd drop in on your little chat here."

"Welcome, Mr. President," Joint Chiefs of Staff chairman Taylor Bain said. He was obviously perturbed at this very unexpected interruption of his meeting, but tried hard not to show it. "We'd be happy to start the briefing over again, sir."

"Not necessary," the President said. "I have information that is pertinent to the purpose of this meeting, and I thought the best and most expeditious way to get it to you was to just break in."

"You're welcome at any time, sir," Bain said. "Please go on. The floor is yours."

"Thanks, Taylor," the President said. "I just got off the phone with Russian president Zevitin. General McLanahan?"

"Yes, sir."

"He claims you fired a missile at one of his reconnaissance planes in international airspace, and when the missile missed you seriously damaged the aircraft with high-powered radioactive beams called T-waves or some such thing. He also claims a missile fired by one of your aircraft killed several dozen innocent civilians in Tehran, including women and children. Care to explain?"

"He's lying, sir," McLanahan replied immediately. "None of that is true."

"Is that so?" He held up a piece of paper. "I have a copy of the Air

Force chief of staff's summary of the incident which seems to say pretty much the same thing. So both the president of Russia and the chief of staff are lying, and *you're* telling me the truth, General? Is that what you want me to believe?"

"We've just discussed the incident and the issues brought forth by General Huffman, sir," Bain said, "and I've ruled that McLanahan acted properly and as directed and was not responsible for the civilian deaths—"

"And as for Zevitin or anyone else at the Kremlin, sir," McLanahan cut in, "I wouldn't believe *one* word any of them said."

"General McLanahan, scores of innocent Iranians are dead by chemical weapons and a Russian reconnaissance pilot is badly injured by radiation fired at him by one of your bombers," the President retorted. "The world thinks you're starting another shooting war with Russia in the Middle East and is demanding answers and accountability. This is no time for your bigoted attitude." Patrick shook his head and turned away, reaching for his water bottle, and the President's eyes widened in anger. "You have something else to say to me, General?" Patrick turned back to the camera, then looked at his outstretched arm in confusion, as if he had forgotten why he had extended it. "Is something the matter with you, McLanahan?"

"N—no, sir . . ." Patrick responded in a muted voice. He missed the water bottle, felt for it, grasped it, then used too much force to rip it from its Velcro mooring and sent it spinning across the module.

"What? I can't hear you." Gardner's eyes squinted in confusion as he watched the water bottle fly away out of sight. "What's going on there? Where are you, General? Why are you moving like that?"

"He's on Armstrong Space Station, sir," General Bain said.

"*On the space station?* He's in *orbit?* Are you kidding me? What are you doing up there?"

"As the commander of his task force operating from space, I authorized General McLanahan to oversee the operation from the space station," Bain explained, "just as any commanding officer would take charge of his forces from a forward-deployed command ship or—"

"On the bridge or CIC of a destroyer, yes, but not on a damned *space station*!" President Gardner shot back. "I want him off that thing *immediately*! He's a three-star general, for God's sake, not Buck Rogers!"

"Sir, if I may, can we address the question of the air strike on the insurgent rocket launcher and the actions against the Russian aircraft?" General Bain said, worriedly looking on as Valerie Lukas checked on Patrick. "We've conducted a review of the reconnaissance data, and we've determined—"

"It couldn't have been a very thorough review if the incident happened just a couple hours ago, General," the President said. He turned to the National Security Adviser seated beside him. "Conrad?"

"It's a preliminary review of the same sensor data from the Global Hawk unmanned recon plane and the space station's radars that General McLanahan and his crew saw before they attacked, sir," Carlyle responded. "General Bain and his experts at the Pentagon reviewed the images as if they had been asked *before* the attack if the target was legitimate based on the rules of engagement established by us under the attack order, as is required if there is any uncertainty as to the safety to noncombatants due to weapon effects or collateral damage. The videoconference was convened as a preliminary incident review to determine if a more detailed investigation would be warranted."

"And?"

"General Bain has ruled that, although it could have been possible for General McLanahan to anticipate civilian casualties, his order to engage was justified and proper based on the information at hand, the threat of more civilian deaths at the hands of the insurgents, and his authority under the attack plan," Carlyle responded. "He is recommending to the Secretary of Defense and to you that no further investigation is warranted and that McLanahan be allowed to continue his operation as planned, with the full complement of missile launch bombers instead of just one."

"Is that so?" The President paused for a moment, then shook his head. "General Bain, you're telling me that you thought it was proper that McLanahan attack a target knowing that so many civilian noncombatants were nearby, and that such an attack is within the letter and spirit of my executive order authorizing a hunt for insurgents in Iran?" he retorted. "I think you have grossly misinterpreted my orders. I thought I was being very plain and specific: I don't want *any* noncombatant casualties. Was that not clear to you, General Bain?"

"It was, sir," Bain responded, his jaw hardening and his eyes narrowing under the scolding, "but with the information General McLanahan had at the time, and with the threat posed by these insurgent rockets, I felt he was fully justified in making the decision to—"

"Let's get this straight right here and now, General Bain: *I* am the commander-in-chief, and *I* make the decisions," the President said. "Your job is to carry out my orders, and my orders were *no civilian casualties*. The only proper order in this instance was to withhold because of the numbers of civilians around that launcher. Even if they had been told to leave the immediate area, you should have anticipated that they would be near enough to be hurt or killed by the explosion. They—"

"Sir, there was *no* explosion, at least not one caused by us," Bain protested. "The SkySTREAK missile is a kinetic-energy weapon only—it was designed to—"

"I don't care what it was *designed* to do, General—McLanahan knew there were civilians in the immediate area, and according to General Huffman, you were briefed that some rockets might have chemical weapons on them, so he obviously should have withheld. End of discussion. Now what is this about McLanahan firing a missile at the Russian fighter? McLanahan's bombers have air-to-air missiles on them?"

"That's standard defensive armament for the EB-1D Vampire aircraft, sir, but McLanahan didn't—"

"So why did you fire on that Russian reconnaissance plane, General McLanahan?"

"We did not fire any missiles, sir," McLanahan responded as firmly as he could, nodding to Lukas that he was all right, "and it was not a reconnaissance plane: it was a MiG-29 tactical fighter."

"What was it doing up there, McLanahan?"

"Shadowing our bomber over the Caspian Sea, sir."

"I see. Shadowing . . . as in, performing *reconnaissance*? Am I interpreting this correctly, General?" Patrick rubbed his eyes and swallowed hard, licking dry lips. "We're not keeping you up, are we, General?"

"No, sir."

"So the Russian aircraft was just performing reconnaissance after all, correct?"

"Not in my judgment, sir. It was—"

"So you fired a missile at it, and it returned fire, and you then hit it with a radioactive beam of some sort, correct?"

"No, sir." But something was wrong. Patrick looked at the camera, but seemed to be having trouble focusing. "It . . . we didn't . . ."

"So what happened?"

"Mr. President, the MiG fired on us first," Boomer interjected. "The Vampire just defended itself, nothing more."

"Who is that?" the President asked the National Security Adviser. He turned to the camera, his eyes bulging in anger. "Who are you? Identify yourself!"

"I'm Captain Hunter Noble," Boomer said, getting to his feet, staring in shock at the image of Patrick being helped by Lukas, "and why the hell don't you stop badgering us? We're only doing our jobs!"

"What did you say to me?" the President thundered. "Who the hell are *you* to talk to me like that? General Bain, I want him fired! I want him discharged!"

"Master Sergeant, what's going on?" Bain shouted, ignoring the President. "What's happening to Patrick?"

"He's having trouble breathing, sir." She found a nearby intercom switch: "Medical detail to the command module! Emergency!" And then she terminated the videoconference with a keypress on the communications control keyboard.

"McLanahan is having a *heart attack*?" the President exclaimed after the video images from the space station cut off. "I knew he shouldn't be up in that thing! General Bain, what kind of medical facilities do they have up there?"

"Basic, sir: just a medically trained technician and first aid equipment. We've never had anyone have a heart attack on an American military spacecraft."

"Great. Just fucking great." The President passed a hand through his hair in sheer frustration. "Can you get a doctor and some medicine and equipment up there right away?"

"Yes, sir. The Black Stallion spaceplane can rendezvous with the space station in a couple hours."

"Get on it. And terminate those bomber missions over Iran. No more cruise missile shots until I know for sure what happened."

"Yes, sir." Bain's videoconference link cut off.

The President sat back in his chair, loosened his tie, and lit up a cigarette. "What a clusterfuck," he breathed. "We kill a bunch of innocent civilians in Tehran with a hypersonic missile fired from an unmanned bomber controlled from a military space station; Russia is screaming mad at us; and now the hero of the American Holocaust has a damned heart attack in space! What's next?"

"McLanahan's situation might turn out to be a blessing in disguise, Joe," Chief of Staff Walter Kordus said. He and Carlyle had known Joseph Gardner since their years in college and Kordus was one of the few allowed to ever address the President by his first name. "We've been looking for ways to cut funding for the space station despite its popularity in the Pentagon and Capitol Hill, and this might be it."

"But it has to be done delicately—McLanahan is too popular

with the people to be used as an excuse to cut his favorite program, especially since he's been touting it all over the world as the next big thing, the impregnable fortress, the ultimate watchtower, yada yada yada," the President said. "We have to get some congressmen to raise the question of safety on that space station, and if it needs to be manned at all in the first place. We'll have to 'leak' this incident to Senator Barbeau, the Armed Services Committee, and a few others."

"That won't be hard," Kordus said. "Barbeau will know how to stir things up without slamming McLanahan."

"Good. After it comes out in the press, I want to meet with Barbeau privately to discuss strategy." Kordus tried hard to control his discomfort at that order. The President noted his friend and chief political adviser's warning tenseness and added quickly, "Everyone's going to have their hand out for the money once we start the idea of killing that space station, and I want to control the begging, whining, and arm-twisting."

"Okay, Joe," Kordus said, not convinced by the President's hasty explanation, but not wanting to press the issue. "I'll set it up."

"You do that." He took a deep drag of his cigarette, crushed it out, then added, "And we need to get our ducks in a row soon, just in case McLanahan kicks the bucket and Congress kills his program before we can divvy up his budget."

CHAPTER THREE

One does what one is; one becomes what one does.

— ROBERT VON MUSIL

AZADI SQUARE, OUTSIDE MEHRABAD INTERNATIONAL AIRPORT, TEHRAN, DEMOCRATIC REPUBLIC OF PERSIA

DAYS LATER

"No bread, no peace! No bread, no peace!" the protesters chanted over and over again. It seemed the crowd, now numbering around two or three hundred, was growing bigger and exponentially louder by the minute.

"If they have no bread, where do they get all the energy to stand out here and protest?" Colonel Mostafa Rahmati, commander of the Fourth Infantry Brigade, muttered as he studied the security barriers and observed the crowds getting ever closer. Just two weeks earlier, Rahmati, a short, rather round man with bushy dark hair that seemed to grow thickly across every inch of his body except the top of his head, was executive officer of a transportation battalion, but the way commanding officers were disappearing—presumably killed by insurgents, although no one could rule out desertion—promotions came quickly and urgently in the army of the presumptive Democratic Republic of Persia.

"More smoke," one of Rahmati's lookouts reported. "Tear gas, not an explosion." Seconds later, they heard a loud *bang!* strong enough to rattle the windows of the airport office building he and his senior staff members were seated in. The lookout sheepishly glanced at his commanding officer. "A *small* explosion, sir."

"So I gather," Rahmati said. He didn't want to show any displeasure or exasperation—two weeks ago he wouldn't have been able to tell a grenade explosion from a loud fart. "Watch the lines carefully—it could be a diversion."

Rahmati and his staff were on the upper floor of an office building that once belonged to the Iranian Ministry of Transportation at Mehrabad International Airport. Since the military coup and the start of the Islamist insurgency against the military government in Iran, the coup leaders had decided to take over Mehrabad Airport and had established a tight security perimeter around the entire area. Although most of the city east of Tehran University had been left to the insurgents, taking over the airport turned out to be a wise decision. The airport was already highly secure; the open spaces around the field were easy to patrol and defend; and the airport could be kept open to receive and send supplies by air.

Besides, it was often pointed out, if the insurgents ever got the upper hand—which could be any day now—it would be that much easier to get the hell out of the country.

The windows rattled again, and heads turned farther southeast along Me'raj Avenue northeast toward Azadi Square, about two kilometers away, where another billow of smoke, this one topped with a crown of orange fire, suddenly rose. Bombings, arson, intentional accidents, mayhem, and frequent suicide bombings were commonplace in Tehran, and none more common than the area between Mehrabad Airport, Azadi Square, and the famous Freedom Tower, the erstwhile "Gateway to Iran." Freedom Tower, first called Shahyad Tower, or the King's Tower, commemorating the two thousand five hundredth anniversary of the Persian Empire, was built in 1971 by Shah Reza Pahlavi as a symbol of the new, modern Iran. The tower was renamed after the Islamic Revolution and, like the U.S. Embassy, was seen more as a symbol of the decadent monarchy and a warning to the people not to embrace the Western enemies of Islam. The square became a popular area for anti-Western demonstrations and speeches and so became a symbol of the Islamic revolution, which was probably why the marble-clad monument to Iran's last monarchy was never torn down.

Because the entire area was heavily fortified and well patrolled by the military, trade and commerce had started to revive here, and even some luxuries like restaurants, cafés, and movie theaters had reopened. Unfortunately these were frequent targets by Islamist insurgents. A few brave pro-theocratic protesters would organize a rally occasionally in Azadi Square. To their credit, the military did not crack down on these rallies and even took steps to protect them against counterprotesters that threatened to get too violent. Buzhazi and most of his officers knew that they had to do everything possible to demonstrate to the people of Persia, and to the world, that they were not going to replace one brand of oppression with another.

"What's happening over there?" Rahmati asked as he continued to scan the avenue for more signs of an organized insurgent offensive. Every insurgent attack of late had been preceded by a smaller innocuous-looking one nearby, which diverted the attention of police and military patrols just enough to allow the insurgents to create even more havoc somewhere else.

"Looks like that new ExxonMobil gasoline station off the Sai-di Highway, across from Meda Azadi Park, sir," a lookout reported. "A large crowd running toward Azadi Avenue. The smoke is getting thicker—perhaps the underground tanks are on fire."

"Damn it all, I thought we had enough security around there," Rahmati cursed. The station was the government's first experiment into allowing foreign investment and part ownership in businesses in Persia. With the world's fourth-largest oil reserves, petroleum companies around the world were eager to move into the newly freed country and tap its wealth, almost untouched for decades since the Western embargoes against the theocratic Iranian government following the takeover of the U.S. Embassy in 1979. It was much, much more than a simple gasoline station—it was a symbol of a reborn, twenty-first-century Persia.

Everyone understood that, even soldiers like Rahmati, whose main goal in life was to look out for number one—himself. He came from a privileged family and joined the military because of its prestige and benefits after it was apparent that he wasn't smart enough to become a doctor, lawyer, or engineer. After Ayatollah Ruhollah Khomeini's revolution, he saved his skin by swearing fealty to the theocrats, informing on his fellow officers and friends to the Pasdaran i-Engelab, the Revolutionary Guards Corps, and by giving up much of his family's hard-earned riches in bribes and tributes. Although he hated the theocracy for taking everything he had, he didn't join the coup until it was obvious that it was going to succeed. "I want a reserve platoon to go in with the firefighters to put out those fires," he went on, "and if any protesters get near, they are to push them back north of Azadi Avenue and northwest of the square, even if they have to crack some skulls. I don't want—"

"If you were going to say, 'I don't want to let this get out of control,' Colonel, cracking skulls is not the way to accomplish that," a voice said behind him. Rahmati turned, then snapped to and called the room to attention as the leader of the military coup, General Hesarak al-Kan Buzhazi, entered the room.

The struggle to free his country from the grip of the theocrats and Islamists had aged Buzhazi well beyond his sixty-two years. Tall and always slender, he now struggled to take time to eat enough to maintain a healthy weight amidst his twenty-hour-a-day duties, infrequent and sparse meals, and the necessity of staying on the move to confuse his enemies—inside his cadre as well as outside— that were relentlessly hunting him. He still wore a closely cropped beard and mustache, but had shaved his head so he didn't have to take the time to keep his former flowing gray locks looking good. Although he had traded his military uniform for a suit and French-styled Gatsby shirt, he did carry a military-style greatcoat

without decorations and wore spit-shined paratrooper's boots under
his slacks, and he wore a PC9 nine-millimeter automatic pistol in a
shoulder rig under his jacket. "As you were," he ordered. The others in the room relaxed. "Report, Colonel."

"Yes, sir." Rahmati quickly ran down the most serious events of
the past few hours; then: "Sorry for that outburst, sir. I'm just a little
frustrated, that's all. I put extra men on that station just to prevent
such an occurrence."

"Your frustration sounded like an order to retaliate against
anti-government protesters, Colonel, and that won't help the situation," Buzhazi said. "We'll deal harshly with the perpetrators, *not*
the protesters. Understood?"

"Yes, sir."

Buzhazi looked carefully at his brigade commander. "Looks like
you need some rest, Mostafa."

"I'm fine, sir."

Buzhazi nodded, then looked around the room. "Well, you can't
run your brigade from here all the time, can you? Let's go see what
happened out there." Rahmati gulped, then nodded, reluctantly following the general out the door, wishing he had agreed to take a
nap. Traveling the streets of Tehran—even in broad daylight, within
the portion of the city Buzhazi controlled, and with a full platoon of
battle-hardened security forces—was never a safe or advisable
move.

Every block of the two kilometers from the airport to Meda Azari
Park was a maze of concrete and steel chicanes designed to slow the
heaviest vehicles down; there was a new checkpoint every three blocks,
and even Buzhazi's motorcade had to stop and be searched each time.
Buzhazi didn't seem to mind one bit, using the opportunity to greet
his soldiers and the few citizens out on the street. Rahmati didn't want
to get that close to anyone, choosing instead to keep his AK-74 assault
rifle at the ready. As they got closer to the park and the crowds got
larger, Buzhazi strode down the street, shaking hands with those who
offered their hand, waving to others, and shouting a few words of en-
couragement. His bodyguards had to step lively to keep up with him.

Rahmati had to hand it to the guy: the old warhorse knew how to work a crowd. He waded into the crowds fearlessly, shook hands with those who might just as well be holding a gun or trigger for a bomb vest, spoke to reporters and gave statements in front of TV cameras, had his picture taken with civilians and military men, kissed babies and old toothless women, and even acted as a traffic officer when fire trucks tried to enter the area, urging the crowds back and directing confused motorists away. But now they were just a few blocks from the gas station fire, and the crowds were getting thicker and much more restive. "Sir, I suggest we interview the security patrols and find out if any witnesses saw what happened or if any security cameras were operating," Rahmati said, making it clear that *here* would be a good place to do that.

Buzhazi didn't seem to hear him. Instead of stopping he kept on walking, heading right for the largest and noisiest gaggle gathering on the northwest side of the park. Rahmati had no choice but to stay with him, rifle at the ready.

Buzhazi didn't turn around, but seemed to sense the brigade commander's anxiety. "Put the weapon away, Mostafa," Buzhazi said.

"But sir—"

"If they wanted a shot at me they could have done it two blocks ago, before we were looking at each other eye to eye," Buzhazi said. "Tell the security detail to shoulder their weapons as well." The team leader, an impossibly young air force major by the name of Haddad, must have heard him, because the bodyguards' weapons had already disappeared by the time Rahmati turned to relay the order.

The crowd visibly tensed as Buzhazi and his bodyguards approached, and the small knot of men, women, and even some kids quickly grew. Rahmati was no policeman or expert on crowd psychology, but he noticed as more onlookers came closer to see what was going on, the others would be pressed farther and farther forward, toward the source of danger, causing them to feel trapped and scared for their life. Once panic started to set in, the crowd would quickly and suddenly turn into a mob; and when some soldier or armed individual felt his life was in danger, the shooting would start and the casualties would quickly mount.

But Buzhazi seemed oblivious to the obvious: he kept on marching forward—not threateningly, but not with any kind of false bravado or friendliness either; all business, but not confrontational like a soldier or glad-handed like a politician. Did he think he was going to drop in on some friends and discuss the issues of the day, or sit down to watch a football match? Or did he think he was invulnerable? Whatever his mental state, he was not reading this crowd correctly. Rahmati began thinking about how he was going to get to his rifle . . . and at the same time trying to decide which way he could run if this situation completely went to hell.

"Salam aleikom," Buzhazi called when about ten paces from the growing crowd, raising his right hand in greeting as well as to show he was unarmed. "Is anyone hurt here?"

A young man no more than seventeen or eighteen stepped forward and jabbed a finger at the general. "What does a damned soldier care if anyone is—?" And then he stopped, his finger still extended. *"You!* Hesarak Buzhazi, the new emperor of Persia! The reincarnation of Cyrus and Alexander himself! Are we required to genuflect before you, or is a simple bow sufficient, my lord?"

"I said, is anyone—?"

"What do you think of your empire now, General?" the young man asked, motioning to the clouds of acrid smoke swirling not too far away. "Or is it 'Emperor' Buzhazi now?"

"If no one is in need of assistance, I need volunteers to keep others away from the blast site, locate witnesses, and gather evidence until the police arrive," Buzhazi said, turning his attention away—but not *completely* away—from the loud firebrand. He sought out the eldest person in the crowd. "You, sir. I need you to ask for volunteers and to secure this crime scene. Then I need—"

"Why should we help you, lord and master sir?" the first young man shouted. "You were the one who brought this violence upon us! Iran was a peaceful and secure country until you came in, slaughtered everyone who didn't agree with your totalitarian ideas, and took over. Why should we cooperate with *you*?"

"Peaceful and secure, yes—under the heel of the clerics, Islamists, and crazies who killed or imprisoned anyone who didn't comply with their edicts," Buzhazi said, unable to avoid being drawn into a debate he knew was not going to be won. "They betrayed the people like they betrayed myself and everyone in the army. They—"

"That's what this is about, isn't it, Mr. Emperor: *you*?" the man said. "You don't like the way you were treated by your former friends, the clerics, so you slaughtered them and took over. Why do we care what you say now? You'll tell us anything to stay in power until you're done raping the country, and then you'll fly off right from your very conveniently located new headquarters at Mehrabad Airport."

Buzhazi was silent for a few moments, then nodded, which surprised everyone around. "You're right, young man. I was angry at the deaths of my soldiers, who had worked so hard to get rid of the radicals and nutcases in the Basij and make something of themselves, their unit, and their lives." After Buzhazi had been dismissed as chief of staff, following the American stealth bomber attacks against their Russian-made aircraft carrier years earlier, he had been demoted to commander of the Basij-i-Mostazefin, or "Mobilization of the Oppressed," a group of civilian volunteers who informed on neighbors, acted as lookouts and spies, and roamed the streets terrorizing others to conform and cooperate with the Revolutionary Guards Corps.

Buzhazi purged the Basij of the gangsters and rabble-rousers and transformed the remainder into the Internal Defense Force, a true military reserve force. But their success challenged the domination of the Revolutionary Guards Corps, and they acted to try to discredit—or preferably destroy—Buzhazi's fledgling national guard force. "When I learned it was the Pasdaran that had staged the attack against my first operational reserve unit, making it look like a Kurdish insurgent action, just to hurt and discredit the Internal Defense Force, I got angry and lashed out.

"But the Islamists and the terrorists the clerics have brought into our country are the real problem, son, not the Pasdaran," Buzhazi went on. "They have gutted the minds of this nation, emptied them of all common sense and decency, and filled it with nothing but fear, contempt, and blind obedience."

"So what is the difference between you and the clerics, Buzhazi?" another young man shouted. Rahmati could see the crowd was getting bolder, more vocal, and not afraid to get closer every second. "You kill off the clerics and take down the government—*our* government, the one we elected!—and replace it with your junta. We see your troops breaking down doors, burning buildings, stealing, and raping every day!"

The crowd noisily voiced its agreement, and Buzhazi had to raise his hands and voice to be heard: "First of all, I promise you, if you bring me evidence of a theft or rape by any soldier under my command, I will personally put a bullet in his head," he shouted. "No tribunal, no secret trial, no hearing—bring me the evidence, convince me, and I will drag the man responsible before you and execute him myself.

"Second, I am not forming a government in Persia, and I am not a president or emperor—I am commander of the resistance forces temporarily in place to quell violence and establish order. I will stay in command long enough to root out the insurgents and terrorists and supervise the formation of some form of government that will draft a constitution and enact laws governing the people, and then I will step down. That is why I set up my headquarters at Mehrabad— not for a quick escape, but to show that I'm not going to occupy legitimate government offices and call myself a president."

"That's what Musharraf, Castro, Chávez, and hundreds of other dictators and despots said when they engineered their coups and took over the government," the young man said. "They said they fought for the people and would leave as soon as order was established, and before you knew it they had installed themselves in office for life, placed their friends and thugs in positions of power, suspended or tossed out the constitution, taken over the banks, nationalized all the businesses, taken away land and wealth from the rich, and closed any media outlets that opposed them. You will do the same in Iran."

Buzhazi studied the young man for a moment, then carefully scanned the others around him. Those, he observed, were some very good points—this guy was very intelligent and well read for such an age, and he suspected most of the others were too. He was not among normal street kids here.

"I judge a man by his actions, not his words—friend as well as enemy," Buzhazi said. "I could promise you peace, happiness, security, and prosperity, just like any politician, or I could promise you a place in heaven like the clerics, but I won't. All I can promise is that I will fight as hard as I can to stop the insurgents from tearing our country apart before we've had a chance to form a government of the people, whatever that government will be. I will use all my skills, training, and experience to make this country secure until a government by the people stands up."

"Those sound like pretty words to me, Mr. Emperor, the kind you just pledged you wouldn't use."

Buzhazi smiled and nodded, looking at those who seemed the angriest or most distrustful directly in the eye. "I see many of you have cell phone cameras, so you have video proof of what I say. If I was the dictator you think I am, I'd confiscate all those phones and have you tossed in prison."

"You could do that tonight after you break into our homes and roust us out of bed."

"But I won't," Buzhazi said. "You are free to send the videos out to anyone on the planet, post it on YouTube, sell it to the media. The video will be documentation of my promise to you, but my actions will be the final proof."

"How do we send out any videos, old man," a young woman asked, "when power is only on for three hours a day? We are lucky if the phones work for a few minutes each day."

"I read the postings, I surf the Internet, and I lurk on the blogs, just like you," Buzhazi said. "The American satellite global wireless Internet system works well even in Persia—may I remind you that it was jammed by the clerics in order to try to prevent you from receiving contrary news from the outside world—and I know many of you enterprising young people have built pedal-powered generators to recharge your laptops when the power goes out. I may be an old man, young lady, but I'm not *completely* out of touch." He was pleased to see a few smiles appear on the faces of those around him—finally, he thought, he was starting to speak their language.

"But I remind you that the power goes out because of insurgent attacks on our power generators and distribution networks," he went on. "There's an enemy out there who doesn't care about the people of Persia—all they want is to regain power for themselves, and they'll do it any way they can think of, even if it hurts or kills innocent citizens. I took power away from them and allowed the citizens of this country to communicate with the outside world again. I allowed foreign investment and aid to return to Persia, while the clerics shut out the rest of the world for over thirty years and hoarded the wealth and power of this nation. That's the action I'm talking about, my friends. I can say absolutely nothing, and those actions would speak louder than a thousand thunderstorms."

"So when will the attacks stop, General?" the first man asked. "How long will it take to drive the insurgents out?"

"Long after I'm dead and buried, I think," Buzhazi said. "So then it'll be up to you. How long do you want it to take, son?"

"Hey, *you* started this war, not me!" the man thundered, shaking his fist. "Do not lay this at my feet! You say you'll be dead long before this is over—well, why don't you just go to hell *now* and save us all a lot of time!" A few in the crowd blinked at the man's violent outburst, but said or did nothing. "And I am *not* your son, old man. My father was killed in the street outside the shop my family has owned for three generations, during a gun battle between your troops and the Pasdaran, right before my eyes, my mother's, and my baby sister's."

Buzhazi nodded. "I am sorry. Then tell me your name."

"I don't feel like telling you my name, old man," the young man said bitterly, "because I see you and your forces just as capable of arresting me or shooting me in the head as the Pasdaran reportedly were."

" 'Reportedly?' You doubt that the Pasdaran are killing anyone who opposes the clerics?"

"I saw plenty of violence and bloodthirstiness on both sides in the gun battle in which my father was killed," the young man went on, "and I see very little difference between you and the clerics except perhaps the clothes you wear. Are you correct or justified in your actions just because the Americans swooped in and helped you drive the Pasdaran temporarily out of the capital? When *you* are driven out, will you be the new insurgents then? Will you make war on the innocent because you think you are correct?"

"If you truly believe that I'm no better or worse than the Islamic Revolutionary Guards, then no amount of words will ever convince you otherwise," Buzhazi said, "and you will blame your father's death on any convenient target. I am sorry for your loss." He turned and scanned the others around him. "I see a lot of angry faces out here in the street, but I hear some extremely intelligent voices as well. My question to you is: If you're so smart, what are you doing out here just standing around? Your fellow citizens are dying, and you do nothing but shuffle from attack to attack shaking your fists at my soldiers while the insurgents move to the next target."

"What are *we* supposed to do, old man?" another man asked.

"Follow your head, follow your heart, and take *action,*" Buzhazi said. "If it's the clerics you truly believe have the best interests of the nation in mind, join the insurgency and fight to drive me and my men out of the country. If you believe in the monarchists, join them and create your own insurgency in the name of the Qagev, battling both the Islamists and my soldiers, and bring the monarchy back to power. If you think what I say and do makes sense, put on a uniform, pick up a rifle, and join *me*. If you don't want to join anyone, at least keep your damn eyes open and when you see an attack against your family or your neighbors, take action . . . *any* action. Fight, inform, assist, protect—do *something* rather than just stand around and complain about it."

He scanned their faces once again, letting them look directly into his eyes and he into theirs. Most of them did. He saw some real strength in this bunch, and it gave him hope. They *were* worth fighting for, he decided. No matter which side they chose, *they* were the future of this land. "It's your country, dammit . . . it's *our* country. If it's not worth fighting for, go somewhere else before you become another casualty." He fell silent, letting his words sink in; then: "Now I need your help policing this crime scene. My soldiers will set up a perimeter and secure the area, but I need some of you to help the rescuers recover the victims and the police gather evidence and interview witnesses. Who will help?"

The crowd paused, waiting for someone to move first. Then the first young man stepped forward and said to Buzhazi, "Not for you, Emperor. You think you are any different than the insurgents roaming the streets? You're *worse.* You're nothing but a pretentious old man with a gun. That doesn't make you *right.*" And he turned and walked away, followed by the rest.

"Shit, I thought I had gotten through to them," Buzhazi said to Colonel Rahmati.

"They're just a bunch of losers, sir," the brigade commander said. "You asked what they're doing out here on the streets? They're stirring up trouble, that's all. For all we know, *they* are the ones who blew up that gas station. How do we know they're not insurgents?"

"They *are* insurgents, Mostafa," Buzhazi said.

Rahmati looked stunned. "They . . . *are*? How do you know . . . I mean, we should arrest all of them right now!"

"They're insurgents, but not Islamists," Buzhazi said. "If I had a choice as to which I'd want out on the streets right now, it's *definitely* them. I still think they'll help, but not the way I might want them to." He looked in the direction of the still-burning gasoline station to the remnants of a smoldering delivery truck that had been blown several dozen meters across the street. "Stay here and keep your weapons out of sight. Get the perimeter set up. I want no more than two soldiers positioned at any intersection, and they should be stationed on opposite corners, not together."

"Why, sir?"

"Because if there are more, informants will not approach them—and we need information, fast," Buzhazi said. He started walking toward the smoking truck. Rahmati started to follow, not wanting to appear any more frightened than he was already, but Buzhazi turned and growled, "I said stay here and get that perimeter set up." Rahmati was only too glad to comply.

A fire truck had approached the burning hulk and two very young-looking firefighters—probably children of dead or injured *real* firemen, a common practice in this part of the world—started to fight the fire, using a weak stream of water from the old surplus fire truck. It was going to be a long and smoky job. Buzhazi stepped around the fire truck, just far enough from the smoke so he wouldn't be choked by it, but was mostly screened from view. Now that the cleanup job had started, the crowds had started to disperse. Another, larger fire crew was attacking the blaze at the gas station itself, which was still very hot and fierce, rapidly driving huge columns of black smoke skyward. It was unbelievable to Buzhazi that the flames seemed to drink in even that huge volume of water—the fire was so intense that the fire actually seemed to—

"Quite a speech back there, General," he heard a voice say behind him.

Buzhazi nodded and smiled—he had guessed correctly. He turned and nodded formally to Her Highness Azar Assiyeh Qagev, the heir presumptive of the Peacock Throne of Persia. He glanced behind the young woman and spotted Captain Mara Saidi, one of Azar's royal bodyguards, standing discreetly near a lamppost, expertly blending in with the chaos around them. Her jacket was open and her hands clasped before her, obviously shielding a weapon from sight. "I thought I saw the captain there in the crowd, and I knew you'd be nearby. I assume the major is nearby with a sniper rifle or RPG, correct?"

"I believe he's armed with both weapons today—you know how he likes to come prepared," Azar said, bowing in return, not bothering to point out her chief of internal security Parviz Najar's hiding place—just in case Buzhazi's little rendezvous here was really a trap. She couldn't afford to trust this man—alliances changed so quickly in Persia. "I have promoted Najar to lieutenant colonel and Saidi to major for their bravery in getting me out of America and back home."

Buzhazi nodded approvingly. Azar Assiyeh Qagev, the youngest daughter of the pretender to the Peacock Throne, Mohammed Hassan Qagev—still missing since the beginning of Buzhazi's coup against the theocratic regime of Iran—had just turned seventeen years old, but she had the self-confidence of an adult twice her age, not to mention the courage, martial skills, and tactical foresight of an infantry company commander. She was also turning into a woman very nicely, Buzhazi couldn't help but notice, with long shiny black hair, graceful curves starting to bud on her slender figure, and dark, dancing, almost mischievous eyes. Her arms and legs were covered but with a white blouse and "chocolate chip" desert fatigue trousers, not a *burka,* to protect herself from the sun; her head was covered but with a TeamMelli World Cup Football team "doo-rag," not a *hijab.*

But his eyes were also automatically drawn to her hands. Every other generation of men of the Qagev dynasty—possibly the women too, but they were probably discarded as newborns rather than have them grow up with any sort of deficiency—had suffered from a genetic defect called bilateral hypoplastic thumb, or missing a thumb on both hands. She had pollicization surgery as a young child, which makes the index fingers function as thumbs, and left her with only four fingers on both hands.

But rather than becoming a handicap, Azar had made the deformity a source of strength, toughening her up beginning at a very young age. She had more than made up for her perceived deficiency: rumor was that she could outshoot most men twice her age and was an accomplished pianist and martial artist. Azar reportedly rarely wore gloves, letting others see her hands both as a symbol of her legacy and as a distraction to her adversaries.

Azar had secretly lived in the United States of America since she was two years old, under the protection of her bodyguards Najar and Saidi, who posed as her parents, separated from her real parents for security reasons, who had also lived in hiding as guests of the U.S. Department of State. When Buzhazi's coup erupted, the Qagevs immediately activated their war council and headed back to Iran. The king and queen—who were supposed to be in hiding yet ran a Web site, regularly appeared in the media blasting the theocratic regime in Iran, and openly vowing to someday return and take control of the country—were still missing and presumed killed by the Iranian Revolutionary Guards Corps or al-Quds terrorist forces, with the help of the Russians and Turkmenis. But Azar did make it into Iran, using her wits, natural-born leadership skills—and a lot of help from the American Battle Force and a small army of armored commandos—and joined up with the royal war council and their thousands of jubilant followers.

"I'm impressed, Highness," Buzhazi said, taking off his helmet and pouring a bit of water on his face before taking a deep drink. "I was looking specifically for you, but you blended into the crowd perfectly. Obviously the others had no idea who you were, because no one tried to form a defensive shield around you when I approached. You hid your *mun* well."

"I've been hanging around the city trying to listen to these young people to find out what they want and what they expect," Azar said. Her American accent was still thick, making her Farsi hard to understand. She removed the Iranian national soccer team headband to reveal the long waist-length ponytail, the *mun,* typical of Persian royalty for centuries. She shook her hair, glad to be free from the self-imposed but traditional bonds. Major Saidi, a horrified look on her face, stepped toward her, silently urging her to hide her *mun* before anyone on the streets noticed. Azar rolled her eyes in mock exasperation and tied the ponytail up again under the doo-rag. "They know me as one of the displaced, that's all—like them."

"Except with a hundred armed bodyguards, a council of war, a secret war chest bigger than the gross national product of most of central Asia, and several hundred thousand followers who would gladly step in front of a line of machine guns to see you back on the *Takht-e-Tavous,* the Peacock Throne."

"I'd trade all that I control to convince you and your brigades to join me, Hesarak," she said. "My followers are loyal and dedicated, but we are still far too few, and my followers are loyalists, not fighters."

"What do you think is the difference between a so-called loyalist and a soldier, Highness?" Buzhazi asked. "When your country's in danger, there *is* no difference. In times of war, citizens become fighters, or they become slaves."

"They need a general . . . they need *you.*"

"They need a leader, Highness, and that person is *you,*" Buzhazi said. "If half your loyalists are as smart, fearless, and daring as that bunch that you were hanging around with back there, they can easily take control of this country."

"They won't follow a girl."

"Probably not . . . but they'll follow a *leader.*"

"I want you to lead them."

"I'm not taking sides here, Highness—I'm not in the business of forming governments," Buzhazi said. "I'm here because the Pasdaran and the insurgents they sponsor are still a threat to this country, and I will hunt them down until every last one of them is dead. But I'm not going to be the president. John Alton said, 'Power corrupts, and absolute power corrupts absolutely.' I know my power comes from my army, and I don't want the people to be ruled by its military. It should be the other way around."

"If you won't be their president, be their general," Azar said. "Lead your army under the Qagev banner, train our loyalists, draft more fighters from the civilian population, and let us put our nation back together."

Buzhazi looked seriously at the young woman. "What of your parents, Highness?" he asked.

Azar swallowed at the unexpected question, but the steel quickly returned to her eyes. "Still no word, General," she replied firmly. "They are alive—I know it."

"Of course, Highness," Buzhazi said softly. "I have heard your council of war won't approve of you leading your forces until you reach the age of majority."

Azar sneered and shook her head. "The age of majority was *fourteen* for centuries—Alexander was fourteen when he led his first army into battle," she spat. "When projectile warfare became more advanced and weapons and armor got thicker and heavier, the age of majority—the word comes from *majour,* the leader of a regiment—was raised to eighteen because anyone younger could not lift a sword or wear the armor. What relevance does that have in today's world? Nowadays a five-year-old can use a computer, read a map, talk on a radio, and understand patterns and trends. But my esteemed council of stuffed-shirt old men and cluck-clucking old women won't let anyone younger than eighteen lead the army— especially one that is female."

"I recommend someone get your battalion commanders to-gether, nominate a commander, get it approved by your war coun-cil, and get organized . . . *soon,*" Buzhazi warned. "Your raids are completely uncoordinated and don't seem to have any purpose other than random killings and mayhem that keep the population on edge."

"I've already said that to the council, but they're not listening to a little girl," Azar complained. "I'm just a figurehead, a symbol. They would rather quibble over who has seniority, who has more followers, or who can bring in more recruits or cash. All they want out of me is a male heir. Without a king, the council will make no decisions."

"Then be the *Malika.*"

"I don't like being called 'Queen,' General, and you know it, I'm sure," Azar said hotly. "My parents *are not dead.*" She said those last words angrily, defiantly, as if attempting to convince herself as well as the general.

"It's been almost two years since they've disappeared, Highness— how much longer are you going to wait? Until you turn eighteen?

Where will Persia be in fifteen months? Or until a rival dynasty asserts its claim to the Peacock Throne, or some strongman takes over and has all the Qagevs back on the run?"

Obviously Azar had asked herself all these questions already, because it pained her that she didn't have any answers. "I know, General, I know," she said in a tiny voice, the saddest one he had ever heard her use. "That's why I need you to go before the council of war, join us, take command of our loyalists, and unite the anti-Islamist forces against Mohtaz and his bloodthirsty *jihadis*. You are the most powerful man in Persia. They would not hesitate to approve."

"I'm not sure if I'm ready to be the commanding general in a monarchist army, Highness," Buzhazi said. "I need to know what the Qagev stand for before I'll throw my support behind them." He looked at Azar somberly. "And until your parents appear, or until you turn eighteen—maybe not even then—the council of war speaks for the Qagev . . ."

"And they cannot even decide if the royal flag should be raised *before* or *after* morning prayers," Azar said disgustedly. "They argue about court protocol, rank, and petty procedures rather than tactics, strategies, and objectives."

"And you want *me* to take my orders from *them*? No thank you, Highness."

"But if there was a way to convince them to support you if you announced that you would form a government, Hesarak—"

"I told you, I'm not in the business of forming governments," Buzhazi snapped. "I took down the clerics, the corrupt Islamist leadership, and their hired goons the Pasdaran because they are the true obstacles to freedom and law in this country. But may I remind you that we still have a Majlis-i-Shura that we elected that supposedly have the constitutional authority to take control and form a representative government? Where are they? Hiding, that's what. They're afraid they'll be targeted for assassination if they poke their little heads out, so they'd rather watch in their comfortable villas with their bodyguards surrounding them while their country tears itself apart."

"So it sounds like you just want someone to *ask* you to help them, is that it, General? You crave the honor and respect of having a politician or princess beg for help?"

"What I crave, Highness, is for the persons who supposedly lead this country to get off their fat asses and *lead*," Buzhazi said hotly. "Until the Majlis, your so-called war council, or someone else decides it has the stomach to squash the Islamist insurgency, take charge, and form a government, I'll keep doing what I do best—hunting down and killing as many of the enemies of Persia as I can to save innocent lives. At least *I* have an objective."

"My followers share your vision, General . . ."

"Then prove it. Help me do my job until you can talk some sense into your war council."

Azar wanted to argue, for her people and their struggle as well as for her own legitimacy, but she knew she had run out of answers. Buzhazi was right: they had the will to resist the Islamists, but they just couldn't get the job done. She nodded resignedly. "All right, General, I'm listening. How can we help you?"

"Tell your loyalists to join my army and pledge to follow my orders for two years. I'll train and equip them. After two years they are free to return to you, with all the equipment and weapons they can carry on their backs."

Azar's eyebrows raised in surprise. "A very generous offer."

"But they must swear during their two-year enlistment to obey my commands and fight for *me*, all the way and then some, upon penalty of death—not by any war council, court, or tribunal, but by *me*. If they are caught passing information to *anyone* outside my ranks, including *you,* they'll die in humiliation and disgrace."

Azar nodded. "What else?"

"If they will not join my army, they must agree to pass on clear, timely, and actionable information to me, on a constant basis or on demand, and to support my army with everything they have to give—food, clothing, shelter, water, money, supplies, anything," Buzhazi went on. "I've ordered my security details spread out to make it easier for your people to pass notes, photos, or other information to them, and I will provide you with blind drops and secure voice and e-mail addresses for you to use to leave us information.

"But you must help us, *all* of you. Your loyalists can follow the Qagev, such as you are, but they *will* help me, or they will stand out of the way while my men and I fight. They either agree that I fight for Persia and I am deserving of their complete and total support, or they will lay down their weapons and stay off the streets—no more raids or bombings, no more roving gangs, and no more assassinations that serve only to terrorize the innocents and cause the Pasdaran and Islamists to increase their attacks against the civilian population."

"That will be . . . difficult," Azar admitted. "I simply don't know all of the resistance leaders out there. I frankly doubt if anyone on the council knows all of the cells and their leaders."

"You attend the war council meetings, don't you?"

"I'm allowed to attend general meetings of the war council, but I'm not allowed to vote, and I'm discouraged from attending strategy meetings."

Buzhazi shook his head in exasperation. "You're probably the smartest person in that council meeting—why you're not allowed to participate is a damned mystery to me. Well, it's your problem, Highness. I'm telling you that your loyalists are part of the problem, not part of the solution. I don't know if the person with the gun at the other end of the block is an Islamist or one of your loyalists, so I'm going to blow his head off regardless before he tries to do the same to me. That's not the way I want it, but that's the way I'll play it if I have to."

"I'm sorry I can't be of more help, General."

"You can, Highness, if you just drag yourself back into the twenty-first century like I know you can," Buzhazi said, donning his helmet again and pulling the straps tight.

"What?"

"Come on now, Highness—you know exactly what I'm talking about," Buzhazi said irritably. "You're a smart woman as well as a natural-born leader. You've lived in America most of your life and you've obviously learned that the old ways won't work any-more. You know as well as I that this court of yours and this so-called council of war is what's hamstringing you. You've vol-untarily imprisoned yourself in this six-hundred-year-old cage called your 'court' and you've committed to cede authority to a bunch of spineless cowards—half of which aren't even *in* this country right now, am I correct?" He could tell by her expression that he was.

Buzhazi shook his head in disappointment quickly turning to disgust. "Pardon me for saying this, Highness, but get your royal head out of your pretty little ass and get with the program before we all die and our country becomes a mass graveyard," he said angrily. "*You're* the one out here on the streets, Azar. You can see the prob-lems and are smart enough to formulate a response, but you won't take charge. Why? Because you don't want your parents to think you're taking over their thrones? This is the twenty-first century, Azar, for God's sake, not the *fourteenth*. Besides, your parents are either dead or cowards themselves if they haven't shown themselves in almost two—"

"*Shut up!*" Azar screamed, and before Buzhazi could react, she had spun around and planted her right foot solidly in his solar plexus, knocking the wind out of him. Buzhazi went down on one knee, more embarrassed at being taken by surprise than hurt. By the time he got back on his feet and was able to take at least a half of a normal breath, Mara Saidi was shielding Azar, an automatic ma-chine pistol pointed at him.

"Good kick, Highness," Buzhazi grunted, rubbing his abdomen. Obviously, he guessed, one of her accommodations for having de-fects of the hands was her ability to fight with her feet. "The rumors said you could take care of yourself—I see that's true."

"The meeting is over, General," he heard a man say behind him. Buzhazi turned and nodded at Parviz Najar, who had run out of hiding in the blink of an eye and had another machine pistol pointed at him. "Go quickly."

"*After* you both lower your weapons," they heard another voice shout. They all turned to see Major Qolom Haddad hidden behind the rear end of the smoldering truck, an AK-74 rifle leveled at Najar. "I'm not going to repeat myself!"

"Everyone, lower your weapons," Buzhazi said. "I think we've both said what we needed to say here." No one moved. "Major, you and your men, stand down."

"Sir—"

"Colonel, Captain, stand down as well," Azar ordered. Slowly, reluctantly, Najar and Saida complied, and when their weapons were out of sight, Haddad lowered his. "There are no enemies here."

Buzhazi took his first full deep breath, smiled, nodded again respectfully, then extended his hand. "Highness, it was good to speak with you. I hope we can work together, but I assure you, I'm going to keep fighting."

Azar took his hand and bowed her head as well. "It was good to speak with you too, General. I have much to think about."

"Don't take too long, Highness. *Salam aleikom.*" Buzhazi turned and headed back to his men, with Haddad and two more soldiers who had been carefully hidden nearby covering his back.

"Peace be unto you as well, General," Azar called after him.

Buzhazi turned halfway to her, smiled, and called out, "Unlikely, Highness. But thanks anyway."

THE WHITE HOUSE RESIDENCE

THAT SAME TIME

Chief of Staff Walter Kordus knocked on the door of the President's sitting room on the third-floor family residence of the White House. "Sir? She's here."

President Gardner looked up over his reading glasses and set down the papers he was reviewing. He had a large flat-screen TV on to a boxing match but with the sound muted. He wore a white shirt and business slacks, with his tie loosened—he rarely wore anything else but business attire until moments before bed. "Good. Where?"

"You said you didn't want to meet in the West Wing, so I had her brought up to the Red Room—I thought that was appropriate."

"Cute. But she asked to see the Treaty Room. Have her brought up."

Kordus took a step into the sitting room. "Joe, are you sure you want to do this? She's the chairwoman of the Senate Armed Services Committee, probably the most powerful woman in the country besides Angelina Jolie. It's got to remain business . . ."

"This *is* business, Walt," Gardner said. "I'll be there in a few minutes. Got those notes I asked you for?"

"They're on the way."

"Good." Gardner went back to studying his papers. The chief of staff shook his head and departed.

A few minutes later, Gardner made his way down the Center Hall, now wearing his suit jacket, straightening his tie as he walked. Kordus intercepted him and passed him a folder. "Hot off the press. Want me to—?"

"Nope. I think we're done for the night. Thanks, Walt." He breezed past the chief of staff and entered the Treaty Room. "Hello, Senator. Thanks for meeting me at this ungodly hour."

She was standing beside the immense mahogany U. S. Grant Cabinet table, lovingly running her long fingers across the inlaid cherry features. The steward had placed a tray of tea on the coffee table on the other side of the room. Her eyes widened and that camera-magnetizing smile appeared when she saw Gardner enter the room. "Mr. President, it is certainly my honor and privilege to be with you tonight," Senator Stacy Anne Barbeau said in her famous silky Louisiana accent. "Thank you so much for the invitation." She stood, embraced the President, and exchanged polite kisses on the cheek. Barbeau wore a white low-cut business suit which subtly but effectively displayed her breasts and cleavage, accented for the evening by a shimmering platinum necklace and dangling diamond earrings. Her red hair bounced as if motorized in tune with her smile and batting eyelashes, and her green eyes flashed with energy. "You know that you may call upon me at any time, sir."

"Thank you, Senator. Please." He motioned to a Victorian couch and took her hand as he led her to it, then took an ornate chair to her right, facing the fireplace.

"I hope you give my best to the First Lady," Barbeau said as she arranged herself just so on the couch. "She's in Damascus, if I'm not mistaken, attending the international women's rights conference?"

"Exactly, Senator," the President said.

"I wish my duties in the Senate would have allowed me to attend," Barbeau said. "I sent my senior staffer Colleen to attend, and she's bringing a resolution of support from the full Senate for the First Lady to present to the delegates."

"Very thoughtful of you, Senator."

"Please, sir, will you not call me 'Stacy,' here in the privacy of the residence?" Barbeau asked, giving him one of her mind-blowing smiles. "I think we've both earned the right to a little downtime and relief from the formalities of our offices."

"Of course, Stacy," Gardner said. He did not offer to let her call him "Joe," and she knew enough not to ask. "But the pressure is never really off, is it? Not in our lines of work."

"I've never considered what I do 'work,' Mr. President," Barbeau said. She poured him a cup of tea, then sat back and crossed her legs as she sipped hers. "It's not always pleasurable, to be sure, but doing the people's business is never a chore. I suppose the stress is part of what makes one feel alive, don't you agree?"

"It always seemed to me you thrive on the pressure, Senator," Gardner commented. He suppressed a grimace after he sipped the tea. "In fact, if I may say so, it looks to me like you enjoy *creating* a bit of it."

"My responsibilities many times dictate that I do things above and beyond what most folks might call 'politic,'" Barbeau said. "We do whatever we need to do in the best interest of our constituents and our country, isn't that right, Mr. President?"

"Call me Joe. Please."

Barbeau's green eyes flashed, and her head bowed without her eyes leaving his. "Why, thank you for the honor . . . Joe."

"Not at all, Stacy," Gardner said with a smile. "You're right, of course. No one likes to admit it, but the end often justifies the means, as long as the end is a safer and more secure nation." He picked up a telephone sitting on the Monroe desk. "Could you have the libation table brought to the Treaty Room, please?" He hung up the phone. "It's after nine P.M., Stacy, and I'm not in the mood for tea. Hope you don't mind."

"Not at all, Joe." The smile was back, but it was more introspective, more reserved. "I may just join you."

"I know what might convince you." A steward brought a rolling table with several crystal decanters. Gardner poured himself a glass of Bacardi Dark on ice and fixed Barbeau a drink. "I thought I read in *People* magazine that you preferred a 'Creole Mama,' correct? I hope I got it right . . . bourbon, Madeira, and a splash of grenadine, topped with a cherry, right? Sorry, we only have red cherries, not green."

"You are a real surprise sometimes, Joe," she said. They touched glasses, their eyes locked together. She tasted hers, her eyes glistened again, and she took a deeper sip. "My my, Mr. President, a little intelligence work, even after hours, and a skilled hand at the bar. I'm again impressed."

"Thank you." Gardner took a deep sip of his drink as well. "Not as sophisticated as a Creole Mama, I'm sure, but when you're a politician from Florida, you'd better know your rum. Cheers." They touched glasses and sipped their drinks once more. "Do you know the origin of touching glasses, Stacy?"

"I'm sure I don't," Barbeau replied. "I didn't even realize there *was* an origin to it. It's not just a cute little noisemaker then?"

"In medieval times, when adversaries met to discuss terms of treaties or alliances, when they drank after negotiations were concluded they tipped a bit of the contents of their cups into the other's to show neither was poisoned. The custom evolved into a sign of friendship and camaraderie."

"Why, how fascinating," Barbeau said, taking another sip, then letting her tongue run across her full lips. "But I certainly hope you don't see me as an adversary, Joe. I'm anything but. I have been an admirer of yours for years, as was my father. Your political skills are exceeded only by your intelligence, charm, and true dedication to the service of the nation."

"Thank you, Stacy." He let his eyes drift across Barbeau's body as she took another sip. Even as it appeared that she was concentrating on enjoying her drink, she noticed he was looking her over . . . again. "I knew your father when we were in the Senate together. He was one *power*ful man, very strong-willed and passionate in his pursuits."

"He counted you among his most trusted friends, even though you and he were on opposite sides of the political and ideological aisle then," Barbeau said. "After I was elected to the Senate, he often reminded me that if I wanted some straight talk from the other side, I shouldn't hesitate to come to you." She paused, adopting a rather wistful expression. "I wish he was still here now. I could use his strength and wisdom. I love him so much."

"He was a fighter. A tough opponent. You knew where he stood and he wasn't afraid to tell you. He was one hell of a man."

Barbeau put her hand on Gardner's and pressed it. "Thank you, Joe. You're a sweet man." She took an instant to look at him deeply, then let her lips part slightly. "You . . . look very much like I remember him in his younger, more fiery years, Joe. We had a dining room very much like this in Shreveport, and we used to spend endless hours together, just like this. I wanted to talk politics and he wanted to find out about who I was dating."

"Daddies and daughters always stay close, eh?"

"He made me tell him my most intimate secrets," she said, a mischievous smile spreading across her face. "I couldn't deny him anything. He made me tell him everything—and I was a *very* naughty girl growing up. I dated all the politicians' boys. I wanted to learn everything about politics: strategies, planning, fund-raising, candidates, issues, alliances. They wanted . . ." She paused, giving him another sly smile and a bat of her eyes. ". . . well, you *know* what *they* wanted." Gardner swallowed hard as he imagined what they got from *her*. "It was a mutually beneficial relationship. Sometimes I think my daddy set me up on some of those dates just so I could be his spy—the Cajun political version of turning your daughter out, I suppose."

Gardner chuckled, and unconsciously let his eyes roam her body again, and this time Barbeau allowed herself to show that she noticed, smiled, and blushed—she was one of those women who could blush anytime, anywhere, in any situation, at will. He sat back in his chair, wanting to get this meeting under way so they could concentrate on other things, if the opportunity presented itself. "So, Stacy, we both know the issue before us. Where does the White House stand with the Armed Services Committee? Are we going to have a fight over the military budget, or can we come to an agreement and form a united front?"

"Unfortunately we're more confused than ever, I'm afraid, Joe," Barbeau replied. She took her hand away, watching a sudden pang of loss cloud his face. "This is all confidential, Mr. President?"

"Of course." He touched her hand, and her eyes fluttered. "On both sides. Strictly confidential."

"My lips are sealed." Barbeau smiled, then put her red lips together, made a locking motion with her long fingers, and tucked the invisible key in the ample cleavage between her breasts. Gardner took that as open permission to look at her chest this time, and he did so liberally. "The committee is in an uproar, Joe. They're concerned about General McLanahan's health and well-being, of course. Have you heard anything more about him?"

"Not much. The doctors originally told me not to expect him back to duty for several months. Some kind of heart thing."

That jibed with what her sources at Walter Reed National Military Medical Center told her, she thought—so far, Gardner wasn't lying to her. That was a good sign. "For such a strong young man to be suddenly rendered unconscious like that, the stresses of living on that space station and making repeated trips back and forth in the Black Stallion spaceplane must be enormous, far more than anyone could have possibly anticipated."

"McLanahan's a tough guy, but you're right—although he is over fifty and has a family history of heart disease, he was incredibly fit. Shuttle astronauts usually get several days between liftoff and re-entry—McLanahan has taken five round-trips to the space station in the past four weeks. That's unprecedented, but for the past few months it's been the norm. We're restricting travel to the space station and are in the process of doing extensive physicals on everyone involved. We need answers as to what's happened."

"But that's exactly my point, Joe. McLanahan is tough and strong, especially for a middle-aged man, and he's a combat veteran and national military figure—my God, he's a *hero!*—who I'm sure gets regular fitness checkups. Yet he was still incapacitated and God knows what sort of injury he has sustained. It calls into question the safety and utility of the proposed military space plan. For heaven's sake, Joe, why are we risking good men on such a project? I grant you it's modern and exotic and exciting, but it's technology that just hasn't been perfected and probably won't be for another ten years—not to mention the fact that it's four-fifths fewer aircraft and one-tenth the payload for the same money. If a strong guy like General McLanahan is knocked senseless by flying the thing, is it safe for other crewmembers?"

"What does the committee think, Stacy?"

"It's simple and logical, Joe," Barbeau said. "It's not about impressing the folks with global Internet access or half-meter resolution photographs of everyone's backyards—it's about creating value and benefit for our country's defense. As far as I can see, the space-planes benefit only the handful of contractors assigned to the project, namely Sky Masters and their subcompanies. We have a dozen different space booster systems with proven track records that can do a better job than the Black Stallion." She rolled her eyes. "For God's sake, Joe, who else is McLanahan in bed with?"

"Certainly not Maureen Hershel anymore," Gardner chuckled.

Barbeau rolled her eyes in dramatized disbelief. "Oh, that *dreadful* woman—I'll never understand why President Martindale chose *her* of all people to be his Vice President," Barbeau retorted. She looked inquisitively, then playfully at Gardner over the rim of her glass, then asked, "Or was the cold-fish routine just for public consumption, Joe?"

"We became close friends because of the demands of the job, Stacy, just business. All the rumors floating around about us are completely bogus."

Now he was lying, Barbeau thought, but she expected nothing less than a complete and outright denial. "I completely understand how the working conditions in Washington thrust two people together, especially ones who seem complete opposites," Barbeau said. "Combine power politics with a brewing war in the Middle East and long nights attending briefings and planning sessions, and sparks can fly."

"Not to mention McLanahan was obviously not getting business done back at home," Gardner added. They both laughed, and Gardner used that opportunity to clasp Barbeau's hand again. "He was too busy playing space cadet to pay any attention to her." He affixed Barbeau with a deep, serious stare. "Look, Stacy, let's get right down to it, okay? I know what you want—you've been lobbying for it since you set foot inside the Beltway. With most of the rest of the Air Force bomber bases destroyed by the Russians in the '04 Holocaust nuclear attacks, Barksdale Air Force Base is the natural home for a new long-range bomber fleet—"

"If the Pentagon doesn't keep on dumping money into that dust-bowl desert base in Battle Mountain, black programs in Dreamland—another Nevada base that mostly falls outside congressional oversight, I might point out—or the space station."

"It's no secret McLanahan's stock rose to all-time highs after his actions in the counterattacks against Russia," Gardner said, "and his pet projects were the unmanned bombers at Battle Mountain, his high-tech laser gizmos at Dreamland, and now the space station. It gave Martindale something to point at and brag to the American people that he devised and supported—"

"Even though President Thomas Thorn was the one who authorized their construction, not Martindale," Barbeau pointed out.

"Unfortunately, President Thorn will always and forever be known as the president who allowed the Russians to pull off a sneak attack against the United States that killed thirty thousand men, women, and children and injured another quarter million," Gardner said. "It won't matter that he was just as interested in high-tech toys as Martindale: Thorn will always be thought of as the weaker president.

"But the question is, what do we think is in the best interest of the American people and national defense, Stacy—these fancy spaceplanes that can't carry as much as the Secret Service's Suburbans, or proven technology like stealth bombers, unmanned combat aerial vehicles, and aircraft carriers? McLanahan has convinced Martindale that spaceplanes are better, even though he used unmanned bombers almost exclusively in his attacks on Russia—"

"And as you've pointed out many times, Joe," Barbeau added, "we can't afford to put all our eggs in one basket again. The Russian attack was so successful because all the bombers were located at a small handful of undefended bases, and unless they're all in the air, they're vulnerable to attack. But aircraft carrier battle groups deployed to bases all around the world, or far out at sea, are heavily equipped for self-protection and are far less vulnerable to sneak attack."

"Exactly," Gardner said, nodding with pleasure that Barbeau had brought up the aircraft carriers. "That's the point I've been trying to make for all these years. We need a mix of forces—we can't dump all the money for new weapon systems on one unproven technology. An aircraft carrier battle group is no more expensive that what McLanahan is proposing we spend on these spaceplanes, but they are far more versatile and battle-proven."

"The Senate Armed Services Committee *needs* to hear that argument from you and your administration, Joe," Barbeau said, giving his hand another caress and leaning forward toward him sympathetically, exposing more of her ample cleavage. "McLanahan was the hero of the war to avenge the American Holocaust, but that was in the past. A lot of senators may be afraid to cross McLanahan for fear there will be a backlash against them if the American people wonder why they're not supporting America's most famous general. But with McLanahan silenced, if they get the direct support of the President, they'll be more inclined to break ranks. Now is the time to act. We *must* do something, and it has to be now, while McLanahan is . . . well, with all due respect, while the general is out of the picture. Undoubtedly the committee's confidence in the spaceplane program is rattled. They are much more amenable to a compromise."

"I think we need to get together on this, Stacy," Gardner said. "Let's hammer out a plan that both the committee and the Pentagon will support. We should present a united front."

"That sounds marvelous, Mr. President, really marvelous."

"Then I have the full support of the Senate Armed Services Committee?" Gardner asked. "I have allies in the House I can call on too, but the backing of the Senate is crucial. Together, united, we can go before the American people and Congress and make a convincing argument."

"What if McLanahan pulls out of this? He and that ex-senator astronaut science geek Ann Page are a formidable team."

"McLanahan is out—he'll surely retire, or be forced to retire."

"That man is a bulldog. If he recovers, he won't retire."

"If he won't do it for his own good, he'll do it because I'll *order* him to do it," Gardner said. "And if he still fights it, I'll make sure the world understands how dangerous the man has been over the years. He *is* a loose cannon—the world just doesn't know about it. The man killed dozens of innocent civilians in Tehran, for Christ's sake."

"He did?" She hated to let it slip that the majority leader of the U.S. Senate didn't know something, but she couldn't help it. It *was* a surprise, and she didn't like surprises. Would Gardner fill her in? "When?"

"On the very mission we were discussing when he had his episode, the operational test mission he was running from the Armstrong Space Station," Gardner replied. "He set off a missile that released chemical weapons outside an apartment building in Tehran, killing dozens including women and children, and *then* he attacked a Russian reconnaissance plane with some kind of death ray— probably to cover up the attack on Tehran."

Thank God Gardner was a blabbermouth. "I had no idea . . . !"

"That's not the half of what this joker does, Stacy. I know a dozen different criminal infractions and outright acts of war he's responsible for over the years—including an attack that probably made Russian president Gryzlov plan the atomic attacks against the United States."

"What?"

"McLanahan is a loose cannon, a complete wild card," Gardner said bitterly. "He attacked Russia with absolutely no authorization; he bombed a Russian bomber base simply for personal revenge. Gryzlov was a former Russian bomber pilot—he knew it was an attack against *him,* a personal attack." Gardner was on a roll—this was better than the Congressional Research Service, Barbeau thought. "That's why Gryzlov went after bomber bases in the United States—not because our bombers were any great strategic threat to Russia, but because he was trying to get McLanahan."

Barbeau's mouth was open in shock . . . but at the same time, she was tantalized, even aroused. Damn, she thought, McLanahan seemed like such a milquetoast, a Boy Scout—who the hell knew he was some kind of maverick action hero? That made him more appealing than ever. What else lurked underneath that impossibly quiet, unassuming frame? She had to shake herself out of her sudden reverie. "Wow . . ."

"The Russians are scared of him, that's for sure," Gardner went on. "Zevitin wants me to have him arrested. He demands to know what he's been doing and what he intends to do with the space station and those spaceplanes. He's madder than hell, and I don't blame him."

"Zevitin sees the space station as a threat."

"Of course he does. But is that the only damned benefit of the thing? It's costing us as much as two aircraft carrier battle groups to keep that thing up there . . . for *what*? I've got to reassure Zevitin that the space stuff is no direct offensive threat to Russia, and *I* don't know exactly what the thing can do! I didn't even know McLanahan was *on board* the thing!"

"If it's only a defensive system, I don't see any reason not to tell Zevitin all there is to tell about the space station, if it'll help defuse tensions between us," Barbeau said. "The McLanahan situation may have solved itself."

"Thank God," Gardner grunted. "I'm sure for every crime I *know* McLanahan is guilty of, there are ten more I don't know about . . . yet," Gardner went on. "He's got weapons at his disposal from dozens of different black research programs that I don't even fully know about, and *I* was the damned *Secretary of Defense!*"

She looked at Gardner carefully. "McLanahan will certainly retire on his own, or you can have him medically retire," she said. "But he could be even more dangerous to us on the outside."

"I know, I know. That's why Zevitin wants him put away."

"If I can help you put pressure on McLanahan, Joe, just tell me," Barbeau said sincerely. "I'll do whatever I can to turn him, or at least make him think about what his opinions mean to others in the government and around the world. I'll make him realize it's personal, not just business. I'll ruin him if he persists, but I'm sure I can convince him to see it our way."

"If anyone can convince him, Stacy, it's you."

They looked into each other's eyes for a long moment, each silently asking and answering the questions they dared not verbalize. "So, Stacy, I know this isn't your first time in the residence. I assume you've seen the Lincoln Bedroom before?"

Barbeau's smile was as hot as a bonfire, and she unabashedly looked Gardner up and down hungrily as if sizing him up in a pickup bar. She slowly rose from her seat. "Yes, I've seen it," she said in a low, breathy voice. "I played there as a young girl when my father was in the Senate. It was a children's playroom back then. Of course it has an entirely different connotation now—still a playroom, but not for children."

"It's still the best fund-raiser in town—twenty-five grand a night per person is the going rate."

"It's too bad we've been reduced to such tawdry acts, isn't it?" Barbeau asked. "It spoils the feel of this place."

"The White House is still a house," Gardner said distractedly. "It's impossible for me to see it as more than just a workplace. I haven't seen a tenth of the rooms in here yet. They tell me there are thirty-five bathrooms here—I've seen *three*. Frankly I don't have much desire to explore the place."

"Oh, but you should, Joe," Barbeau said. "I think you will, when you get over the tumultuous first few months in office and get a chance to relax."

"If McLanahan can stop stirring the shit, maybe I could."

She turned, her arms outstretched, looking around the room. "I asked Mr. Kordus if we could meet here, in the Treaty Room, because I don't recall ever being in here although it's right next door to the Lincoln Bedroom. But the history in this place is so strong you can *feel* it. The Treaty Room has been used as a Cabinet meeting room, reception and waiting room, and as the President's study. It's historically been the place in the White House where the real political business gets done, even more so than the Oval Office."

"I've had a few informal meetings in here, but mostly the staff uses it."

"The staff is usually too busy to appreciate the energy that flows through this room, Joe," Barbeau said. "You should take the time to sense it." With her arms still outstretched, she closed her eyes. "Imagine: Ulysses S. Grant conducting his half-drunken Cabinet meetings here, followed by a card game and arm-wrestling matches with his friends; Teddy Roosevelt nailing animal hides to the walls; Kennedy signing the Nuclear Test Ban Treaty here, then days later seducing Marilyn Monroe in the same place, right down the hall from where his wife and children slept."

Gardner stepped behind her and lightly put his hands on her waist. "I never heard *that* story before, Stacy."

She took his hands and pulled them around her waist, drawing him closer. "I just made that last one up, Joe," she said in a whisper, so quiet that he moved his cheek to hers and pulled her tightly to him to hear. "But I'll bet it happened. And who knows what a man like Kevin Martindale did in here after his divorce—the divorce that should have wrecked his political career but only *enhanced* it—with all his Hollywood starlets flitting in and out of here all the time at all hours?" She took his hands, swirled them around her belly, then took his fingers and gently lifted them to her breasts, encircling her nipples. She could feel his body stiffen and could practically hear his mind whirring as he tried to decide what to do about her sudden advance. "He probably had a different bitch in here every night of the year."

"Stacy . . ." She could feel Gardner's breath on her neck, his hands gently caressing her breasts, barely touching . . .

Barbeau whirled around toward him and roughly pushed him away. "Martindale was an *imbecile,* Joe, but he spent two terms as president and two terms as vice president and became a damned *fixture* in the White House—and he got to fuck Hollywood starlets in here! What are *you* going to do to beat that, Joe?"

Gardner was frozen in shock. "What the hell is wrong with you, Stacy?" he finally managed to blurt out.

"What is it you want, Mr. President?" Barbeau asked loudly. "What is your game plan? Why are you *here*?"

"What are you talking about?"

"You're the President of the United States of America. You live in the White House . . . but you've *only used three bathrooms*? You don't know what's been done in this room, this house, the enormous history of this place? You have a three-star general under your command that has twice the voter approval rating you do, with a heart condition no less, and he's *still* in uniform? There's a space station orbiting the planet that you don't want and it's *still up there*? You have a woman in your arms but you touch her like some sweaty lovestruck adolescent on his first date trying to get to second base? Maybe all you *really* did with Maureen Hershel is 'business,' is that it?"

Gardner was flustered, then angry, then indignant. "Listen, Senator, this is no damned game. You're hot as hell, but I came here to discuss business."

"You've been honest with me since I called you for this meeting, Joe—don't fucking lie to me now," Barbeau snapped, taking one step away from him and letting her green eyes bore into him. Her sudden change in persona, from seductress to barracuda, startled him. "I didn't have to threaten you to invite me to the residence; I didn't drag you down that hallway and into this room. We're not children here. We're talking about joining forces to get an important job done, even if it means siding with the Russians and ruining a distinguished military career. What did you think we'd do—shake hands on it? Sign a contract? Cross our hearts and hope to die? Not on your life. Now, if you don't want to do this, you let me know right now, and we'll both go back to our offices and responsibilities and forget this meeting ever took place."

"What is this shit—?"

"Don't give me the innocent-waif routine either, Gardner. I know this is the way politics is played in Louisiana—don't tell me you've never played it like this in Florida or Washington. We're going to do it, right here, right now, or you can just tuck your tail between your legs and crawl back to your nice safe cozy apartment down the hall. What's it going to be?" When he didn't answer, she sighed, shook her head, and tried to step around him . . .

. . . but when she felt his arm across her chest and his hand on her breast, she knew she had him. He pulled her close, grasped her behind the head with his other hand, and pulled her lips to his, kissing her deeply, roughly. She returned the kiss just as forcibly, her hand finding his crotch, massaging him impatiently. Their lips parted, and she smiled at him confidently, assuredly. "That's not going to be enough, Mr. President, and you know it," she said. She smiled at his quizzical expression, darkly this time, confidently, and his mouth opened when he realized what she meant, what she wanted. "Well?"

He scowled at her, then moved his hands back to her breasts, then to her shoulders, pushing her down. "Let's seal the deal, Senator," he said, leaning back against the Grant conference table, steadying himself.

"Good boy. Get over here." She dropped to her knees and quickly began to undo his belt and pants. "My, my, look what we have here. Are you sure you don't have a little coonass in you, Mr. President?" He didn't reply as she began her vigorous, rhythmic ministrations.

CHAPTER FOUR

A man who has to be convinced to act before he acts is not a man of action....You must act as you breathe.

— George Clemenceau

ABOARD ARMSTRONG SPACE STATION

THE NEXT MORNING, EAST COAST TIME

"Joining us live from Armstrong Space Station, orbiting two hundred some odd miles above Earth, is a man that needs no introduction: Air Force Lieutenant General Patrick McLanahan," the cable news morning show host began. "General, thanks for joining us today. The question everyone wants an answer to, of course, is: How are you, sir?"

There was a second or two delay because of the satellite relay, but Patrick was accustomed to waiting those few seconds to make sure he wasn't talking over the host. "It's nice to be with you, Megyn," Patrick responded. He was Velcroed as usual to the station commander's console, wearing his trademark black flight suit with black insignia. "Thanks for having me on the show again. I'm doing fine, thank you. I feel pretty good."

"All of America is relieved to see you up and around, General. Have they determined what exactly happened?"

"According to Navy Captain George Summers at Walter Reed National Medical Center, who reviewed all my tests remotely from up here, it's called long-QT syndrome, Megyn," Patrick replied. "That's an infrequent prolongation of the electrical activation and inactivation of the heart's ventricles, caused by stress or shock. Apparently, other than eyesight, it's one of the most common disqualifying conditions in the astronaut corps."

"So you've been disqualified from flying ever again?"

"Well, I hope I won't be," Patrick said. "Officially I'm not really an astronaut in the conventional sense. I'm hoping that the docs will determine that incapacitation due to long-QT syndrome is most likely to occur just while traveling in space and won't stop me from all other flying activities."

"You do have a history of heart disease, is that correct?"

"My dad did die of heart problems, yes," Patrick replied somberly. "Dad suffered from what they used to call 'heart flutters' and was treated for anxiety and stress. Long-QT is hereditary. Apparently in my dad's case it was the police department and running a family business that triggered it; in my case, it was flying in space."

"And he died around the same age as you are now?"

A cloud passed briefly over Patrick's face that was clearly visible to millions of viewers around the world. "Yes, a couple years after retiring from the Sacramento Police Department and opening up McLanahan's in Old Town Sacramento."

"A shameless plug for your family tavern, eh, General?" the host asked, trying to liven up the conversation.

"I'm not ashamed of McLanahan's in Old Town Sacramento at all, Megyn."

"Another plug. Good. Okay, that's enough, General, you did your job fantastically," the host said, laughing. "Was this heart condition already noted on your records, and if so what were you doing flying repeatedly to Armstrong Space Station?"

"I did report the family history on my medical records," Patrick replied, "and I get a Class One Air Force flight physical twice a year, plus pre- and post-space flight checkups, and no problems have ever been detected before. Even though long-QT syndrome is a common disqualifying condition in the astronaut corps, I wasn't specifically tested for it because, as I said, technically I'm not an astronaut—I'm a unit commander and engineer who just happens to get to ride on his unit's research vehicles whenever I feel it's necessary."

"So do you feel that your lack of astronaut training and screening contributed to onset of this medical condition?"

"One of the things we're trying to prove with the Black Stallion spaceplane and Armstrong Space Station program, Megyn, is to make space more accessible to everyday folks."

"And it appears that the answer might be, 'No, they can't,' is that right?"

"I don't know all there is to know about long-QT syndrome, Megyn, but if it's commonly found only in combat aviators over the age of fifty who have to go into space frequently, perhaps we can test for it and exclude only those who show a proclivity for that disease," Patrick said. "I don't see why it has to disqualify everyone."

"But it is disqualifying for you?"

"I'm not ready to throw in the towel yet," Patrick said with a confident smile. "We have some incredible technology at our disposal, and new and better technologies being developed every day. If I can, I'll keep on flying, believe me."

"You haven't seen enough combat and orbited the Earth enough times already, General?" the host said with an amused laugh. "As I understand it, you've been on the station several times just in the past few months. That's more than a NASA astronaut goes into space in his entire career, isn't that true? John Glenn only flew in space twice."

"Pioneers like Senator John Glenn will always be the inspiration our future astronauts need to summon the courage and fortitude to undergo the rigorous preparation for space," Patrick replied, "but as I said, one goal of our military space program is to gain greater access to space. I don't consider episodes like mine a setback. It's all part of the learning experience."

"But you have to think of yourself and your family too, don't you, General?"

"Of course—my son sees me on TV more than he does in person," Patrick said gamely. "But no aviator likes to lose his wings, Megyn—we have an inbred aversion to doctors, hospitals, weight scales, eye charts, sphygmomanometers, and anything else that can keep us from flying . . ."

"Okay, General, you lost me there. Sphygmo . . . sphygmo . . . what is that, one of your high-tech laser ray guns?"

"A blood pressure tester."

"Oh."

"It'll be up to the flight docs, but you can bet I'll be fighting disqualification the whole way," Patrick said. A beep in his communications earset got his attention, and he turned and briefly activated his command monitor and read the display. "Sorry, Megyn, I have to go. Thanks for having me on this morning." The host was able to get out a confused and startled "But General, we're *live* around the—!" before Patrick terminated the link. "What do you have, Master Sergeant?" he asked on the command module intercom.

"COMPSCAN alert in the target region, sir, and it says it's a big one, although we might have nothing but a big glitch on our hands," Master Sergeant Valerie "Seeker" Lukas replied. The COMPSCAN, or Comparison Scans, collected and compared radar and imaging infrared data during sensor sweeps and alerted the crew whenever there was a significant buildup of personnel or equipment in a particular target region—thanks to the power and resolution of Armstrong's space-based radar and other satellites and unmanned aircraft, the target region could be as large as continent, and the change between comparison scans could be as small as four or five vehicles.

"What's the target?"

"Soltanabad, a highway airfield about a hundred miles west of Mashhad. Imaged recently by the new Night Owl unmanned reconnaissance plane Captain Noble just launched." Seeker studied the reconnaissance file on the area before continuing: "Attacked once by the Air Battle Force with a Vampire bomber with runway-cratering munitions last year because it was suspected of being used to fly in weapons and supplies to the Islamists operating out of Mashhad. The highway portion of the base was reopened by the Revolutionary Guards Corps, reportedly for relief and humanitarian supply shipments. We put the entire base on the 'watch' list and launched the Night Owl over the area to be sure they weren't repairing the ramps and taxiways or flying military stuff in there."

"Let's see what they're doing," Patrick said. A few moments later an incredibly detailed overhead image of the spot came up on his monitor. It clearly showed the four-lane highway with aircraft distance marks, taxi lines, and touchdown zone designations—it looked like a typical military runway, only with cars and trucks running on it. On both the north and south sides of the highway/airstrip were wide paved areas with aircraft taxiways, large aircraft parking areas, and the remnants of bombed-out buildings. Many of the destroyed buildings had been razed and a number of tents of various sizes put in their place, some with the seal of the Red Crescent humanitarian relief organization on them. "Do those tents look like they have open sides to you, Master Sergeant?" Patrick asked.

Seeker peered closer at the image, then magnified it until it started to lose resolution. "Yes, sir," she replied, unsure of why the general had asked—it was fairly plain to her. Per agreement between the United Nations, Buzhazi's Persian occupying force, and the Iranian government-in-exile, large tents set up in certain combat areas servicing refugees or others traveling through the Iranian deserts had to have open sides during reconnaissance flyover time periods so all sides could see inside, or they could be designated as hostile emplacements and attacked.

"Looks like a big shadow on that side, that's all," Patrick said. "This photo was taken during nighttime, correct?" Lukas nodded. "The sides look open, but the shadows on the ground from the nearby floodlights are making it look . . . I don't know, they just don't look right to me, that's all." He zoomed in again on the former aircraft parking ramps. Both paved areas were dotted with dozens of bomb craters, from several yards to over a hundred feet wide, with huge chunks of concrete heaved up around the edges. "Still looks busted up to me. How old is this image?"

"Just two hours, sir. No way they could have repaired all those craters and brought in aircraft in two hours."

"Let's see the scans compared by the computer." The image split first into two, then four, then sixteen shots of the same spot taken over a period of several days. The pictures appeared identical.

"Looks like a glitch—false alarm," Seeker said. "I'll reset the images and take a look at the comparison parameters for—"

"Wait a minute," Patrick said. "What is the computer saying has changed?" A moment later, the computer had drawn rectangles around several of the craters. The craters were precisely the same—the only difference was that the rectangles were not exactly oriented the same in all the images. "I still don't get what COMP-SCAN is flagging."

"Me neither, sir," Seeker admitted. "Could be just a looking-angle computation error."

"But we're sun-synchronous on this part of the world, right?"

"Yes, sir. We're precisely over Tehran at the same time—approximately two A.M. local—every day."

"So the looking angle should be the same except for minor station or sensor attitude changes, which the computer should be correcting for," Patrick said.

"Obviously something's screwed up in the adjustment routine, sir," Seeker said apologetically, anchoring herself at her terminal to begin work. "Don't worry, I'll get it straightened out. Sorry about that, sir. These things need recalibrating—obviously a bit more often that I thought. I should probably look at the station attitude gyro compensation readouts and fuel consumption figures to see if there's a major shift taking place—we might have to make a gross alignment change, or just throw out all the old attitude adjustment figures and come up with new ones. Sorry, sir."

"No problem, Master Sergeant," Patrick said. "We'll know to look for things like that more often from now on." But he continued staring at the images and the computer's comparison boxes. The boxes disappeared as Lukas erased the old comparison data, leaving very clear images of the bomb craters on the ramps and taxiways. He shook his head. "The space-based radar's pictures are stunning, Seeker—it's like I can measure the thickness of those concrete blocks heaved up by the bombs. Amazing. I can even see the colors of the different layers of concrete, and where the steel reinforcing mesh was applied. Cool."

"The SBR is incredible, sir—it's hard to believe it's almost twenty-year-old technology."

"You can clearly see where the concrete ends and the road base begins. It's—" Patrick looked closely at the images, then put on a pair of reading glasses and peered closer. "Can you enlarge that image for me, Seeker?" he asked, pointing at a large crater on the south side of the highway.

"Yes, sir. Stand by."

A moment later the crater filled the monitor. "Fantastic detail, all right." But now something was niggling at him. "My son loves those 'I Spy' and 'Where's Waldo?' books—maybe he'll be an imagery analyst someday."

"Or he'll design the computers that will do it for us."

Patrick chuckled, but he still felt uneasy. "What is wrong with this picture? Why did the computer ring the bell?"

"I'm still checking, sir."

"I spent a short but insightful period of time as a detachment commander in the U.S. Air Force's Air Intelligence Agency," Patrick said, "and the one thing I learned about interpreting multispectral overhead imagery was not to let the mind fill in too many blanks."

"Analysis 101, sir: Don't see what isn't there," Seeker said.

"But never ignore what *is* there but isn't right," Patrick said, "and there is something not right about the position of those craters. They're different . . . but how?" He looked at them again. "They look to me like they're turned, and the computer said they moved, but—"

"That's not possible for a crater."

"No . . . unless they're *not* craters," Patrick said. He zoomed in again. "I might be seeing something that's not there, but those craters look *too* perfect, too uniform. I think they're decoys."

"Decoy *craters*? I've never heard of such a thing, sir."

"I've heard of every other kind of decoy—planes, armored vehicles, troops, buildings, even runways—so why not?" Patrick remarked. "That might explain why COMPSCAN flags them—if they're moved and not placed in exactly the same spot, COMPSCAN flags it as a new target."

"So you think they've rebuilt that base and are secretly using it, right under our noses?" Lukas asked, still unconvinced. "If that's true, sir, then the space-based radar and our other sensors should have picked up other signs of activity—vehicles, tire tracks, storage piles, security personnel patrolling the area . . ."

"If you know exactly when a satellite is going to pass overhead, it's relatively easy to fool it—just cover the gear with radar-absorbent camouflage, erase the tracks, or disguise them with other targets," Patrick said. "All those tents, trucks, and buses out there could be housing an entire battalion and hundreds of tons of supplies. As long as they offload the planes, get the men and vehicles out of the area, and sweep up the area within the two-to-three-hour span between our overflights, they're safe."

"So all our gear is practically useless."

"Against whoever is doing this, yes—and I'll bet it's not the Islamist clerics or even the remnants of the Revolutionary Guards Corps," Patrick said. "There's only one way to find out: we need eyes on the ground. Let's get a report ready for STRATCOM and I'll append my recommendations for action . . . but first I want to get Rascal working on a plan." While Lukas began downloading sensor data and adding her observations—and reservations—about the activity at Soltanabad, Patrick selected the command channel on his encrypted satellite communications system. "Odin to Rascal."

A moment later the image of a large, blond-haired, blue-eyed, powerful-looking man appeared on Patrick's monitor: "Rascal here, sir," replied Air Force Major Wayne Macomber rather testily. Macomber was the new commander of the Battle Force ground forces based at Elliott Air Force Base in Nevada, replacing Hal Briggs, who had been killed while hunting down mobile medium-range

ballistic missiles in Iran a year earlier. Macomber was only the second person ever to take charge of the Battle Force. He had big
shoes to fill, and that, in Patrick's mind, would never happen.

Macomber was not Patrick's first choice to lead "Rascal" (which
had been Hal's call-sign and was now the new unclassified call-sign
of the Battle Force). To put it mildly, Macomber had serious problems dealing with authority. But he had somehow managed to use
that personality glitch to propel himself into more and more challenging situations in which he was ultimately able to adapt, overcome, and succeed.

He was kicked out of public middle school in Spokane, Washington, because of "behavioral incompatibilities" and was sent off to the
New Mexico Military Institute in Roswell in hopes of having round-
the-clock military discipline straighten him out. Sure enough—after a
difficult first year—it worked. He graduated near the top of his class
both academically and athletically and won a nomination to attend the
Air Force Academy in Colorado Springs, Colorado.

Although he was a nationally ranked linebacker for the Falcons
football team, where he earned his nickname "Whack," he was
kicked off the squad in his senior year for aggressive play and "personality conflicts" with several coaches and teammates. He used the
extra time—and probationary period—to improve his grades and
again graduated with honors with a bachelor of science degree in
physics and a pilot training slot. Once again he dominated in his un-
dergraduate pilot training class, graduating top of his class, and won
one of only six F-15E Strike Eagle pilot slots awarded straight out of
flight school—almost unheard of for a first lieutenant at the time.

But again, he couldn't keep his drive and determination in check.
An F-15 Eagle air superiority fighter is a completely different bird
with an offensive systems operator, big radar, conformal long-range
fuel tanks, and ten thousand pounds of ordnance on board, and for
some reason Wayne Macomber couldn't figure out that airframes
bend in unnatural directions when an F-15E Strike Eagle pilot
loaded up with bombs tries to dogfight with another fighter. It didn't
matter that he was almost always the winner—he was racking up

victories at the expense of bending expensive airframes, and was
eventually . . . ultimately . . . asked to leave.

But he was not orphaned for long. One organization in the Air
Force welcomed and even encouraged aggressive action, out-of-the-
box thinking, and virulent leadership: Air Force Special Operations.
To his dismay, however, the unit that wanted rude and crude
"Whack" the most was the Tenth Combat Weather Squadron at
Hurlburt Field, Florida: because of his physics education, the Air
Force quickly made him a combat weather parachutist. He got to wear
the coveted green beret and parachutist wings of an Air Force com-
mando, but it still grated on him to be known as a "weatherman."

Although he and his squadron mates always took a lot of ribbing
from other commando units for being "combat weather-guessers" or
"groundhogs," Macomber soon learned to like the specialty not only
because he happened to like the science of meteorology but also because he got to parachute out of perfectly good planes and helicopters, carry lots of guns and explosives, learn how to set up airfields
and observation posts behind enemy lines, and how to kill the enemy at close quarters. Whack performed more than a hundred and
twenty combat jumps in the next eight years and rose quickly
through the ranks, eventually taking command of the squadron.

When Brigadier General Hal Briggs was planning the assault and
occupation of Yakutsk Air Base in Siberia in Patrick McLanahan's retaliatory operation against Russia following the American Holocaust,
he turned to the one nationally recognized expert in the field to assist in
mission planning for operations behind enemy lines: Wayne Macomber.
At first Whack didn't like taking orders from a kid eight years younger
than he, especially one who outranked him, but he quickly recognized
Briggs' skill, intelligence, and guts, and they made a good team. The
operation was a complete success. Macomber won a Silver Star for saving dozens of personnel, Russians as well as Americans, by getting
them into fallout shelters before Russian president Gryzlov's bombers
attacked Yakutsk with nuclear-tipped cruise missiles.

"I'm sending you the most recent shots of a highway airbase in
northeastern Iran, Wayne," Patrick said. "I think it's being secretly

repaired, and I'm going to ask permission for you to go in, recon it, and render it unusable again—permanently."

"A ground op? About time," Macomber responded gruffly. "Almost all I've been doing since you brought me here is sweating— either out doing PT or tryin' to squeeze into one of those damned Tin Man union suits."

"And complaining."

"The sergeant major been yakkin' about me again?" Marine Corps Sergeant Major Chris Wohl was the noncommissioned officer in charge of Rascal, the Air Battle Force ground team, and one of the most senior members of the unit. Although Macomber was commander of Rascal, everyone fully knew and understood that Chris Wohl was in charge—including Macomber, a fact which really rankled him. "I wish that sumbitch would retire like I thought he would do so I can pick my own first shirt. He's ready to be put out to pasture."

"I'm the commander of the Air Battle Force, Wayne, and even *I* wouldn't dare say that to the sergeant major's face," Patrick said, only half jokingly.

"I told you, General, that as long as Wohl is around, it'll be his unit and his baggage I'll have to drag around," Whack said. "All he does is mope around after Briggs." Patrick couldn't remotely picture Wohl moping for a second, but he didn't say so. "Guys die in special ops, even in tin can suits like that robot thing he was in—he better get used to that. Retire his ass, or at least reassign him, so I can spin up this unit *my* way."

"Wayne, you're in charge, so *be* in charge," Patrick said, not liking the way this conversation was going. "You and Chris can make a great team if you learn to work together, but you're still the man in charge whether you use him or not. I expect you to get your team ready to fly and fight, *soonest*. If it's not set up the way you want it in time for the next op, put Wohl in charge until—"

"*I* lead the unit, General, not the no-cock," Macomber retorted, using his own personal term "no-cock" instead of the Air Force acronym NCOIC, or "noncommissioned officer in charge."

"Then lead it, Wayne. Do whatever you need to do to accomplish the mission. Chris Wohl, the Cybernetic Infantry Devices, and the Tin Man armor can all be part of the problem or part of the solution—it's up to you. The men are pros, but they need a leader. They know Chris and will follow him into hell—you have to prove you can lead them along with the NCOIC."

"I'll whip them into line, General, don't worry about that," Macomber said.

"And if you haven't done it already, I'd suggest you not use that term 'no-cock' in front of Wohl, or you two might be standing before me bloody and broken. Fair warning."

Macomber's expression gave absolutely no indication that he understood or agreed with McLanahan's warning. That was unfortunate: Chris Wohl didn't tolerate most officers below flag rank and was not afraid to risk his career and freedom to straighten out an officer who didn't show the proper respect to a veteran noncommissioned officer. If the situation wasn't resolved properly, Patrick knew, those two were heading for a confrontation. "It would be a lot easier if I didn't have to train in that Tin Man getup."

"The 'getup,' as you call it, allows us to go into hot spots no other special ops team would ever consider," Patrick said.

"Excuse me, General, but I can't recall *any* hot spot I ever considered *not* going into," Macomber said testily, "and I didn't wear the long undies."

"How many men would you need to go in and take out an airfield, Major?"

"We don't 'take out' airfields, sir—we reconnoiter or disrupt enemy air ops, or we build our own airfields. We call in air strikes if we want it—"

"The Battle Force *takes them out,* Major," Patrick interjected. "Remember Yakutsk?"

"We didn't destroy that airfield, sir, we occupied it. And we brought in a hundred guys to help us do it."

"The Battle Force was prepared to destroy that base, Major—if *we* couldn't use it, the Russians weren't going to, either."

"Destroy an *airfield*?" The skepticism in Macomber's voice was obvious, and Patrick could feel the heat rise up under the collar of his black flight suit. He didn't want to waste time arguing with a subordinate, but Macomber had to be made aware of what was expected of him, not just busted because he was a junior officer. "How can a handful of lightly armed men destroy an airfield?"

"That's what you're here to learn, Wayne," Patrick said. "I told you when we first talked about taking over the command that I needed you to think outside the box, and around there it means not just learning to use the gadgets that you have at your disposal but embracing and expanding the technology and developing new ways to use it. Now I need you up to speed quick, because I've got an airfield in Iran I might want destroyed . . . tomorrow."

"*Tomorrow?* How can that happen, General? I just learned about the target location *just now*—if we hustled, we might make it off the base by tomorrow, and that's with no intel and no rehearsals on how to assault the target! You can't run a successful infiltration on a military base with no intel and no practice runs! I'll need at least a week just to—"

"You're not hearing what I'm telling you, Major: you have to start thinking differently around here," Patrick insisted. "We locate targets and attack them, *period*—little or no rehearsal, no strategic intel, first-cut organic intel received while en route, no joint support packages, and small but mobile and high-tech ground units with minimal but devastating air support. I told you all this when I first briefed you on Rascal, Wayne . . ."

"I assumed you got your intel and tasking from higher headquarters, sir," Macomber argued. "You mean you launch on an operation without gathering strategic intel from—?"

"We don't get *any* help from *anyone,* and we still launch and get the friggin' job done, Whack," Patrick interjected pointedly. "Are you finally getting the picture?" Patrick waited a heartbeat and got no response—considering Macomber's mercurial, almost rabid personality, the silence was a real stunner. "Now I know you're accustomed to Air Force special ops tactics and methodology, and I know you're a good operator and leader, but you have to get with the program at the Lake. I know PT is important, but knowing the hardware and resources we have is *more* important. It's a mind-set as well as a job. Understand?"

"Yes, sir," Macomber said—probably the first real hint of acquiescence Patrick had sensed from this guy. "Looks to me like I'll need Wohl's help after all if I'm going out on a mission . . . tomorrow?"

"Now you're getting the idea, Major."

"When can I get the intel you have, sir?"

"I'm sending it now. I need a game plan drawn up and ready to brief to the powers that be in an hour."

"An *hour* . . . ?"

"Is there something wrong with this connection, Major?"

"No, sir. I heard you. One hour. One more question?"

"Hurry it up."

"What about my request to change the unit call-sign, sir?"

"Not again, Major . . ."

"That was Briggs' call-sign, sir, and I need to change that name. Not only do I hate it, but it reminds the guys of their dead former boss, and that detracts from their mission focus."

"Bill Cosby once said if it was up to him he would never have picked a name for his kids—he would just send them out onto the street and let the neighborhood kids name him," Patrick said.

"Bill who?"

"When it's time to change the unit's name, Major, the entire unit will come to *me* with the request."

"It's *my* unit, sir."

"Then prove it," Patrick said. "Get them ready to roll immediately, learn how to use the tools I've busted my butt to get you, and show me a plan—drawn up *as a unit*—that will get the job done and get approved right away. Get on it, Major. Genesis out." He broke the connection with a stab at the button so hard that it almost detached him from his Velcro perch. For Pete's sake, Patrick thought, he never realized how lucky he was to be working with the men and women under his command and not true prima donnas like Macomber. He might be one of America's premier specials ops commandos, but his interpersonal skill set needed some serious re-evaluation.

After taking an exasperated sip of water from a squeeze tube, he reopened the satellite link: "Odin to Condor."

"Condor here, secure," the senior controller at the Joint Functional Component Command-Space (JFCC-Space) command post at Vandenberg Air Force Base, California, responded. "Saw you on the news a bit ago. You looked A-OK, sir. Good to see you're feeling okay. That Megyn is a fox, isn't she?"

"Thanks, Condor, but unfortunately I never saw the host, so I'll have to take your word for it," Patrick responded. "I have an urgent reconnaissance assessment alert and request for ground ops tasking message for the boss."

"Roger that, sir," the senior controller responded. "Ready to copy whenever you're ready."

"I've detected a possible covert re-establishment of an illegal Iranian air base in the Persian Republic, and I need eyes-only confirmation and tasking authority for a shutdown if it's verified." Patrick quickly ran down what he knew and what he surmised about the Soltanabad highway airbase.

"Got it, sir. Sending to JFCC-Space DO now." The DO, or deputy commander of operations for Joint Functional Component Command-Space, would report to his commander after assessing the request, investigating availability of forces, gathering intelligence, and computing an approximate timeline and damage expectancy. It was time-consuming, but probably kept the commander from being inundated with requests for support. "We should get a message back soon if the DO wants to act. How do you feel, sir?"

"Just fine, Condor," Patrick responded. "Sure wish I could upload my requests directly to STRATCOM or even SECDEF," Patrick remarked.

"I hear you, sir," the controller said. "I think they're afraid you'll bury them with data. Besides, no one wants to give up their kingdoms." In a convoluted and rather frustrating mix of responsibilities, tasking and coordination for air missions involving

Armstrong Space Station and HAWC's unmanned B-1 and B-52 bombers flying over Iran had to be channeled through two different major commands, who both reported directly to the President through the national security staff: JFCC-Space in California, who upchanneled the information to U.S. Strategic Command (STRATCOM) in temporary headquarters in Colorado and Louisiana; and to U.S. Central Command (CENTCOM) at MacDill Air Force Base in Florida, which handled all military operations in the Middle East and central Asia. CENTCOM and STRATCOM's different intelligence, plans, and operations staffs would go over the data separately, make their own recommendations, and present them to the Secretary of Defense and the President's National Security Adviser, who would then make recommendations to the President.

"I don't understand why these reports should go to STRATCOM at all," Patrick groused. "CENTCOM is the theater commander—they should get reports, draw up a plan of action, get approvals, and then task everyone else for support."

"You don't need to convince me, sir—if you ask me, your reports should go directly to SECDEF," the senior controller said. There was a slight pause; then: "Stand by for Condor, Odin. Good to talk with you again, General."

A moment later: "Condor-One up, secure," came the voice of the Fourteenth Air Force's commanding officer, Air Force Major General Harold Backman. The commander of the U.S. Air Force's Fourteenth Air Force, Backman was "dual-hatted" as Joint Forces Component Command-Space, or JFCC-S, a unit of U.S. Strategic Command (which had been destroyed in the Russian air attacks against the United States and was being reconstituted in various locations around the country).

JFCC-S was responsible for planning, coordinating, equipping, and executing all military operations in space. Before McLanahan, his High-Technology Aerospace Weapons Center, and the XR-A9 Black Stallion spaceplanes, "military operations in space" generally meant the deployment of satellites and monitoring space activities of other nations. No longer. McLanahan had given JFCC-Space a global strike and ultra-rapid mobility capability, and frankly he didn't feel they were yet up to the task.

"Odin here, secure and verified," Patrick said. "How are you doing, Harold?"

"Up to my eyeballs as usual, sir, but better than you, I'm guessing. The duty officer said he saw you on TV but you cut off the interview suddenly without warning. You okay?"

"I got a COMPSCAN warning and got right on it."

"If it scared the piss out of one of my controllers, it's going to panic the brass, you know that, right?"

"They should learn to relax. Did you get my data?"

"I'm looking at it right now, Muck. Give me a sec." A few moments later: "I've got my intel chief looking it over now, but it just looks like a bombed-out highway airbase to me. I take it you don't think so?"

"I think those craters are decoys, Harold, and I'd like some of my guys to go out there and take a look."

Another slight pause. "Khorasan province, just a hundred miles from Mashhad—that area is controlled by Mohtaz and his Revolutionary Guards Corps," Backman said. "Well within armed-response distance from Sabzevar, which certainly has a lot of Pasdaran hiding out there. If Soltanabad is really vacant, you'll still be in the teeth of the storm if the bad guys spot you—and if it's active like you said, it'll be a meat grinder. I assume you want to go in with just a couple of your robots, right?"

"Affirmative."

"Thought so. Your gizmos up there can't give you any more detailed imagery?"

"Our only other option is a direct flyover by a satellite or unmanned aircraft, and that'll alert the bad guys for sure. I'd like to get a peek first before I plan on blowing the place, and a small force would be the fastest and easiest."

"How fast?"

"I haven't looked at the orbital geometry, but I'm hoping we can launch them within four, have them on the ground in seven, airborne again in eight, and home within twelve."

"Days?"

"Hours."

"Shit," Backman cursed. "Pretty friggin' unbelievable, sir."

"If I had my guys *based* up here, Harold, like I briefed you and STRATCOM I'd like to do, I could possibly be out of there and back home in *four* hours."

"A-friggin'-mazing. I'm all for that, Muck, but I think that idea is just boggling too many minds down here on plain old planet Earth. You know that we've been directed by the National Command Authority to restrict all spaceplane missions to resupply and emergency only, right?"

"I consider this an emergency, Harold."

"I know you do . . . but is it *really* an emergency?"

Patrick swallowed down a flare of anger at being questioned about his judgment, but he was accustomed to everyone second- and third-guessing him, even those who knew and liked him. "I won't know for sure until I get some of my guys out there."

"I don't think it'll be authorized, sir. You still want me to ask the question?"

Patrick didn't hesitate: "Yes."

"O-kay. Stand by." The wait was not very long at all: "Okay, Muck, the DO of STRATCOM says you can get your guys moving in that direction, but no one puts boots—or whatever the hell your robots wear on their feet—on the ground, and no aircraft crosses any lines on any maps, without a go-ahead from CENTCOM."

"Can I load up a few Black Stallion spaceplanes and put them in orbit?"

"How many, and loaded up with what?"

"One or two with operators, staggered and in different orbits until I can get a firm A-hour; one or two cover aircraft, loaded with precision-guided weapons; perhaps one or two decoys that will double as in-orbit retrieval backups; and one or two Vampire bombers airborne from Iraq ready to destroy the base if we find it to be operational."

"That many spacecraft might be a hard sell—and the armed spacecraft might be a deal-breaker."

"The more I can forward-deploy, and the more support stuff I get into orbit, the quicker this will be over, Harold."

"I get it," Backman said. The pause was longer this time: "Okay, approved. No one crosses any political boundaries in the atmosphere without a go-ahead, and keep the re-entry weapons tight until given the green light." He chuckled, then added, "Jeez, I sound like friggin' *Battlestar Galactica* Commander Adama or something. Never thought I'd be okaying an attack from outer space in *my* lifetime."

"It's the way things need to be from now on, my friend," Patrick responded. "I'll have the complete package plan out to you within the hour, and the air tasking order for movement of spacecraft will be out to you sooner. Thanks, Harold. Odin out."

Patrick's next videoconference call was to his battle management area at Elliott Air Force Base: "Macomber notified us that you had given him a ground op in Iran and that he was in a time crunch to do some planning, so we've already jumped in," his deputy commander, Brigadier General David Luger, said. The two navigators had been together for over two decades, first as fellow B-52G Stratofortress crewmembers and then assigned to the High-Technology Aerospace Weapons Center as aircraft and weapon flight test engineers. Tall, lean, quiet, and deliberate in personality as well as appearance, Luger's best attribute was acting as Patrick McLanahan's conscience whenever his irascible, determined, single-minded side threatened to obliterate all common sense. "We should have something for you in no time. The guy's fast and pretty well organized."

"I knew you'd be on it, buddy," Patrick said. "Surprised to hear from Whack?"

"Surprised? How about thunderstruck?" Luger deadpanned. "Everyone in the Air Battle Force goes out of their way to avoid the guy. But when he gets down to business, he does okay."

"Any thoughts on Soltanabad?"

"Yeah—I think we should skip the prelims and just put a couple spreads of SkySTREAKs or Meteors with high explosives down there, instead of wasting time inserting a Battle Force team," Luger replied. "If the Iranians are hiding something there, our guys will be landing right on top of them."

"As much as I like blowing things up, Texas," Patrick responded, "I think we should get a look first. If those craters are really decoys, they're the best I've ever seen, which means—"

"They're probably not Iranian," Luger said. "You thinking maybe the Russians?"

"I think Moscow would like nothing better than to help Mohtaz destroy Buzhazi's army and station a few brigades there as his reward," Patrick said.

"You think that's what Zevitin wants to do?"

"An American-friendly state in Iran would be completely unacceptable," Patrick said. "Mohtaz is a nutcase, but if Zevitin can convince him to allow Russian troops into Iran to help defeat Buzhazi's army—or for any other reason such as defending against American aggression—Zevitin will be able to send in troops to counterbalance American domination in the region. At the very least, he can put pressure on President Gardner to back away from supporting former Soviet bloc countries that are drifting into the American sphere of influence."

"All that geopolitical stuff makes my head hurt, Muck," Dave said with mock weariness. Patrick could see Dave's attention diverted away from the videoconference camera. "I have the first draft of the plan ready—I'll upload it to you," he said, entering instructions into his computer.

"Okay, Muck, here's the preliminary status reports," Luger went on moments later. "We have two Black Stallion spaceplanes available within four hours along with their dedicated tankers and enough fuel and supplies for orbital missions, and three available in seven hours if we cancel some training sorties. Macomber says he can get loaded up in time to launch. How do you want to build the air tasking order?"

Patrick made fast mental calculations, working the timing backward from when he wanted the Black Stallion off the ground and out of Persian airspace. "I'd sure like to have decoys, backups, more intel, and more rehearsals for Whack and the ground forces, but my primary concern is getting a good look at that base soon without the Revolutionary Guards being alerted," he said. "I'll see if I can get approval for two Studs to go in right away. If we launch in four hours, we'll be over the objective by midnight to one A.M. local time—let's call it two A.M. to be safe. We recon for one hour max, blast off before civil sunrise, refuel somewhere over western Afghanistan, and head home."

"The 'Duty Officer' is spitting out the preliminary guesstimate for the air tasking order," Luger said. The "Duty Officer" was the central computer system based at the High-Technology Aerospace Weapons Center that tied in all of the various departments and laboratories around the world and could be securely accessed by any member of HAWC anywhere in the world—or, in the case of Armstrong Space Station, *around* it. "The biggest question mark we have right now is the KC-77 tanker support for the exfiltration aerial refueling. Our closest XR-A9-dedicated tanker is at Al Dhafra Air Base in the United Arab Emirates, which is two hours' flight time to the closest possible refueling point over Afghanistan. If everything worked absolutely perfectly—they loaded the tanker without mishap, got all the diplomatic and air traffic clearances in a timely manner, et cetera—they'd make a possible rendezvous spot over western Afghanistan just as the Black Stallion goes bingo fuel."

"And when was the last time we ever had a mission go completely flawless?"

"I don't recall that *ever* happening," Luger reassured him. "There are several emergency landing sites in that area we can use, but they are very close to the Iranian border, and we would need a lot of ground support to secure the base until fuel arrived. We can move recovery teams into Afghanistan to assist in case the Stud has to make an emergency landing, or we can push the mission back a couple days . . ."

"Let's push ahead with this plan," Patrick said. "We'll present it as is and bring in as many contingency assets as we can—hopefully we won't need any of them."

"You got it, Muck," Dave said. "I need to . . . stand by, Patrick . . .

I have a call from your flight surgeon at Walter Reed. He wants to talk with you."

"Plug me in, and stay on the line."

"Roger that. Stand by . . ." A moment later the video image split in two, with Dave on the left side and the image of a rather young-looking man in Navy Work Uniform camouflage blue digital fatigues, typical of all military personnel in the United States since the American Holocaust. "Go ahead, Captain, the general is on the line, secure."

"General McLanahan?"

"How are you, Captain Summers?" Patrick asked. U.S. Navy Captain Alfred Summers was the chief of cardiovascular surgery at Walter Reed National Military Medical Center and the man in charge of Patrick's case.

"I saw your interview this morning," the surgeon said testily, "and with all due respect, General, I was wondering where you got your medical degree from?"

"You have some problems with what I told the interviewer, I take it?"

"You made it sound like long-QT syndrome can be cured by taking a couple aspirin, sir," Summers complained. "It's not as easy as that, and I don't want my staff blamed in case your request to remain on flight status is denied."

"Blamed by whom, Captain?"

"Frankly, sir, by the great majority of Americans who think you are a national treasure that should not be sidelined for any reason whatsoever," the physician responded. "I'm sure you know what I mean. In short, sir, long-QT syndrome is an automatic denial of flight privileges—there's no appeal process."

"My staff has been researching the condition, Captain, as well as the medical histories of several astronauts who have been disqualified from space duties but still retained flight status, and they tell me that the condition is not life-threatening and might not be serious enough to warrant a denial of—"

"As your doctor and the leading expert on this condition in the

United States, General, let me set it straight for you if I may," Summers interjected. "The syndrome was most likely caused by what we call myocardial stretch, where severe G-forces deform the heart muscles and nerves and create electrical abnormalities. The syndrome has obviously lain dormant for your entire life until you flew into space, and then it hit full force. It's interesting to me that you obviously experienced some symptoms during some or perhaps all of your space flights, but then it lay dormant again until you had a mere videoconference confrontation—I'd guess it was equally as stressing as flying in space, or maybe just stressful enough to provide the trigger for another full-blown episode."

"The White House and Pentagon can do that, Doctor," Patrick said.

"No doubt, sir," Summers agreed. "But do you not see the danger in this condition, General? The stress of that simple videoconference episode, combined with your repeated trips into orbit, sparked electrical interruptions that eventually created an arrhythmia. It was so severe that it created cardiac fibrillation, or irregular heartbeat, a true heat 'flutter,' which like a cavitating pump means that not enough blood gets circulated to the brain even though the heart hasn't stopped. It goes without saying, sir, that any stressor now can bring on another episode, and without constant monitoring we have absolutely no way of knowing when or how severe it would be. Allowing you to stay on flight status would jeopardize every mission and every piece of hardware under your control."

"I assume you were going to add, 'not to mention your *life*,' eh, Captain?" Patrick added.

"I assume we're all thinking of your welfare first, sir—I could be mistaken about that," Summers said dryly. "Your life is at risk every minute you spend up there. I cannot stress that too strongly."

"I get it, I get it, Doctor," Patrick said. "Let's move on past the dire warnings now. What's the treatment for this condition?"

" 'Treatment?' You mean, other than avoiding stress at all costs?" Summers asked with obvious exasperation. He sighed audibly. "Well, we can try beta blockers and careful monitoring to see if any electrical abnormalities crop up again, but this course of treatment is recommended only for non-syncopic patients—someone who has never passed out before from the condition. In your case, sir, I would strongly recommend an ICD—implantable cardioverter-defibrillator."

"You mean, a pacemaker?"

"ICDs are much more than just a pacemaker, sir," Summers said. "In your case, an ICD would perform three functions: carefully monitor your cardiac condition, shock your heart in case of fibrillation, and supply corrective signals to restore normal rhythm in case of any tachycardia, hypocardia, or arrhythmia. Units nowadays are smaller, less obtrusive, more reliable, and can monitor and report on a wide variety of bodily functions. They are extremely effective in correcting and preventing cardiac electrical abnormalities."

"Then it doesn't affect my flight status, right?"

Summers rolled his eyes in exasperation, completely frustrated that this three-star general wouldn't let go of the idea of getting back on flying status. "Sir, as I'm sure you understand, installing an ICD is a disqualifier for all flight duties except under FAA Part 91, and even then you'd be restricted to solo day VFR flights," he said, taken aback simply by the fact that anyone who had an episode like this man did would even *think* about flying. "It is, after, all an electrical generator and transmitter that can momentarily cause severe cardiac trauma. I can't think of any flight crewmember, military or civilian, who's been allowed to maintain flight status after getting an ICD."

"But if they're so good, what's the problem?" Patrick asked. "If they clear up the abnormalities, I should be good to go."

"They're good, much better than in years past, but they're not foolproof, sir," Summers said. "About one in ten patients suffer pre-syncopic or syncopic episodes—dizziness, drowsiness, or unconsciousness— when the ICD activates. Three in ten experience enough discomfort to make them stop what they're doing—truck drivers, for example, will feel startled or uncomfortable enough that they will pull off to the side of the road, or executives in meetings will get up and leave the room. You can't pull off to the side of the road in a plane, especially a spaceplane. I know how important flying is to you, but it's not worth—"

"Not worth risking my life?" Patrick interrupted. "Again, Doctor, with all due respect, you're wrong. Flying is essential to my job as well as an important skill and a source of personal pleasure. I'd be ineffective in my current position."

"Would you rather be *dead,* sir?"

Patrick looked away for a moment, but then shook his head determinedly. "What are my other alternatives, Doctor?"

"You don't have any, General," Summers said sternly. "We can put you on beta blockers and constant monitoring, but that's not as effective as an ICD, and you'd still be restricted in flight duties. It's almost guaranteed that within the next six months you'll have another long-QT episode, and the odds are greater that you'll suffer some level of incapacitation, similar or probably more severe than what you experienced before. If you're in space or at the controls of an aircraft, you'd become an instant hazard to yourself, your fellow crewmembers, innocent persons in your flight path, and your mission.

"General McLanahan, in my expert opinion, your current job or just about any military position I can think of is too stressful for a man in your condition, even if we install an ICD. More than any treatment or device, what you need now is rest. If there is no history of drug abuse or injury, long-QT syndrome is almost always triggered by physical, psychological, and emotional stress. The damage done to your heart by your position, duties, and space flights will last the rest of your life, and as we saw, the stress of just one simple videoconference meeting was enough to trigger a syncoptic episode. Take my advice: Get the ICD installed, retire, and enjoy your son and family."

"There have to be other options, other treatments," Patrick said. "I'm not ready to retire. I've got important work to do, and maintaining flying status is a big part of it—no, it's a big part of who *I* am."

Summers looked at him for a long moment with a stern and exasperated expression. "Bertrand Russell once wrote, 'One symptom of an approaching nervous breakdown is the belief that one's work is terribly important,'" he said, "except in your case, you won't suffer a nervous breakdown—you'll be *dead.*"

"Let's not get too dramatic here, Captain . . ."

"Listen to me carefully, General McLanahan: I'm not being dramatic—I'm being as honest and open with you as I can," Summers said. "It is my opinion that you have suffered unknown but serious damage to your cardiac muscles and myocardium as a result of your space flight that is triggering long-QT episodes that are causing arrhythmia and tachycardia resulting in pre-syncoptic and syncoptic occurrences. Is that undramatic enough for you, sir?"

"Captain—"

"I'm not finished, sir," Summers interjected. "The likelihood is that even with rest and medication you will suffer another syncoptic event within the next six months, more severe than the last, and without monitoring and immediate medical attention, your chances of survival are twenty percent, at *best*. With an ICD, your chances of surviving the next six months go up to seventy percent, and after six months you have a ninety percent chance of survival."

He paused, waiting for an argument, and after a few moments of silence he went on: "Now if you were any other officer, one who didn't use to date the Vice President of the United States with the Secret Service in tow, I would simply advise you that I will recommend to your commanding officer that you be confined to the hospital for the next six months. I will—"

"Six months!"

"I will *still* advise your commanding officer so," Summers went on. "Whether you decide to get an ICD installed is your decision. But if you insist on not getting the ICD installed and you are not on 24/7 monitoring, you have virtually *no chance* of surviving the next six months. *None.* Do I make myself clear to you, sir?" Patrick momentarily looked like a rapidly deflating balloon, but Dave Luger could see his dejection quickly being replaced with anger—anger at *what,* he wasn't quite certain yet. "It appears to me that the final decision is up to you. Good day, General." And Summers logged out of the videoconference with a rueful shake of his head, certain that the three-star general had no intention of complying with his orders.

Once Summers left the conference, Patrick sat back in his chair, took a deep breath, then stared at the conference room table. "Well, shit," he breathed after several long moments in silence.

"You okay, Muck?" Dave Luger asked.

"Yeah, I guess so," Patrick replied, shaking his head in mock puzzlement. "I always thought it was Will Rogers who made that quote about mental breakdowns, not Bertrand Russell."

Dave laughed—this was the guy he was familiar with, making jokes at a time when most sane men would be on the verge of tears. "I guess Mark Twain was right when he said, 'It's not what you know, it's what you know that ain't so.'"

"It wasn't Mark Twain, it was Josh Billings."

"Who?"

"Never mind," Patrick said, turning serious again. "Dave, I need to learn *everything* about long-QT syndrome and treatment for heart arrhythmias before I can make a decision about what I can handle and what I can't. There are probably a dozen companies doing research on modern ICDs, or whatever the next generation of those things becomes—I should know about the latest advances before I decide to get any old technology installed. Jon Masters probably has an entire lab devoted to treating heart disorders."

"Excuse me for saying so, buddy, but you just *had* probably the best heart doc in the country on the line, ready to answer any questions you have, and you pretty much blew him off."

"He wasn't ready to help me—he was standing by ready to punch my ticket to a medical retirement," Patrick said. "I need to handle this in my own way."

"I'm worried about how much time you have to make this decision, Patrick," Dave said. "You heard the doc: most patients who have this condition either start continual monitoring and drugs or get an ICD installed, *right away*. The others *die*. I don't see what other research you need to do on this."

"I don't know either, Dave, but it's the way I always do things: I check them out for myself, using my own sources and methods," Patrick said. "Summers may be the best heart doc in the military, maybe even the country, but if that's so, then my own research will tell me that too. But riddle me this, bro: What do guys like Summers do with active-duty cardiac victims who are still alive?"

"They retire them, of course."

"They retire them," Patrick echoed, "and then they're cared for by the Veterans Administration or private doctors paid for in part by the government. Summers is doing what he always does: discharging sick guys and pushing them off to the VA. Most of his patients are so thankful to be alive that they never give retirement a second thought."

"Aren't you glad to still be alive, Muck?"

"Of course I am, Dave," Patrick said, giving his longtime friend a scowl, "but if I'm going to punch out, I'm doing it on *my* terms, not Summers'. In the meantime, maybe I'll learn something more about the condition and possible treatments that these docs don't know, something that will let me keep my flying status. Maybe I'll—"

"Patrick, I understand flying is important to you," Luger said sincerely, "but it's not worth risking your life to—"

"Dave, I risk my life just about every time I go up in a warplane," Patrick interrupted. "I'm not afraid of losing my life to—"

"The enemy . . . the *outside* enemy," Dave said. "Hey, Patrick, I'm just playing devil's advocate here—I'm not arguing with you. You do what you want. And I agree: it's worth risking your life using your skills, training, and instincts to battle an adversary who's out to destroy the United States of America. But the enemy we're talking about here is *you*. You can't outfly, outguess, or outsmart *yourself*. You're not equipped or trained to handle your own body trying to kill you. You should approach this battle like any battle you've ever prepared for . . ."

"That's exactly what I intend to do, Dave," Patrick said flatly. "I'm going to study it, analyze it, consult with experts, gather information, and devise a strategy."

"Fine. But take yourself off flight status and check into the hospital for round-the-clock monitoring while you do it. Don't be stupid."

That last comment took Patrick aback, and he blinked in surprise. "You think I'm being stupid?"

"I don't know what you're thinking, man," Luger said. He knew Patrick wasn't stupid, and he was sorry he said it, but the one thing that his longtime friend had taught him was to speak his mind. Patrick was scared, and this was his response to fear, just as it had been in the cockpit of a strategic bomber all these many years: Fight the fear, focus on the objective, and never stop fighting no matter how awful the situation appears.

"Look at it from the doc's point of view, Muck," Luger went on. "I heard the doctors tell you that this thing is like a ticking time bomb with a hair trigger. It might not go off at all, but the odds are it could go off in the next ten seconds as we're standing here arguing. Hell, I'm afraid you could vapor-lock on me as I'm arguing with you *right now,* and there's not a damned thing I could do from down here but watch you die."

"My chances of dying up here in Earth orbit are just a little bit greater than average with this heart thing—we can be blasted wide open and sucked out into space by a hypersonic piece of debris the size of a pea at any friggin' time, and we'd never know it," Patrick said.

"If you're not sure about an ICD, then go ahead and research it; talk to Jon Masters or the dozen or so brainiacs on our list, and think it over," Dave said. "But do it from the safety of a private hospital room where the docs can keep an eye on you." Patrick's eyes and features remained determined, stoic, impassive. "C'mon, Muck. Think about Bradley. If you continue to fly without the ICD, you might die. If you don't stress yourself out, you'll probably live on. What's the question?"

"I'm not going to give in, Dave, and that's *it*. I'm up here to do an important job, and I'm—"

"A *job*? Muck, do you want to risk hurting yourself over a *job*? It's important, sure, but dozens of younger, stronger guys can do it. Give the job to Boomer, or Raydon, or even Lukas—anyone else. You haven't figured it out yet, Patrick?"

"Figure what out?"

"We're *expendable,* General McLanahan. We're all disposable.

We're nothing but 'politics by other means.' When it comes right down to it, we're just hard-core hard-assed type-A gung-ho military prima donnas in ill-fitting monkey suits, and nobody in Washington cares if we live or die. If you blow a gasket tomorrow there'll be twenty other hard-asses waiting to take your place—or, more likely, Gardner could just as easily order us shut down the day after you croaked and spend the money on more aircraft carriers. But there are those of us who *do* care, your son being at the top of the list, but you're not paying attention to us because you're focusing on the *job*—the job that doesn't care one *whit* about *you*."

Luger took a deep breath. "I know you, man. You always say that you do it because you don't want to order another flyer to do something you haven't done yourself, even if the flyers are trained test crewmembers, the best of the best. I've always known that's bullshit. You do it because you love it, because you want to be the one to pull the trigger to take down the bad guys. I understand that. But I don't think you should be doing it anymore, Muck. You're unnecessarily risking your life—not by flying a mostly untested machine, but by exposing yourself to stresses that can kill you long before you reach the target area."

Patrick was silent for a long time; then he looked at his old friend. "I guess you do know what it's like to face your own mortality, don't you, Dave?"

"Unfortunately, yes," Luger said. As a young navigator-bombardier flying a secret mission to destroy the old Soviet Union's Kavaznya ground-based laser site, Dave Luger had been captured by the Russians, interrogated, tortured, and imprisoned for several years, then brainwashed into believing he was a Russian aerospace engineer. The effects of that treatment affected him emotionally and psychologically—stress would cause him to unexpectedly enter a detached fugue state that left him nearly incapacitated with fear for minutes, sometimes hours—and he voluntarily took himself off active flight status years ago. "It was a hell of a ride . . . but there are *other* rides out there."

"Don't you miss flying?" Patrick asked.

"Hell no," Dave said. "When I want to fly, I pilot one of the un-manned combat air vehicles or my radio-controlled model planes. But I have enough things going on where I don't have the desire anymore."

"I'm just not sure how it would affect me," Patrick said honestly. "I think I'd be okay—no, I'm sure I would—but would I always be demanding one more flight, one more mission?"

"Muck, you and me both know that manned aircraft are going the way of the dinosaur," Dave said. "Are you all of a sudden get-ting some kind of romantic notion about aviation, some kind of weird 'slip the surly bonds' idea that somehow makes you forget everything else? Since when did flying ever become anything more than 'plan the flight, then fly the plan' for you? Man, if I didn't know you, I'd swear you cared more about flying than you did about Bradley. That's not the Patrick Shane McLanahan I know."

"Let's drop it, okay?" Patrick asked irritably. He hated it when Luger (or his former girlfriend, Vice President Maureen Hershel) brought up his twelve-year-old son Bradley, believing it was a too-oft-used argument to try to get Patrick to change his mind about something. "Everyone's all worried about my heart, but no one stops arguing with me." He made sure to give Luger a smile when he added, "Maybe you're all trying to make me crash. Change the damned subject, Texas. What's going on at the Lake?"

"The rumor mill is churning, Muck," Dave said. "Guess who might be back at HAWC?"

"Martin Tehama," Patrick responded. Dave blinked in surprise—this was a guy who was rarely surprised. "I saw a strange e-mail address on a CC from SECDEF and checked to see who was in that office. I think he's going to be reinstated as HAWC commander."

"With his buddy in the White House? No doubt." Air Force Colonel Martin Tehama was designated the commander of the High-Technology Aerospace Weapons Center after Major Gen-eral Terrill "Earthmover" Samson's departure, bypassing Patrick

McLanahan. A well-respected test pilot and engineer, Tehama wanted to rein in the "extracurricular" activities HAWC often got involved with—such as using experimental aircraft and weapons in "operational test flights" around the world—and get back to the serious business of flight test. When Patrick left his White House adviser position he was awarded command of HAWC, bumping Tehama out. He retaliated by delivering reams of information on HAWC's classified missions to members of Congress. "After Summers files a full report on your condition, he'll reappear and take charge as soon as you announce your retirement—or the President announces that you're being medically retired."

"The President and Senator Barbeau will use my heart thing to cancel the Black Stallion program, citing health concerns, and their errand boy Tehama will promptly shut it down within months."

"Not even that long, Muck," David said. "The word from the Senate is that they're going to push the White House to move quicker to shut us down."

"Barbeau wants her bombers, that's for sure."

"It's not just her, but she's the loudest voice," Dave said. "There are lobbyists for every weapon system imaginable—carriers, ballistic missile subs, special ops, you name it. President Gardner wants another four aircraft carrier battle groups at least, maybe six, and he's likely to get them if the space program is canceled. Everyone's got their own agenda. The spaceplane lobby is practically nonexistent, and your injury just casts a shadow on the program, which delights the other lobbyists no end."

"I hate this political shit."

"Me too. I'm surprised you lasted as long as you did working in the White House. You definitely weren't made for wearing a suit, listening to meaningless speeches while wasting weeks testifying before another congressional committee, and being jerked around by lobbyists and so-called experts."

"Copy that," Patrick said. "Anyway, the heat's been turned up, and Tehama will turn it up even more—right in our faces. All the more reason to accomplish this Soltanabad mission, bring the crew back safely, and get some good intel all before tomorrow morning. The Russians are up to something in Iran—they can't be content to just sit in Moscow or Turkmenistan and watch Iran become democratic, or disintegrate."

"I'm on it," Dave said. "The air tasking order will be ready by the time you get the green light. I'll send you the orbital game plan and the complete force timing schedule right away. Genesis out."

CHAPTER FIVE

Integrity is praised and starves.

—DECIMUS JUNIUS JUVENALIS

HIGH-TECHNOLOGY AEROSPACE WEAPONS CENTER, ELLIOTT AIR FORCE BASE, NEVADA

A SHORT TIME LATER

"It's ten times more boring than playing video games," Wayne Macomber complained, "because I can't even *play* the thing."

"Pretty deep wash ahead, Whack," U.S. Army National Guard Captain Charlie Turlock said. "It angles away from the objective, so we'll eventually have to get out. We should—"

"I see it, I see it," Macomber grumbled. "Wohl, clear those railroad tracks again."

"Roger," Marine Corps Sergeant Major Chris Wohl responded in his usual gravelly whisper. A moment later: "Rails are clear, Major. Satellite reports the next train is twenty-seven miles to the east, heading in our direction at twenty-five miles an hour."

"Copy," Macomber responded, "but I keep on seein' a return at my three o'clock, five miles, right in front of you somewhere. It's there for a second and then it disappears. What the hell is it?"

"Negative contact, sir," Wohl radioed.

"This is nuts," Macomber muttered, knowing that both Turlock and Wohl could still hear him but not caring one bit. This was not how he envisioned doing mission planning . . . although he had to admit it was pretty darned cool.

As incredible as the spaceplane was, even the passenger module was a pretty nifty device. It served to not only carry passengers and cargo inside the Black Stallion but also as a docking adapter between the spaceplane and a space station. In an emergency the module could even be used as a spacecraft crew lifeboat: it had maneuvering thrusters to facilitate retrieval by repair spacecraft while in orbit and to keep it upright during re-entry; little winglets for stability in case it was jettisoned in the atmosphere; enough oxygen to allow six passengers to survive for as long as a week; enough shielding to survive re-entry if the module was jettisoned during re-entry; and parachutes and flotation/impact attenuation bags that would cushion the module and its passengers upon land or water impact. Unfortunately all this protection was only available to the passengers—there was no way for the Black Stallion's flight crew to get inside the module after takeoff except by spacewalking while in orbit and using the transfer tunnel.

Macomber and Wohl were wearing a full Tin Man armor system, a lightweight suit made of BERP, or ballistic electronically reactive process material which was totally flexible like cloth but protected the wearer by instantly hardening to a strength a hundred times greater than steel when struck. The suit was completely sealed, affording excellent protection even in harsh or dangerous environments, and was supplemented with an extensive electronic sensor and communications suite that fed data to the wearer through helmet visor displays. The Tin Man system was further enhanced by a micro-hydraulic exoskeleton that gave the wearer superhuman strength, agility, and speed by amplifying his muscular movements.

Charlie Turlock—"Charlie" was her real name, not a call-sign, a young woman given a boy's name by her father—was not wearing a Tin Man suit, just a flight suit over a thin layer of thermal underwear; her ride was in the cargo compartment behind their seats. She wore a standard HAWC flight helmet, which displayed sensor and computer data on an electronic visor similar to the sophisticated Tin Man displays. Trim, athletic, and of just slightly more than average height, Turlock seemed out of place with a unit full of big, muscular, commandos—but she brought something along from her years at the Army Research Laboratory's Infantry Transformational Battle- lab that more than made up for her smaller physical size.

All three were watching a computer animation of their planned infiltration of the Soltanabad highway airfield in Persia. The anima- tion used real-time satellite sensor images to paint an ultra-realistic view of the terrain and cultural features in the target area, complete with projections of such things as personnel and vehicle movement based on past information, lighting levels, weather predictions, and even soil conditions. The three Battle Force commandos were spread out approximately fifty yards apart, close enough to support one an- other quickly if necessary but far enough apart to not give one an- other away if detected or engaged by a single enemy patrol.

"I can see the fence now, range one point six miles," Charlie re- ported. "Moving over the wash now. The 'Goose' reports thirty minutes of flight time left." The "Goose" was the GUOS, or Grenade-launched Unmanned Observation System, a small pow- ered flying drone about the size of a bowling pin, launched from a backpack launcher, that sent back visual and infrared images to the commandos by a secure datalink.

"That means we're behind," Macomber groused. "Let's pick it up a little."

"We're right on schedule, sir," Wohl whispered.

"I said we're behind, Sergeant Major," Macomber hissed. "The drone will be running out of fuel and we'll still be inside the damned compound."

"I've got another Goose ready," Charlie said. "I can launch it—"

"When? When we get close enough for the Iranians to hear it?" Macomber growled. "How noisy are those things anyway?"

"If you'd show up for my demos, Major, you'd know," Charlie said.

"Don't give me any lip, Captain," Macomber spat. "When I ask you a question, give me an answer."

"Outside a couple hundred yards of engine ignition, they won't hear a thing," Charlie said, not disguising her exasperation at all, "unless they have audio sensors."

"If we had proper intel before starting this mission, we'd *know* if the Iranians had audio sensors," Macomber groused some more. "We need to plan delaying the drone launch until we're within two miles of the base, not three. You got that, Turlock?"

"Roger," Charlie acknowledged.

"Next I need—" Macomber stopped when he noticed a flicker of a target indicator appearing again in the very periphery of his electronic visor's field of view. "Dammit, there it is again. Wohl, did you see it?"

"I saw it that time, but it's gone," Wohl responded. "I'm scanning that area . . . negative contact. Probably just a momentary sensor sparkle."

"Wohl, in my book, there's no such thing as 'sensor sparkle,'" Macomber said. "There's something out ahead of you causing that return. Get on it."

"Roger," Wohl responded. "Moving off-track." He used a small thumbwheel mouse to change direction in the animation, waiting every few meters until the computer added available detail and plotted more warnings or cautions regarding whatever lay ahead. The process was slow because of all the wireless computer activity, but it was the only available means they had of rehearsing their operation and getting ready to fly it at the same time.

"We're supposed to be commandos—there's no such thing as a 'track' for us," Macomber said. "We have an objective and a million different ways of getting there. It should be a damned piece of cake with all these pretty pictures floating in front of us—why is this making my head hurt?" Neither Turlock nor Wohl replied—they had grown quite accustomed to Macomber's complaining. "Anything yet, Wohl?"

"Stand by."

"Looks like tire tracks just past the wash," Charlie reported. "Not very deep—Humvee-sized vehicle."

"That's new," Macomber said. He checked the source data tags. "Fresh intel—downloaded in just the past fifteen minutes by a low-altitude SAR. A perimeter patrol, I'd guess."

"No sign of vehicles."

"That's the reason we're doing this, isn't it, kids? Maybe the general was right after all." It sounded to both Wohl and Turlock as if Macomber hated to admit that the general could be right. "Let's proceed and see what—"

"Crew, this is the MC," the mission commander, Marine Corps Major Jim Terranova, cut in over the intercom, "we've commenced our countdown to takeoff, T-minus fifty-six minutes and counting. Run your pre-takeoff checklists and prepare to report in."

"Roger, S-One copies," Macomber responded . . . except, as he noted himself with not a small bit of shock, that his words came out through an instantly dry, raspy throat and vocal cords, with barely enough breath for the words to escape his lips.

If there was one thing these guys at the High-Technology Aerospace Weapons Center and the Air Battle Force were *really* good at, Macomber had learned early on, it would definitely be computer simulations. These guys ran simulations on everything—for every hour of real flight time, these guys probably did twenty hours on a computer simulator beforehand. The machines ranged from simple desktop computers with photo-realistic displays to full-scale aircraft mockups that did everything from drip hydraulic fluid to smoke and catch on fire if you did something wrong. Everyone did them: air crews, maintenance, security, battle staff, command post, even administration and support staffs conducted drills and simulations regularly.

A good percentage of all the personnel at both Elliott and Battle Mountain Air Bases, probably one-tenth of the five thousand or so at both locations, were involved solely in computer programming, with other private and military computer centers tied in all around the world contributing the latest codes, routines, subroutines, and devices; and at least a third of all the code these top secret super-geeks wrote 24/7 had to be involved solely with simulations. This was his first *real* trip into space, but the simulations were so realistic and so numerous that he truly felt as if he had done this dozens of times before . . .

. . . until *just now,* when the mission commander announced they were less than an hour from takeoff. He had been so busy preparing for the approach and infiltration into Soltanabad—just three hours to get ready, when he demanded no less than three *days* to prepare in the Combat Weather Squadron!—that he had completely forgotten that they were going to be *blasted into space* to get there!

But now that frightening reality hit home with full force. He was not going to just pile his gear into a C-17 Globemaster II or C-130 Hercules for a multiday trip to some isolated airstrip in the middle of nowhere—he was going to be shot almost a hundred miles into space, then flutter down through the atmosphere through hostile airspace to a landing in a desert in northeastern Iran, where quite possibly an entire brigade of Iranian Revolutionary Guards Corps fighters, the elite of the former theocratic regime's terror army, could be waiting for them.

In the time it would normally take for him to just *arrive* at his first transition base en route to his destination, this mission would be *completed*! That simple fact was absolutely astounding, almost unbelievable. The time compression was almost too much to comprehend. And yet, here he was, sitting in the actual spacecraft— not a simulator—and the clock was ticking. By the time the sun rose again, this mission would be over, and he'd be debriefing it. He would have entered low-Earth orbit, traveled halfway across the globe, landed in Iran, scoped it out, blasted off again, re-entered low-Earth orbit, and hopefully landed at a friendly base . . .

. . . or he'd be dead. There were a million unforeseen and

un-simulatable things that could kill them, along with the hundred or so simulatable things they practiced dealing with day after day, and even when they *knew* something bad was going to happen, sometimes they couldn't deal with it. It would either work out okay, or they'd be dead . . . or a hundred other things could happen. Whatever would happen, it was all going to happen *now*.

Macomber certainly felt the danger and the uncertainty . . . but as it so often did, the frenetic pace of every activity dealing with McLanahan and everyone at the High-Technology Aerospace Weapons Center and the Air Battle Force quickly pushed every other feeling of dread out of his conscious mind. It seemed a dozen voices—some human, but most computerized—were speaking to him at the same time, and all needed acknowledgment or an action, or the speaking quickly changed to "demanding." If he didn't respond quickly enough, the computer usually ratted on him, and a rather irate human voice—usually the mission commander but sometimes Brigadier General David Luger, the deputy commander himself, if it was critical enough—repeated the demand.

He was accustomed to performing and succeeding under intense pressure—that was the common denominator for any Special Operations commando—but this was something entirely different: because at the end of all the sometimes chaotic preparation, *they were going to shoot his ass into space*! It seemed Terranova made the announcement just moments earlier when Macomber felt the Black Stallion move as four Laser Pulse Detonation Rocket System engines, or "leopards," in full turbofan propulsion mode, easily propelled the aircraft to Dreamland's four-mile-long dry lake bed runway.

Whack was not afraid of flying, but takeoffs were definitely his most fearsome phase of flight—all that power behind them, the engines running up to full power sucking up tons of fuel per minute, the noise deafening, the vibration its most intense, but the aircraft still moving relatively slowly. He had done many Black Stallion takeoffs in the simulator, and he knew that the performance numbers even with the spacecraft still in the atmosphere were impressive, but for this part he was definitely on pins and needles.

The initial takeoff from the dry lake bed runway at Elliott Air Force Base was indeed spectacular—a massive shove as the LPDRS engines in turbofan mode moved into full military thrust, then a rapid, high-angle climb-out at well over ten thousand feet per minute after a short takeoff roll. The first few seconds of the run-up and takeoff roll seemed normal . . . but that was it. At full military power in turbofan mode, the four LPDRS engines developed one hundred thousand pounds of thrust *each*, optimized by solid-state laser igniters that superheated the jet fuel before ignition.

But high-performance takeoffs were nothing new to Whack or to most commandos and others who flew in and out of hostile airstrips. He had been in several huge C-17 Globemaster II and C-130 Hercules transport planes where they had to do max-performance takeoffs to get out of range of hostile shoulder-fired anti-aircraft missiles in the vicinity of the airstrip, and those planes were many times larger and far less high-tech than the Black Stallion. There was nothing more frightening than the feel of a screaming five-hundred-thousand-pound C-17 Globemaster III cargo plane standing on its tail clawing for every foot of lifesaving altitude.

The Tin Man outfit actually helped his body take some of the G-forces and even gave him a little extra shot of pure oxygen when it sensed his heart and breathing rates jumping up a bit. Because the thrust was so powerful and the air so dense at lower altitudes, the laser igniters had to be "pulsed," or rapidly turned off and on again, to avoid blowing up the engines. This created the distinctive "string of pearls" contrails across the Nevada skies that conspiracy theorists and "Lakespotters"—guys who sneaked into the classified test ranges in hopes of photographing a top secret aircraft for the first time—associated with the Air Force's Aurora hypersonic spy plane.

They had a short high subsonic cruise out over the Pacific coast to the refueling area, and then a rendezvous with an Air Battle Force KC-77 tanker. The secret of the Black Stallion spaceplane program was the inflight refueling, where they took on a full load of jet fuel and oxidizer right before blasting into orbit—instead of launching from zero altitude in the thickest part of the atmosphere, they would begin the cruise into space from twenty-five thousand feet and three hundred knots, in far less dense air.

Refueling always seemed to take forever in every aircraft Whack had ever flown in, especially the big intercontinental-range jet transports, but the Black Stallion took even longer because they actually required three consecutive refuelings: the first to top off the jet fuel tanks, since they didn't take off with a full load and needed a refueling right away; the second to top off the large borohydrogen tetroxide oxidizer—BOHM, nicknamed "boom"—tanks; and a third to top off the jet fuel tanks once more right before the boost into space. Filling the JP-7 jet fuel tanks went fairly quickly each time, but filling the large BOHM tanks took well over an hour because the boron and enhanced hydrogen peroxide mixture was thick and soupy. It was easy to feel the XR-A9 get heavier and noticeably more sluggish as the tanks were being filled, and every now and then the pilot needed to stroke the afterburners on the big LPDRS engines to keep up with the tanker.

Macomber spent the time checking intel updates downloaded to his on-board computers on their target area and studying the maps and information, but he was starting to get frustrated because precious little new data seemed to be coming in, and boredom was setting in. That was dangerous. Although they didn't have to prebreathe oxygen before this flight, as they would if they were going to wear a space suit, they couldn't take their helmets off during refueling operations; and unlike Wohl, who could take a combat catnap anywhere and anytime, like right now, Macomber couldn't sleep before a mission. So he reached into his personal kit bag attached to the bulkhead and . . .

. . . to Turlock's stunned amazement, pulled out a ball of red yarn and two knitting needles, which already had a section of knitted material strung on them! He found it amazingly easy to manipulate the needles with the Tin Man armored gloves, and before long he was picking up speed and almost at his normal work pace.

"Crew, this is S-Two," Turlock said on intercom, "you guys are not going to believe this."

"What is it?" the spacecraft commander, U.S. Navy Lieutenant Commander Lisette "Frenchy" Moulain asked, the concern thick in her voice. There was normally very little conversation during aerial refueling—anything said on the open ship-wide intercom was usually an emergency. "Do we need a disconnect . . . ?"

"No, no, SC, not an emergency," Charlie said. She leaned forward in her seat to get a better look. Macomber was seated ahead of her and on the opposite side of the passenger module, and she strained in her straps to see all the way into his lap. "But it *is* definitely a shocker. The major appears to be . . . *knitting*."

"Say again?" Jim Terranova asked. The Black Stallion spaceplane burbled momentarily as if the spacecraft commander was momentarily so stunned that she almost flew out of the refueling envelope. "Did you say 'knitting'? Knitting . . . as in, a ball of yarn, knitting needles . . . *knitting?*"

"Affirmative," Charlie said. Chris Wohl, who was seated beside Macomber, woke up and looked over at Macomber for a few seconds, the surprise evident even through his helmet and Tin Man body armor, before he dropped back off to catnap again. "He's got the needles, the red ball of yarn, the 'knit one purl two' thing going, the whole show. Martha friggin' Stewart right over here."

"Are you shitting me?" Terranova exclaimed. "Our resident bad-ass snake-eating commando is *knitting?*"

"He looks *sooo* cute, too," Charlie said. Her voice changed to that of a young child's: "I can't tell if he's making a cute widdle doily, or maybe it's a warm and cozy sweater for his widdle French poodle, or maybe it's a—"

In a blur of motion that Turlock never really saw, Macomber withdrew another knitting needle from his kit bag, twisted to his left, and threw it at Turlock. The needle whistled just to the right of her helmet and buried itself three inches deep into her seat's headrest.

"Why, you motherfucker . . . !" Turlock exclaimed, pulling the needle out. Macomber waved at her with his armored fingers, grinning beneath his bug-eyed helmet, then turned and went back to his knitting.

"What in hell is going on back there?" Moulain asked angrily.

"Just thought since the captain was talking baby talk that maybe she wanted to try knitting too," Whack said. "You want the other one, Turlock?"

"Take off that helmet and I'll give it back to you—right between your eyes!"

"You jerks knock it off—maintain radio discipline," Moulain ordered. "The most critical part of aerial refueling and you bozos are farting around like little snot-nosed kids. Macomber, are you really *knitting?*"

"What if I am? It relaxes me."

"You didn't get clearance from me to bring knitting stuff on board. Put that shit away."

"Come back here and make me, Frenchy." There was silence. Macomber glanced over at Wohl—the only one on the spacecraft who probably *could* make him, if he wanted to—but he looked like he was still asleep. Whack was sure he wasn't, but he made no move to intervene.

"You and I are going to have a little talk when we get home, Macomber," Moulain said ominously, "and I'll explain to you in terms I hope you can understand the authority and responsibilities of the spacecraft commander—even if it takes a swift kick in your ass to make it clear."

"Looking forward to it, Frenchy."

"Good. Now knock off the horseplay, put away any nonauthorized equipment in the passenger module, and cut the chatter on the intercom, or this flight is terminated. Everyone got it?" There was no response. Macomber shook his head but put away his knitting stuff as directed, smiling at the feeling of Turlock's angry glare on the back of his helmet. The rest of the refueling was carried out with only normal call-outs and responses.

After refueling was completed, they subsonically cruised north-ward along the coast for about an hour, flying loose formation with the KC-77—it was now easy for the tanker to keep up with the Black Stallion since the spaceplane was so heavy. They hooked up with the tanker once again to top off the JP-7 tanks, which didn't take long, and then the tanker headed back to base. "Orbital inser-tion checklist programmed hold, crew," Terranova reported. "Re-port in when your checklist is complete."

"S-One, wilco," Macomber growled. Yet another checklist. He called up the electronic checklist on his helmet's electronic data visor and used the eye-pointing cursor and voice commands to check off each item, which mostly dealt with securing loose items, checklisting the oxygen panel, cabin pressurization, yada yada yada. It was all busywork that a computer could check easily, so why have humans do it themselves? Probably some touchy-feely human engineering thing to make the passengers feel they were something else other than exactly what they were: passengers. Whack waited until Turlock and Wohl completed their check-lists, checked his off as complete, then spoke, "MC, S-One, check-list complete."

"Roger. Checklist complete up here. Stand by for orbital insertion burn, crew."

It all sounded very routine and quite boring, just like the endless simulator sessions they made him take, so Macomber began think-ing about the target area in Soltanabad once again. Updated satellite images confirmed the presence of heavy-vehicle tire tracks again but did not reveal what they were—whoever was down there was very good at keeping the vehicles hidden from satellite view. The Goose drones were not much better than the space-based radar network in detecting very small targets, but maybe they needed to stay away from the highway airstrip and send in the Goose drones first to get a real-time look before . . .

. . . and suddenly the LPDRS engines kicked in, not in turbojet mode but now in hybrid rocket mode, and Macomber was suddenly and violently thrust back into the here and now. No simulator could prepare you for the shove—it felt like hitting a football tackle training sled except it was completely unexpected, the sled was hitting *you* instead of the other way around, and the force was not only sustained but increasing every second. Soon it felt like the entire offensive line had piled on top of him, being joined shortly by the defensive line as well. Whack knew he could call up data readouts about their altitude, speed, and G-force levels, but it was all he could do just to concentrate on his breath control to fight off the G-force effects and keep from blacking out.

The G-forces seemed to last an hour, although he knew the boost into orbit only took seven or eight minutes. When the pressure finally eased, he felt exhausted, as if he had just finished running the stadium stairs at the Academy before football season, or jogging across the Iraqi desert with a hundred-pound pack.

Obviously his labored breathing was loud enough to be heard on the intercom, because a few moments later Charlie Turlock asked, "Still feel like farting around with your knitting needles, Macomber?"

"Bite me."

"Get your barf bag ready, Major," Charlie continued gaily, "because I'm not cleaning up after you if you spew in the module. I'll bet the macho commando didn't take his anti-motion-sickness medication."

"Cut the chatter and run your 'After Orbital Insertion Burn' checklists," Moulain said.

Macomber's breathing quickly returned to normal—more from embarrassment than by will. Damn, he thought, that hit him too suddenly, and a lot harder than he'd expected. Getting back into a routine would surely take his mind off his queasiness, and the Air Battle Force was nothing if not driven by checklists and routine. He used his eye-pointing system to call up the proper checklist by looking at a tiny icon in the upper left corner of his electronic visor and speaking . . .

. . . but instead of issuing a command, all he could manage was a throatful of bile. Scanning the electronic visor with his eyes suddenly gave him the worst case of vertigo he had ever experienced—he felt as if he was being swung upside down by the ankles on a rope, suspended a hundred feet aboveground. He couldn't stop the spinning sensation; he lost all sense of up and down. His stomach churned as the spinning intensified, a thousand times worse than the worst case of the spins and leans he had ever had on the worst all-night party in his life . . .

"Better clear the major off-helmet, Frenchy," Charlie said, " 'cause it sounds like he's ready to blow lunch."

"Screw you, Turlock," Macomber meant to say, but all that came out was a gurgle.

"You're cleared off-helmet, S-One, module pressurization in the green," Moulain said. "I hope you kept a barf bag handy—vomit in free fall is the most disgusting thing you've ever seen in your life, and you might be too sick to do your job."

"Thanks a bunch," Macomber said through gritted teeth, trying to hold back the inevitable until he got the damned Tin Man helmet off. Somehow he managed to unfasten his helmet—he had no idea where it floated off to. Unfortunately the first bag he could reach was not a motion sickness bag—it was the personal bag containing his knitting stuff. To his shock and dismay, he quickly found that vomit in free fall didn't behave as he expected: instead of filling the bottom of his bag in a disgusting but controllable clump, it curled back into a smelly, chunky cloud right back up into his face, eyes, and nose.

"Don't let it out, Whack!" he heard Turlock yell from behind him. "We'll spend the next hour Dustbustering globs of barf out of the module." That bit of imagery didn't help to settle his stomach one bit, nor did the awful smell and feel of warm vomit wafting across his face inside the bag.

"Relax, big guy," he heard a voice say. It was Turlock. She had unstrapped and was holding his shoulders, steadying his convulsions and helping seal the bag around his head. He tried to shrug her

hands off, but she resisted. "I said relax, Whack. It happens to everyone, drugs or no drugs."

"Get away from me, bitch!"

"Shut up and listen to me, asshole," Charlie insisted. "Ignore the
smell. The smell is the trigger. Remove it from your consciousness.
Do it, or you'll be a vegetable for the next three hours minimum. I
know you bad-ass commando types know how to control your
senses, your breathing, and even your involuntary muscles so you
can endure days of discomfort in the field. Hal Briggs fought on for
several minutes after being shot up by the Iranians . . ."

"Screw Briggs, and screw you, too!"

"Pay attention, Macomber. I know you can do this. Now is the
time to turn whatever you got *on*. Concentrate on the smell, isolate
it, and eliminate it from your consciousness."

"You don't know *shit* . . ."

"Just do it, Wayne. You know what I'm telling you. Just shut up
and do it, or you'll be as wasted as if you've been on a three-day
bender."

Macomber was still blindingly angry at Turlock for being right
there with him at this most vulnerable moment, taking advantage
of him, but what she said made sense—she obviously knew something about the agony he was experiencing. The smell, huh? He
never thought about smell that much—he was trained to be hy-
persensitive to sight, sound, and the indefinable sixth sense that
always warned of nearby danger. Smell was usually a confusing
factor, something to be disregarded. Shut it down, Whack. Shut
it *off*.

Somehow, it worked. He knew that breathing through his mouth
cut off the sense of smell, and when he did that a lot of the nausea
went away. His stomach was still doing painful knots and waves of
roiling convulsions, as bad as if he had been stabbed in the gut, but
now the trigger of those awful spasms was gone, and he was back in
control. Sickness was *not allowable*. He had a team counting on him,
a mission to perform—his damned weak stomach was not going to
be the thing that let his team and his mission down. A few pounds

of muscle and nerve endings were *not* going to control him. The mind is the master, he reminded himself, and he *was* the master of the mind.

A few moments later, with his stomach empty and the aroma erased from his consciousness, his stomach quickly started to return to normal. "You okay?" Charlie asked, offering him a towelette.

"Yeah." He accepted the wipe and began to clean up, but stopped and nodded. "Thanks, Turlock."

"Sorry about the shit I gave you about the knitting."

"I get it all the time."

"And you usually bust somebody's head for ragging on you, except it was me and you weren't going to bust my head?"

"I would have if I could've reached you," Whack said. Charlie thought he meant it until he smiled and chuckled. "Knitting relaxes me, and it gives me a chance to see who gets in my shit and who leaves me be."

"Sounds like a screwed-up way to live, boss, if you don't mind me sayin'," Charlie said. He shrugged. "If you're okay, drink some water and stay on pure oxygen for a while. Use the vacuum to clean up any pieces of vomit you see before we re-enter, or we'll never find them and they'll become projectiles. If they stick on our gear the bad guys will smell it yards away."

"You're right, Tur—Charlie," Whack said. As she headed back to her seat, he added, "You're all right, Turlock."

"Yes, I am, boss," she replied. She found his helmet lodged somewhere in the cargo section in the back of the passenger module and handed it back to him. "Just don't you forget it." She then detached the cleanup vacuum from its recharging station and floated it over to him as well. "Now you *really* look like Martha Stewart, boss."

"Don't push it, Captain," he growled, but he smiled and took the vacuum.

"Yes, sir." She smiled, nodded, and returned to her seat.

PRESIDENT'S RETREAT, BOLTINO, RUSSIA

A SHORT TIME LATER

They didn't always meet like this to make love. Both Russian president Leonid Zevitin and minister of foreign affairs Alexandra Hedrov loved classic black-and-white movies from all over the world, Italian food, and rich red wine, so after a long day of work, especially with a long upcoming trip ready to begin, they often stayed after the rest of the staff had been dismissed and shared some time together. They had become lovers not long after they first met at an international banking conference in Switzerland almost ten years earlier, and even as their responsibilities and public visibility increased they still managed to find the time and opportunity to get together.

If either of them was concerned about the whispered rumors of their affair, they showed no sign of it. Only the tabloids and celebrity blogs spoke of it, and those were all but dismissed by most Russians—certainly no one in the Kremlin would ever wag their tongues about such things and about such powerful people in anything louder than a quiet thought. Hedrov was married and was the mother of two grown children, and they long ago learned that their lives, as well as the life of their wife and mother, belonged to the state now, not to themselves.

The president's dacha was the closest to security and privacy than anything else they could ever expect in the Russian Federation. Unlike the president's official residence in the Senate Building at the Kremlin, which was rather unassuming and utilitarian, Zevitin's dacha outside Moscow was modern and stylish, fit for any international business executive. Like the man itself, the place revolved around work and business, but it was hard to discern that at first glance.

After flying in to Boltino to the president's private airport nearby, visitors were driven to the residence by limousine and escorted through a sweeping grand foyer to the great room and dining room, dominated by three large fireplaces and adorned with sumptuous leather and oak furniture, works of art from all over the world, framed photos of world leaders, and mementos from his many celebrity friends, topped off with a spectacular panoramic view of Pirogovskoje Reservoir outside the floor-to-ceiling windows. Special guests would be invited up the double marble curved staircases to the bedroom suites on the second floor, or down to the large Roman-style baths, indoor pool, thirty-seat high-definition movie theater, and game room on the ground floor. But all that was still only a fraction of the square footage of the place.

A guest being dazzled by the grand view outside the great room would miss the dark, narrow cupola on the right side of the foyer, almost resembling a doorless closet, which had small and unimpressive paintings hanging on the curved walls illuminated by rather dim LED spotlights. But if one stepped into the cupola, he would be instantly but surreptitiously electronically searched by X-ray to locate weapons or listening devices. His facial features would be scanned and the data run through an electronic identification system that was able to detect and filter out disguises or impostors. Once positively identified, the hidden door inside the cupola would be opened from within, and you would be admitted to the main part of the dacha.

Zevitin's office was as large as the great- and dining rooms combined, large enough for a group of generals or ministers to confer with each other on one side and not be heard by a similarly sized meeting of the president's advisers on the other—unheard except for the audio and video recording devices planted everywhere on the grounds, as well as out on the streets, neighborhoods, and roads of the surrounding countryside. Eight persons could expansively dine on Zevitin's walnut and ivory-inlaid desk with elbow room to spare. Video feeds and television reports from hundreds of different sources were fed to a dozen high-definition monitors located in the office, but none were visible unless the president wanted to view them.

The president's bedroom upstairs was the one made up for show:

the bedroom adjoining the office suite was the one Zevitin used most of the time; it was also the one Alexandra preferred, the one that she thought best reflected the man himself—still grand, but warmer and perhaps plusher than the rest of the mansion. She liked to think he made it so just for her, but that would be foolish arrogance on her part, and she often reminded herself not to indulge in any of that around this man.

They had slipped beneath the silk sheets and down comforter of his bed after dinner and movies and just held each other, sipping tiny glasses of brandy and talking in low intimate voices about everything but the three things both mostly cared about: government, politics, and finances. Phone calls, official or otherwise, were expressly forbidden; Alexandra couldn't remember ever being interrupted by an aide or a phone call, as if Zevitin could somehow make the rest of the world instantly comatose while they were together. They touched each other occasionally, exploring each other's silent desires, and mutually deciding without a word that tonight was for companionship and rest, not passion. They had known each other a long time, and she never considered that she might not be fulfilling his needs or desires, or he was disregarding hers. They embraced, kissed, and said good night, and there was no hint of tension or displeasure. All was as it should be . . .

. . . so it was doubly surprising for Alexandra to be awakened by something she had never heard before in that room: a beeping telephone. The alien sound made her sit bolt upright after the second or third beep; she soon noticed that Leonid was already on his feet, the bedside light on, the receiver to his lips.

"Go ahead," he said, then listened, glancing over to her. His eyes were not angry, quizzical, confused, or fearful, as she was certain hers were. He obviously knew exactly who was calling and what he was going to say; like a playwright watching a rehearsal of his latest work, he was patiently waiting for something he already knew would be said.

"What is it?" she mouthed.

To her surprise, Zevitin reached down to the phone, touched a button, and hung up the receiver, activating the speakerphone. "Repeat that last, General," he said, catching and arresting her gaze with his.

General Andrei Darzov's voice, crackling and occasionally fading with interference as if talking across a vast distance, could still clearly be heard: "Yes, sir. KIK Command and Measurement Command sites have detected an American spaceplane launch over the Pacific Ocean. It crossed over central Canada and was inserted safely into low-Earth orbit while over the Arctic ice pack of Canada. If it stays on its current trajectory, its target area is definitely eastern Iran."

"When?"

"They could be starting their re-entry burn in ten minutes, sir," Darzov replied. "It possibly has enough fuel to fly to the same target area after re-entering the atmosphere after a complete orbit, but it is doubtful without a midair refueling over Iraq or Turkey."

"Do you think they discovered it?" Hedrov didn't know what "it" was, but she assumed, because Zevitin had allowed her to listen in on the conversation, that she would find out soon enough.

"I think we should assume they have, sir," Darzov said, "although if they positively identified the system, I am sure McLanahan would not hesitate to attack it. They may have just detected activity there and are inserting more intelligence-gathering assets to verify."

"Well, I'm surprised they took *this* long," Zevitin remarked. "They have spacecraft flying over Iran almost every hour."

"And those are just the ones we can positively detect and track," Darzov said. "They could have many more that we can't identify, especially unmanned aircraft."

"When will it be within striking range for us, General?"

Hedrov's mouth opened, but at a warning glare from Zevitin, she said nothing. What in hell were they thinking of . . . ?

"By the time the spaceplane crosses the base's horizon, sir, they'll be less than five minutes from landing."

"Damn, the speed of that thing is mind-boggling," Zevitin muttered. "It's almost impossible to move fast enough against it."

He thought quickly; then: "But if the spaceplane stays in orbit instead of re-entering, it will be in perfect position. We have one good shot only."

"Exactly, sir," Darzov said.

"I assume your men are preparing for an assault, General?" Zevitin asked seriously. "Because if the spaceplane successfully lands and deploys its Tin Man ground forces—which we *must* assume they will have on board—"

"Yes, sir, we must."

"—we will have no time to pack up and get out of Dodge."

"If I understand you correctly, sir—yes, we would undoubtedly lose the system to them," Darzov acknowledged, not knowing what or where "Dodge" was but not bothering to reveal his own ignorance. "The game will be over."

"I see," Zevitin said. "But if it does not re-enter and stays in orbit, how long will you have to engage it?"

"We should acquire it with optronic observation sensors and laser rangefinders as soon as it crosses the horizon, at a range of about eighteen hundred kilometers or about four minutes away," Darzov replied. "However, we need radar for precise tracking, and that is limited to a maximum range of five hundred kilometers. So we will have a maximum of two minutes at its current orbital altitude."

"Two minutes! Is that enough time?"

"Barely," Darzov said. "We will have radar tracking, but we still need to hit the target with an air data laser that will help compute focusing corrections to the main laser's optics. That should take no longer than sixty seconds, assuming the radar stays locked on and the proper computations are made. That will give us a maximum of sixty seconds' exposure time."

"Will it be enough to disable it?"

"It should, at least partially, based on our previous engagements," Darzov replied. "However, the optimum time to attack is when the target is directly overhead. As the target moves toward the horizon the atmosphere grows thicker and more complex, and the laser's optics cannot compensate quickly enough. So—"

"The window is very, very small," Zevitin said. "I understand, General. Well, we must do everything we can to be sure the space-plane stays in that second orbit."

There was a noticeable pause; then: "If I can help in any way, sir, please do not hesitate to call on me," Darzov said, obviously completely unsure as to what he could do.

"I'll keep you posted, General," Zevitin said. "But for now, you are cleared to engage. Repeat, you are cleared to engage. Written authorization will be sent to your headquarters via secure e-mail. Advise if anything changes. Good luck."

"Luck favors the bold, sir. We cannot lose if we take the fight to the enemy. Out."

As soon as Zevitin hung up the phone, Hedrov asked, "What was that all about, Leonid? What is going on? Was it about Fanar?"

"We are about to create a crisis in space, Alexandra," Zevitin responded. He turned to her, then ran the fingers of both hands through his hair as if wiping his thoughts completely clear so he could start afresh. "The Americans think they have unfettered access to space—we are going to throw some roadblocks up in their faces and see what they do. If I know Joseph Gardner, as I think I do, I think he will stomp on the brakes of McLanahan's vaunted space force, and stomp on them *hard*. He would destroy one of his own just to keep someone else from having a victory he couldn't claim for himself."

Alexandra rose from the bed, kneeling before him. "Are you so sure of this man, Leonid?"

"I'm positive I've got this guy pegged."

"And what of his generals?" she asked softly. "What of McLanahan?"

Zevitin nodded, silently admitting his own uncertainty about that very factor. "The American attack dog is on his leash, and he is apparently hurt . . . for now," he said. "I don't know how long I can count on that leash holding. We've got to prompt Gardner to put McLanahan out of commission . . . or be prepared to do it ourselves."

He picked up the phone. "Get me American president Gardner on the 'hot line' immediately."

"It is a dangerous game you are playing, no?" Hedrov asked.

"Sure, Alexandra," Zevitin said, running the fingers of his left hand through her hair as he waited. He felt her hands slip from his chest to below his waist, soon tugging at his underwear and then ministering to him with her hands and mouth, and although he heard the beeps and clicks of the satellite communications system quickly putting the "hot line" call through to Washington, he didn't stop her. "But the stakes are that high. Russia can't allow the Americans to claim the high ground. We need to stop them, and this is our best chance right now."

Alexandra's efforts soon increased both in gentleness and urgency, and Zevitin hoped that Gardner was preoccupied enough to allow him a few more minutes with her. Knowing the American President as he did, he knew he very well might be similarly distracted.

ABOARD AIR FORCE ONE, OVER THE SOUTH-EAST UNITED STATES

THAT SAME TIME

Relaxing in his newly reupholstered seat at his desk in the executive office suite aboard Air Force One, on his way to his "southern White House" oceanside compound outside St. Petersburg, Florida, President Gardner was studying the very ample bosom and shapely fanny of the female Air Force staff sergeant who had just brought a pot of coffee and some wheat crackers into the office. He knew she knew he was checking her out, because every now and then she would cast a glance over to him and a tiny smile would appear. He had a newspaper on his lap but was angled over just enough to surreptitiously watch her. Yep, he thought, she was taking her sweet time setting out his stuff. Damn, what an *ass* . . .

Just as he was going to make his move and invite her to bring those tits and ass over to his big desk, the phone beeped. He was tempted to push the DO NOT DISTURB button, cursing himself that he hadn't done so after he finished his last meeting with the staff and settled in, but something told him that he should take this call. He reluctantly picked up the receiver. "Yes?"

"President Zevitin of the Russian Federation calling for you on the 'hot line,' sir," the communications officer responded. "He says it's urgent."

He held the MUTE button on the receiver, groaned aloud, then gave the stewardess a wink. "Come back in ten minutes with fresh stuff, okay, Staff Sergeant?"

"Yes, *sir*," she replied enthusiastically. She stood to attention, thrusting her chest out to him, before glancing at him mischievously, slowly turning on a heel, and departing.

He knew he had her pegged, he thought happily as he released the button. "Give me a minute, Signals," he said, reaching for a cigarette.

"Yes, sir."

Shit, Gardner cursed to himself, what in hell does Zevitin want *now*? He pressed the buzzer button to summon his chief of staff Walter Kordus. He was going to have to review the policy he'd established of immediately taking calls from Zevitin, he thought—he was starting to speak with him almost on a daily basis. Ninety seconds and a half a cigarette later: "Put him through, Signals," he ordered, stubbing out the cigarette.

"Yes, Mr. President." A moment later: "President Zevitin is on the line, secure, sir."

"Thank you, Signals. Leonid, this is Joe Gardner. How are you?"

"I'm fine, Joe," Zevitin replied in a not-so-pleasant tone. "But I'm concerned, man, real concerned. I thought we had a deal."

Gardner reminded himself to stay on guard while talking to this guy—he sounded so much like an American that he could be talking to someone from the California congressional delegation or some Indiana labor union leader. "What are you talking about, Leonid?" The chief of staff entered the President's office, picked up the dead extension so he could listen in, and turned on his computer to start taking notes and issuing orders if necessary.

"I thought we agreed that we would be notified whenever you'd fly manned spaceplane missions, especially into Iran," Zevitin said. "This is really worrisome, Joe. I'm working hard to try to defuse the situation in the Middle East and keep the hard-liners in my government in check, but your activities with the Black Stallions only serve to—"

"Hold on, Leonid, hold on," Gardner interrupted. "I have no idea what you're talking about. What Black Stallion missions?"

"C'mon, Joe—do you think we can't see it? Do you think it's invisible? We picked it up as soon as it crossed the horizon over the Greenland Sea."

"One of the spaceplanes is flying over Greenland?"

"It's over southwestern China now, Joe, according to our space surveillance and tracking units," Zevitin said. "C'mon, Joe, I know you can't talk about ongoing classified military missions, but it's not hard to guess what they're going to do, even if it is the Black Stallion spaceplane we're talking about. Orbital mechanics are as predictable as sunrise and sunset."

"Leonid, I—"

"I know you can't confirm or deny anything—you don't have to, because we know what's going to happen," Zevitin went on. "It is obvious that in the next orbit, in about ninety minutes, it will be directly over Iran. We expect it to begin deorbit maneuvers in about forty-five minutes, which will put it directly over the Caspian Sea when its atmospheric engines and flight controls will become active. You're obviously flying a mission into Iran, Joe. I thought we had an agreement: hands off Iran while we pursue a diplomatic solution to the military coup and the murder of the elected Iranian officials."

"Hold on, Leonid. Stand by a sec." Gardner hit the MUTE button. "Get Conrad in here," he ordered, but Kordus had already hit the button to page the National Security Adviser. Gardner released the MUTE button. "Leonid, you're right, I can't talk about any ongoing operations. You just have to—"

"Joe, I'm not calling to discuss anything. I'm pointing out to you that we can clearly see one of your spaceplanes in orbit right now, and we had no idea you were going to launch one. After all we've discussed over the past several weeks, I can't believe you'd do this to me. When they find out about this, my Cabinet and the Duma will think I've been duped, and they'll demand I take action, or else I'll lose all the support for our cooperative efforts and rapprochement I've taken months to cultivate. You cut the rug out from under me, Joe."

"Leonid, I'm in the middle of an important meeting, and I need to finish up what I'm doing first," the President lied, impatiently rising to his feet and resisting the urge to yell outside his door for Carlyle and Kordus to tell him what in hell was going on. "I assure you, we don't have any actions under way against Russia anywhere, in any fashion—"

"'Against Russia?' That sounds like an alarming equivocation, Joe. What does that mean? Are you launching an operation against someone else?"

"Let me clear my desk and finish this briefing, Leonid, and I'll fill you in. I'll—"

"I thought we agreed, Joe: essential flights only until we had a treaty governing military travel in space," Zevitin pressed. "As far as we can tell, the spaceplane isn't going to dock with the space station, so this is not a logistical mission. I know things are bad in Iran and Iraq, but bad enough to stir up widespread fear by launching a Black Stallion? I think not. This is a complete disaster, Joe. I'm going to get butchered by the Duma and the generals—"

"Don't panic, Leonid. There's a rational and completely benign explanation. I'll call you back as soon as I can and—"

"Joe, you had better be straight with me, or else I won't be able to rein in the opposition leaders and some of the more powerful generals—they'll all be clamoring for an explanation and a strong response in kind," Zevitin said. "If I can't give them a plausible answer, they'll start searching for one themselves. You know I'm holding on by a shoestring out here. I need your cooperation or everything we've worked for will unravel."

"I'll call you right back, Leonid," Gardner said. "But I assure you, on my honor, that nothing is going on. Absolutely *nothing.*"

"So our ambassadors and observers on the ground in Tehran shouldn't be worried about another hypersonic missile slamming through the ceiling any moment now?"

"Don't even joke about that, Leonid. It's not going to happen. I'll call you back." He impatiently hung up the phone, then wiped the beads of sweat off his upper lip. "Walter!" he shouted. "Where the hell are you? And where's Conrad?"

The two advisers trotted into the executive suite moments later. "Sorry, Mr. President, but I was downloading the latest spacecraft status report from Strategic Command," National Security Adviser Conrad Carlyle said. "It should be on your computer." He accessed the computer on the President's desk, opened a secure file location, and quickly scanned the contents. "Okay, it's right here . . . yes, General Cannon, commander of U.S. Strategic Command, authorized a spaceplane launch about four hours ago, and the mission was approved by Secretary Turner."

"Why wasn't I notified of this?"

"The mission is described as 'routine,' sir," Carlyle said. "Crew of two, three passengers, six orbits of the Earth and return to Elliott Air Force Base, total mission duration ten hours."

"What is this, a fucking *joy ride*? Who are the passengers? I ordered essential missions only! What in hell is going on? I thought I grounded all of the spaceplanes."

Carlyle and Kordus exchanged puzzled expressions. "I . . . I'm not aware of an order grounding the spaceplanes, sir," Carlyle responded feebly. "You did recall the SkySTREAK bombers from their patrols, but not the space—"

"I had a deal with Zevitin, Conrad: No more spaceplane launches without first notifying him," Gardner said. "He's hopping mad about the launch, and so am I!"

Carlyle's brows knitted, and his mouth opened and closed with confusion. "I'm sorry, Joe, but I'm not aware of any agreement we made with Zevitin to inform him of anything dealing with the spaceplanes," he said finally. "I know he's been *clamoring* for that—he rants and raves to every media outlet in the world that the spaceplanes are a danger to world peace and security because they can be mistaken for an intercontinental ballistic missile, and he's demanding that we notify him before we launch one—but there's been no formal agreement about—"

"Didn't I order Cannon to be sure that those spaceplanes and any space weapons didn't enter sovereign airspace, even if it meant keeping them on the ground?" the President thundered. "They were to stay out of any country's airspace at all times. Didn't I give that order?"

"Well . . . yes, sir, I believe you did," Kordus replied. "But the spaceplanes can easily fly *above* a country's airspace. They can—"

"How can they do that?" the President asked. "*We* have airspace that's restricted from the surface to *infinity*. Sovereign airspace is all the airspace above a nation."

"Sir, as we've discussed before, under the Outer Space Treaty no nation can restrict access or travel through outer space," Carlyle reminded the President. "Legally space begins one hundred kilometers from Earth's surface. The spaceplane can climb into space quickly enough while over friendly countries, open ocean, or the ice packs, and once up there can fly around without violating anyone's sovereign airspace. They do it—"

"I don't give a shit what it says in an obsolete forty-year-old treaty!" the President thundered. "For many months we have been involved in discussions with Zevitin and the United Nations to come up with a way to alleviate the anxiety felt by many around the world to spaceplane and space station operations without restricting our own access to space or revealing classified information. Until we had something worked out, I made it clear that I didn't want the spaceplanes flitting around unnecessarily making folks nervous and interfering with the negotiations. Essential missions *only,* and that meant resupply and national emergencies—I had to personally approve all other missions. Am I mistaken, or have I *not* approved any other spaceplane flights recently?"

"Sir, General Cannon must have felt it important enough to launch this flight without—"

"Without my approval? He thinks he can just blast off into space without anyone's permission? Where's the emergency? Is the spaceplane going to dock with the space station? Who are the three passengers? Do you even *know?*"

"I'll put in a call to General Cannon, sir," Carlyle said, picking up the phone. "I'll get all the details right away."

"This is a damned nightmare! This is out of control!" the President thundered. "I want to know who's responsible for this, and I want his ass *out!* Do you hear me? Unless war has been declared or aliens are attacking, I want whoever's responsible for this *shit-canned!* I want to speak with Cannon myself!"

Carlyle put his hand over the phone's mouthpiece as he waited and said, "Sir, I suggest I speak with General Cannon. Keep an arm's-length distance from this. If it's just a training flight or something, you don't want to be perceived as jumping off the deep end, especially after just speaking with the president of Russia."

"This is serious, Conrad, and I want it clear to my generals that I want those spaceplanes under tight control," the President said.

"Are you sure that's how you want to handle it, Joe?" Kordus asked in a quiet voice. "Reaching down past Secretary Turner to dress down a four-star general is bad form. If you want to beat someone up, pick on Turner—he was the final authority for that spaceplane launch."

"Oh, I'll give Turner a piece of my mind too, you can bet on that," the President said angrily, "but Cannon and that other guy, the three-star—"

"Lieutenant General Backman, commander of CENTAF."

"Whatever. Cannon and Backman have been fighting me too hard and too long over this space defense force idea of McLanahan's, and it's about time to bring them back into line—or, better, get rid of them. They're the last holdouts of Martindale's Pentagon brain trust, and they want the space stuff because it builds up *their* empires."

"If you want them gone, we'll get rid of them—they all serve at the pleasure of the commander-in-chief," Kordus said. "But they're still very powerful and popular generals, especially with congressmen who are for the space program. They may push their own plans and programs while in uniform, but as disgraced and disgruntled retired generals, they'll attack *you* openly and personally. Don't give them a reason."

"I know how the game is played, Walter—hell, I made most of the rules," the President said hotly. "I'm not afraid of the generals, and I shouldn't be worried about tiptoeing around them—I'm the damned commander-in-chief. Get Turner on the line right away." He reached over and snatched the phone out of the National Security Adviser's hand. "Signals, what the hell is going on? Where's Cannon?"

"Stand by, sir, he should be connecting any second now." A few moments later: "Cannon here, secure."

"General Cannon, this is the President. Why the hell did you authorize that spaceplane to launch without my authority?"

"Uh . . . good afternoon, sir," Cannon began, perplexed. "As I explained to the Secretary of Defense, sir, it's a pre-positioning flight only while we await final approval for a mission inside Iran. With the spacecraft in orbit, if we got approval it would be easy to insert the team, do their job, then get them out again. If it was not approved, it would be equally easy to return them to base."

"I specifically ordered no spaceplanes to cross foreign borders without my approval."

"Sir, as you know, once the spaceplane is above the sixty-mile threshold, it's—"

"Don't give me that Outer Space Treaty crap!" the President thundered. "Do I have to spell it out for you? I don't want the spaceplanes in orbit unless it's to support the space station or it's an emergency, and if it's an emergency it had better be a damned serious one! The rest of the world thinks we're getting ready to launch attacks from space . . . which apparently is *exactly* what you are planning, *behind my back!*"

"I'm not hiding anything from anyone, sir," Cannon argued. "Without orders to the contrary, I launched the spaceplanes on my own authority with strict orders that no one crosses into any sovereign airspace. That is my standing general order from SECDEF. Those instructions have been complied with to the letter."

"Well, I'm rescinding your authority, General," the President said. "From now on, *all* movements of *any* spacecraft will need my direct permission before execution. Do I make myself clear, General? You had better not put so much as a *rat* in space without my permission!"

"I understand, sir," Cannon said, "but I don't recommend that course of action."

"Oh? And why not?"

"Sir, keeping that level of control on any military asset is dangerous

and wasteful, but it's even more critical with the space launch systems,"
Cannon said. "Military units need one commander to be effective,
and that should be a theater commander with instantaneous and constant access to information from the field. The spaceplanes and all of
our space launch systems are designed for maximum speed and flexi-
bility, and in an emergency they'll lose both if final authority remains
in Washington. I strongly recommend against taking operational
command of those systems. If you're not happy with my decisions, sir,
then may I remind you that you can dismiss me and appoint another
theater commander to have control of the spaceplanes and other
launch systems."

"I'm well aware of my authority, General," Gardner said. "My
decision stands."

"Yes, sir."

"Now who the hell is aboard that spaceplane, and why wasn't I
informed of this mission?"

"Sir, along with the two flight crewmembers, there are three
members of General McLanahan's Air Battle Force ground operations unit aboard the spaceplane," Cannon responded tonelessly.

"*McLanahan?* I should have known," the President spat. "That
guy is the *definition* of a loose cannon! What was *he* up to? Why did
he want that spaceplane launched?"

"They were being pre-positioned in orbit pending approval for a
reconnaissance and interdiction mission inside Iran."

" 'Pre-positioned'? You mean, you sent a spaceplane and three commandos over Iran without my permission? On your *sole* authority?"

"I have the authority to pre-position and forward-deploy forces
anywhere in the world to support my standing orders and fulfill my
command's responsibilities, sir," Cannon said testily. "The spaceplanes were specifically directed not to enter any foreign airspace
without permission, and they have fully complied with that order. If
they do not receive authorization to proceed with their plan, they
are directed to return to base."

"What kind of nonsense is this, General? This is the spaceplane we're talking about—loaded with McLanahan's armed robots, I assume, correct?"

"It's not nonsense, sir—it's how this command and all major theater commands normally operate," Cannon said, trying mightily to keep his anger and frustration in check. Gardner was the former Secretary of the Navy and Secretary of Defense, for God's sake—he knew this better than anyone . . . ! "As you know, sir, I give orders to pre-position and forward-deploy thousands of men and women all over the world every day, both in support of routine day-to-day operations as well as in preparation for contingency missions. They all operate within standing orders, procedural doctrine, and legal limits. They don't deviate *one iota* until given a direct execution order by myself, and that order isn't given until I receive a go-ahead from the national command authority—you, or the Secretary of Defense. It doesn't matter if we're talking about one spaceplane and five personnel, or an aircraft carrier battle group with twenty ships, seventy aircraft, and ten thousand personnel."

"You seem to believe that the spaceplanes are simple little windup toy planes that no one notices or cares about, General," the President said. "You may think it's routine to send a spaceplane over Iran or an aircraft carrier battle group off someone's coastline, but I assure you, the entire world is in mortal fear of them. Wars have been started by far less. It's obvious your attitude toward the weapons systems under your command has to change, General, and I mean *now*." Cannon had no response. "What members of McLanahan's Battle Force are aboard?"

"Two Tin Men and one CID unit, sir."

"Jesus . . . that's not a recon team, that's a damned *strike team*! They can take on an entire infantry company! What were you thinking, General? Did you think McLanahan was going to fly that kind of force all that way and not use them? What in hell were McLanahan's robots going to do in Iran?"

"Sensors picked up unusual and suspicious activity at a remote highway airbase in eastern Iran that had previously been used by the Iranian Revolutionary Guards," Cannon said. "General McLanahan believes the base is secretly being reopened either by the Iranians or by the Russians. His satellite imagery can't give him precise enough pictures to tell for sure, so he requested an insertion of a three-person Battle Force squad to take a look and, if necessary, destroy the base."

"Destroy the base?" the President thundered, angrily slapping the handset into an open hand. "My God, he authorized McLanahan to send an armed spaceplane over Iran to destroy a military base, and *I didn't know about it?* Is he in*sane?*" He raised the receiver: "And when were you going to let the rest of us know about McLanahan's little plan, General—after World War Four was under way?"

"McLanahan's plan has been passed along to us here at Strategic Command, and my operations staff is reviewing it and will be presenting a recommendation to the Secretary of Defense," Cannon replied. "We should be making a decision any moment—"

"I'll make a decision for you *right now,* General: I want that spaceplane to land as soon as possible back at their home base," the President said. "Do you understand me? I don't want those commandos deployed, or that spaceplane to land, anywhere but back in Nevada or wherever the hell it's from, unless it's a life-or-death emergency. And I don't want one thing to be launched, ejected, or otherwise leave that spacecraft that might be considered an attack on anyone . . . *noth-ing.* Am I making myself perfectly clear, General Cannon?"

"Yes, sir."

"And if that spaceplane crosses one political boundary anywhere on the planet under that damned sixty-mile altitude limit, you will lose your stars, General Cannon . . . *all* of them!" the President went on hotly. "You overstepped your authority, General, and I hope to hell I don't have to spend the rest of my first term in office explaining, correcting, and apologizing for this monumental blunder. Now get on it."

The President slammed the phone down, then took his seat, fuming. After a few moments of muttering to himself, he barked, "I want Cannon fired."

"Sir, technically he *does* have the authority to move his assets any-where he wants to on routine missions," National Security Adviser Carlyle said. "He doesn't need permission from the national defense authority—you or the Secretary of Defense—for day-to-day opera-tions."

"But we usually tell the Russians before we move any weapon systems that might be confused as an attack, correct?"

"Yes, sir—that's always a wise precaution," Carlyle said. "But if the theater commander needed to position his assets in preparation for an actual mission, we aren't obligated to tell the Russians any-thing. We don't even have to lie to them and tell them it's a training mission or something."

"Part of the problem with these spaceplanes, Conrad, is that they move *too* quickly," Chief of Staff Kordus said. "Even if this was a routine mission, they're around the world in the blink of an eye. We've got to put stricter controls on those guys."

"If Cannon had something going, something *important,* he should have told me or Turner before launching that spaceplane," the Presi-dent said. "Walter's right: those spaceplanes are too fast and too threatening to just launch them anytime, even on a perfectly peace-ful, benign, routine mission—which this certainly was *not.* But I thought I made it clear to everyone that I didn't want the spaceplanes up unless it was an emergency or a war. Am I mistaken about that?"

"No, sir, but apparently General Cannon thought this was a pretty serious indication, because he moved very quickly. He—"

"It doesn't matter," the President insisted. "The Russians spotted him, and I'm sure they're radioing the Iranians, Turkmenis, and half the spies in the Middle East to be on the lookout for the Battle Force. The gig is blown. The Russians are hopping mad, and so will the United Nations, our allies, the media, and the American people be as soon as they find out about this—"

"Which will probably be any minute now," Kordus added, "be-cause we know Zevitin runs and leaks his information to the Euro-pean press, who can't wait to excoriate us on the most trivial matter.

On something this big, they'll have a field day. They'll roast us alive for the next month."

"Just when things were starting to settle down," the President said wearily, lighting another cigarette, "Cannon, Backman, and especially McLanahan have managed to stir it all up again."

"The spaceplane will be on the ground before the press can run with this, Joe," the chief of staff said, "and we'll just refuse to confirm or deny any of the Russians' allegations. The thing will die out soon enough."

"It'd better," Gardner said. "But just to be sure, Conrad, I want the spaceplanes grounded until further notice. I want all of them to stay put. No training, no so-called routine missions, *nothing*." He looked around the suite and, raising his voice just enough to show his irritation and let anyone outside the suite hear, asked, "Is that clear enough for everyone? No more unauthorized missions! They stay grounded, and *that's that*!" There was a chorus of muted "Yes, Mr. President" responses.

"Find out exactly when that spaceplane will be on the ground so I can notify Zevitin before someone impeaches or assassinates his ass," the President added. "And find out from the flight docs when McLanahan can get off that space station and be brought back to Earth so I can fire his ass too." He took a deep drag of his cigarette, stubbed it out, then reached for his empty coffee mug. "And on your way out, have that stewardess bring me something hot."

CHAPTER SIX

It is difficult to overcome one's passions, and impossible to satisfy them.

— MARGUERITE DE LA SABLIÈRE

ABOARD THE XR-A9 BLACK STALLION SPACEPLANE

THAT SAME TIME

"Two minutes to re-entry initiation, crew," Major Jim Terranova announced. "Re-entry countdown initiated. First auto countdown hold in one minute. Report when your checklist is complete."

"S-One, roger," Macomber responded.

"How are you feeling, Whack?" Terranova asked.

"Thanks to copious amounts of pure oxygen, a little Transcendental Meditation, not using the eye-pointing electronic checklists, and the mind-numbing routine of still more damned checklists to perform, I feel pretty good," Macomber responded. "Wish this thing had windows."

"I'll put it on the wish list, but don't count on it anytime soon."

"It's a pretty spectacular sight, guys," Frenchy Moulain said. "This is my eleventh flight in orbit and I never get tired of it."

"It looks pretty much the same after the first orbit," groused Chris Wohl. "I've been on the station three times, and it just feels like you're standing on a *really* tall TV tower, looking down."

"Only the sergeant major could minimize a sight like *this,*" Moulain said. "Ask to spend a couple nights on the station, Whack. Bring lots of data cards for your camera. It's pretty cool. You'll find yourself waking up at all times of the night and scheduling window time a day in advance just to take a picture."

"I doubt that very much," Macomber said dryly. He received a notification beep in his helmet. "I'm getting another data dump from the NIRTSats, guys." NIRTSats, or Need It Right This Second Satellites, were small "microsatellites," no bigger than a refrigerator, designed to do a specific task such as surveillance or communications relay from low-Earth orbit. Because they were smaller, carried less positioning thruster fuel, and had substantially less solar radiation shielding, the NIRTSats stayed in orbit for very short periods of time, usually less than a month. They were launched from aircraft aboard orbital boosters or inserted into orbit from the Black Stallion spaceplanes. A constellation of four to six NIRTSats had been put into an eccentric orbit designed to maximize coverage of Iran, making multiple passes over Tehran and the major military bases throughout the country since the military coup began. "Finish your checklists and let's go over the new stuff before we get squished again."

"I don't think we'll have time unless we delay re-entry for another orbit," Terranova said. "You'll have to review the data after we land."

"Listen, we have time . . . we'll *make* the time, MC," Macomber said. "We already launched on this mission without any proper mission planning, so we need to go over this new data right away."

"Not another argument," Moulain said, exasperated. "Listen, S-One, just run your checklists and get ready for re-entry. You know what happened last time you weren't paying attention to the flight: your stomach gave you a little warning."

"I'll be ready, SC," Macomber said. "Ground team, finish your checklist, report when complete, and let's get on the new data dump. S-One is complete." Turlock and Wohl reported complete moments later, and Macomber reported that the passengers were ready for re-entry. Moulain acknowledged the call and, tired of arguing with the zoomie again right before an important phase of flight, said nothing else.

Cautiously, Macomber opened the new satellite data file using voice commands instead of the faster but vertigo-causing eye-pointing system, allowing the data to flow onto the old imagery so he could see changes to the target area. What he got was a confusing jumble of images. "What the hell . . . looks like the data's corrupted," he said over private intercom, which allowed him to talk to his Ground Force team members without disturbing the flight crew. "Nothing's in the right place. They'll have to resend."

"Wait one, sir," Wohl said. "I'm looking at the computer frame-holders on the two shots, and they're matching up." As Macomber understood them—which meant he didn't understand them hardly at all—the frameholders were computer-derived marks that aligned each image with known, fixed landmarks that compensated for dif-ferences in photograph angle and axis and allowed more precise comparisons between images. "Recommend you do not delete the new data yet, sir."

"Make it quick. I'll rattle HQ's cage." Macomber cursed into his helmet, then switched over to the secure satellite communications network: "Rascal to Genesis. Resend the last TacSat images. We got garbage here."

"Stand by, Rascal." Jeez, I *really* hate that call-sign, Macomber complained to himself. A few moments later: "Rascal, this is Gene-sis, set code Alpha Nine, repeat, Alpha Nine. Acknowledge."

"*What?* Is that the *abort code?*" Macomber thundered. "Are they telling us we're not going in?"

"Shut up, S-One, until we get this figured out," Moulain snapped. "MC, did the authentication come in?"

"Affirmative—got it just now," Terranova said. "The mission's

been scrubbed, crew. We're directed to remain in present orbit until
we get a flight plan change to a transfer orbit that will bring us back
for a refueling and landing ASAP. Canceling re-entry procedure
checklist . . . 'leopards' secure, checklist canceled."

Macomber punched a fist into his hand and was instantly sorry
he did so—it felt as if he punched a steel wall. "What in hell is going
on? Why didn't we get a clearance? This is bull—"

"Rascal, this is Genesis." This time it was David Luger himself,
calling from the battle management area at HAWC. "That data
dump was valid, Rascal, I repeat, *valid*. We're looking it over, but it
looks like the landing zone is hot."

"Well, that's the reason we're going in, isn't it, Genesis?" Macomber asked. "Let us drop in there and we'll take care of business."

"Your mission was scrubbed by the White House, Whack, not us,"
Luger said, the tension obvious in his voice. "They want you guys back
home right away. We're computing a re-entry schedule now. It's looking like you'll have to stay up for at least another day before we can—"

"Another *day*! You've gotta be shitting me—!"

"Stand by, Rascal, stand by—"

There was a moment's pause, with a lot of encryption clicking and
chattering on the frequency; then a different voice called: "Rascal,
Stud, this is Odin." This was from McLanahan, up on Armstrong
Space Station. "Recon satellites are picking up strong India-Juliet radar signals coming from your target area. Looks like a long-range
search radar. We're analyzing now."

"A radar, eh?" Macomber commented. He started studying the
new NIRTSat images again. Sure enough, it was the same Soltanabad highway airbase . . . but now all the craters were gone, and several semi tractor-trailers, troops and supply trucks, helicopters, and a
large fixed-wing aircraft were parked on the ramp. "Looks like you
were right, Odin. The bastards are setting the place up again."

"Listen to me, guys," McLanahan said, and the tone of his voice
even over the encrypted satellite link was plainly very ominous indeed.
"I don't like the smell of this. You'd be safer if you deorbited, but you've
been ordered to return to base, so we have to keep you up there."

"What's the problem, sir?" Moulain asked. "Is there something you're not telling us?"

"You cross the target's horizon in eleven minutes. We're trying to compute if we have enough time to deorbit you and have you land in central Asia or the Caucasus instead of overflying Soltanabad."

"*Central Asia!* You want us to land *where* . . . ?"

"Button it, Whack!" Moulain shouted. "What's going on, Odin? What do you think is down there?"

There was a long pause; then McLanahan responded simply: "Stud One-One."

He could have not made a more explosive response. Stud One-One was the XR-A9 Black Stallion that was shot down over Iran in the early days of the military coup, when the Air Battle Force was hunting down and destroying Iranian medium- and long-range mobile ballistic missiles that threatened not only the anti-theocratic insurgents but all of Iran's neighbors as well. The spaceplane was downed not by a surface-to-air missile or fighter jet but by an extremely powerful laser similar to the Kavaznya anti-satellite laser built by the Soviet Union over two decades earlier . . . that had appeared not over Russia, but in Iran.

"What do we do, sir?" Moulain asked, the fear thick in her voice. "What do you want us to do?"

"We're working on it," Patrick said from Armstrong Space Station. "We're trying to see if we can start you down right now in time to stay out of line of sight, or at least out of radar coverage."

"We can translate right now and get ready," Terranova said.

"Do it," Patrick said immediately. He then spoke, "Duty Officer, get me the President of the United States, immediately."

"*Yes, General McLanahan,*" the computer-synthesized female voice of Dreamland's virtual "Duty Officer" responded. A moment later: "*General McLanahan, your call is being forwarded to the Secretary of Defense. Please stand by.*"

"I want to speak with the President of the United States. It's urgent."

"Yes, General McLanahan. Please stand by." Another long moment later: *"General McLanahan, your 'urgent' request has been forwarded to the President's chief of staff. Please stand by."*

That was probably the best he was going to do, Patrick thought, so he didn't redirect the Duty Officer again. "Inform the chief of staff that it's an emergency."

"The 'urgent' request has been upgraded to an 'emergency' request, General. Please stand by."

Time was running out, Patrick thought. He thought about just having the Black Stallion crew declare an inflight emergency—there were dozens of glitches occurring on every flight that could constitute a *real* no-shit emergency—but he needed to be sure the Stud had someplace to land before ordering them to drop out of orbit.

"This is Chief of Staff Kordus."

"Mr. Kordus, this is General McLanahan. I'm—"

"I don't like being called by your computerized staffers, General, and neither does the President. If you want to talk to the President, show us the simple courtesy of doing it yourself."

"Yes, sir. I'm on board Armstrong Space Station, and I'm—"

"I know where you are, General—my staff was watching the live broadcast with great interest until you abruptly cut it off," Kordus said. "When we give you permission to do a live interview we expect you to finish it. Mind telling me why you cut it off like that?"

"I believe the Russians have placed an anti-spacecraft weapon of some kind, possibly the same laser that downed the Black Stallion over Iran last year, in an isolated highway airbase in Iran once used by the Revolutionary Guard Corps," Patrick responded. "Our sensors picked up the new activity at the base and alerted us. Now our unmanned reconnaissance aircraft are picking up extremely high-powered radar signals from that very same location that are consistent with the anti-spacecraft laser's acquisition and tracking system. I believe the Russians will attack our Black Stallion spacecraft if it passes overhead still in orbit, and I need permission to deorbit the spacecraft and divert it away from the target area."

"You have positive proof that the Russians are behind this? How do you know this?"

"We have satellite imagery showing the base is now completely active, with fixed-wing aircraft, trucks, and vehicles that appear similar to the vehicles we detected in Iran where we believe the laser that downed the Black Stallion came from. The radar signals confirm it. Sir, I need permission immediately to divert that flight. We can have it come out of orbit and maneuver it as much as possible with all but emergency fuel until it reaches the atmosphere, and then we can fly it away from the target area to an alternate landing site."

"The President has already ordered you to land the spaceplane back in the United States at its home base, General. Did you not copy that order?"

"I did, sir, but complying with that order means flying the spaceplane over the target base, and I believe it will be attacked if we do so. The only way we can protect the crew now is to deorbit the spaceplane to keep it as low as possible on the horizon until we can—"

"General, I don't understand a word of what you just said," Kordus said. "All I understand is that you have a strong hunch that your spaceplane is in danger, and you're asking the President to countermand an order he just issued. Is this correct?"

"Yes, sir, but I need to stress the extreme danger of—"

"I got that part loud and clear, General McLanahan," Kordus said, the exasperation thick in his voice. "If you start bringing the spaceplane down, will you be overflying anyone's airspace, and if so, whose?"

"I don't know precisely, sir, but I'd say countries in eastern Europe, the Middle East—"

"Russia?"

"Possibly, sir. Extreme western Russia."

"Moscow?"

Patrick paused, and when he did he could hear the chief of staff say something under his breath. "I don't know if it will be below the sixty-six-mile limit, sir, but depending on how fast and how successful we are at maneuvering the—"

"I'll take that as a yes. Perfect, just perfect. Your spaceplane coming out of orbit right over the capital of Russia will look like an ICBM attack for damned sure, won't it?" He didn't wait for an answer. "This is precisely the nightmare scenario the President was afraid of. He's going to tear your throat out, McLanahan." He paused for a moment; then: "How long does the President have to decide this, General?"

"About five minutes, sir."

"*For God's sake, McLanahan!* Five minutes? Everything is a crisis with you!" Kordus shouted. "But poor planning on your part doesn't constitute an emergency on our part!"

"Lives could be at stake, sir."

"I'm well aware of that, General!" Kordus snapped. "But if you had bothered to wait and have this plan approved by the White House and the Pentagon before launching the spaceplane, none of this would be happening!" He muttered something else under his breath; then: "I'll take this request to the President right away. In the meantime, stay on the line because you will have to explain all this to the National Security Adviser so he can properly advise the President, because I doubt if *you* have the capacity to explain it clearly enough to him to his satisfaction—or that he would even listen to you if you tried. Stand *by*."

"Crew, be advised, we're doing a *y*-translation in preparation for deorbit. Stand by." Using her multifunction display and her piloting skills, Moulain used the Black Stallion's hydrazine thrusters to flip the spaceplane around so it was flying tailfirst. The maneuver took almost two minutes—a record for her. Everything felt exactly the same to the crewmembers in the passenger module, and even Macomber's stomach didn't complain. "Maneuver complete, Genesis. When do we start down? When can we fire the 'leopards'?"

"We need to find out if you can reach a safe landing runway if you deorbited right now," Dave Luger interjected. "We're also looking for a tanker that can refuel you in case you can't reach a suitable airport, and we need permission from the White House to bring you down over national boundaries."

"You need *what?*" Macomber retorted. "You think the Russians are going to shoot at us with a fucking laser, and you need *permission* to get us the hell out of here?"

"We're running the calculations, Major—put a sock in it and let us do our work," Luger said sternly, unaccustomed to being yelled at by a field-grade officer. Still, the tone in his voice made it obvious he wasn't all that happy about the circumstances either. "Stand by."

"Do it, Frenchy," Macomber said on intercom. "Get us the hell out of here."

"I can't do that without authorization, S-One."

"The hell you can't. You're the spacecraft commander—you made that real clear to *me,* remember? Exercise some of your authority and *get us the hell out of here!*"

"I can't just drop us out of the sky without knowing where we go once we re-enter the atmosphere," Moulain said. "I need to know where we'll be when we resume atmospheric flight, what our best range will be, which runway we'll approach, what the terrain is, how long the runway is, what the political, diplomatic, and security situation will—"

"For Christ's sake, Frenchy, stop asking questions and hit the damned button!" Macomber shouted. "Don't wait for some politician to wave his hand or give us the finger—just *do it!*"

"Shut up and stand by, Macomber!" Moulain shouted. "We can't just pull over and shut off the engine. Just hold your water, will you?"

"We'll be crossing the target area's horizon in about two minutes," Terranova reported.

"We briefed several recovery, alternate, and emergency bases in eastern Europe, India, and the western Pacific," Macomber persisted. "We *know* we have alternates. Just declare an emergency and land at one of them."

"We've already passed most of the safe emergency bases," Terranova said. "The alternate landing sites we had picked were designed in case of failure to insert into orbit, failure of re-entry burn engines, or alternate landing sites if we started deorbit but weren't authorized to go into the target area. We're past that point now. If we didn't deorbit by now, the plan was to overfly the target area, transfer orbits if we had enough fuel, or stay in orbit until we could land back at Dreamland. We can't just turn on a dime and head back the other way."

"So we're screwed," Turlock said. "We've got to overfly the target area now."

"Not necessarily, but the longer we delay firing the 'leopards,' the fewer options we have," Terranova said. "We can always bleed off more energy and drop faster through the atmosphere to try to stay as low to the horizon as possible, then once we're back in the atmosphere we can use the rest of the available fuel to fly away from the tracking radar."

"Then do it!"

"If we bleed off all our energy and don't have enough fuel to make it to a suitable landing site, we're dead," Moulain said. "This bird glides just a little bit better than a damned *brick*. I'm not going to throw away all our options unless there's a plan! Besides, we don't even know if there's a Russian anti-satellite laser down there. This could all be just a bad case of paranoia."

"Then there's one more option . . ."

"No way, MC."

"What's the last option?" Macomber asked.

"Jettisoning the passenger module," Terranova said.

"What?"

"The passenger module is designed to be its own re-entry vehicle and lifeboat . . ."

"I'm not releasing the module except in an emergency," Moulain insisted. "Absolutely not."

"There's no way we can make it down by ourselves!" Macomber cried.

"The simulations say it can, although we've never tested it for real," Terranova said. "The passenger module has its own reaction control system, high-tech heat shields better than the Stud, parachutes and impact attenuation bags for landing, a pretty good environmental system—"

" 'Pretty good' isn't good enough, MC—the captain doesn't have any armor on," Chris Wohl interjected.

"It'll work, Sergeant Major."

"I'm not jettisoning anything, and *that's that,*" Moulain cut in. "That's the last resort only. I'm not even going to consider it unless all this fearmongering comes true. Now everyone shut up for a minute." On the command channel: "Genesis, Odin, what do you got for us?"

"Nothing," Patrick responded. "I've spoken to the chief of staff, and he's going to talk to the President. I'm waiting to talk to SECDEF or the National Security Adviser. You're going to have to—"

"I've got it!" Dave Luger suddenly cut in. "If we deorbit now and use max-G maneuvers to lose altitude, we should have enough energy to make it to Baku on the Caspian coast of Azerbaijan. If not, you can make it to Neftcala, which is an Azerbaijan border and coastal patrol base. Turkey and the United States are expanding an airstrip there and you might have enough runway to make it. The third option—"

"Jettison the passenger module into the Caspian Sea, then ditch the Stud in the Caspian Sea or eject before hitting the water depending on how out of control we become," Moulain intoned.

"Stand by, Stud," Patrick said after a short pause. "Genesis, I'm studying the latest images of the target area, and I'm concluding that the trucks and setup at Soltanabad are virtually identical to the ones we saw in Kabudar Ahang in Iran. I believe the Russians set up their mobile anti-spacecraft laser in Soltanabad. Can you verify?"

"General, are you sure this Russian threat is for real? If we do this, there's no turning back."

"No, I'm not sure of any of this," Patrick admitted. "But the signs are looking just like Stud One-One. Genesis?"

"I'm double-checking, Odin," Dave Luger said. "Remember they faked the setup at Kabudar Ahang to suck in the Battle Force. They could be doing the very same thing again."

"We'll know in about sixty seconds, crew," Terranova said.

"We can't wait," Patrick said finally. "Stud, this is Odin, I'm ordering you to deorbit, do a max-rate re-entry interface profile, and attempt an emergency landing at Baku or Neftcala, Azerbaijan. Genesis, upload the flight plan to the Black Stallion and be sure it's executed. Do you copy?"

"Odin, I copy, but are you sure about this?" Moulain asked. "It doesn't make any sense."

"Just do it, Frenchy," Macomber said. "If he's wrong and everything goes snafu, we might take a swim in the damned polluted Caspian Sea with the caviar. Big deal. Been there, done that. If he's right, we'll still be alive in an hour. Do it."

"Flight plan uploaded," Luger reported. "Awaiting execution."

"Stud, advise when you execute deorbit procedures."

"What are you waiting for, Frenchy?" Macomber shouted. "Start us down! Fire the rockets!"

"I don't want to crash into the Caspian Sea," Moulain said. "If we don't make it, we'll have no option but to ditch—"

"Dammit, Frenchy, get us down *now!*" Macomber shouted. "What's with you?"

"*I don't believe General McLanahan, that's why!*" Moulain cried out. "I don't believe any of this!"

"Stud, I'm sure this is a trap," Patrick said. "I think we stumbled onto a Russian anti-spacecraft laser weapon site in Iran. If you don't get out of there, any way you can, their laser will burn through your heat shielding and destroy the spacecraft. I don't want to take that risk. Deorbit the spacecraft and get out of there."

"Crossing the target's horizon, *now,*" Terranova said.

"Stud, that was an order: deorbit the spacecraft," Patrick said. "Your objection is noted. I take full responsibility. Now *do it.*"

"I'm sorry, sir, but I copied valid and authenticated orders to the contrary from the national command authority: stay in orbit until we're in a position to return to Groom Lake," Moulain said. "Those orders supersede yours. We're staying. MC, remove the deorbit flight plan and reload the previous one."

"Frenchy—"

"Do it, MC," Moulain said. "That's an order. I'll stay in this ori-entation to conserve thruster fuel, but we're staying in orbit, and that's final."

The radios and intercoms got very quiet after that, with Luger and McLanahan feeding the crew and each other a steady stream of radar threat warnings and updated reconnaissance imagery. Time seemed to drag on forever. Finally, Macomber said, "What the hell is going on, Genesis, and how long until we're out of the shit?"

"Four minutes ten seconds until we cross back below the target area horizon," Dave Luger responded.

"I'm sorry, Odin," Moulain said, "but I had to make a decision. I'm following orders."

"I hope I'm wrong, SC," Patrick responded. "You did what you thought was right. We'll talk about it after you're home safe."

"How are we doing on that Baku landing site, Genesis?" Ter-ranova asked.

"You'll lose it in thirty seconds. You won't have enough energy to make it to Forward Operating Base Warrior in Kirkuk, Iraq, after you re-enter the atmosphere—Herat, Afghanistan, is your best op-tion, but you'll still have to overfly Soltanabad. Another option might be the deserts of southern Turkmenistan—we can get a special ops team from Uzbekistan in to help you quickly."

"You suggesting we land in Turkmenistan, sir?"

"I didn't say 'land,' MC."

Terranova gulped. Luger obviously meant for them to "jettison the aircraft"—let it crash-land in the desert. "What's the next abort base?"

"Karachi and Hyderabad beyond that."

"We're ready to fire the 'leopards,'" Terranova said. "Ten-second checklist hold. Should I set the re-entry for maximum decelera-tion?"

"We're not going to deorbit," Moulain said. "The Russians wouldn't dare take a shot at us. Leonid Zevitin's not crazy. The guy can *dance,* for God's sake!" The radios sparkled with low chuckles. But she looked at her aft-cockpit camera and nodded to Terranova, silently ordering him to program the computers for a maximum-rate speed and altitude loss. "I mean, think about it, everyone: no male who knows how to dance would be nutty enough to—"

Suddenly they heard, *"Warning, warning, laser detected . . . warning, warning, hull temperature increasing, stations two hundred fifty through two-ninety . . . warning, hull temperatures approaching operational limits . . . !"*

"The Kavaznya laser!" Patrick McLanahan exclaimed. "They're attacking from extreme range. Stud, get out of there *now!*"

"Initiate deorbit procedures!" Moulain shouted. "Crew, stand by to deorbit immediately! 'Leopards' engines throttling up!"

". . . hull temperature rate warning, stations two-seventy through two-ninety . . . warning, warning . . . !"

The crew was slammed back into their seats as the Laser Pulse Detonation Rocket System engines fired at full power. The immense power of the hybrid rocket engines immediately and dramatically decelerated the Black Stallion aircraft, and it quickly began its fall to Earth. Macomber cried out as the G-forces quickly increased, far past anything he had previously experienced. Soon he could no longer muster the strength to make any noise at all—it took all of his concentration to inflate his lungs enough to keep from passing out.

"Passing twenty-eight thousand feet per second," Terranova said amidst the almost-constant warning messages. "Passing ninety miles' altitude . . . 'leopards' at ninety percent power, three point zero Gs . . ."

"Go to one hundred and ten percent power," Moulain grunted through the pressure.

"That's over five Gs, SC," Terranova said. "We'll have to sustain that for—"

"Do it, MC," Moulain ordered. "Crew, SC, it's going to get real uncomfortable for a few minutes. Keep ahead of it the best you can." A few moments later, her words were cut off by a feeling that her chest was going to implode as the G-forces nearly doubled. Cries of anguish and surprise were evident. "Hang . . . on . . . crew . . ."

"Five point three Gs," Terranova gasped. "Jesus . . . passing twenty-five K, passing eighty miles . . ."

"Oh God, how much longer?" someone murmured—it was impossible to tell who was speaking now.

STRATEGIC AIR FORCES ALTERNATE OPERATIONS COMMAND CENTER, POLDOSK, RUSSIAN FEDERATION

THAT SAME TIME

With the destruction of Engels Air Base near Saratov and the bombing of R'azan underground command center by the Americans, air forces chief of staff General Andrei Darzov had reactivated and modernized an old civil defense shelter and reserve forces reconstitution center southwest of Moscow called Poldosk for use as his evacuation and alternate command post. It didn't have an air base or even room for a large helicopter landing pad, but it had underground rail lines adjacent to the facility, plenty of freshwater supplies (as fresh as could be expected in the Greater Moscow area) . . .

. . . and—more importantly, Darzov believed—it was sufficiently close to large numbers of city dwellers that even someone as crazy as the American bomber commander Lieutenant General Patrick McLanahan might think twice about bombing the place.

Because of its mostly modern high-speed data and communications upgrades, Poldosk today served yet another purpose: as the monitoring and command center for the *Molnija* anti-spacecraft air-launched missile and *Fanar* anti-spacecraft laser systems. From a simple room with a bank of four computers, Darzov maintained contact with his forces in the field via secure high-speed Internet and voice-over-IP connections. The command center was completely mobile, could be packed up in less than an hour and set up elsewhere in about as much time, and in an emergency could be run from a single laptop computer and secure cellular or satellite phone anywhere on the planet.

This evening, the focus was on Soltanabad. It was unfortunate that the Americans found *Fanar* so quickly—it had to be blind luck, or maybe some Iranian Revolutionary Guards Corps members turned traitor and informed on them to the coup leader Hesarak

Buzhazi or to the Americans. But he had set up *Fanar* at Soltanabad precisely because so many American spacecraft overflew the area so often. It was, as the Americans put it, a "target-rich environment."

Darzov scowled at a new readout and hit the TRANSMIT button on the computer keyboard: "Striker, this is Keeper. Say status. You terminated the attack . . . why?"

"We had full optronic lock on the target and opened fire as ordered, General," the chief engineer and project officer at Soltanabad, Wolfgang Zypries, replied. "But seconds after we initiated the attack we lost contact." Zypries was a German laser engineer and scientist and formerly a colonel in the German air force. Unknown to him, Zypries' longtime girlfriend was a Russian spy, hacking into his computer at home and transferring volumes of classified material to Moscow. When his girlfriend informed him of who she was and that the German Militärischer Abschirmdienst, or Military Screen Service's counterespionage group, was on his tail, he allowed himself to be whisked off to Russia. Darzov immediately plied him with everything he desired—money, a house, and all the women he could handle—to work on improving and mobilizing the Kavaznya anti-spacecraft laser system. After over five years' work, he was more successful than even Darzov dared to hope.

"The spacecraft appears to be descending rapidly," Zypries went on. "We suspect our optics were blinded when the spacecraft fired its retrorockets."

"You did brief me that might happen, Colonel," Darzov said. To avoid detection they had decided to use a telescopic electro-optical acquisition and tracking system and keep their extreme long-range space tracking radar in standby. They locked onto the American spaceplane seconds after it crossed the horizon and tracked it with ease. As they hoped, it had not started its descent through the atmosphere, although the highly magnified image showed it was indeed turned in the proper direction to begin slowing down, flying tailfirst. It was still in the perfect position, and Darzov ordered the attack to commence.

The next step in the laser engagement was to hit the target with a higher-powered laser to measure the atmosphere and apply corrections to the main laser's optics, allowing it to focus more precisely on the target before firing the main chemical-oxygen-iodine laser. Darzov and Zypries decided, since the spacecraft was turned in position to fire its retrorockets, to use the main laser itself to make its own corrections in order to engage more rapidly.

"The crew was obviously expecting an attack," Zypries said, "because they fired their main engines seconds after our laser hit. We were able to maintain contact for about fifteen seconds, but the optics were still fine-focusing so we were probably only laying sixty percent power on their hull. Then the optronic system broke lock. They must be squishing their crewmembers like bugs inside that thing—they are decelerating at three times the normal rate. I am tracking them on infrared scanners but that's not precise enough for the main laser, so I need permission to use the main radar to reacquire and engage."

"Are they still in range and high enough to engage?"

"They are at one hundred thirty kilometers' altitude, sixteen hundred kilometers downrange, decelerating quickly below seven thousand eight hundred meters per second—they are dropping like a stone, but they are well within the laser's engagement envelope," Zypries assured him. "The structure of that spacecraft must be incredibly strong to withstand that kind of stress. They will be in the atmosphere soon but they will not be able to fly away fast enough now. I will get him for you, General."

"Then permission granted to continue the attack, Colonel," Darzov said immediately. "Good hunting."

"Five point seven Gs . . . twenty-two K feet per second . . . seventy-five miles . . . five point nine Gs . . ." It seemed to take forever for Terranova to grunt out each readout. "Passing seventy miles . . . sixty-five miles, reaching entry interface, crew, 'leopards' cutoff." The G-forces suddenly were reduced, followed by a chorus of moans and swearing from throughout the spacecraft. Macomber couldn't believe he hadn't passed out from that sustained pressure. He still felt the deceleration forces as the spaceplane continued to lose energy, but it wasn't nearly as bad as it was when the "leopards" were firing. "Crew, report."

"You guys okay?" Macomber asked the others in the passenger module. "Sing out."

"S-Two, I'm okay," Turlock said weakly.

"S-Three, okay," Wohl responded, sounding as if nothing at all had just happened. The jarhead bastard was probably sound asleep through it, Macomber thought.

"S-One is okay too. SC, passengers are okay, everything back here's in the green. That was some ride."

"Roger that," Moulain said. "The laser looks like it's broken lock for now. We've initiated maneuvering to entry interface attitude." The Black Stallion began to turn so it was nose-forward again, then pitched up to forty degrees above the horizon for atmospheric entry, presenting its bottom heat shields to the onrushing atmosphere to protect the ship against the heat built up by friction. "MC, let's brief the approach."

"Roger," Terranova said. "We've passed the terminal alignment cylinder for Baku, so I've programmed in Herat, Afghanistan, as our landing site. We are still on max-energy descent profile, and Herat is fairly close—around thirteen hundred miles—so we have plenty of energy to reach the base. In sixty seconds the airflow pressure will be great enough for the adaptive surfaces on the Stud to take effect, and we'll shut down the reaction control system, transition to maximum-drag profile, and deviate east over Turkmenistan to stay away from Soltanabad. Once we pass one hundred thousand feet we can transition to atmospheric flight, shut down the 'leopards,' start up the turbojets, and head down on a normal approach profile."

"How much gas do we have, MC?" Macomber asked.

"After we start up the turbojets, we'll have less than an hour of fuel, but we'll be gliding in at around Mach five so we'll have plenty of energy to get rid of before we need the turbojets," Terranova replied. "We'll start securing the thrusters and get ready to secure the 'leopards' so when we—"

"Warning, warning, search radar, twelve o'clock, nine hundred sixty miles, India-Juliet band," the computerized voice of the threat warning receiver suddenly blared. Seconds later: *"Warning, warning, target tracking radar, twelve o'clock, nine hundred fifty miles . . . warning, warning, pulse-Doppler target tracking radar, twelve o'clock, nine hundred forty miles . . . warning, warning, laser detected, twelve o'clock . . . warning, warning . . . !"*

"They hit us with radar at almost a *thousand miles?*" Terranova blurted out. "That's impossible!"

"It's the Kavaznya radar, crew," Patrick McLanahan said. "The range of that thing is incredible, and now it's mobile."

"Warning, warning, emergency cooling system activated . . . warning, warning, spot hull temperature increasing, station one-ninety . . ."

"What do we do, Odin?" Lisa Moulain cried on the radio. "What do I do?"

"The only choice you have is to roll the spacecraft to keep the laser energy from focusing on any one spot for too long," Patrick said. "Use the reaction control system to roll. Once your mission adaptive system is effective, you can use max bank angle to fly away from the laser and do heading changes as much as possible to keep the laser off you. Dave, I need you to launch the Vampires from Batman Air Base and knock out that laser site! I want Soltanabad turned into a smoking *hole!*"

"They're on the way, Odin," Luger responded.

But as the seconds ticked by, it was obvious that nothing Moulain could do was going to work. They were getting almost constant overtemperature warnings from dozens of spots on the hull, and some began reporting leaks and structural integrity losses. Once Moulain accidentally looked directly at the laser light shining through the cockpit windshield and was partially blinded even though they both had their dark visors lowered.

Terranova finally muted the threat warnings—they were doing them no good anymore. "Frenchy, you okay?"

"I can't see, Jim," Moulain said on the "private" intercom setting so the crewmembers in the passenger compartment couldn't hear.

"I glanced at the laser beam for a split second, and all I see are big black holes in my vision. I screwed up. I killed us all."

"Keep rolling, Frenchy," Terranova said. "We'll make it."

Moulain began nudging the side control stick back and forth, using the thrusters to turn and roll the spacecraft. Terranova fed her a constant stream of advisories when she was going too far. The temperature warnings were almost constant no matter how hard she tried. "We've got to jettison the passenger module," Moulain said, still on "private" intercom. "They might have a chance."

"We're way over the G-force and speed limits for jettison, Frenchy," Terranova said. "We don't even know if they'll survive even if we slowed down enough—we've never jettisoned the module before."

"There's only one way to find out," Moulain said. "I'm going to initiate a powered descent to try to slow us down enough to jettison the passenger module. We'll use every drop of fuel we have left to slow us down. I'll need your help. Tell me when we're ass-end backward." She gently rolled wings-level, then with Terranova's assistance turned the Black Stallion so they were flying tailfirst again. On full intercom she spoke, "Crew, prepare for max retrorocket fire, powered-descent profile. 'Leopards' coming online."

"What?" Macomber asked. "You're firing the 'leopards' again? What—?"

He didn't get to finish his question. Moulain activated the Laser Pulse Detonation Rocket System engines and immediately pushed them up to powered-descent profile power, then to maximum power, far exceeding the normal G-limits for passengers and crewmembers. Their speed dropped dramatically—they were still flying at over Mach 5, but that was over half of the speed they would normally be flying. Everyone in the passenger module was hit with G-forces so severe and so unexpected that they immediately blacked out. Jim Terranova blacked out too . . .

. . . and so did Lisa Moulain, but not before she opened the cargo bay doors on the upper fuselage of the XR-A9 Black Stallion, unlocked the securing bolts holding the module to the cargo bay, lifted a red-guarded switch, and activated it . . .

. . . and at the very instant the doors were fully open, the securing bolts were free, and the module's jettison rockets fired, the Black Stallion exhausted every pound of propellant left in its tanks . . . and it was ripped apart by the Russian laser and exploded.

"Target destroyed, General," Wolfgang Zypries reported from Soltanabad. "Showing massive speed loss, multiple large targets probably debris, and quickly losing radar and visual contact. Definite kill."

"I understand," General Andrei Darzov responded. Many of the technicians and officers in the room triumphantly raised fists and gave low cheers, but he silenced them with a warning glare. "Now I suggest you get out of there as fast as you can—the Americans have certainly sent a strike force out to destroy that base. They could be there in less than an hour if they launch from Iraq."

"We will be out of here in thirty minutes, General," Zypries said. "Out."

Darzov broke the connection, then activated another and spoke: "Mission accomplished, sir."

"Very well, General," Russian president Leonid Zevitin responded. "What do you expect will be their reaction?"

"They are undoubtedly launching unmanned B-1 bombers from Batman Air Base in Turkey, fitted with the hypersonic attack missiles to attack and destroy the base in Iran," Darzov said. "They could be in position to fire in less than an hour—even as quickly as thirty minutes if they had a plane ready to launch. The target will be struck less than a minute later."

"My God, that's incredible—we need to get our hands on that technology," Zevitin muttered. "I assume your people are haulin' ass and getting away from that base."

"They should be well away before the Americans attack—I assure you, they feel those hypersonic missiles on the backs of their necks even now."

"I'll bet they do. Where was the spaceplane when it went down, General?"

"Approximately one thousand kilometers northwest of Soltana-bad."

"So by chance does that place it . . . over Russia?"

There was a short pause as Darzov checked his computerized maps; then: "Yes, sir, it does. One hundred kilometers northwest of Machackala, the capital of Dagestan province, and three hundred kilometers southeast of the Tupolev-95 bomber base at Mozdok."

"And the debris?"

"Impossible to say, sir. It will probably be scattered for thousands of kilometers between the Caspian Sea and the Iran-Afghanistan border."

"Too bad. Track that debris carefully and advise me if any reaches land. Order a search team from the Caspian Sea Flotilla to begin a search immediately. Have our radar stations alerted our air defense systems?"

"No, sir. The normal air defense and air traffic radar systems would not be able to track a target so high and traveling so fast. Only a dedicated space tracking system would be able to do so."

"So without such radar, we wouldn't know anything has happened yet, would we?"

"Unfortunately not, sir."

"When would you expect the debris to be detected by a regular radar system?"

"We are not tracking the debris anymore since we are breaking down the *Fanar* radar system at Soltanabad," Darzov explained, "but I would guess that within a few minutes we might be able to start picking up the larger pieces as they re-enter the atmosphere. I will have our air defense sites in Dagestan report immediately when debris is detected."

"Very good, General," Zevitin said. "I wouldn't want to complain about the latest American attack against Russia too soon, would I?"

ABOARD AIR FORCE ONE

THAT SAME TIME

"My, my, Mr. President," the female staff sergeant said as she rose from her knees and began rebuttoning her uniform blouse, "you certainly get *my* vote."

"Thank you, Staff Sergeant," President Gardner said, watching her rearrange herself as he zipped his fly. "I think there's a position available on my . . . staff for someone as skilled as you." She smiled at the very much intended double entendre. "Interested?"

"Actually, sir, I've been waiting for an opening in Officer Training School," she replied, looking the commander-in-chief up and down hungrily. "I was told a slot might not open up for another eighteen months. I finished my bachelor's degree and put in my application just last semester. I'm *very* determined to get my commission."

"What was your degree in, sugar?"

"Political science," she replied. "I'm going for a law degree, and then I'd like to get into politics."

"We could sure use someone of your . . . *enthusiasm* in Washington, Staff Sergeant," the President said. He noticed the CALL light blinking on the phone—an urgent call, but not urgent enough to override the DO NOT DISTURB order. "But OTS is in Alabama?"

"Yes, sir."

"That's too bad, honey," the President said, acting disappointed—the *last* thing he wanted was for this one to show up in Washington. Maxwell Air Force Base in Alabama would be perfect—far enough away from Washington to avoid rumors, but close enough to Florida for her to sneak down when he was at his estate in Florida. "I'd sure like to work with you more often, but I admire your dedication to the service. I'm sure I heard of an OTS slot opening up in the next class, and I think you'd fit in perfectly. We'll be in touch."

"Thank you *very* much, Mr. President," the steward said, smoothing out the rest of her hair and uniform, then departing without even a backward glance.

That's the way he liked them, Gardner thought as he took a sip of juice and started to get his heart rate and thoughts back in order: the ones bold and aggressive enough to do anything necessary to get an advantage over all the others, but wise enough to go back to work and avoid getting emotionally involved—*those* were the real powerhouses in Washington. Some did it with talent, brains, or political connections—there was nothing wrong, or different, about the ones who did it on their knees. Plus, she understood the same as he that *both* their careers would be finished if word ever got out about their little rendezvous, so it benefited both of them to do what the other wanted and, more important, keep their mouths shut about it. That one was going to go *very* far.

Seconds later, his mind quickly refocused on the upcoming events and itinerary, he punched off the DO NOT DISTURB button. Moments later his chief of staff and National Security Adviser knocked, checked the peephole to be sure the President was alone, waited a moment, then entered the suite. Both had cell phones up to their ears. Air Force One could act as its own cellular base station, and unlike passengers on commercial airliners there were no restrictions on the use of cell phones inflight on Air Force One—users could light up as many terrestrial cell towers as they liked. "What's going on?" the President asked.

"Either nothing . . . or the shit has just hit the fan, Mr. President," Chief of Staff Walter Kordus said. "Air forces in Europe headquarters got a call from the Sixth Combined Air Operations Center in Turkey requesting confirmation for an EB-1C Vampire bomber flight of two scramble launch out of Batman Air Base in southern Turkey . . . the same ones we grounded after the missile attack in Iran. USAFE called the Pentagon for confirmation since there was no air tasking order for any bomber missions out of Batman."

"You mean, *McLanahan's bombers?*" Kordus's panicked face had the answer. "McLanahan ordered two of his bombers to launch . . . after I ordered them *grounded*? What the hell is going on?"

"I don't know yet, sir," Kordus said. "I told USAFE that no bombers were authorized to launch for any reason, and I ordered them to deny launch clearance. I have a call in to McLanahan and to his deputy Luger out in Nevada, trying to find out what's going on."

"Are the bombers armed?"

"We don't know that yet either, sir. This mission was totally unauthorized."

"Well, we should assume they are—knowing McLanahan, he would keep weapons on his planes even though they're all grounded, unless we specifically ordered him *not* to, and even then he might do it. Just keep them on the ramp until we find out what's going on. What's the story with the spaceplane? Is it still in orbit?"

"I'll check as soon as McLanahan picks up the phone, sir."

"It'd better be, or I'll nail his hide to my bathroom door," the President said, taking another sip of orange juice. "Listen, about the 'meet-and-greet' thing in Orlando . . ." And then he heard Carlyle swear into his phone. "What, Conrad?"

"The B-1 bombers launched," the National Security Adviser said. The President's jaw dropped in surprise. "The tower controller at the air base told the crew to hold their position, but *there is no crew* on those planes—they're remotely controlled from Elliott Air Force Base in Nevada—"

"McLanahan."

"McLanahan is still aboard the space station, so it's his deputy, Brigadier General Luger, in charge of the bombers out of Elliott," Carlyle said. "I've got a call in to Secretary of Defense Turner to order Luger to get those bombers back on the ground. Je-*sus* . . . !"

"He is *out of control*!" the President snapped. "I want him off that space station and in custody immediately! Send a damned U.S. Marshal up there if you have to!"

"Send a U.S. Marshal—into *space*?" Kordus asked. "I wonder if that's ever been done before . . . or if we could get a marshal to volunteer to do that?"

"I'm not kidding around, Walter. McLanahan has to be slapped down before he starts another damned war between us and Russia. Find out what in hell is going on, and do it *fast*. Zevitin will be on the phone before we know it, *again,* and I want to assure him everything is under control."

BATTLE MANAGEMENT AREA, BATTLE
MOUNTAIN AIR RESERVE BASE, NEVADA

THAT SAME TIME

"Headbanger Two-One flight of two is level at flight level three-one-oh, due regard, Mach point nine-one, thirty minutes to launch point," the mission commander reported. "Due regard" meant that they had terminated all normal air traffic control procedures and were flying without official flight-following or civil aviation monitoring . . . because they were going to war.

Two officers sat side by side in a separate section of the BAT-MAN, or battle management area, at Battle Mountain Air Reserve Base in northern Nevada, seated at what appeared to be a normal computer workstation that might be used by a security guard or securities day trader . . . except for the jet-fighter-style joysticks. On each side of the officers were two enlisted technicians with their own bank of computer monitors. The men and women in the room talked into their microphones in muted voices, bodies barely moving, eyes scanning from monitor to monitor. Only an occasional flick of a finger on a keyboard or hand rolling a cursor with a trackball led anyone to believe anything was really happening.

The two officers were piloting two unmanned EB-1C Vampire supersonic "flying battleships" which had launched from their forward operating base in eastern Turkey across northern Iran. Three high-resolution monitors showed the view in front and to the sides of the lead bomber, while other monitors showed performance, systems, and weapons readouts from both planes. Although the two bombers were fully flyable, they were usually flown completely on computer control, reacting autonomously to mission commands entered before the flight and deciding for themselves what to do to accomplish the mission. The ground crew monitored the flight's progress, made changes to the flight plan if necessary, and could take over at any time, but the computers made all the decisions. The technicians watched over the aircraft's systems, monitored the electromagnetic spectrum for threats, and looked over incoming intelligence and reconnaissance data along the route of flight that might affect the mission.

"Genesis copies," David Luger responded. He was back at the battle staff area at Elliott Air Force Base in south-central Nevada, watching the mission unfold on the wall-sized electronic "big boards" before him. Other displays showed enemy threats detected by all High-Technology Aerospace Weapons Center aircraft and satellites and other allied sensors operating in the region. But Luger's attention was drawn to two other displays: the first was the latest satellite imagery of the target area in eastern Iran . . .

. . . and the second was of the satellite space tracking data, which at the moment was blank.

"They're taking down the laser stuff in a pretty big damned hurry," Dave commented. "They must have guessed we'd send bombers to blast the hell out of that base. I'm not sure if we'll get there in time, Muck."

"Push 'em up, Dave," Patrick McLanahan said. He was monitoring the mission as well from the command module on Armstrong Space Station. "Get a tanker airborne to meet the bombers on the way back, but I want those missiles on the way before the Russian cockroaches scatter."

"Roger, Muck. Stand by. Headbanger, this is Genesis. Odin wants the bombers to attack before the target scatters. Push up the bombers and say status of the support tankers."

"Already got the alert tankers taxiing out, Dave," the commander of the Air Battle Force's air forces from Battle Mountain, Major General Rebecca Furness, responded. "He'll be airborne in five minutes."

"Roger that. Odin wants the Vampires pushed up as much as you can."

"As soon as the tanker's within max safe range, we'll push the Vampires up to Mach one point two—that's the max launch speed for the SkySTREAKs. Best we can do with the current mission parameters."

"Suggest you erase the one-hour fuel reserve for the tanker and push up the Vampires now," Luger said.

"Negative—I'm not going to do that, Dave," Rebecca said. Rebecca Furness was the U.S. Air Force's first female combat pilot and first female commander of a tactical combat air unit. When Rebecca's Air Force Reserve B-1B Lancer unit at Reno, Nevada, was closed and the bombers transferred to the High-Technology Aerospace Weapons Center for conversion into manned and unmanned "flying battleships," Furness went along. Now she commanded the five tactical squadrons at the new Reserve base at Battle Mountain, Nevada, composed of converted manned and unmanned B-52 and B-1 bombers, unmanned QA-45C stealth attack aircraft, and KC-76 aerial refueling tankers. "We'll get them, don't worry."

Luger glanced again at the latest satellite image of the highway air base at Soltanabad, Iran. It was only five minutes old, but it already showed a few of the larger trucks gone and what appeared like an entire battalion of workers taking down the rest. "We're running out of time, ma'am. The cockaroaches are scattering quick."

"I know, Dave—I see the pictures too," Rebecca said, "but I'm not risking losing my bombers."

"Like we lost the Stud?"

"Don't give me that crap, Dave—I know what's going on here, and I'm just as mad about it as you are," Rebecca snapped. "But may I remind you that our bombers are the only long-range strike aircraft we have now, and I'm not going to risk them on . . . an unauthorized mission." It was no exaggeration, and Dave Luger knew it: since the American Holocaust, the Russian cruise missile attack on American bomber and intercontinental missile bases four years earlier, the only surviving long-range bombers had been the handful of bombers deployed overseas and the converted B-52 and B-1 bombers based at Battle Mountain.

Furness's bombers soon racked up casualties of their own. All of

Battle Mountain's bombers had been sent to a Russian aerial refueling tanker base in Yakutsk, Siberia, from where Patrick McLanahan led attack missions against nuclear ballistic missile bases throughout Russia. When the American bombers were discovered, then–Russian president General Anatoliy Gryzlov attacked the base with more nuclear-tipped cruise missiles. Half the force had been lost in the devastating attack. The remaining bombers successfully attacked dozens of Russian missile bases, destroying the bulk of their strategic nuclear force; McLanahan himself, aboard one of the last EB-52 Megafortress battleships, attacked and killed Gryzlov in his underground bunker southeast of Moscow in a grueling twenty-hour-long mission that took him across the entire breadth of the Russian Federation.

After the conflict, Rebecca Furness had been given command of the Air Force's few remaining bombers; consequently, no one knew better than she the incredible responsibility placed upon her. The surviving planes, and the few unmanned stealth bombers built since the American Holocaust, were the only air-breathing long-range strike aircraft left in the American arsenal—if any bombers were going to be built ever again, it might take decades to build the force back up to credible levels.

"Ma'am, I'm sure the strike mission will be approved once the national command authority gets our report on what happened to our spaceplane," Dave said. "That mobile Kavaznya laser is the biggest threat facing our country right now—not just to our spacecraft, but possibly to anything that flies." He paused, then added, "And the Russians just killed five of our best, ma'am. It's time for some payback."

Rebecca was silent for a long moment; then, shaking her head, she said wryly, "Three 'ma'ams' out of you in one conversation, General Luger—I believe that's a first for you." She punched some instructions into her computer. "I'll authorize a change to thirty minutes' bingo fuel."

"Odin to Headbanger, I said, push them up, General Furness,"

Patrick interjected from Armstrong Space Station. "Take them up to Vmax, then slow them down to one point two for weapon release."

"What if they don't make it to the air refueling anchor on the way back, General?" she asked. "What if there's a navigation error? What if they can't hook up on the first go? Let's not lose sight of—"

"Push 'em up, General. That's an order."

Rebecca sighed. She could legally ignore his order and be sure her bombers were safe—that was her job—but she certainly understood how badly he wanted retribution. She turned to her Vampire flight crew and said, "Push them up to one point five, recompute bingo fuel at the air refueling control point, and advise."

The crew complied, and a moment later reported: "Headbanger flight of two now at flight level three-one-oh, on course, speed Mach one point five, due regard, in the green, twenty minutes to launch point. Bingo fuel at the ARCP is gone; we're down to ten minutes' emergency fuel. We should make up a few more minutes after we get the tanker's updated ETE."

"That's ten minutes after the *second* bomber cycles on the boom, right?" Rebecca asked. The grim, ashen expression and silent no on the face of the tech told her that they were in really deep shit.

CHAPTER SEVEN

In war, there are no unwounded soldiers.

— JOSE NAROSKY

ABOARD ARMSTRONG SPACE STATION

MINUTES LATER

"McLanahan here, secure."

"McLanahan, this is the President of the United States," Joseph Gardner thundered. "What in hell do you think you're doing?"

"Sir, I—"

"This is a direct order, McLanahan: Turn those bombers around *right now.*"

"Sir, I'd like to give you my report before—"

"You're not going to do a damned thing except what I order you to do!" the President snapped. "You've violated a direct order from the commander-in-chief. If you want to avoid life in prison, you'd better do what I tell you. And that spaceplane had better still be in orbit, or by God I'll—"

"The Russians shot down the Black Stallion spaceplane," Patrick quickly interjected. "The spaceplane is missing and presumed lost with all souls."

The President was silent for a long moment; then: "How?"

"A mobile laser, the same one that we think shot down our spaceplane last year over Iran," Patrick replied. "*That* was what the Russians were hiding at Soltanabad: their mobile anti-spacecraft laser. They brought it into Iran and set it up at an abandoned Revolutionary Guards Corps base, one we thought had been destroyed—they even placed fake bomb craters on it to fool us. The Russians set up the laser in a perfect spot to attack our spacecraft overflying Iran. They got the second-biggest prize of them all: another Black Stallion spaceplane. The positioning suggests their real target was Armstrong Space Station."

Again, silence on the other end of the line . . . but not for long: "McLanahan, I'm very sorry about your men . . ."

"There were two women on board too, sir."

". . . and we're going to get to the bottom of this," the President went on, "but you violated my orders and launched those bombers without permission. Turn them around immediately."

Patrick glanced up at the time remaining: seven-plus minutes. Could he stall the President that long . . . ? "Sir, I had permission to launch the spaceplane into standard orbit from STRATCOM," he said. "We suspected what the Russians were up to, but we were awaiting permission to go in. Our worst fears were confirmed . . ."

"I gave you an order, McLanahan."

"Sir, the Russians are packing up and moving the laser and their radar out of Soltanabad as we speak," he said. "If they are allowed to slip away, that laser will be an immense threat to every spacecraft, satellite, and aircraft in our inventory. We're just a few minutes away from launch, and it'll be over in less than a minute. Just four precision-guided missiles with kinetic-kill warheads—no collateral damage. It'll take out the components that haven't been moved yet. The Russians can't complain about the attack because then they'd be admitting moving attack troops into Iran to kill Americans, so there won't be any international backlash. If we can get Buzhazi's troops in there to start a forensic search as soon as possible after the attack, we might uncover evidence that—"

"I said, turn those bombers around, McLanahan," the President said. *"That's an order.* I'm not going to repeat myself. This conversation is being recorded and witnessed and if you don't comply it'll be used against you in your court-martial."

"Sir, I understand, but I ask you to reconsider," Patrick pleaded. "Five astronauts aboard the spaceplane were killed. They're *dead,* blasted apart by that laser. It was an act of war. If we don't get direct evidence that Russia has commenced direct offensive military action against the United States of America, they'll get away with murder and we'll never be able to avenge their deaths. And if we don't destroy, damage, or disable that laser, it'll pop up somewhere else and kill again. Sir, we *must*—"

"You are in violation of a direct order from the commander-in-chief, General McLanahan," the President interrupted. "I'll give you one last chance to comply. Do it, and I'll let you retire quickly and quietly without a public trial. Refuse, and I'll strip you of your rank and throw you in prison at hard labor for *life.* Do you understand me, General? One last chance . . . which is it going to—?"

Six minutes left. Could he get away with the "scratchy radio" routine? He decided he was far, far beyond that point now: he had no choice. Patrick cut off the transmission. Ignoring the stunned expressions of the technicians around him, he spoke: "McLanahan to Luger."

"Just got off the phone with the SECDEF, Muck," Dave said from Elliott Air Force Base via their subcutaneous global transceiver system. "He ordered the Vampires recalled immediately."

"My phone call trumps yours, buddy: I just heard from the President," Patrick said. "He ordered the same thing. He offered me a nice quiet retirement or a lifetime breaking big rocks into little ones at Leavenworth."

"I'll get them turned—"

"Negative . . . they continue," Patrick said. "Bomb the crap out of that base."

"Muck, I know what you're thinking," Dave Luger said, "but it might already be too late. The latest satellite image shows at least a fourth of the vehicles already gone, and that was over ten minutes ago. Plus we're already past bingo fuel on the Vampires and well into an emergency fuel situation—they might not reach the tanker before they flame out. It's a no-win scenario, Muck. It's not worth risking your career and your freedom. We lost this one. Let's pull back and get ready to fight the next one."

"The 'next one' could be an attack against another spaceplane, a satellite, a reconnaissance aircraft over Iran, or Armstrong Space Station itself," Patrick said. "We've got to stop it, *now*."

"It's too late," Luger insisted. "I think we've missed it."

"Then we'll leave 'em with a little calling card in their rearview mirrors, if that's the best we can do," Patrick said. "Nail it."

"He's going to *what*?"

"You heard me, Leonid," the President of the United States said on the "hot line" from Air Force One, just minutes after the connection was broken to the space station—he had to let loose a string of epithets for a full sixty seconds after the line went dead before he could speak with anyone else. "I think McLanahan is going to launch an air strike on a place called Soltanabad in northeastern Iran. He insists you have set up a mobile anti-spacecraft laser there and you used it to shoot down his Black Stallion spaceplane just a few moments ago."

Russian president Leonid Zevitin furiously typed instructions on a computer keyboard to Russian air forces chief of staff Darzov while he spoke, warning him of the impending attack and ordering him to get fighters airborne to try to stop the American bombers. "This is unbelievable, Joe, simply unbelievable," he said in his most convincing, sincere, outraged tone of voice. "Soltanabad? In Iran? I've never heard of the place! We don't have *any* troops *anywhere* in Iran except the ones guarding our temporary embassy in Mashhad, and it's there because our embassy in Tehran has been blasted to hell and Mashhad is the only secure place in the entire country right now, thanks to Buzhazi."

"I'm just as flabbergasted as you are, Leonid," Gardner said. "McLanahan must have flipped. He must've suffered some kind of brain injury when he had that heart flutter episode. He's unstable!"

"But why does an unstable officer have control of supersonic bombers and hypersonic missiles, Joe? Maybe you can't get your hands on McLanahan, but you can shut down his operation, can't you?"

"Of course I can, Leonid. It's being done as we speak. But those bombers may get off a few missiles. If you have any forces on the ground out there, I suggest you get them out pronto."

"I thank you for the call, Joe, but we don't have forces in Iran, period." Still no reply from Darzov, he noticed—damn, he'd better get that laser out of there, or else their game was going to be over. "And we certainly don't have some kind of magic super-laser that can shoot down a spacecraft orbiting Earth at seventeen thousand miles per hour and can then disappear like smoke. The United Nations investigated those reports last year and came up with nothing, remember?"

"I believe they said there were inconclusive results because—"

"Because President Martindale didn't allowed them to interview anyone at Dreamland, and Buzhazi and his insane rebel insurgents didn't allow them access to debris or the suspected site where the laser was supposedly set up," Zevitin said. "The bottom line is that there is not one scrap of evidence out there pointing to some damned super-laser. McLanahan is obviously whipping up a lot of fear in Congress, in the media, and with the American public in order to keep his expensive and dangerous secret programs afloat."

"Well, that's going to be put to a halt *real* quick," Gardner said. "McLanahan is finished. The bastard hung up on me and ordered that attack to continue."

"Hung up on you?" That was *perfect,* Zevitin thought happily. Not only was McLanahan going to be removed, but he was going to be portrayed as a lunatic . . . *by his own commander-in-chief*! No way his supporters in the military or Congress were going to support him now! He choked down his glee and went on in a low, ominous voice, "That is *insane*! Is he *crazy*? You can't allow this to continue!

This unstable, insubordinate man has got to be stopped, Joe. You're making a lot of folks real scared out here. Wait until the Duma and the Cabinet hears about another hypersonic missile attack in Iran. They're going to shit their pants."

"Convince them not to worry, Leonid," Gardner said. "McLanahan is done for, and so is his private military force."

"Shut it down, Joe," Zevitin urged. "Shut it all down—the space station, those hypersonic missiles, the unmanned bombers with their EMP death rays—before it's too late. Then let's get together and present the world with a unified, peaceful, cooperative front. That's the only way we're going to ratchet down the tension around here."

"Don't worry about a thing," Gardner insisted. "In case your Caspian Sea ships are in the vicinity, you might tell them that the bombers might launch high-speed missiles."

"Joe, I'm concerned about the backlash in Iran if those missiles hit that area," Zevitin said. "The last I recall, that base was being used by the Red Crescent to fly in relief supplies, and by United Nations monitors—"

"Oh no," Gardner moaned. "This is a damned nightmare."

"If McLanahan blasts that base, he'll be killing dozens, perhaps hundreds of innocent civilians."

"Damn," Gardner said. "Well, I'm sorry, Leonid, but McLanahan's out of control for the time being. There's nothing else I can do."

"I have one radical suggestion, my friend—I hope you don't think I'm crazy," Zevitin said.

"What's your—?" And then Gardner stopped, because he soon figured it out for himself. "You mean, you're asking my *permission* to—?"

"It's the only way, Joe," Zevitin said, almost unable to contain his amazement at the direction this conversation was taking. "You know it, and I know it. I don't believe even a stressed-out schizoid like McLanahan would ever dare launch missiles against a humanitarian relief airfield, but I can't think of any other way to stop this madness, can you?" There was no response, so Zevitin quickly went on: "Besides, Joe, the bombers are unmanned, correct? No one will get hurt on your side, and we'll be saving many lives." There was a very long pause. Zevitin added, "I'm sorry, Joe, I shouldn't have brought up such a crazy idea. Forget I said—"

"Hold on, Leonid," Gardner interrupted. A few moments later: "Do you have jets nearby, Leonid?" he heard the President of the United States ask.

Zevitin almost doubled over with disbelief. He swallowed his shock, quickly composed himself, then said, "I don't know, Joe. I'll have to ask my air force chief of staff. We normally patrol this area, of course, but since our MiG was shot down by McLanahan's bomber with the EMP nuclear T-wave thing we've pulled back quite a bit."

"I understand," Gardner said. "Listen to me. My National Security Adviser tells me that the bombers launched from Batman Air Base in Turkey and are undoubtedly heading directly to a launch point over the southern Caspian Sea. We can't tell you any more because we simply don't know."

"I understand," Zevitin said. He could scarcely believe this— Gardner was actually telling him where the bombers had launched from and where they were going!

"We don't know their weapons either, but we'll assume they have the same hypersonic cruise missiles they used before, so the launch point is a couple hundred miles from Soltanabad."

"I agree with your assumptions, Joe," Zevitin said, trying to disguise the surprise in his voice and stay calm and serious. "We can search for them where you suggest. But if we do find them . . . Joe, should I proceed? I think it's the only way to avoid a disaster. But it's got to be *your* call, Mr. President. Tell me what you'd like me to do."

Another pause, but this one shorter: "Yes, Leonid," Gardner said, obviously racked with great anger. "I hate to do it, but that bastard McLanahan has left me no choice."

"Yes, Joe, I understand and agree," Zevitin said. "What about the T-wave weapon? Will they use it again to attack our fighters?"

"You must assume they will, and launch your attack from maximum range," Gardner said. "I'm sorry, but I don't have any control over that, either."

"I know it's not your doing, my friend," Zevitin said as solemnly as he could muster through his glee. Hell, now the guy was giving him *suggestions* on how to successfully attack *his own people*! "We'll do everything possible to avert a disaster. I'll be in touch shortly with an update."

"Thank you so much, my friend."

"No, thank *you* for the responsible notification, my friend. I don't know if I can be in time, but I'll do everything I can to avoid an embarrassing situation from getting worse. Wish me luck. Good-bye." Zevitin hung up the phone . . . then resisted the impulse to take a little victory dance around the desk. He snatched up the phone again and asked to be connected immediately to Darzov. "Status, General?"

"We are moving as fast as we can," Darzov said. "We are prioritizing the main components first—the radar, laser chamber, and adaptive optics. The fuel tanks and power generators will have to wait."

"Do you have any fighters on patrol over the Caspian, General?"

"Of course, sir."

"Are you shadowing the American B-1 bombers?"

"I have an entire squadron of MiG-29s airborne to try to keep up with them," Darzov said. "The unmanned Vampires are much faster than a regular B-1 Lancer, so we've loaded a few of the fighters up with *Molnija* missiles adapted to work at reduced range with the MiG-29's fire control radar. They might be able to take down their hypersonic attack missiles if they can be fired—"

"I've just received permission from the President of the United States for you to *shoot the bombers down*," Zevitin said happily.

"The President of the United States told us to shoot down his own bombers?"

"He doesn't consider them *his* bombers—to him they're McLanahan's bombers now, and they might as well be invading Martians," Zevitin said. "Do it. Shoot them down . . . but *after* they launch their missiles."

"*After?*" Darzov asked incredulously. "Sir, if we cannot move our equipment out in time, or if they target the main *Fanar* components, we could lose billions of rubles of precious equipment!"

"Do the best you can, General," Zevitin said, "but let those missiles launch and *hit the base*. You do have the screening implements in place, as we discussed earlier?"

"Yes, sir, of course," Darzov replied. "But we also have—"

"If any part of *Fanar* gets hit, your first priority is to get it out of there while you continue to set the stage as planned," Zevitin went on breathlessly, "because minutes after the missiles hit, I'm going to tell the whole world about it. The world media will want to see for themselves, and it's important that they see it right away. Do you understand me, General?"

"Yes, sir," Darzov replied. "I will do as you ask. But I hope we are not sacrificing our most important assets for mere public relations purposes."

"You'll do as I tell you for whatever reason I devise, General, whether you understand it or not," Zevitin snapped. "Just make sure when the media descends on Soltanabad—which I am going to work very hard to see happen—they see nothing but senseless ruin and destruction, or I'll have your ass. Do I make myself clear?"

"Sir, we're picking up a locator beacon signal!" Master Sergeant Lukas shouted from her station in the command module of Armstrong Space Station. "It's from the passenger module."

"My God, they made it," Patrick said breathlessly. "Any data yet?"

"Nothing yet . . . yes, sir, yes, we're receiving location and environmental readouts!" Lukas said. "It's intact! Stabilizers have deployed and it is under computer guidance! Telemetry says the passenger module is still pressurized!"

"Good God, it's a miracle," Patrick said. "Moulain and Terranova must have ejected the module just before the Black Stallion was destroyed. Rebecca—"

"We're readying two more Vampires for launch to provide air

cover for the recovery," Rebecca Furness said. "They'll be airborne
in twenty minutes."

"Dave—"

"We're talking to Special Operations Command right now about
launching a CSAR mission from Afghanistan, Muck," Dave Luger
said. "As soon as we know where they might come down, they'll
launch. We're hoping they'll land in western Afghanistan. A Pave
Hawk is standing by at Herat Air Base. We're trying to get a couple
Predators and Reapers retasked to fly over the area." The MQ-1
Predator and MQ-9 Reaper were unmanned reconnaissance aircraft, each configured to carry air-to-surface attack missiles; both
were controlled via satellite from control stations in the United
States.

"Sixty seconds to the launch point," Dave Luger reported. "Airspeed coming back to one point two Mach." He was by himself at
the command console in the Batman, but he still lowered his voice
as if not wanting anyone else to hear as he went on: "Muck, now
would be a good time to turn them around."

"Continue," Patrick McLanahan responded.

He sounded every bit as resolute and confident as when he first
made the decision to attack—that, at least, made him feel a little
better. If Patrick showed the slightest hesitation in his decision, Dave
vowed he would've turned the bombers around on his own authority to make sure the planes made it back to the refueling control
point—as well as to save Patrick's career.

In seconds, it was going to be too late . . .

On the command-wide net he spoke, "Roger, Odin, copy, continue. Forty-five seconds. No threats, no surveillance radar. Airspeed
steady at one point two Mach. Thirty seconds . . . twenty . . . ten,
doors coming open on Headbanger Two-One . . . missile one away . . .
doors coming open on Two-Two . . . missile two away, doors coming
closed . . . missile one away from Two-Two . . . missile two away,
doors coming closed, the flight is secure, heading westbound to the
ARIP."

"How are the Vampires doing on fuel, Dave?" Patrick asked.

"We'll make it—barely," Luger responded. "If the hookups go smoothly, Two-One will be able to get on the boom, take on emergency fuel, cycle off, and Two-Two will start to take on fuel with ten minutes left to dry tanks."

"Good going, Headbanger," Patrick breathed with audible relief. No reply from Rebecca Furness—this was not over, not by a long shot, and he knew she was still angry about her decision being overruled.

"Thirty seconds to impact . . . SkySTREAK speed Mach ten point seven, all in the green . . . scramjet motor burnout, warhead coasting . . . flight controls active and responding, steering control good . . . twenty TG, datalink active." They all watched as the composite millimeter-wave radar and imaging infrared picture flared to life, revealing Russian transport planes and helicopters on the runway, several lines of men handing boxes and packages from various parts of the base to waiting trucks, several large unidentifiable buildings on trailers . . .

. . . and several large tents with clearly identifiable Red Cross and Red Crescent logos on the tops. "Jesus!" Dave Luger gasped. "They look like relief worker tents!"

"Target the large trailers and portable buildings!" Patrick shouted. "Stay away from those tents!"

"We got it, Odin," Rebecca said. She had commander's override authority and could take over targeting from the weapons officer, but she didn't need to—the weapons officer smoothly centered the aiming reticle over the four largest trailers. The SkySTREAK's millimeter-wave radar was able to look through the outer steel shell of each truck, and it verified that the trailers under the aiming reticle were indeed dense and not hollow or less densely packed, like a partially empty cargo trailer might be. Otherwise, the trailers all looked the same and were being attended to by equivalent-looking numbers of workers.

"Five seconds . . . targeting locked . . . breakapart charge initiated." The final image from the SkySTREAK missiles showed nearly direct hits on the center of each trailer . . . all except one, which had skittered off-target to land in a clear area somewhere beside the targeted trailer. The computer's estimate of the area of damage, approximately fifty feet in diameter, showed nothing except some soldiers carrying rifles and boxes and perhaps one lone individual standing nearby, probably a supervisor—it didn't hit any of the relief tents. "Looks like one missed, but it hit in a clearing beside the trailer."

"Good shooting, Headbanger," Patrick said. "Those trailers looked identical to the ones that attacked Stud One-One."

"They looked like a billion other trailers around the world—there's no way of knowing what we got, sir," Rebecca Furness said, the exasperation obvious in her voice. "We didn't see any radar arrays or anything that looked like laser fuel storage tanks or laser optics. We could've hit anything . . . or nothing."

"Our first priority is to set up a rescue and recovery operation for the passenger module and a search for any debris and remains of the Black Stallion and its crew," Patrick said, ignoring Furness's exasperated remarks. "I want a Battle Force team sent out immediately to Afghanistan, along with every support aircraft we have available. I want unmanned vehicles and NIRTSats set up for immediate deployment to search along all possible trajectories for survivors or debris. Recall every asset we have for the search. I want a progress update in one hour. Do you copy, Headbanger?"

"Stand by, Odin," Rebecca responded, concern thick in her voice. Patrick immediately turned his attention back to the mission status monitors . . . and immediately saw the new threat: a swarm of missiles barreling down on the Vampire bombers. "We did a post-turn long-range LADAR sweep and spotted them," she said. The LADAR, or laser radar, was a system of electronically agile laser emitters embedded throughout the fuselage of the Vampire bombers that instantaneously "drew" a high-resolution image of everything around the plane for a hundred miles, then compared the three-dimensional picture to a catalog of images for immediate identification. "Look at the speed of those things—they have to be traveling at greater than Mach seven!"

"Countermeasures!" Dave Luger shouted. "Knock them out of the sky!"

But it was soon clear that it was too late. Traveling at more than fourteen miles per *second,* the Russian missiles ate up the distance long before the Vampire bombers' microwave emitters could activate, lock on, and disrupt their guidance systems. Three of the four hypersonic missiles scored direct hits, quickly sending both bombers spiraling into the Caspian Sea.

"Damn it," Dave swore. "Looks like the Russians have a new toy for their MiGs. Well, I guess we won't have to worry if the bombers will make their tanker, will we, Rebecca?"

"We just lost one-fourth of our remaining B-1 bomber inventory, Dave," Rebecca Furness radioed from Battle Mountain Air Reserve Base. "It's not a laughing matter. We only have two Vampires at Batman now."

"Get 'em airborne to provide air cover for the CSAR guys out of Herat, Rebecca," Patrick ordered. "Use active LADAR to scan for intruders. If anyone comes within a hundred miles of your planes, fry 'em."

"With pleasure, Muck," Rebecca said. "I'm ready for a little payback. They'll be ready to taxi in about fifteen." But just a few minutes later she called back: "Odin, this is Headbanger, we have a problem. Security Forces are parked in front of the hangar and preventing the Vampire from taxiing. They're ordering us to shut down or they'll disable the plane."

Patrick was on the secure videoconference line in a heartbeat, but he was beaten to the punch by an incoming call: "General McLanahan, you are either deranged or suffering from some sort of mental breakdown," Secretary of Defense Miller Turner said. "This is an order directly from the commander-in-chief: stand down all your forces immediately. You are relieved of command. Do I make myself clear?"

"Sir, one of my Black Stallion spaceplanes has been shot down by a Russian anti-satellite laser based in eastern Iran," Patrick said. "We have indications that the passengers may have survived. I want air cover . . ."

"General, I'm sympathetic, but the President is pissed and he's not listening to any arguments," Turner said. "You hung up on him, for God's sake! Do you expect him to listen to you now?"

"Sir, the passenger module is intact, and it'll be on the ground in less than fifteen minutes," Patrick said.

"What? You mean, someone *ejected* from the spaceplane . . . ?"

"The passenger module is jettisonable and is designed to act as a lifeboat for the space station crewmembers," Patrick explained. "It can withstand re-entry, fly itself to a landing spot, safely glide in for a landing, and save the crew. The module is intact, sir, and we're hoping the crew is safe. We're zeroing in on the possible landing zone right now, and as soon as we compute the exact landing spot we can deploy a rescue team there right away—that's the only advantage we'll have over the enemy. But it'll take at least ninety minutes for a rescue team and air cover to arrive in the recovery area. We have to launch right away."

"General, you have already disobeyed direct orders from the President," Turner said. "You're already on your way to prison, do you understand that? Don't compound it by arguing anymore. For the last time: *Stand down.* I'm directing General Backman to take command of all of your forces. I'm telling you—"

"And I'm telling *you,* sir," Patrick interrupted, "that most of the Middle East and central Asia will have seen the Black Stallion fall to Earth, and the Iranian Revolutionary Guards Corps, the al-Quds forces, all of the terrorists that have flooded into Iran since the military coup, and probably the Russians will be on their way to the crash site to retrieve whatever they can find. We must get every aircraft and combat search and rescue team possible airborne to find the survivors before the enemy does."

"Central Command will coordinate that, McLanahan, not *you.* You are ordered to *stand down.* Take no further actions whatsoever. You will do or say *nothing* to *anyone.* You are relieved of your command and will be placed under arrest as soon as you can be brought off that station."

For the second time that day, Patrick hung up on a civilian military leader. His next call was directly to General Kenneth Lepers, the four-star Army general in charge of U.S. Central Command, the major combat command overseeing all military operations in the Middle East and central Asia, to try to convince him to allow the bombers to take off.

"General McLanahan, your ass is in a really big sling right now," Lepers' deputy said. "The general has been directed not to speak with you, and this call will be reported to SECDEF. I advise you to straighten this thing out with SECDEF before the whole world cuts you off." And he hung up.

Patrick's next call was back to Rebecca Furness at Battle Mountain Air Reserve Base. "I was just going to call you, sir," Rebecca said. "I'm sorry about the Black Stallion. I wish we could've done more."

"Thanks, Rebecca. I'm sorry about your Vampires."

"Not your fault, sir." It was, she reminded herself: if he hadn't ordered to launch on this unauthorized mission, she'd still have her bombers. But the Vampires were unmanned, and the Black Stallion wasn't, so she didn't feel the need to rub salt on a wound. "We should have been scanning for bandits—I made the call to go in completely silent. I don't know how the Russians knew we were coming or when, but they are going to get it back in spades, I guarantee *that*."

"Are you still being stopped by the sky cops?"

"Affirmative. We've shut down as ordered and are holding our position inside the hangar."

Patrick thought for a moment; then: "Rebecca, I tried calling General Lepers at CENTCOM to get his permission to launch the Vampires, and he's not talking to me. I would guess if I tried to call STRATCOM I'd get the same response."

"Cannon's an okay guy," Rebecca commented. "The others think you're gunning for their jobs." Or nuts, she silently added.

"If we don't launch some air cover, our guys and maybe the CSAR troops will get chewed apart by the Pasdaran," Patrick said.

"I'm going to clear those Security Forces away from the hangar. I want you ready to launch as soon as they're away."

"But you said Lepers won't talk to you, and you haven't spoken to CENTAF yet, so who's going to—?" Furness paused for a moment, then said simply, "That's crazy. Sir."

"The question is, Rebecca: Will you launch?"

The pause was very, very long; just when Patrick was going to repeat himself, or was wondering if Furness was dialing SECDEF's number on another line, she said, "Get 'em out of my ships' way, General, and I'll launch."

"Thank you, General." Patrick hung up the phone, then spoke, "Odin to Genesis."

"Go ahead, Muck," Dave Luger responded via their subcutaneous global transceiver.

"Move those security guys away from the bombers."

"They're moved, Muck. Out." Luger turned to his command radio: "Saber, this is Genesis."

BATMAN AIR BASE, REPUBLIC OF TURKEY

THAT SAME TIME

"Saber copies, go ahead, Genesis," Air Force First Lieutenant James "JD" Daniels, commander of the Battle Force ground operations team code-named "Saber," responded. Daniels had been sent to Batman Air Base to provide security for the EB-1C Vampire bombers, but also because the base was an isolated, well-equipped place to train with new CID pilots in real-world scenarios. As a technical sergeant the thirty-year-old tall, brown-eyed, brown-haired rancher's son from Arkansas was one of the first of the Battle Force commandos to check out as a Cybernetic Infantry Device pilot. After being injured from radiation sickness after fighting in Yakutsk Air Base in Russia following the American Holocaust, Daniels used his recovery time to get a bachelor's degree, then attended Officer Training School and earned his commission. Now he was the senior training officer and, except for Charlie Turlock herself, the resident expert in the CID weapon system.

"I have a task for you, Saber, but you might not like it," Dave Luger said. "Odin wants to launch the Vampire bombers."

"Yes, sir. We were ready to go a moment ago, but the Security Forces guys showed up at the hangar, and the planes shut themselves down. The base commander ordered us to assist and protect the Security Forces from any remote-controlled actions by you regarding the aircraft. We verified the orders. Sorry, sir. What is it I won't like?"

"One of our spaceplanes has been shot down in eastern Iran, and there are survivors. We need air cover for a rescue operation. The NCA still says no. We want to launch the Vampires anyway."

"Why won't the NCA approve the mission, sir?"

"I don't know why, Saber, but we believe the NCA is worried that our actions over Iran are inciting fear and intimidating everyone in the region."

"Sir, I received authenticated orders to stand down—us as well as the Vampires. The base commander ordered us to help secure you. You're asking me to violate those orders."

"I know, Saber. I can't order you to violate valid orders. But I'm telling you that the survivors of the spaceplane will be caught and captured or killed if we don't do something."

"Who shot down the spaceplane, sir?"

"We believe the Russians did, Saber."

"Yes, sir," Daniels said. That was enough for him. Daniels had spent a year in the hospital recovering from radiation poisoning which occurred when the Russian air force used tactical nuclear weapons to destroy their own air base, Yakutsk, that was being used by McLanahan and the Air Battle Force to hunt down and destroy Russian mobile intercontinental ballistic missiles that were being readied to launch a second nuclear attack on the United States. He endured severe dehydration, nausea for days on end, incredible pain, and eventually a liver transplant—but he survived, won the right to go back on active duty, requalified for field operations, rejoined the Battle Force, and took command of a CID team.

He had won, then lost, then won back all the things he ever wanted to do in his life, except one: get some payback for what the Russians did to him, his comrades, and to their own people in Yakutsk.

"You still there, Saber?"

"I'm sorry, sir, but I have my orders," Daniels said in a deep monotone voice, quite different from his normally energetic, upbeat tone. "If those planes were to move, I and my team would do everything in our power to protect the Security Forces from harm. Good night, sir."

"Genesis to Headbanger."

"Go ahead, Dave," Rebecca Furness replied.

"Get ready."

"Can't. My grounds crews say the sky cops are still blocking the hangar and taxiways."

"Get ready anyway."

"Did you order your guys to *take out the sky cops?*"

"No, ma'am, I did not. The base commander ordered the Battle Force team to assist and protect the Security Forces from unauthorized aircraft movement, and that's what they will do."

This is crazy, Rebecca told herself for the umpteenth time, utterly *crazy*. She turned to her operations officer, Brigadier General Daren Mace: "Daren, start 'em up and launch the Vampires immediately." She closed her eyes and saw herself standing in front of a court-martial, being sentenced to prison for the rest of the best years of her life; then, thinking about her fellow airmen on the ground in Iran being chased by Pasdaran and Muslim insurgents, opened her eyes and said, "Stop for nothing."

"Yes, ma'am," Mace said. He adjusted the mike on his headset and spoke: "Headbanger, start 'em up and launch without delay. Stop for nothing. Repeat, stop for nothing."

"Affirmative, Panther, the APUs are still on, both planes," the Air Force Security Forces detail team leader reported to NATO base headquarters. It was creepy enough that the APU started and stopped by itself, but ten times more so when the engines did the same. The crew chiefs and assistants for each plane were outside the hangars, per the base commander's orders.

"This is Panther. Put the fucking senior crew chief on," the base commander, a Turkish army colonel, ordered in very good English.

"Stand by, Panther." The SF officer handed his radio to the head crew chief, an Air Force technical sergeant. "It's the base commander, and he's steamed."

"Tech Sergeant Booker here, sir."

"I ordered those planes shut down, and I mean *completely* shut down—APUs also."

"Yes, sir, I know, but you ordered us not to hook the ground power units up either, and without power the command center at Battle Mountain can't talk to the planes, so I think that's why the APUs are—"

"Sergeant, I am giving you a direct order: I want those planes *completely* shut down, *immediately,* or I will have you arrested!" the base commander screamed. "I do not care if no one can talk to the planes—I do not *want* anyone to talk to the planes! Now turn off those APUs, and do it *now!*"

"Yes, sir," Booker said, and he handed the radio back to the SF officer.

"Detail One here, Panther."

"I just ordered that tech sergeant to completely shut down those planes, including the APUs—the power units in the tail," the base commander said. If they do not comply right away, place them all under arrest." Mallory swallowed hard, then made a gesture to his team members, a sign that said "Get ready for action." "Do you understand me, Detail One?"

"Yes, sir, I do."

"What is that tech sergeant doing right now?"

"He's going over to the other crew chiefs . . . he's gesturing to the planes . . . they're putting on gloves, like they're getting ready to go to work."

They were sure taking their sweet time, the Security Forces officer thought—the colonel's going to have a shit fit if they don't get their rears in gear. Sure enough, moments later the base commander called: "What are they doing, dammit? Are those planes shut down yet?"

"Negative, sir. They're just standing there talking right now, sir," Mallory replied. "One of them has a radio, and another one has a checklist. Maybe they're discussing shutting down the APUs from here."

"Well, go find out what is taking them so damned long."

"Roger, Panther. Stand by." He holstered his radio and started walking toward the crew chiefs. The three men and one woman crew chiefs saw him coming . . . and then, without a backward glance, they started walking toward their end unit hangar which served as the Air Battle Force's headquarters. "Hey, you jerkoffs, get back here and shut those power units off, colonel's orders." Just as he was about to yell at them again, to his complete surprise, they started *running* toward the hangar! *"Where the hell are you going?"* he shouted. He pulled his radio out of its holster. "Panther, the crew chiefs are *running away toward their headquarters building!"*

"They are *what?"* the base commander shouted. "Arrest those sons of bitches!"

"Roger that, sir. Break. Detail One to Control, signal Alert Red, Alpha Seven ramp area, repeat, Alert Red, Alpha—" Then Mallory heard a sound, much louder than the APUs, and realized moments later what it was. His hand shaking, he raised his radio again: "Control, Detail One, be advised, the articles in the Alpha Seven hangars are starting engines, repeat, *starting engines!* Requesting a Code Niner-Niner alert, full response, repeat, full—"

And then he saw them, emerging from the hangar the crew chiefs had just run toward, sprinting like linebackers from hell . . . and he nearly fell over backward in shock, surprise, and a mad scramble to get the hell out of there. He had seen them before, of course, but usually just walking around or being folded or unfolded near a truck or helicopter—never *running right at him!*

"Saber Four and Five responding!" one of the Cybernetic Infantry Device manned robots said in a loud computer-synthesized voice. "Say status!" Mallory was still on his hands and knees cowering in terror as the first robot ran right up to him. Both had him surrounded within moments. They were wearing huge backpacks, with what appeared to be grenade launchers deployed over their shoulders aimed right at him. "Team leader, I say again: say status!"

"I . . . uh . . . the bombers . . . they've started engines!" Mallory stammered. The muzzle of the grenade launcher was just a few feet from his nose. "Get that weapon out of my face!"

The robot ignored the order. "Have they taxied yet?" the robot blared at him. Mallory couldn't respond. "Five, report to Alpha-Seven-Two, I'll take Alpha-Seven-One. Protect the Security Force units." The second robot nodded and ran off, just like a football player breaking from a huddle except it was gone literally in the blink of an eye. "Are you hurt, Team Leader?"

"I . . . no," Mallory said. He scrambled to his feet. "Get in those hangars and find some way to disable those—"

At that instant they heard an impossibly loud roar of aircraft engines and a tremendous blast of jet exhaust from the open rear of both occupied shelters. "The bombers are taxiing!" the robot said. "Five, bombers are moving! Protect the Security Force units!"

"No! Stop the bombers! Find some way to—!" But the robot had sped off toward the hangar entrance. Well, he thought, the bombers weren't going anywhere, and if for some reason the Humvees didn't stop them, the robots certainly could. "Detail One units, the CID units are headed inside the hangars. Assist them if possible, but monitor and report if—"

At that instant, Mallory saw an object fly out of the near hangar. At first he thought it was a cloud of smoke or perhaps an explosion of some kind . . . and then seconds later realized it was the Humvee that had been stationed inside blocking the hangar! Moments later the robot ran out of the hangar clutching a Security Forces officer in each hand, carrying him out as easily as someone might carry a beach towel. Directly behind him, the B-1 bomber careened out of the hangar and sped up the throat toward the main taxiway.

"*What in hell is going on?*" Mallory shouted. "What happened? What are you . . . ?" But the robot kept coming. It scooped up the Security Forces team leader with a bone-jarring tackle and ran him a hundred yards away in the blink of an eye, finally depositing the three stunned officers in a heap near the security fence surrounding the detachment area. The robot huddled over them as if shielding them from something. "What the hell are you doing? Get off me!"

"The bomber is transmitting its microwave weapon system," the robot said. "I had to get the Humvee out of the hangar before it exploded, and then I evacuated you. At close range the MPW can be lethal, and I had to get away or else it could have disabled my electronics too."

"What are you talking about?" Mallory struggled to get a better look. "The second bomber is moving too! They're taxiing for takeoff!" He fumbled for his radio, realizing he'd dropped it when the robot tackled him. "Call security control!" he told the robot. "Alert the base commander! Get units on the taxiways and runways before those things can get into takeoff position!"

"Roger," the robot responded. "I'll call it in, then see what I can do to stop them." And the robot stood up and was gone, running away with amazing speed, the muzzle of the grenade launcher swiveling back and forth searching for targets. It cleared the twelve-foot fence surrounding the detachment area—he just noticed that the gate across the throat was wide open—and was out of sight within seconds.

"What the fuck are those things doing? Who's in control of those things—ten-year-olds?" Mallory ran back to the first hangar and found his radio. "Control, Detail One, the bombers are taxiing out. There are two CID units in pursuit. They said the bombers were transmitting some kind of microwave weapon."

"Control, Knifepoint West, the bombers are crossing Taxiway Foxtrot on the way to Runway One-Niner," another Security Force unit radioed. "I'm parking my vehicle in the middle of Taxiway Alpha at the intersection of Hotel taxiway. I'm going to dismount. Those fuckers are coming this way awfully damned fast!" Mallory and the other Security Forces officers ran up the throat to the main taxiway to see what was going on . . .

. . . and just as they reached Taxiway Alpha they saw a Humvee fly into the air to the north, and the B-1 bombers roar past it! "Knifepoint West, Knifepoint West, do you copy?" Mallory radioed as he watched the nearly five-thousand-pound Humvee hit and tumble across the ground like a child's toy. "What happened? Say status!"

"*Those robots threw my Humvee off the taxiway!*" the officer radioed a few moments later. "They're not trying to *stop* them—they're *helping* them escape!"

"*Those bastards!*" Mallory swore. "I knew something screwy was going on! Control, Detail One, those robots are engaging our security units!"

"Detail One, this is Panther," the base commander cut in. "I do not care what you have to do, but stop those bombers from leaving the ground! Do you read me? *Stop those bombers!* Then place that entire Headbanger contingent under arrest! I want some butts, and I want them *now*!"

But as he listened, Mallory saw the first unmanned B-1 bomber leave the ground and streak across the night sky, trailing four long afterburner flames behind it, followed just a few short seconds later by the second. "Ho-lee *shit*," he cried aloud as the twin afterburner booms rolled over him. "What in hell is going on?"

It took almost a minute for the noise to subside enough so he could talk on the radio: "Control, Panther, Detail One, the bombers have launched, repeat, they've *launched*. All available patrol and re-sponse units, report to the Alpha Seven special detachment area with restraints and transport. Control, notify the base hospital and all command units that a special security enforcement operation has commenced." His ears were buzzing and his head felt as if it was going to explode from the tension and sheer disbelief over what had just happened. "Notify all responding units that there are two of those CID robot units that assisted the bombers to launch and are armed and dangerous. Do not approach the CID units, only report and observe. Do you copy?"

The two bombers were just bright dots in the night sky, and soon those telltales winked out as the afterburners were cut off. This was unbelievable, Mallory told himself over and over again, simply *unbe-lievable*. Those Saber guys had to be nuts or on drugs, he thought, wiping sweat from his forehead. The robot guys had to be crazy . . . or maybe the robots had been hijacked by terrorists? Maybe they weren't Air Force after all, but fucking Muslim terrorists, or maybe Kurdish terrorists, or maybe . . . ?

And then he realized he wasn't *thinking* all this, but *screaming* it at the top of his lungs! His skin felt as if it was going to burst into flames, and his head felt ready to explode! What in God's name was happening? He turned . . .

. . . and then he saw the shape of one of the robots, about thirty yards away, slowly heading toward him. He raised his radio to his suddenly sweat-stained lips: "Control, Detail One, one of the CID units is heading toward me, and I am engaging," he said, wiping yet another rivulet of sweat away from his eyes. "Request backup, Alpha Seven and Taxiway Alpha, get backup out here *now*." He unholstered his sidearm, but he couldn't summon enough strength to lift it. The burning sensation increased, completely disrupting his vision and creating an intense headache, the pain finally forcing him to his knees. "Control . . . Control, how do you copy?"

"I'm sorry, Sergeant Mallory, but no one is here to take your call right now," he heard a strange voice say. "But don't worry. You and your friends will wake up in a nice cozy cell, and you won't have a care in the world." The robot advanced toward him menacingly, the muzzle of the grenade launcher aimed right between his eyes . . . but then, just before his vision completely shut down in a cloud of stars, he saw the robot wave "bye-bye" to him with his huge armored but incredibly lifelike fingers. "Nightie-night, Sergeant Mallory," he heard over the radio lying somewhere on the ground, and then everything went blank.

"Odin, Headbanger, Genesis, this is Saber, we have control of the base," Lieutenant Daniels reported a few minutes later. "Those new microwave emitters built into the CID units worked great out to thirty yards or so." The nonlethal microwave emitters broadcasted an intense feeling of heat, pain, disorientation, and eventually unconsciousness but did no actual injury to a human target. "The bombers are away and we're securing the perimeter. The base commander is pretty sore at us but he opened up his hidden liquor cabinet so he's not quite as verbal as before."

"Roger that," Patrick McLanahan responded from Armstrong Space Station. "Thank you, Saber."

"Our pleasure, sir," Daniels responded. "Maybe we can all share a cell in Leavenworth together."

"Or Supermax, if we're not so lucky," Rebecca added.

"We received a coded locator beacon and status data dump from the Black Stallion's passenger module," Luger said. "It's intact, its parachute and impact attenuation bags have deployed, and it's coming down in eastern Iran, about a hundred and twenty miles northwest of Herat, Afghanistan."

"Thank God."

"No indications if anyone inside made it yet, but the module is intact and still pressurized. We've got an Army Special Forces team in Herat gearing up for a rescue mission."

"The bombers will be in maximum SkySTREAK launch position in sixty minutes, and overhead in ninety—if they're not jumped by Russian fighters again," Rebecca Furness said. "We'll be on the lookout for them this time."

"That's probably the same amount of time it'll take the Special Forces team to chopper in—if they get permission to launch," Luger added.

"I'll speak to the commander myself," Patrick said. "I don't have much pull with the Army, but I'll see what I can do."

"Wait a minute, wait a minute—are you boys forgetting something?" Rebecca Furness interjected. "We just *took over* a Turkish-NATO military base by force and ignored direct orders from the commander-in-chief. You guys are acting as if that's no big deal. They are going to come after us, *all* of us—even the general, even though he's up on a space station—and they are going to haul us off to prison. What do you propose we do about this?"

"I propose we rescue our crewmembers on the ground in Iran, then hunt down any parts of that anti-spacecraft laser the Russians fired at us, General Furness," Patrick said immediately. "Anything else is background noise at this point."

"'Background noise'? Do you call the Turkish and U.S. governments—possibly our own military—coming after us just 'background noise'? We'll be lucky if they just send in an infantry battalion to drag us out of here. Do you intend on continuing to disregard orders and take down anyone who gets in your way, General? Are we going to war against our own people now?"

"Rebecca, I'm not ordering you to do anything—I'm asking," Patrick said. "We have crewmembers down in Iran, the Russians blasting away with a laser, and the President doing nothing about any of it except telling *us* to stand down. Now if you don't want to help, just say so, recall the Vampires, and call the Pentagon."

"And tell them what, Patrick—that you *forced* me to launch those planes? You're two hundred miles up on the space station, probably on the other side of the planet. I'm already committed, General. I'm screwed. My career is over."

"Rebecca, you did what you did because we have friends and fellow warriors on the ground in Iran, and we wanted to save and protect them if possible," Patrick said. "You did it because you had the forces standing by and ready to respond. If we'd followed orders, the survivors would be captured, tortured, then killed—you know it, and I know it. You acted. That's more than I can say for the Pentagon and our commander-in-chief. If we're going to lose our freedom, I'd rather it be because we tried to make sure our fellow airmen kept theirs."

Rebecca fell silent for a long moment, then shook her head ruefully. "I hate it when you're right, General," she said. "Maybe I can tell them that you threatened to blast me with Skybolt if I didn't do as you ordered."

"Maybe they'll laugh so hard they'll forget what we did."

"We need a plan, General," Rebecca said. "The Turks are going to send a force to retake Batman Air Base, and if they don't there's an entire U.S. airborne division in Germany that could be dropping on our heads within half a day. We've only got three CID units and four Tin Men at Batman, plus the security and maintenance troops. And we all know that Battle Mountain and probably Elliott will be next."

"We should move the Air Battle Force units to Dreamland," Patrick said. "We can hold that base a lot easier than Battle Mountain."

"Do you hear what you're saying, Patrick?" Rebecca asked incredulously. "You're conspiring to organize and direct U.S. military forces against the orders of the commander-in-chief, illegally marshal them under your own command without any authority, and directly oppose and engage with American military forces. That's sedition! That's *treason*! You won't go to prison, Patrick—you could be *executed*!"

"Thanks for the legal primer, Rebecca," Patrick said. "I'm hoping it won't come to this. After the survivors are rescued and the Russian anti-spacecraft laser is destroyed or at least discovered, all of this will be over. I understand if you don't want to do as I suggest, Rebecca. But if you want to take the Air Battle Force and assist, you can't stay at Battle Mountain. They could be rolling up outside to take you down as we speak."

Everyone on the secure video teleconference could see the tortured expression on Rebecca Furness's face. Out of all of them, she probably had the most to lose in this, and it was obvious she didn't want this. But just a moment later, she nodded. "All right. In for a dime, in for a dollar—in for twenty to life. Maybe the court-martial will take pity on me because I'm a woman. I'll get the planes moving right away, Dave. Make room for me."

"Yes, ma'am," Dave Luger responded from Elliott Air Force Base. Then: "What about the personnel and equipment at Batman Air Base, Muck? The Turks and our own guys could be waiting for them to return . . . if Turkey doesn't try to shoot them down when they cross back into Turkish airspace."

"I've got an idea for them, Dave," Patrick said. "It's going to be risky, but it's our only chance . . ."

PRIVATE RESIDENCE OF LEONID ZEVITIN, BOLTINO, RUSSIA

THAT SAME TIME

"Calm yourself, Excellency," Leonid Zevitin said. He was in his private study with Foreign Minister Alexandra Hedrov, making phone calls and sending secure e-mails to military and diplomatic units around the world alerting them to the events unfolding over Iran. The phone call from Iranian supreme leader Hassan Mohtaz happened much later than expected, but that was undoubtedly because it was probably very hazardous for anyone to wake the guy up with bad news.

"Calm myself? We are under attack—and it is because of *you!*" Mohtaz cried. "I allowed you to put your weapons on my soil because you said it would protect my country. It has done just the opposite! Four bombs have destroyed one of my Revolutionary Guards Corps bases, and now my air defense forces tell me that American bombers are flitting freely across our skies!"

"There are no bombers over Iran, Excellency—we have seen to that," Zevitin said. "As far as your base: remember that Russia paid to refurbish and disguise that base so we could use it temporarily, and we agreed that it would be turned over to you after we were done with it . . ."

"And now you are done with it because the Americans have *destroyed* it!" Mohtaz said. "Will you leave us a smoking hole in the ground now?"

"Calm yourself, Mr. President!"

"I want anti-aircraft weapons, and I want them *now!*" Mohtaz screamed. "You told me six units of the S-300 and another dozen Tor-M1 missile vehicles were waiting for pre-delivery checkout in Turkmenistan. How long ago was that, Zevitin? Eight, ten weeks? How long does it take to unpack a few missile launchers, turn them on, and see if all the pretty lights come on? When are you going to deliver on your promises?"

"They will be delivered, Mr. President, do not worry," Zevitin said. He didn't want to deliver missiles, especially the advanced S-300 strategic anti-aircraft and anti-ballistic missile system, until he was sure he could not get any more concessions from American President Joseph Gardner in exchange. Zevitin was perfectly willing to let Mohtaz rant and rave if he could get the Americans to agree not to put troops in Poland or the Czech Republic, or agree to veto any resolution in the United Nations that might allow Kosovo to break away from Serbia, in return. Those negotiations were in a critical stage, and he wasn't going to let Mohtaz screw them up.

"I want them now, Zevitin, or you can take all of your planes and tanks and radars back to Russia!" Mohtaz said. "I want the S-300 and Tor protecting Mashhad *tomorrow*. I want an impenetrable shield of missiles around that city when I return in triumph with my exiled government."

"That is impossible, Excellency. It takes time to test those advanced weapon systems properly before deployment. I will have Minister Ostenkov and chief of staff General Furzyenko brief your military advisers on—"

"No! No! No more briefings and wasted time!" Mohtaz shouted. "I want them deployed *immediately* or I will see to it that the entire world knows of your duplicity! What would your American friends say if they learn that you agreed to sell Iran anti-aircraft missiles, chemical weapons, and anti-personnel rockets?"

"You agreed not to share any information . . ."

"And you agreed to give me anti-aircraft missiles, Zevitin," Mohtaz interjected. "Break your promises further, and we are finished. Your infantry and tanks can rot in Turkmenistan for all I care." And at that the connection was broken.

TORBAT-E-JAM UNITED NATIONS REFUGEE CAMP, IRAN

A SHORT TIME LATER

"Easy now, lass, you're hurt. Don't move, eh?"

Captain Charlie Turlock opened her eyes . . . and immediately what little vision she had was shattered in a cloud of stars as the pain shot through her lower back, up through her spine, and into her brain. She gasped, the pain doubled, and she cried aloud. She felt a cool hand hold her forehead. "My God, my God . . . !"

"Believe it or not, lass, you shouting in pain is music to me ears," the man said, his thick Irish brogue slowly becoming clearer and soothing in a way, "because if you were'na cryin' out so, I'd believe your spine was broken. Where does it hurt, lass?"

"My back . . . my lower back," Charlie gasped. "It feels like . . . like my whole back is on fire."

"On fire . . . that's funny, lass," the man said. "I'm na surprised." Charlie looked at the man in confusion. She could see the stethoscope dangling around his neck now. He was very young, like an older teenager, with closely cut reddish-blond hair, bright green eyes, and an ever-present smile—but his eyes showed deep concern. The glare of a single overhead lightbulb hurt her eyes, but she was thankful that at least her eyes were working. "You might say you're an angel from heaven . . . or maybe a fallen angel?"

"I don't understand, Doctor . . . Doctor . . ."

"Miles. Miles McNulty," the man replied. "I'm na a doctor, but everyone out here believes I am, and that's good enough for all of us for now."

Charlie nodded. The pain was still there, but she was starting to get accustomed to it, and found that it even subsided a bit if she moved just so. "Where are we, Mr. McNulty?" she asked.

"Och, c'mon, lass, you're makin' me feel old callin' me by what they call me old man," Miles said. "Call me Miles, or Wooz if you like."

"Wooz?"

"Some of the docs gave me the nickname after I got here—I guess I'd get a little woozy seein' some of the shit that goes on around here: the blood, the putrid water, the injuries, the infant deaths, the starvation, the damned evil that someone can do to another human bein' in the name of God," Miles said, his young features momentarily turning hard and gray.

Charlie chuckled. "Sorry." She was pleased when his smile returned. "I'll call you Miles. I'm Charlie."

"Charlie? I know I've been here in the desert for a while, lass, but you na look like a 'Charlie' to me."

"Long story. I'll tell it to you sometime."

"Love to hear it, Charlie." He found a bottle in his jacket pocket and shook out some tablets. "Here. It's just over-the-counter NSAIDs—all the pain medication I dare give you until I do some more tests to find out if you're bleeding internally or if anything's broken."

A large armored hand reached out and completely surrounded the man's hand—Charlie couldn't turn her head, but she knew who it was. "I'll have a look at those first," he heard Chris Wohl's electronically synthesized voice say.

"Ah, it speaks," Miles said. He took his hand and the pills back. Wohl undid his helmet, exercising a kink out of his neck. "Pardon me for saying, bub, but ye looked better with the helmet on," he quipped, smiling broadly until he saw Wohl's warning glare. He put the tablets back into the bottle, shook it up, took one out, and popped it in his mouth. "I'm tryin' to help the lady, na hurt her." Wohl allowed him to give Charlie three tablets and a sip of water.

"How do you feel?" Wohl asked.

"Not bad if I don't . . . move," she said, gasping through a surge of pain. "I can't believe we made it." Wohl's warning glance reminded her not to talk any more about what they had just experienced. "How long have we been here?"

"Not long," Wohl responded. "About an hour."

"Where's Three?" Wohl motioned to Charlie's left. Charlie's mouth instantly turned dry. The pain forgotten, she followed the big Marine's glance beside her . . . and she saw the other Tin Man, Wayne Macomber, lying on another table beside her as if laid out on a funeral bier. "Is he dead?" she asked.

"No, but he's been unconscious awhile," Wohl said.

"I asked your comrade here if there's an on-off switch or latch or can opener to peel him open and check him out—I'm not even sure if it's a 'him' or a machine."

"We've got to get out of here as soon as possible," Wohl said.

"I think I'd like to give the lass a look, if you don't mind," Miles said to Wohl. "Ten minutes to look you over first, eh?"

"Five minutes."

"All right, all right." He turned to Charlie, smiling confidently. "I hate to do this while you're hurting, lass, but it'll help me isolate the injured areas. Ready?"

"I guess so."

"There's a game lass. I'm going to try not to move you too much myself, so try to move yourself along with me as much as you can—you're the best judge about how much is too much, yes? We'll start with the head and work our way down. Ready? Here we go." With surprising gentleness, McNulty examined her head, turning it ever so carefully, stooping down with a flashlight as low as he could go to look behind her head and neck without her having to turn her head as much.

"Well, I'm na seein' anything sticking out," Miles said after a few minutes. "You have a fun number of bruises and cuts, but so far nothing critical. I've seen much worse around here."

"Where are you from, Miles?"

"I'm from God's back porch: Westport, County Mayo." He didn't have to specify "Ireland." "And you?" Charlie turned her eyes away and down, and Wohl changed position—not very much, just enough for everyone to remember he was present and not let the conversation drift into unwanted territory. "Ah, that's okay, lass, I figured as much anyway. The only whites in these parts are relief workers and spies, and you're na dressed like a nurse."

"Where are we?"

"You're here at Torbat-e-Jam, the United Nations refugee camp, originally set up for the poor bastards fleein' the Taliban in Afghanistan, and now used by the other poor bastards fleein' the Muslim insurgents," Miles said. "I volunteered to help bring in a load of food and supplies about six months ago, but when the doctor's assistant went missing, I stayed. About a month ago, the doctor went missing—if the Taliban or al-Quds forces need a doctor, they don't send fer one, they *take* one—so I'm fillin' in until the next flight comes in. No tellin' when that will be, so I play the doc and help as best I can. I lose a few more than the doc did, but I'm startin' to get the hang of it, I think."

"Tobat-e-Jam?"

"Iran," Miles said. "Around here they still call it 'Iran'—the insurgency hasn't reached this far yet, so they don't call it 'Persia' yet, although the Revolutionary Guards Corps and al-Quds forces are gettin' pretty nervous, like the rebels are nippin' at their heels a wee bit. We're about sixty klicks from the border."

"Inside Iran?"

"Afraid so, lass," Miles said. "About two hundred kilometers from Mashhad, the capital of Khorasan province."

"God, this is the *last* place we want to be," Charlie moaned. She attempted to get up off the hard plywood board she was resting on and nearly passed out from a surging wave of pain that eclipsed anything else she had felt since awakening. "I'm not sure if I can make it yet," she told Wohl. "Where's my . . . briefcase?"

"Right here," Wohl said, without indicating where or what they were really talking about.

"You're in no shape to go anywhere, lass, and neither is your friend—as far as I can tell, at least," Miles said.

"I'll make it," Charlie said. "How far are we from the crash site?"

"About ten klicks," Miles replied. "What is that thing, anyway . . . Mercury's chariot? It's not exactly an airplane, is it—more like a tin can with balloons on it. It was badly burned but intact."

"How did you find us?"

"That wasn't a problem, lassie—we saw you streak across the sky and fall to Earth like a lightning bolt from Zeus himself!" Miles said, his eyes twinkling as the memory of seeing that sight came back. "Like the biggest meteor ever seen! You must have been trailing a tail of fire fifty kilometers long if it was an inch! It was a miracle to see three human beings still recognized as such in the wreckage, and even more amazing to find you still alive! We nearly shit our pants watchin' you blazin' down right toward us—thought the good Lord was going to end all of our sufferin' right then and there on the spot—but ya missed us. Findin' you alive was nothin' short of a miracle."

"Unfortunately that means that the Pasdaran probably saw us as well."

Miles nodded. "They di'na come around too often, but they're surely be sniffin' around out this way, for sure. The faster we get you folks out of here, the better for all of us. You should be well enough to travel after the painkiller kicks in. It won't be easy, but I think you can do it." He turned to the Tin Man lying beside her. "Now this gent, I'm still not so sure. Can you tell me how to . . . unlock him, unscrew him, unbolt him, whatever, so I can have a look and check him over?"

"We don't have time, Miles," Charlie said. "We'll carry him." Choking back the pain, she managed to sit up on her cot. "We'll be going now, Miles. I want to thank you for all you've done for us."

"I'll be sad to see you go, Charlie, but frankly I'd rather not have you around when the Pasdaran or al-Quds goons track you down here." He looked carefully at Wohl and the Tin Man suit. "I think I've read about these things lately, haven't I? The American anti-terrorist outfit." Charlie didn't respond. "Oh, I see—you could tell me, but then you'd have to kill me, right?" She laughed, causing a ripple of pain through her back, but she still welcomed the humor.

"All right, no more questions, Charlie. I'll go out and see if the coast is clear. Good luck to you, lass."

"Thanks." She grimaced at the pain as she started to pull herself up, but the stuff McNulty gave her must've started working because the pain wasn't debilitating this time. After McNulty departed, Charlie lowered her voice and spoke, "Odin, Stud Four."

"We read you loud and clear, Four," Patrick McLanahan responded via the subcutaneous global transceiver system. Every member of the Air Battle Force had the communications and data transceiver system implanted into their bodies for the rest of their lives, ostensibly for situations like this but realistically to allow the government to monitor each member's whereabouts for *life*. "Thank God you're alive. We read Five is with you."

"Affirmative—he's alive but still unconscious," Charlie said. Wohl started to put his helmet on, preparing to move out. "I'm going to mount up and we'll—"

Suddenly McNulty ran back into the tent, completely out of breath. "Soldiers, just outside the camp," he said frantically. "Hundreds of them."

"Odin, do we have a ride yet?" Charlie radioed.

"Stud, this is Genesis," Dave Luger cut in. "We have a CSAR team on the way from Herat, ETE ninety minutes. We're launching cover aircraft from Batman Air Base in Turkey, but they'll take about the same amount of time. What's your situation?"

"Getting tense," Charlie said. "We'll give you a call when we're safe. Stud Four, out." Charlie went over to the large box lying on the dirt floor. "Any backpacks or rifles, Five?"

"Negative," Wohl replied. "Sorry."

"That's okay—you had your hands full," Charlie said. "Let's get moving."

Miles motioned to the large box that Wohl had been carrying with him when he entered the camp. "Are those your weapons? Now would be a good time to get them out, lass."

"Not exactly," Charlie said. "CID One, deploy."

As Miles watched in amazement, the box began to move, quickly shifting size and shape like a magician's wand changing into a bouquet of flowers. In seconds, the large but ordinary-looking metal box had transformed into a ten-foot-tall robot, almost bursting out the top of the tent, with smooth black "skin," a bullet-shaped head with no discernible eyes or ears, and large, fully articulating arms, legs, and fingers.

"CID One, pilot up," Charlie spoke. The robot assumed a leaning-forward stance as if on a sprinter's starting block, but with one leg and both arms extended backward. Grimacing from the pain, Charlie stepped around the robot and climbed up the extended leg, using the arms as handrails. She entered a code into a tiny keypad somewhere behind the robot's head, a hatch popped open on its back, and she slipped herself inside. The hatch closed . . .

. . . and moments later, to the Irishman's amazement, the robot came to life and stood, resembling a regular person in everything but its appearance—its movements were so smooth, fluid, and lifelike that Miles immediately found himself forgetting it was a machine!

Charlie scooped up the still-unconscious Wayne Macomber. "Now is a very bad time to be out of it, Whack," she said. She activated the Cybernetic Infantry Device's millimeter-wave radar and scanned the area outside the tent. "Looks like they're trying to surround us," she said. "The south side looks like our best escape route—just one truck set up down that way."

"How about a little diversion to the north and west?" Wohl asked, studying the radar image data being transmitted to him from Charlie's CID unit. "Looks like a machine-gun squad getting set up on the north side. I can use one of those."

"Sounds good." She reached a fist out, and he punched it in return with his own. "As a hunky Australian actor said in a movie once: 'Unleash hell.'"

"On the way. Better give him some cover." Wohl sprinted out the front of the tent. Charlie knocked Miles to the ground and covered him just as a hail of automatic gunfire shredded the tent apart.

"Hop on, Miles," Charlie's electronically synthesized voice said. Still bent over, she shifted the inert form in her arms aside, far enough to form a space between her body and the Tin Man. He hesitated, still dumbfounded by what he had just seen. "You can't stay here. The Revolutionary Guards Corps will think you're one of us."

"Can ye carry us both?"

"I can carry twenty of you, Miles. Let's go." He lay across her arms, and she rolled Macomber back on top of him and tightened her grip, sandwiching him in securely. "Hang on."

But when she got up, there was obviously something wrong—Miles felt a high-frequency vibration within the machine, and Charlie's gait was unsteady. "What's wrong?" he shouted.

"The CID unit is damaged," Charlie said. "Must've been from the crash."

"I copy," Wohl radioed. Charlie could see his position in her electronic data visor—he was moving rapidly through the Iranian Revolutionary Guards Corps' positions, stopping briefly at each concentration of troops. "Head out the best you can. I'll be beside you in a moment."

The next few minutes were sheer torture. Wohl had drawn some of their fire away briefly, but it returned full force just moments after Charlie burst from the tent, seemingly all aimed at them. The sounds were deafening. They were consumed with clouds of smoke, occasional blasts of fire, and continuous gunfire. McNulty screamed when a round hit his left leg, and screamed again when a crushing explosion knocked Charlie to the ground. They were up again within moments, but now the smooth running rhythm was replaced by an awkward limping shuffle, like an automobile with a flat tire and bent rim.

Wohl ran beside Charlie, a Chinese Type 67 machine gun in his right hand, a metal can of ammunition in his left. "Can you travel, Captain?"

"Not for long."

"What the hell is going on?" they heard.

"Whack!" Thankfully, Macomber was awake, although he sounded sluggish and doped-up. "Are you okay?"

"My head feels like it's been cracked open," Macomber said thickly. Charlie suspected a concussion. "Am I alive?"

"So far—hopefully it'll stay that way," Charlie said. "Can you walk?"

"Do I still have legs? I can't feel anything down there."

"Stay put and try not to move—you'll squish the other passenger."

"Other passenger?"

Charlie tried to run, but things were definitely getting worse. A rocket-propelled grenade exploded on her back, sending them flying again. "Power is down to forty percent already," Charlie said as Wohl helped them up, "my primary hydraulic system is out, and I can't move my right leg."

"Can you keep moving?"

"Yes, I think so," Charlie said. Using her right leg as a crutch, she limped along, with Wohl laying down suppression fire with his machine gun until he ran out of ammunition. He half supported, half carried Charlie, and they were able to move faster up a low ridgeline. They could easily see their pursuers below them, advancing slowly, with more and more units joining the pursuit.

Charlie set Macomber and McNulty down, then dismounted from the CID unit. "It's getting ready to shut down," she said. "It's done. There's just enough power left to start erasing the firmware. Once we move away, it'll automatically self-destruct."

"It looks like they're not sure where we are," Wohl said, scanning the desert below them with night-vision optics. He zoomed in on a few of the details. "Let's see . . . infantry . . . infantry . . . ah, got one, another machine-gun squad. I'll be right back." He raced off into the darkness.

Macomber struggled to his hands and knees. "Okay, I'm starting to tell up from down," he said. "Who's our guest?"

"Miles McNulty, a UN relief worker," Charlie replied, filling in the details.

A few minutes later, Wohl ran back with an even larger weapon than the first, a Russian DshK heavy machine gun with a huge drum magazine on top, along with a wooden box of more magazines. "Looks like they brought some anti-aircraft weapons with them—they were obviously expecting company. How are you doing, Major?"

"Peachy, Sergeant Major," Macomber replied. He looked at McNulty. Charlie was busy tying a scrap of cloth torn from her uniform around his leg. "The passenger is hurt. Where's the cavalry?"

"At least sixty mike out."

"Where are we headed?"

"East toward the Afghanistan border," Charlie said. "About thirty miles away. Hilly and pretty open. No towns or villages for fifty miles."

"How are you doing on power, Sergeant Major?" Macomber asked.

"Down to thirty percent."

"Here—I can't use it yet." He unclipped one of his circular batteries from his belt and swapped it for one of Wohl's more depleted ones. "Can we use the CID unit to charge our batteries?"

"Not when it's in shutdown mode, Whack," Charlie said.

"Can't we tap into a power or telephone pole?" Macomber asked. Charlie looked at him with astonishment. "Hey, I *have* been studying these things—I may not like them, but I do read the manuals. We're not going to follow the highway, but if we spot a breaker box or control junction, I think I can rig up a jumper. Let's get—"

"I hear helicopters," Wohl said. He used his night-vision and enhanced hearing systems to sweep the skies, pinpointing the approaching aircraft's position. "Two light scout helicopters, about three miles away," he said, raising the DshK machine gun.

"Let's spread out," Macomber said. But he soon found out that was all but impossible: Charlie was still in pain from her injuries, and McNulty was hurt badly and going into shock, so he had to carry both of them even though he still wasn't a hundred percent himself, so it was slow-going. Wohl moved about ten yards away from them, close enough to support them if they came under attack but not close enough that one explosive round fired from a helicopter could take them all out at once.

They had run up the ridge just a few hundred yards when Wohl shouted, "Take cover!" Macomber found the largest piece of rock nearby and threw his charges and then himself behind it, placing himself between the helicopters and the others to shield them the best he could with his armored body. The Tin Man armor system featured an electronically actuated material that stayed flexible but instantly hardened when struck into a protective shield a hundred times stronger than plate steel.

Macomber could hear the oncoming helicopters through his own enhanced hearing system, but his eyes couldn't focus on his electronic displays. "I can't see them, Wohl."

"Stay down." A moment later he opened fire with the DshK machine gun, the muzzle flash of the big 12.7-millimeter cannon illuminating a ten-yard-diameter area around him. They heard a loud metallic screech as several rounds pierced the first helicopter's turbine engine and seized it solid, then an explosion as the engine blew itself apart. Seconds later they heard more explosions as the second scout helicopter opened fire on Wohl's position. He managed to jump out of the way just in time to avoid the full force of the Iranian 40-millimeter rocket attack.

Wohl opened fire on the second helicopter, but the fire soon cut off. "Jammed . . . shit, a round stuck in the chamber . . . won't clear." He was surprised the gun had fired as many rounds as it did—it looked as if it was fifty years old and hadn't been cleaned in half that number of years. He discarded the weapon and scanned the area for more nearby Pasdaran units so he could grab another machine gun, but the three remaining units were hanging back, blindly peppering the ridgeline with occasional rifle and mortar fire and content to let the scout helicopter do some fighting for them.

"The infantry units are hanging back, and there's still one helicopter overhead," Wohl reported. "I'm down to throwing rocks." He wasn't kidding—the microhydraulically actuated exoskeleton on the Tin Man combat system gave him enough power to hurl a five-pound rock almost two hundred yards with enough force to do some damage, which could put him within range of that scout helicopter if he could dash toward it, jump, and throw with perfect timing. He found a softball-sized rock and prepared to do just that . . .

. . . but then his sensors picked up another helicopter, and this time it wasn't a little scout. He'd recognize that silhouette anywhere: "We've got more trouble, ma'am," Wohl said. "Looks like a Mi-24 Hind inbound." The Russian-built Mi-24, NATO code name "Hind," was a large attack helicopter which could also carry up to eight fully outfitted soldiers inside. It carried a formidable array of weapons . . .

. . . the first of which opened fire seconds later, from over three miles away. Wohl immediately dashed away from the rest of his team, then stopped to make sure the anti-tank guided missile was still tracking him. It was, and he realized that the helicopter itself was following him too, which meant that the helicopter crew had to keep him in sight to keep the missile on him. Good. It had to be an older guided missile, probably an AT-6 line-of-sight radio-controlled missile.

Wohl waited another heartbeat, then dashed toward the nearest group of Pasdaran ground pursuers at top speed. He could no longer see the missile, but he remembered that an AT-6's flight time was somewhere around ten seconds when fired from maximum range. That meant he had just seconds to make it. This Pasdaran unit was an armored vehicle with a heavy machine gun on top, which opened fire as he closed in. A few shells hit, but not enough to slow him down. Now he was between the armored vehicle and the helicopter—certainly, Wohl thought, the Hind's gunner had to turn the missile away. His mental stopwatch ran to zero . . .

. . . just as the AT-6 Spiral anti-tank missile slammed into the Pasdaran armored vehicle, setting it afire in a spectacular fireball.

Wohl was thrown skyward by the concussion. The damned Pasdaran gunner got so target-fixated that he lined up and hit his own guys!

Wohl rolled unsteadily to his feet, alive and mostly unhurt except his eyes and throat were clogged with oily smoke. The entire left side of his helmet, along with most of his sensors and communications, had been damaged in the blast. He had no choice but to take the helmet off. The blast had also ruined his hearing, and the acrid smoke burned his eyes and throat. He was a sitting duck. His first order of business was to get away from the burning vehicles behind him, which could be highlighting him . . .

. . . but before he could move, a line of automatic gunfire stitched the ground in front of him, and the big Mi-24 Hind attack helicopter zoomed before him and stopped, the chin-mounted 30-- millimeter cannon trained directly on him. His armor would protect his body, but that would be of no use to him without a head. Wohl had no idea if they would accept a surrender, but if they were distracted long enough it might provide the others a chance to escape, so he raised his hands. The Mi-24 started its descent to touchdown, and he could see the clamshell crew doors open on either side, with soldiers ready to dismount as soon as the big chopper set . . .

. . . and at that instant there was a flash of fire on the right side of the attack chopper, followed by a large plume of smoke, more fire, an explosion, and a scream of metal, and then the big chopper spun to the left and hit the ground. Wohl dashed away just as the helicopter began to disintegrate in several more tremendous explosions. He was about to head back toward the others when he saw several vehicles, including an armored personnel carrier, approach. The lead vehicle, a pickup truck with a machine gunner in back, was flying a flag, but he couldn't make it out yet. He thought about running away from where he last left Turlock, Macomber, and the Irishman . . . until he saw the vehicles veer left away from him and toward the hiding place.

Wohl took off at top speed toward the vehicle at the tail end of the six-vehicle convoy, which had a machine gunner covering the rear of the formation. The other vehicles wouldn't fire toward their own vehicles, and hopefully he could reach the machine gunner, disable him, and take the gun before he could get a shot off. Just a hundred yards to go . . .

. . . and then he saw Turlock coming out of her hiding place, with her arms up. Was she surrendering? It might be good timing after all—if they were concentrating on them he had a better chance of reaching the last pickup truck and . . .

. . . but then as he got closer Wohl realized that Turlock wasn't raising her hands in surrender, but *waving* to him, motioning him back! Why was she doing this? Now she was pointing at the lead vehicle, the one with the flag . . .

. . . and Wohl finally realized what she was trying to tell him. The flag the vehicle was carrying had the green, white, and red stripes of the Islamic Republic of Iran on it, but the center symbol wasn't the "red tulip" stylized word "Allah," but the profile of a lion carrying a sword with the rising sun behind it—the flag representing the pre-revolutionary era and the opposition to the Islamists.

Chris trotted over to Turlock and Macomber, carefully watching to be sure none of the gunners pointed their weapons at him. "Not answering your phone, Sergeant Major?" Turlock asked, pointing to her ear, indicating his subcutaneous transceiver system.

"Got my bell rung back there," Wohl said. He nodded toward the newcomers. "Who are these guys?"

"These are Buzhazi's men," Charlie said. "General McLanahan actually called Buzhazi and asked for help."

"They came right on time. Good thing they brought Stinger missiles with them."

"They didn't shoot down the Hind, Sergeant Major." Charlie pointed to the sky, and they saw the contrails of a very large aircraft high overhead. "Compliments of the general. They'll be on station for another two hours."

"Outstanding. That should get us enough time to get across the border."

"The general suggests we head back toward Tehran with these guys," Charlie said. "They're bringing in a helicopter to pick us up, and the Vampires will cover for us."

"I don't think that's such a hot idea, ma'am."

"I'll explain." She did . . . and Wohl couldn't believe what he had just heard.

CHAPTER EIGHT

You don't hold your own in the world by standing on guard, but by attacking and getting well hammered yourself.

—George Bernard Shaw

CAPITOL HILL, WASHINGTON, D.C.

A SHORT TIME LATER

"Frankly, Brit, I don't care what the Russians say," Senate majority leader Stacy Anne Barbeau said. She was in the second-floor area of the Senate normally used by reporters for "staking out" senators for comments on their way to the floor or between committee meetings. "They have been claiming all sorts of things for many months and none of them have been proven. Although I believe Leonid Zevitin to be a capable and forthright leader, the statements made by his foreign minister Alexandra Hedrov seem more shrill and bombastic every time we see her in the news. President Zevitin is certainly not like that at all, which naturally leads me to the obvious question: Who is telling the truth out there at the Kremlin these days, and who is lying, and for what purpose?"

"But tomorrow there is a key vote in the Senate about funding for the U.S. military," the reporter pressed, "and in the midst of all this wrangling about where to spend the money in the military, President Zevitin's Cabinet members seem to be taking great pleasure in stirring up anxiety about another future confrontation. Are the two activities related, and if so to what end?"

"I'm sure I don't know what is in the mind of a Russian, even one as Westernized, worldly, and charming as Leonid Zevitin," Barbeau said. "I would think they would want to avoid rattling sabers at a time where we in the Congress are trying to determine the proper direction for the world's greatest military force."

"But this is more than just saber-rattling, Senator," the reporter went on. "There is definitely something stirring out there, Senator, and I'm not just talking about the turmoil in Iran, but with American military activities, isn't there? To put it plainly, ma'am: We can't seem to get out of our own way. The civil war in Iran is threatening to blow the entire Middle East into an inferno, and yet we're not doing much of anything except sending unmanned reconnaissance aircraft over the region; oil prices are skyrocketing; the economy is sinking like a rock; Russia accuses us daily of killing civilians, bombing a civil relief base in Iran, and causing unrest and chaos around the world, especially with the Armstrong Space Station and our spaceplanes; the space program seems robust and substantial one day, then completely ineffectual the next. We even have a famous and well-loved American three-star general, the hero of the American Holocaust, in essence *stranded in space* because no one can tell us if he's well enough to be brought back home. My question is, madam: What in the world is happening, what has Congress been told by the White House and the Pentagon, and what are you going to do about it?"

Barbeau gave him her most appealing mind-blowing smile, again defining the phrase "making love to the camera" to millions of viewers as she replied: "Why, sir, what a dreadful picture of doom and gloom you are painting here this morning! Let me assure you, and everyone in your audience around the world, that the Congress of the United States is working very closely with the

President and his department officials not only to deal with current and future crises as they rear their ugly heads, but to chart a course for America's armed forces that is second to none, forward-looking, adaptable, scalable, and affordable. It has been less than five years since the American Holocaust, and three different governments have had to deal with the world as it has become since those awful attacks on our soil. We are making progress, but it will take time."

"So tell us how you envision the debate will develop, Senator. What's on the table?"

"The most important question for us right now is simply this: What is the best force to take the place of the land-based long-range strategic bombers and intercontinental ballistic missiles that were destroyed in the Holocaust?" Barbeau replied, still radiant even while wearing a stern, concerned, determined expression. "President Thorn favored land- and sea-based tactical air forces, both manned and unmanned, along with ballistic missile defense systems. President Martindale favored the same but, as advocated by his special adviser General Patrick McLanahan, also sought to 'skip a generation,' as he said, and develop a fleet of spaceplanes that could strike any target anywhere around the world with amazing speed, launch satellites into orbit whenever needed, and fly troops and equipment anywhere around the planet within hours.

"As the former Secretary of Defense, Joseph Gardner supported those ideas and encouraged development of Armstrong Space Station, the entire constellation of space-based assets, and the Black Stallion spaceplane," Barbeau went on. "The space program has taken some amazing strides and has greatly benefited the entire world—the global Internet access provided by our space program has without question truly changed all of our lives and brought our world together—but it has also suffered some serious setbacks. As President, Joseph Gardner has wisely recognized that perhaps the space-based defense force visualized by Patrick McLanahan wasn't mature enough yet to serve America."

"So where does this leave us, Senator?" the host asked.

"President Gardner has met with the leadership and proposed a more reliable, familiar, proven mix of weapon systems," Barbeau said. "He wants to take the best concepts proposed by previous administrations and combine them in a comprehensive program to quickly stand up a credible force to meet the country's needs."

"And which concepts are those, Senator?"

"I can't give you any specifics, Brit, or I'll have a lot of very angry gentlemen nipping at my heels in short order," Barbeau said sweetly. "But in a nutshell, we have the individual services do what the services do best, what has served the nation and the world so well for the past three generations but also recognizes changes in technology and our vision for the future: fully fund and support an expanded and strengthened Army and Marine Corps as the dominant land and special operations forces; fully support the Navy as the dominant sea and air force; and the Air Force as the dominant global support and space defense force."

"The Air Force wouldn't be the dominant *air force* in the U.S. arsenal? That doesn't seem right."

"Details have yet to be worked out, and of course I'm sure we will adjust and rearrange things as necessary to ensure the absolute best force we can build," Barbeau began, "but it seems to President Gardner and we in the congressional leadership that there is a wasteful and costly overlap between the Air Force and Navy regarding tactical air forces. It all comes down to the basic notion, Brit, that Navy planes can do everything Air Force planes can do, but Air Force planes cannot do everything Navy planes can do—namely, take off and land on an aircraft carrier, which as everyone readily recognizes is the undisputed definition of power projection in the world today."

"And the President as we all know is a big supporter of the Navy, being the former Navy secretary."

"It's a duplication of forces, plain and simple, and now is the time to address this if we want to have a robust, mature, twenty-first century fighting force," Barbeau said. "We're trying to think ahead. The Air Force is the proven expert in long-range strategic attack and rapid resupply, and the Navy has no such equivalent capability—it makes sense to give that mission to the Air Force and let the Navy have the mission of training and equipping tactical fighters for theater commanders around the world."

"Won't your constituents in Louisiana object to this plan, Senator?"

"I represent the finest, most patriotic, and most pro-military folks in the country, Brit: the good people of Barksdale Air Force Base near Bossier City, Louisiana—Bomber Town, USA," Barbeau said. "But even the staunchest bomber supporters, like me, have seen the shift coming for years: the shift from World War Two–era land-based bombers to the importance of global reach, rapid mobility, unmanned aircraft, space technology, and most importantly, information warfare. The Air Force is and will remain the leader in these areas. We've seen this coming for years, and President Gardner and I think it's time to design our twenty-first-century forces around this new reality."

"But the battles are just beginning, aren't they, Senator?"

"With President Gardner's strong leadership and his steadfast pledge to work closely with Congress, I think the battles will be kept to the barest minimum. Together, we'll prevail. The alternative is too awful to consider."

"So does this mean we'll see the end of the Black Stallion space-planes and military space stations watching over us 24/7?"

"The Black Stallion is a remarkable technological advancement, to be sure, but as we've seen with a man like General McLanahan, it has its risks and dangers," Barbeau said, a serious look of concern briefly shadowing her features. "My heart sank when I learned of General McLanahan's illness, and we are doing everything we can to bring him safely home. But my concern is this, Brit: Patrick . . . General McLanahan . . . is a powerful man. You know the stories as well as I, Brit . . ."

"The ones about McLanahan being challenged by visiting heads of state and generals to rip their respective capital's phone books in half?" the reporter filled in with a chuckle. "I thought that was a White House Press Corps rumor."

"It's not a rumor, I assure you!" Barbeau exclaimed. "I've seen it with my own eyes—Patrick can rip a D.C. phone book in half as easily as you or I could rip a page out of your little notebook there. And yet he was still brought down by something difficult to detect, diagnose, or treat, something so debilitating that it could put the lives of every space crewman we have in jeopardy. There is great concern that the injury has affected more than just his heart."

The reporter's mouth opened in surprise. "I haven't heard anything about that, Senator. Would you care to elaborate? What exactly do you mean?"

"It's all just speculation and nonsense, I'm sure," Barbeau said dismissively, acting as if she'd said something completely unintended but riveting the attention of every viewer by looking directly into the camera for a brief moment. "But we do need to fully understand what happened to him. We owe it to him because he is truly a national treasure, a hero in every sense of the word.

"But the fundamental question remains: Can we afford to put our nation's military future on hold while we study this awful catastrophe?" Barbeau asked resolutely, first looking at the reporter and then directly at the camera, right into the hearts of the viewers. "As responsible caretakers of our armed forces, sworn to build the best possible force to protect and defend our homeland and way of life, the answer is simple and obvious: the space defense force is not ready, and so we must turn to proven systems that we know will work. That's our job here today, and with the cooperation of the President and the House, we're going to get it done. The American people expect no less from us."

Stacy Anne Barbeau fielded more questions from the gaggle of reporters, until finally the officials of the Senate Press Gallery and Barbeau's aide shooed them away and let her go. On the way to a late-night meeting in a committee conference room, she took a call on her cellular phone: "I thought you laid on the praise for McLanahan a little too thick, Stacy Anne," President Joe Gardner said. "His ass will be grass here shortly."

"All the more reason to sing his praises, Mr. President," Barbeau said, greeting supporters and colleagues as she walked and talked. "I advise you to do similarly, Mr. President: Let your Secretary of Defense, the pundits, the Russians, and the anti-military media trash him, not us."

"You won't be saying that when you hear what just happened, Senator."

Barbeau's mouth instantly turned dry. "What's happened, Mr. President?" she asked, turning a puzzled expression to her aide, Colleen Morna. As they reached the conference room, Morna immediately shooed everyone else out so Barbeau could talk in private.

"McLanahan lost it, and I mean *completely*," Gardner said. She detected a slight hint of triumph in his voice, like he'd finally gotten something that Barbeau didn't have and expected some quid pro quo for sharing it with her. "His people took over a Turkish air base, captured the base commander and most of the personnel with their manned robots, then launched another air mission over Iran."

Barbeau froze, and her mouth dropped open in complete shock before she exclaimed, *"What!"* Her expression was so alarming that her aide Colleen Morna thought she was having a heart attack. "I . . . I don't believe it . . ."

"What do you say about your knight in shining armor now, Stacy?" the President asked. "But you haven't heard the best part. When the brass sent in some security units from Incirlik Air Base to arrest McLanahan's people, they were gone. The planes and most of their stuff are *gone*. We have *no idea* where they are."

"They . . . they must be on their way back to the States, Mr. President . . ."

"Not that anyone is aware, Stacy," Gardner said. "McLanahan has *stolen* about four experimental attack planes and moved them somewhere. We hope they're on their way back to Dreamland, their main base in south-central Nevada north of Vegas. If they are, McLanahan can be charged with conspiracy and sedition against the U.S. government. How about *them* apples? How's your hero looking now?"

"I . . . I just cannot believe it, Mr. President," Barbeau breathed. Shit, after what she just said to the media, all the nice things about McLanahan . . . God, this could *ruin* her! "We need to meet and discuss this right away, Mr. President. We need to come up with a united stance, both for Congress and for the press."

"We're getting all the information we can, and we'll prepare a briefing for the leadership that we'll give first thing in the morning," the President said. "McLanahan is going down, I promise you, and so is his entire command. He won't be so popular after people find out what he's done. We won't have to look like we're destroying a national hero anymore—he's taking *himself* down."

"We need all the facts first, Mr. President," Barbeau said, her mind racing, trying to make sense of this explosive news. "Why exactly did he launch those bombers? McLanahan doesn't do something for no reason."

"It doesn't matter one bit to me, Stacy," Gardner said. "He's disobeyed orders, ignored my authority, and now he's launched military strike missions overseas, stolen military property, moved and directed military forces without authority, and opposed our own and allied military forces. For all we know, he could be engineering a military coup against the government or even preparing a military strike against Washington. He has to be stopped!"

"Whatever our response is, Mr. President, I suggest we find out all we can first, carefully discuss it, formulate a plan, and carry it out together," Barbeau repeated. "I know your military forces are an executive responsibility, but it would be easier to do what we have to do if we are together on this beforehand."

"Agreed," the President said. "We should meet and discuss strategy, Senator, after we present our findings. Tonight. Private meeting in the Oval Office."

Barbeau rolled her eyes in exasperation. The man's greatest general just stole some bombers and captured a Turkish air base, and all the man could think about was canoodling with the Senate majority leader. But she had been suddenly thrust onto the defensive, especially after her statements to the press, and the President had the upper hand. If she wanted any chance of retaining her bargaining position for the space force funds that were certainly going to be freed up soon, she had to play his game . . . for now. "The Senate has a full schedule, Mr. President, but I'm sure I can . . . squeeze you in," Barbeau said, flipping the phone closed.

"What in the world happened?" her aide, Colleen Morna, asked. "You look as pale as a ghost."

"Possibly the worst thing imaginable . . . or it could be the best," she said. "Set up a meeting with the President after the last agenda conference tonight."

"*Tonight?* It's already past five, and you have that meeting with that law firm that represents those defense and technology industry lobbies at seven. That was scheduled to last until nine. What's the President want? What's going on?"

"We all *know* what the President has got on *his* mind. Set it up."

"It'll be another late night, and with the Armed Services Committee hearings starting tomorrow, you'll be running ragged. What's so important that the President wants to meet so late? He still wants to take McLanahan to the woodshed?"

"Not just to the woodshed—he wants to bury the whole damned ax in his chest," Barbeau said. She filled her in quickly, and soon Morna's expression was even more flabbergasted than her own. "I don't know precisely what happened, but I think I know McLanahan: he's the definition of a goody two-shoes. If he hit something in Iran, he probably had spot-on intelligence that something bad was going down, and he didn't get the green light to take it out, so he did the deed himself. Gardner should be *encouraging* him, not taking him on. But the President wants to show he's still in charge and in control, so he's going to destroy McLanahan." She thought for a moment; then: "We need to find out exactly what's happened, but not from Gardner's perspective. We need our own intel on this. McLanahan's not crazy. If we come to his rescue, we might come out on top of this after all."

"Now you *want* McLanahan to win, Stacy?" Morna asked.

"Of course I want him to win, Colleen, but I want him to win for *me,* not just for himself or even for the country!" Barbeau said. "He's a genuine hero, a knight in shining armor, as Gardner puts it. Gardner's pride is hurt, and he's not thinking clearly. I need to find out what he has in mind, even if it means doin' the dirty with him whenever the First Lady is on the road, but then we need to find out what *really* happened and plan our own strategy. I gotta keep my eye on the prize, honey, and that is getting contracts and perks for my buddies in Louisiana."

"What if he's really flipped out?"

"We need to find out what happened to McLanahan and what he did out in Iran, and *fast,*" Barbeau said. "I'm not going to blindly side with the President and oppose McLanahan unless the guy really has flipped out, which I seriously doubt. Get on the horn and find out all you can about what happened. You still in contact with the space playboy buddy of his . . . what's his name?"

"Hunter Noble."

"Oh yes, the luscious Captain Noble, the young space cowboy. You need to pump him for information, but not make it sound like it. You still screwing him?"

"I'm one of a very long line of Hunter Noble East Coast screw-ees."

"You can do better than that, child," Barbeau said, giving her a pat on the back and then a discreet one on the butt. "Don't just be another squeeze—be his wingman, his confidante. Tell him the Senate Armed Services Committee is going to look in on goings-on in Dreamland, and you'd like to help. Warn him. Maybe he'll give up some useful information."

"It'll be tough to meet up with the guy if he's flying around in space, stuck in that base out there in the desert . . . or in prison."

"We might have to plan a fact-finding trip to Vegas soon so you can *really* put the squeeze on him. Maybe I'll get to join in too." She paused, savoring the thought of a three-way with the Air Force playboy. "Tell him that if he cooperates, we can keep his tight young ass out of prison." She smiled and added, "And if he doesn't cooperate, get me some dirt on the boy that I can use against him. If he won't play nice, we'll use him to start dismantling McLanahan and the rest of those characters at Dreamland."

TEHRAN MEHRABAD AIRPORT, TEHRAN, DEMOCRATIC REPUBLIC OF PERSIA

EARLY THAT EVENING, TEHRAN TIME

The motorcade of armored Mercedes sedans and limousines sped down Me'raj Avenue toward Mehrabad International Airport un- hindered by roadblocks. All along the motorcade route, General Buzhazi had his troops take down the checkpoints and barricades just before the motorcade arrived, let it pass, then hurriedly put them back up. The heavy troop presence throughout western Tehran that night kept citizens and insurgents away from the main thor- oughfares, so few got to see the extraordinary procedures.

The motorcade bypassed the main terminal, where Buzhazi had set up his headquarters, and instead moved quickly down a taxiway and out to a row of Iran Air hangars. Here security appeared rou- tine, almost invisible—unless you had night-vision goggles and a map showing the locations of dozens of sniper and infantry units scattered throughout the airport grounds.

A lone unmarked plain white Boeing 727 sat in front of one of the hangars, its airstair guarded by two security men in suits and ties. The lead sedan pulled forward just beyond the foot of the air- stair, and four men in dark business suits, dark caps similar to chauffeur's hats, white shirts, dark ties, dark slacks and shoes, and carrying submachine pistols exited and took up stations around the stairs and the nose of the aircraft. One by one the two stretch limou- sines pulled up to the foot of the airstair, with more sedans unleash- ing eight more similarly attired and armed security agents to guard the tail and right side of the aircraft. Out of each limo several indi- viduals exited, including an older man in a military uniform, a young woman surrounded by bodyguards, and men and women both in Western-style business suits and Iranian-style high-collared jackets.

In moments all the persons had trotted up the stairs and into the jetliner. The security men stayed in their positions until the jet had started its engines, and then they re-entered their sedans. The big armored cars formed a bubble around all sides of the airliner as it taxied down the empty taxiways and to the main runway, and in minutes the jetliner was airborne. The limousines retreated to a secure fenced area behind the Iran Air hangars and were parked outside a battered-looking repair garage. The Mercedes sedans performed a quick patrol of the ramp and hangar perimeters, then were parked in the same fenced area as the limousines. Minutes after the drivers and security men stepped out and locked their cars, workers came out, used towels to wipe dirt off the vehicles, and covered each of them with elastic-bottomed nylon covers. The lights were turned out, and soon the airport returned to the tense quiet it had become since the insurgency began.

The gaggle of security agents walked across the parking ramp to the main terminal building, weapons slung on their shoulders, most smoking, all saying little. They had their ID badges examined by a security guard outside the terminal and were allowed inside. They walked across the passenger concourse to a door marked CREWMEM-BERS ONLY, had their ID badges checked once more, and were admitted. Other agents inside took their weapons, unloaded and cleared them, and the group went down a dimly lit hallway and inside to a conference room.

"I think everyone played their part as best as could be expected," the first "security guard," General Hesarak al-Kan Buzhazi, said. "Nice to see how the other half lives, eh, Chancellor?"

"I found it uncomfortable, unconvincing, unnecessary, and if my hearing has been damaged by those aircraft engines, I will hold you personally responsible, General Buzhazi," Masoud Noshahr, the Lord High Chancellor of the Qagev royal court, said indignantly. He was tall and thin, in his late forties, with long and slightly curly gray hair, a salt-and-pepper goatee, and long and delicate-looking fingers. Although he was young and appeared healthy, Noshahr, obviously unaccustomed to much physical exertion, was out of breath from their fast walking pace and from climbing stairs instead of taking elevators. He stripped off the jacket and cap and removed the tie as if they were burning his skin with acid, then snapped his fingers to one of the other men in dark suits, one of his real security guards, who went to fetch his ankle-length fur and leather coat. "It was nothing but a petty parlor game that fooled no one."

"We had better hope it worked, Lord Chancellor," another of the "security guards," Princess Azar Assiyeh Qagev, said. Instead of handing her weapon off to a guard, she unloaded and cleared it herself, then began field-stripping the weapon for inspection and cleaning. "The insurgents penetrate our network deeper and deeper every day."

"And we capture and kill more of *them* every day as well, Highness," Noshahr reminded her. "God and time are on our side, Princess, have no fear." Finally his attention was drawn to the weapon disassembly going on in front of him. "What in the world are you doing, Highness?" Noshahr asked in amazement as Azar's deformed but obviously skilled fingers worked the seemingly hidden levers and pins of the weapon. He squinted uncomfortably at the princess working with the submachine gun and nodded to a bodyguard, who went over to the princess, bowed politely at the waist, then reached out to take the gun parts from her hands. She gave him a stern expression and a slight shake of her head, and he bowed again and backed away. In seconds the submachine gun lay in pieces before her on the table.

"You don't carry an unknown or unfamiliar weapon into battle, Lord Chancellor," Azar said. "How do you know if the thing will work when you want it to? How do you even know if it was loaded if you don't bother to check?"

"We carried those things for show, to fool any insurgents who may have been watching us," Noshahr said. "I don't care what shape it's in. That's why we have trained guards with us. Princesses are not supposed to be handling dangerous weapons."

"It's not dangerous now, Lord Chancellor—it looks like it's in good shape to me," Azar said. She began to reassemble the weapon. In less than thirty seconds it was back together, loaded, cocked, and safed, and she slung it over her shoulder. "*I* don't carry weapons for show."

"Very impressive, Highness," Noshahr said, hiding his astonishment with a bored and unimpressed expression. He turned to Buzhazi. "We're wasting time here. Now that we have played along with your charade, General—putting the princes in considerable danger, I will maintain—shall we get down to business?"

"Let's," Buzhazi responded, using the same haughty country-club tone of voice as Noshahr. "I asked you to come here to talk about coordinating our efforts against Mohtaz and his foreign insurgents. Last night's gun battle with what turned out to be *your* assassination squad must never be repeated. We need to start working together."

"The fault was completely *yours,* General," Noshahr said. "Your troops did not allow our freedom fighters to identify themselves. They had just come from a successful raid on an insurgent hideout when your men opened fire. My men discovered more than three dozen high-explosive devices ready for the streets, including a dozen suicide bomber vests and explosives disguised to look like everything from telephones to baby carriages."

"I've had that bomb-making factory under surveillance for days, Noshahr," Buzhazi said. "We were waiting for the master bomb-maker to arrive to arm those bombs. What good does it do to kill a bunch of low-level know-nothing worker bees and let the chief bomb-maker himself escape? Now it'll take us another month or more to locate the new factory, and by then they'll have fabricated another three dozen or more bombs to use against us."

"Do not change the subject, Buzhazi," Noshahr snapped. "Your unit's sneak attack cost us the lives of six of our best agents. We demand reparations, and we demand that you withdraw your troops from the slums and alleys and confine your activities to the avenues, highways, and the airport. Or, better yet, place yourself and your troops under the command of the council of war, which is the legitimate and rightful government of Persia, and we shall ensure that you shall not interfere again with our anti-terrorist missions."

"We bear equal responsibility for their deaths, Lord Chancellor," Azar said.

"You don't have to apologize for the war council's mistakes, Azar—"

"You will address Her Highness properly, Buzhazi!" Noshahr ordered. "You dare not speak to the princess as if she is a commoner!"

"She's not my princess, Noshahr," Buzhazi said, "and I don't take orders from pretend generals or defense ministers like you, either!"

"How dare you! The *Shahdokht* is the rightful heir to the Peacock Throne of Persia, and you will address her as such and show her the proper respect! And I will remind you that I am the appointed chancellor of the Qagev court, royal minister of war, and marshal of the council of war! Have some respect for the office, even if you have no respect for yourself!"

"Noshahr, a year ago you were hanging out in the casinos in Monaco and making up stories about leading freedom fighters against the Pasdaran while trying to boink old rich ladies for their money," Buzhazi said. "In the meantime your loyalists were being captured and tortured because you couldn't keep your drunken mouth shut about their identities and locations—"

"That is preposterous!" Noshahr sputtered.

"The Pasdaran spies in Monaco, Singapore, and Las Vegas were getting a constant stream of information about your network just by sitting near you in the casinos, bars, and whorehouses you frequented, listening to you spin your wild stories about single-handedly freeing Iran."

"You peasant! You insolent pup! How dare you speak to *me* like this!" Noshahr cried. "I serve a king and his queen, directed twenty million loyalists around the world, equip and organize a fighting

force of half a million, and have kept the royal treasury safe and secure for the past twenty years! You are little more than a thief and
murderer, disgraced by your own words and actions over two decades, and demoted and humiliated by the government you served
and then betrayed. You are spurned by your fellow citizens, and you
lead by nothing more than fear of the next murderous rampage you
will embark on, like the hideous massacre at Qom. You dare call
yourself a Persian—!"

"I don't call myself anything *you* call yourself, Noshahr!" Buzhazi shouted. He turned to Azar, his eyes blazing. "I won't have anything to do with you or your so-called court, Princess, as long as *he's*
in charge. I'm not in the mood for playing dress-up and kings and
castles."

"General—"

"Sorry, Princess, but this is a huge waste of my time," Buzhazi
said angrily. "I've got a war to fight. This imbecile who calls himself a marshal and minister of war doesn't know which end of a rifle to point at the enemy. I need fighters, not popinjays. I've got
work to do."

"General, please stay."

"I'm leaving. Good luck to you and your pretty little court jesters,
Princess."

"General, I said *stay*!" Azar shouted. She whipped off the dark
cap, letting her long *mun* whip in the air. The Persians in the room
were stunned into silence by the sudden appearance by the symbol
of royalty in their midst . . . all except Buzhazi, who was stunned
instead by the young woman's commanding tone of voice: part drill
sergeant, part disapproving mother, part field general.

"*Shahdokht* . . . Highness . . . my lady . . ." Noshahr sputtered, his
eyes fixed on the dark shining flowing locks as if a golden scepter
had just appeared before his eyes, "I think it is time for us to depart
and—"

"You will stay and shut your mouth, Chancellor!" Azar snapped.
"We have important business to discuss."

"We cannot conduct business with this . . . this terrorist!"

Noshahr said. "He's nothing but an old tottering fool with delusions of grandeur—"

"I said, *we* have business to discuss with the general," Azar said. This time the word "we" coming from her lips had a different meaning: it no longer referred to *him,* but clearly indicated the imperial "we," meaning *her* alone. "Be silent, Chancellor."

"Be . . . *silent* . . . ?" Noshahr gurgled, his mouth opening and closing indignantly. "Pardon me, *Shahdokht,* but I am the Lord High Chancellor of the royal court, the representative of the king in his absence. I have full and sole authority to negotiate and make agreements and alliances with friendly and allied forces."

"Not any longer, Chancellor," Azar said forcefully. "It has been a year since anyone has heard or seen the king and queen. In the meantime the court has been run by appointed servants who, although true and loyal, do not have the interests of the people in mind."

"I beg your pardon, *Shahdokht*—!"

"It's true, Chancellor, and you know it," Azar said. "Your primary objective has been the organization, security, and placement of the court, in preparation for running the government upon the return of the king and queen. You have done a fine job of that, Chancellor. The court is safe, secure, well run, well financed, and is ready to administer this country when the time comes. But right now the people don't need or want an administrator—they want a leader and a general."

"I am the rightful leader until the king returns, *Shahdokht,*" Noshahr insisted. "And as minister of war and marshal of the council of war, I am the commander-in-chief of our military forces. There are no others permitted."

"You're wrong, Chancellor . . . *I* am," Azar said.

"*You?* But that . . . that is highly irregular, *Shahdokht,*" Noshahr said. "A proclamation of death or abdication has not yet been made. A council must be convened, composed of myself, the religious leaders, and representatives of the eleven royal houses, to investigate the likely whereabouts of the king and queen and decide what actions to take. That is impossible and unsafe to do in time of war!"

"Then, as heir apparent, I will make the proclamation myself," Azar said.

"*You!*" Noshahr repeated. "You . . . that is . . . pardon me for saying so, *Shahdokht,* but that is an insult to the memory of your blessed father and mother, our beloved king and queen. They may be still in hiding, or perhaps injured and healing, or even captured. Our enemies could be waiting for you to do such a thing and then reveal that they are still alive, hoping to throw us into confusion and rebellion against the court and royal family. You cannot . . . I mean, you *should not* do this, *Shahdokht*—"

"I am no longer *Shahdokht,* Chancellor," Azar said. "You will hereby refer to me as *Malika.*"

Noshahr gulped, his eyes bulging. He stole a glance back at his bodyguards, then back at Azar, studying her carefully, trying to decide if she meant what she'd just said and if she would back down or compromise if confronted. "I . . . I am afraid I cannot allow that, Princess," he said, after finally summoning up enough courage. "I have a responsibility to the king and queen to safeguard and preserve the court. In their absence, and without guidance from a council of the royal houses, I'm afraid I cannot do as you wish."

Azar lowered her eyes, nodded, and seemed to even sigh. "Very well, Chancellor. I see your point of view."

Noshahr was filled with relief. He would certainly have to deal with this young Americanized upstart, and soon—she obviously had aspirations far beyond her years, and that could not be tolerated. But he was willing to act the supportive and protective uncle—all the better to keep an eye on her while he . . .

"I see it is time to take back the throne," Azar said. In a blur of motion, she suddenly whipped the German-made Heckler & Koch HK-54 submachine gun up and steadied it from her hip . . . aiming it squarely on Masoud Noshahr's chest. "You are under arrest, Chancellor, for defying my authority." She turned to the Persian bodyguards behind Noshahr. "Guards, place the chancellor under arrest."

"This is preposterous!" Noshahr screamed, more in shock and surprise than anger. "How *dare* you?"

"I dare because I am the *Malika,* Chancellor," Azar said confidently, "and the throne has been vacant long enough." She looked past Noshahr to the bodyguards, who still had their guns slung on their shoulders. "Guards, place the chancellor under arrest. He is forbidden to make any communications with the outside."

"They won't follow you, Azar Assiyeh," Noshahr said. "They are loyal to me and to the king and queen, the *rightful* rulers of Persia. They will not follow a spoiled, bewitched brat from America."

Azar glanced around the conference room, noting that neither Lieutenant Colonel Najar nor Major Saidi, her longtime aides, had raised their weapons—they were unslung, but still pointing at the floor with safeties on. The same with Hesarak Buzhazi and his bodyguard, Major Haddad, and the chief of the infantry brigade based at Mehrabad Airport, Colonel Mostafa Rahmati, both of whom had accompanied them on this diversionary mission. She was the only one with her weapon raised.

"I gave an order, Master Sergeant: Place the chancellor under arrest," Azar commanded. "Allow no outside communications. If he resists, bind and gag him." Still no one moved.

"Master Sergeant . . . all of you, it is time to make a decision," Azar said, affixing each of them with a steady gaze, hoping to hell her hands wouldn't start shaking. "You may follow Chancellor Noshahr and continue on with this so-called revolution as it has been for the past year, or swear loyalty to me and to the Peacock Throne, and follow me in taking back this country for a free Persian republic."

"Follow *you?*" Noshahr sneered. "You're just a girl. You may be a princess, but you're not a queen—and you're *certainly* not a general. The loyalists won't follow a girl into battle. What will you do if no one chooses to accept you as queen?"

"Then I will abdicate my title and join General Buzhazi's forces," Azar replied, to the absolute amazement of all. "It is time to join forces and fight as one nation, and if it won't be done under the

Qagev banner, it will be under the general's flag. If you're ready to take me and my followers, General, we're ready to join you."

"That won't be necessary," Hesarak Buzhazi said . . . and to everyone's great surprise, he unslung his submachine gun, held it before him with arms outstretched . . . and dropped to one knee before Azar. "Because I am surrendering command of my forces and pledging my loyalty to the *Malika* Azar Assiyeh Qagev, the rightful queen of Persia and mistress of the Peacock Throne."

Azar smiled, silently praying that she wouldn't keel over from the surprise or burst into tears herself, then nodded. "We are pleased to accept your oath of loyalty, Hesarak al-Kan Buzhazi." She kissed his forehead, then put her hands on his shoulders. "Rise, sir, take your weapon, and assume leadership of the ministry of war and the council of war of the royal court of Qagev, and command of the combined forces of the Democratic Republic of Persia . . . *Marshal* Buzhazi."

"Thank you, *Malika*," Buzhazi said. He turned to Noshahr. "My first official act shall be to offer an appointment to Masoud Noshahr as deputy minister of war, vice marshal of the army, and my representative to the court. Do you accept?"

"You want *me* to serve under *you?*" Noshahr asked, even more shocked now than before. "You take my position and then you want me back? Why?"

"The queen is a good and astute judge of character, Noshahr," Buzhazi said. "If she says you have served the court well as chancellor and prepared it to lead the country when the time came, I believe her. I want you to keep on doing your job, the one you're best at. Prepare the court to rule a constitutional monarchy, and keep supplies and equipment flowing to my troops. I need someone to represent me in Tehran, because I'll be in the streets suppressing this insurgency and restoring security to the country. That's what I'm good at. And as vice-marshal, you will answer to *me*. Screw up, and you'll have to deal with *me*. Do you accept?"

For a moment Buzhazi thought Noshahr was going to say something crude or insulting; instead, he did something Buzhazi never thought he'd do: he saluted. "Yes, sir, I accept."

"Very good, Vice-Marshal. I want a meeting of the council of war set up immediately." He turned to Azar. "*Malika,* with your permission, I'd like to appoint Lieutenant Colonel Najar as my chief of staff and promote him to full colonel. Major Saidi will remain as your aide-de-camp."

"Permission granted, Marshal," Azar said.

"Thank you, *Malika.* Colonel, work with Vice-Marshal Noshahr to set up a meeting of the war council. Major Haddad is hereby promoted to lieutenant colonel and will be in charge of security." To Azar he said, "*Malika,* I would like you to attend the war council meeting and provide your input on resources and personnel we may be able to recruit from the streets of Tehran and the surrounding towns and villages. We'll need every helping hand we can find to make this work."

"Gladly, Marshal," Azar said.

"Thank you, *Malika,*" Buzhazi said. "If you would, *Malika,* Vice-Marshal Noshahr, I'd like to show you something first before we proceed that could have a bearing on our planning. Colonel Najar, take over."

Azar walked beside Buzhazi through the airport terminal to the exit. "Very dramatic gesture you made back there, Marshal," she said. "I never thought I'd see you kneeling before anyone, let alone *me.*"

"I had to do something to outdo *your* grand gesture, Highness," Buzhazi said. "Besides, if all this fancy froufrou court stuff is what your people know and expect, I guess I had to play along. You were really going to give up your throne and join my ragtag force of outlaws?"

"Did you mean what you said about surrendering your forces to me and swearing allegiance?" They smiled together, knowing each other's reply. "Do you think we can pull it off, Hesarak?" she asked.

"Well, before today, I gave us no more than one chance in ten of winning," Buzhazi said honestly. "Since then, things have improved greatly. I give us perhaps one chance in five now."

"Really? A one hundred percent improvement so fast? We haven't done anything yet except perhaps rearrange the deck chairs on a sinking ship! We have the same forces as before, the same resources—perhaps better organization and a little extra motivation. What else has changed other than our names, titles, and allegiances?"

They had walked outside and were escorted by guards to the nearby Iran Air hangar. After their identities were verified, Buzhazi stepped aside to let Azar pass him. "What else has changed?" he asked with a smile. "Let's just say something from above has dropped into our laps."

"What . . . ?" Azar stepped into the hangar . . .

. . . and was immediately confronted by a ten-foot-tall humanoid robot, wearing some sort of cannon on his shoulders. The robot stepped closer to her with amazing speed and agility, examined them all for a moment, then stood at attention and shouted, "Detail, ten-*hut!*" in a loud computer-synthesized voice, then repeated it again in Farsi. It stepped aside . . .

. . . revealing that the hangar had two sleek, jet-black, massive American bombers inside. Azar recognized them as Air Force B-1 bombers, except the cockpit windows appeared sealed closed. The hangar floor was choked with vehicles, cargo containers of every size and description, and perhaps two hundred American airmen in utility uniforms standing at attention.

"As you were," Azar said. The Americans, men and women alike, relaxed. Many came over to the newcomers, introducing themselves with salutes and handshakes.

A few moments later, a tall man in a strange dark gray all-body suit of armor that Buzhazi recognized as the American Tin Man battle system, without his helmet, came over, stood before Qagev and Buzhazi, and saluted. "General Buzhazi?" he said via his Tin Man suit's on-board electronic translator. "Major Wayne Macomber, U.S. Air Force, detail commander."

Buzhazi returned his salute, then shook hands. "Thank you, Major. May I present Her Highness, Azar Assiyeh Qagev . . ." He paused for effect, giving her a sly wink and nod, then added, "Queen of Persia."

Macomber's eyes widened in surprise, but he recovered quickly enough, snapped to attention again, and saluted. "Nice to meet you, Your Highness." She extended her hand, and he shook it, his armored hand dwarfing hers. "Never met a queen before."

"I have met a Tin Man before, and I take great pleasure and comfort knowing you're here," Azar said in English so perfect, so American that it surprised him. "Welcome to Persia, Major."

"Thanks." He turned his hand and looked down at hers. "Hypoplastic thumb. Nice job fixing it. My youngest sister has it too. Bilateral?"

"Yes, Major," Azar replied rather awkwardly. "I'm surprised at you. Most people I greet look at my hand and then look away, pretending not to notice."

"Ignorance, that's all, ma'am," Macomber said. "Good for you not hiding it. My sister doesn't hide it either. Freaks people out but that's her plan. She still has a wicked tennis backhand."

"You should see me on the rifle range, Major."

The big commando smiled and nodded, his turn to be surprised. "Looking forward to that, ma'am."

"Me too, Major." She looked at another commando in a Tin Man battle armor system approach. "Hello, Sergeant Major Wohl," she said, extending her hand. "Nice to see you again."

"Thank you, Highness," Wohl said. "Nice to see you too." He glanced at Buzhazi. "I hope your new title doesn't mean bad news about your parents."

"I hope so too, Sergeant Major," Azar said, "but the situation has forced my elevation, and so we proceed." Wohl nodded in approval, but still gave Buzhazi a warning glare.

The ten-foot robot came over to them. Macomber motioned to her and said, "Ma'am, I'd like to introduce you to my second-in-command, Captain Charlie Turlock, U.S. Army Reserves, piloting a Cybernetic Infantry Device manned robot battle system she helped develop. She's on patrol now so she can't get out to greet you properly. Captain, meet Queen Azar Qagev of Persia."

"Nice to meet you too, Captain," Azar said, shaking hands with the giant, amazed at her delicate touch despite the size of her mechanical hand. "My minister of war and commander of my armed forces, Marshal Hesarak Buzhazi."

"Nice to meet you, Highness, Marshal," Charlie said from within the CID unit. Macomber's eyes widened at Buzhazi's new title. "All patrols reporting secure, sir. Excuse me, but I'll continue my assignment." The robot saluted and hurried off.

"Incredible, absolutely incredible," Azar remarked. "Thank you so much for the extraordinary job you did in hunting down the Pasdaran's mobile missiles. But now I'm confused. Did Marshal Buzhazi ask you to come to Tehran?"

"We had a little . . . trouble, you might say, with our accommodations in Turkey," Macomber explained. "My commanding officer Lieutenant General Patrick McLanahan got in contact with General—er, Marshal Buzhazi, and he offered to put us up until we get our situation straightened out."

"McLanahan? The general up in the space station?"

"Let's go somewhere and talk, shall we?" Macomber suggested. They moved through the hangar, greeting more airmen, and took a quick tour of the EB-1 Vampire bombers before entering an office just off the main hangar floor. Macomber spoke as if to thin air; a moment later, a telephone rang right beside him. He picked the receiver up and handed it to Azar. "It's for you, Highness."

Azar took the phone, trying to act like impromptu and mysterious phone calls for her were completely normal. "This is Queen Azar Assiyeh Qagev of Persia," she said in English. "Who is this, please?"

"Highness, this is Lieutenant General Patrick McLanahan. How are you tonight?"

"I'm well, General," she responded, trying to sound official and coherent even though her senses were swimming trying to keep up with the amazing otherworldly technology she was being exposed to here at breakneck speed. "We were just talking about you."

"I was listening in—hope you don't mind," Patrick said. "We keep a close eye on our troops all around the world."

"I understand," Azar said. "I hope you are recovered from your space flight injuries. Are you in Persia?"

"No, right now I'm over southern Chile, aboard Armstrong Space Station," Patrick said. "Highness, I was in a little bit of trouble, and I called on General Buzhazi for help. I apologize for not informing you first, but time was of the essence."

"You and your forces are welcome forever and always in Persia, General," Azar said. "You are a hero and champion to all free Persians, and we consider you our brother-in-arms. But perhaps you can explain what's going on."

"We believe Russia has moved military forces into Iran and is working with the theocratic regime to exert influence in the region."

"Well of course they have, General," Azar said matter-of-factly. "Don't tell me that's a surprise to you?" His rather embarrassed pause gave her all the answer she needed. "The Russians have pledged substantial military and economic assistance over the years to the theocratic regime in exchange for presence and to put pressure on them to stop supporting anti-Russian separatist movements inside the Russian Federation and its near abroad, such as in Kosovo, Albania, and Romania. Russia has enjoyed its most-favored-nation status for decades."

"We knew that Russia was using Iran along with the conflict in Iraq to distract the United States from its other activities around its periphery," Patrick said, "but we didn't know their involvement was so widely known and accepted."

"The aid Iran has received from the Russians is reportedly greater than what the United States gives any other nation in the region except perhaps Israel," Azar said. "That was very important not only to keep the theocrats in power but to sustain the Iranian people.

Unfortunately a lot of that aid went to the Revolutionary Guards Corps and their drastic arms buildup, which they used to crack down on any dissent in our country. But has something else changed recently? Is Russia playing a different game?"

"We believe the Russians have brought a new weapon, a powerful mobile anti-spacecraft laser, into Iran and have used it to down one of our spacecraft," Patrick said. "Major Macomber, Captain Turlock, and Sergeant Major Wohl survived such an attack."

"You mean, one of the spaceplanes I've heard so much about?" Azar asked. "They were riding in one in space when it was hit by this laser?"

"Yes, Highness. I would like assistance to hunt down this Russian weapon and neutralize it."

"I don't think that'll be difficult at all," Azar said. She handed the phone to Buzhazi, who put it on a speaker and asked Major Haddad to translate for him.

"Marshal Buzhazi?"

"Greetings, General McLanahan," Buzhazi said through Haddad.

"Hello, Marshal. You got a promotion, I see."

"And I judge by your unexpected call, the sudden appearance of such a large force on my doorstep, and the disturbing lack of information from your military or foreign ministries, that your career has not enjoyed similar success," Buzhazi said. "But you helped me when I was on the run, and I was hoping to one day do the same for you. So. The Russians have shot down your spaceplane?"

"Can you help us find that laser, Buzhazi?"

"Of course. I am sure we can find it quickly, if my men do not already know where it is."

"You sound pretty confident."

"General, we do not automatically distrust the Russians like you do—in fact, we have more reasons to distrust the *Americans*," Buzhazi said. "We are neighbors with Russia, and our borders have been safe and secure for decades; we have purchased many weapons and received substantial military, economic, industrial, and trade assistance from Russia, which was urgently important to us during all the years of the trade embargo with the West; we even still have a mutual defense treaty that is in full force and effect."

"So you're saying that you have been working *with* the Russians, Marshal," Patrick asked with surprise, "including supplying them with information on our activities in Iran?"

"General McLanahan, sometimes the depth of the naïveté of the Americans astounds me," Buzhazi said. "*We* have to live here; you merely influence events here for America's national interests, sometimes from the relative comfort of a battle staff room—or a space station. Of course we supply Russia with information, just as we supply you with information on Russia's activities and assist you when you run into . . . domestic political problems, shall we say?" Again, no response from Patrick.

"We all have our own necessities, pursuits, and agendas," Buzhazi went on. "We hope such cooperation enriches us all and is mutually beneficial, but in the end it is our own objectives that must be attended to first, no?" Again, silence. "General McLanahan? Are you still there?"

"I'm still here."

"I am sorry to have upset or disillusioned you, General," Buzhazi said. "You did save my life and help me defeat the Pasdaran in Qom and Tehran, and for that I would help you until the last of my days. All you had to do was ask. But you should not be so surprised to learn that I would extend similar courtesies to any other country that helps my cause, including *your* adversaries. So. You wish to locate this Russian mobile laser system? Very well. I shall contact you immediately through Major Macomber when I have its precise location. Is that agreeable?"

"Yes, it is, Marshal," Patrick said. "Thank you. And what of my men there in Tehran?"

Buzhazi turned to Azar and spoke in low tones for a few moments; then: "The queen wishes to extend all possible aid and comfort to you and your men. In return, she hopes you will assist us when the time comes."

"So do I have to worry about a Russian attack on that location, Buzhazi?" Patrick asked.

"Patrick, I think I have made myself plain to you," Buzhazi said through his translator. "I hope you are not one of those idealistic men who believe that we help each other because we believe it is the right or just thing to do, or because one side is inherently good and the other is evil. You brought your forces to Tehran for reasons that are not entirely clear to me yet, but I know that we did not invite you. We will learn all soon, God willing. Until then, I will do what I must for our nation and our survival. You will do what you must for your men, your cause, and yourself. Hopefully all those things are mutually beneficial." And he hung up the phone without even a departing salutation.

"Everything okay, sir?" Macomber asked via his subcutaneous transceiver after he had excused himself from Buzhazi and Azar.

"Major, I think we need to trust Buzhazi, but I just can't make myself do it," Patrick admitted. "He may be a patriot, but he's first and foremost a survivor. When he was chief of staff and commander of the Pasdaran, he was fully prepared to sink an American aircraft carrier and kill thousands of sailors just to prove how tough he thought he was. I think he wants to get rid of the theocracy and the Pasdaran, but I think he'll do anything he needs to do—include screwing us both—to survive. You're going to have to make the call."

"Yes, sir," Macomber said. "I'll let you know."

"Well, Major?" Buzhazi asked via the electronic translator when Macomber returned. "What does your commanding officer say? Does he trust me yet?"

"No, sir, he doesn't," Macomber said.

"So. What shall we do?"

Macomber thought for a moment; then: "We take a little ride, Marshal."

CHAPTER NINE

Never contend with a man who has nothing to lose.

—BALTASAR GRACÍAN

OVER SOUTH-CENTRAL NEVADA

EARLY THE NEXT MORNING

"Here's the latest, guys, so listen up," the SEAL team leader, U.S. Navy Lieutenant Mike Harden, said. The fifteen members of his SEAL platoon, all pre-breathing oxygen in the cargo compartment of their C-130 Hercules cargo plane, stopped looking at charts and turned their attention to him. "Our guy on the inside tells us that the place is virtually deserted. He counts a total of twenty Security Forces personnel, mostly centered on the main computer center next to the headquarters building. The battle staff area has been deserted and there is just a skeleton security force stationed there, about six guys. The hangars have been locked up for a couple days. This checks with our own overhead surveillance. So our objective remains the four main offices in the headquarters building: one squad each going for the security operations center, the battle management area, the communications center, and the flight operations center. Unit Bravo is right behind us, and his guys will take the hangars and the weapons storage area.

"Our guy on the inside says he's seen just one of those CID manned robot units around the place patrolling the hangars and weapon storage area. We know they had a total of six CIDs. One was deployed to Iran, two deployed to Turkey, and one surrendered when the Rangers assaulted Battle Mountain, so there's two left, and we have to assume they're both at Elliott. There are approximately a dozen Tin Man units unaccounted for as well.

"Remember, use regular ammo only against the Security Forces guys if they open fire on you—don't waste ammo on the CIDs or Tin Man units." He held up a 40-millimeter grenade round. "These are our best hope of putting those things out of commission: micro-wave pulse generators, like a direct fucking lightning bolt hit. They tell us it should shut down all their systems instantly. Probably lethal for the guy inside, but that's his problem if he chooses to fight. These guys are fast, so stay on your toes and concentrate fire. Questions?" There were none. "All right. We have about five minutes to go. Get ready to kick some zoomie ass." There was a muffled round of "Hoo-ah!" in oxygen masks all around.

It seemed like just a minute later when Harden was notified by the cockpit crew that the jump zone was two minutes out. The SEALs quickly detached themselves from the aircraft oxygen system, hooked up to portable oxygen bottles, got to their feet, and held on tightly to handholds as the rear cargo ramp was lowered. No sooner had the ramp motored down than the red light turned green, and Harden led his platoon out into the frigid darkness. Less than twenty seconds after Harden jumped, all sixteen men deployed parachutes. Harden checked his chute and oxygen, made sure his infrared marker light was operating so the others could follow him in the darkness, then started following the steering indications from his wrist-mounted GPS unit.

This was a HAHO, or High Altitude–High Opening jump. From twenty-seven thousand feet, the team could sail about thirty miles from their jump point to their objective: Elliott Air Force Base, nicknamed "Dreamland." By order of the President of the United States, the two SEAL units had been ordered to assault the base, neutralize the Cybernetic Infantry Devices and Tin Man units patrolling the base, capture all base personnel, and secure the aircraft, weapons, computer center, and laboratories.

The winds were a little squirrelly, definitely different than forecast, which probably explained the hurried jump. Harden found himself steering his canopy in some rather radical maneuvers to get on-course. Each turn soaked up some horizontal speed, so that meant a little more marching once they got on the ground. They would fly for about ten minutes.

Once finally established on-course, Harden started looking for landmarks using his binocular night-vision goggles. He quickly saw that things weren't looking quite as planned. The first visual target was Groom Lake, the big dry lake bed south of the base that had the majority of Elliott's twenty-thousand-foot-long runway embedded in it. It was soon obvious they were too far west—they had jumped way too early. The GPS said they were right on-course, but the landmarks didn't lie. They had planned for this contingency, but Harden was going to give the flight crew a good chewing-out when this mission was over. He had studied the entire surrounding area in his pre-jump target study and was confident he could find a good place to land, even if it had to be on the dry lake bed itself.

He couldn't quite reach the dry lake bed, but he was able to find a flat area about fifty yards north of a dirt road. The landing was a lot harder than he anticipated—again, the GPS was lying about the wind direction and he landed with the wind instead of into it, which increased his ground speed and the force of the landing. Fortunately they were wearing so much cold-weather gear for the long HAHO jump, and the extra impact force was mostly soaked up. He formed up the team in less than three minutes, and it took them less than five to get their parachutes, harnesses, and extra cold-weather gear off and stowed, and their weapons, comm gear, and night-vision systems checked and ready.

Harden checked his GPS and motioned their direction of movement, but the assistant officer in charge, who had the backup GPS, waved his hand and indicated a different direction. They put their GPS receivers side by side, and sure enough, their readouts were completely different . . . in fact, they were different by about three miles!

That explained them being off-course and landing in the wrong direction based on GPS-derived winds: their GPS receivers were being spoofed. Harden knew that GPS jammers were being developed, but a jammed GPS receiver could be disregarded and alternate navigation methods used right away before significant errors were made. On the other hand, a spoofed GPS receiver would *appear* to be working properly. Even the C-130's GPS receivers had been spoofed. He had to remember that they were up against a unit that developed and tested next-generation weapons of all kinds, top secret stuff that probably wouldn't be seen by the rest of the world for years but would revolutionize warfare when it did hit the streets.

The platoon chief pulled out a lensatic compass, ready to take some fixes on terrain landmarks and cross-check their position on his map, but it must've taken a hit in the accelerated landing because the compass dial was spinning as if it were attached to an electric motor. Harden wouldn't be surprised if the eggheads here had developed a way to jam or spoof *compasses* too! He decided that since they landed west of the edge of the dry lake bed they would just head east until they found the lake, then they'd move north until they found the inner perimeter fence. He again signaled their direction of movement, overriding all queries, and headed off at a trot.

They had stripped off the cold-weather gear and left their parachutes behind, greatly lightening their load, but soon Harden found himself wiping sweat from his eyes. Jeez, he thought, it had to be below freezing out here in the high desert, but he was sweating to death! But he ignored it and kept on . . .

"Windward," he heard in his headset. He dropped to his belly and scanned the area. That was the code word for a team member in trouble. He crawled back along his direction of movement and found the platoon chief on his back, with the AOIC checking him over. "What in hell happened?" he whispered.

"He just collapsed," the assistant officer in charge said. He wiped sweat from his face. "I don't feel too good either, LT. Would they use nerve gas on us?"

"Stay down," someone said on the secure FM tactical radio.

Harden looked down the line of SEALs spread out in the desert. "Radios tight!" he whispered. The AOIC passed the word back to the others. He had briefed to use code words only on the radios on this mission unless they were in a firefight and the whole team was compromised.

The platoon chief sat up. "You feeling okay, Chief?" Harden asked. The chief signaled he was, and they prepared to move out again. But this time it was Harden who felt woozy—the minute he stood up, he was bathed in warm, dry heat, as if he had just opened the door to a red-hot oven. The feeling subsided when he dropped to a knee. What in hell . . . ?

And then he realized what it was. They had been briefed on the incident in Turkey, where the guys from Dreamland used nonlethal microwave weapons to knock out the base security personnel—they reported that it felt like intense heat, like their skin was on fire, and soon their brains got scrambled so bad that they passed out. "Crocodile, crocodile," Harden spoke into his whispermike, the code word for "enemy nearby."

"Just stay down and don't move," they all heard in their headsets.

Shit, the Air Force guys had found their FM frequency, decoded the encryption routine, and were talking over their whispermike channel! He turned and made a hand signal to switch to the secondary frequency, and the word was passed down to the others. In the meantime, Harden pulled out his satellite phone and punched up the other SEAL unit's secure channel: "Silver, this is Opus, crocodile."

"Did you know," they heard in their headsets on the new channel, *"that there are no words that rhyme with 'silver' and 'opus,' just like 'orange'?"*

Harden wiped a rivulet of sweat out of his eyes. Comm discipline completely forgotten, he angrily switched back to the whispermike: "Who the hell is this?"

"Ah ah ah, Lieutenant, beadwindow, beadwindow," the voice said again, using the old code word warning of inappropriate radio transmissions. *"Listen, guys, the exercise is over. We already took down the other unit heading to the flight line and weapon storage area—you guys did much better than they did. We have some nice comfy rooms ready for you. Stand up with your hands in the air and we'll take a little drive back to base. We have a truck on the way to come get you."*

"Fuck you!" Harden shouted. He got into a low crouch and scanned the area, ignoring the growing pain radiating throughout his body . . . and then he saw it, a huge robot, less than twenty meters in front of him. He raised his rifle, flicked off the safety, and fired a grenade round. There was a tremendous flash, the smell of high-tension electricity frying the air, and a feeling of millions of ants crawling across his body . . . but the sensation of heat had vanished, replaced by bone-chilling cold as his sweat-soaked uniform quickly released body heat to the frigid night air.

He trotted back to his men. "Everybody okay?" he whispered. They all signaled they were fine. He checked his GPS receiver—it was completely dead, but the platoon chief's compass was working properly again, and he quickly plotted their position on his map, got a bearing toward their destination, and headed out.

On the way they passed the robot. It looked as if its limbs, torso, and neck had twisted in different and very unnatural directions all at once, and it smelled of a short-circuited and burned-out power drill. Harden was at first sorry for the guy inside—after all, he was a fellow American and soldier—but he wasn't going to stick around to check on him in case he was just stunned.

It was completely dark as they approached the inner perimeter fence, a double-layered fifteen-foot-high chain-link fence topped with razor wire. No lights around the fence meant either dogs or infrared sensors, Harden knew. He gave the order for the team to break into squads and begin their approach to . . .

. . . and at that moment he heard a whirring sound, like a high-speed fan, and he looked up. Through his night-vision goggles he saw an object about the size of a garbage can about twenty feet in the sky and just thirty or forty yards away, with a wide round shroud on the bottom, long legs, and two metallic arms which held white flags—and incredibly it had a lighted LED scrolling display on the top that read DON'T SHOOT JUST TALK WE'RE LISTENING.

"What the hell is this?" Harden asked. He waited until the flying robot got about ten yards away, then shot it down with a single burst from his MP5 submachine gun. He was sure he hit it, but it managed to fly down in a more or less controlled manner, landing awkwardly a few yards away, the scrolling LED message still visible. He repositioned his whispermike to his lips. "Who is this?"

"This is Brigadier General David Luger," the voice on the other end replied. "You know who I am. This has got to end, Lieutenant Harden, before anyone else gets hurt or killed."

"I have orders to take you into custody and secure this base, sir," Harden said. "I'm not leaving until my mission is accomplished. On authority of the President of the United States, I'm ordering you to deactivate all of your base defenses and surrender yourselves immediately."

"Lieutenant, there are a dozen more drones flying overhead right now carrying stun grenades," Luger said. "We can see you and each of your fifteen comrades, and we can hit each one of them with a stun grenade. Watch carefully. In front of you, right near the fence." A moment later he heard a tiny metallic *ping!* sound from almost directly overhead . . . and seconds later there was a tremendous flash of light, followed moments later by an impossibly loud *craack!* of sound and then a wall of pressure like a hurricane-force wind lasting a fraction of a second.

"Now that was about a hundred yards away, Lieutenant," Luger said. The ringing in Harden's ears was so loud he had trouble hearing him over the radio. "Imagine what that'll feel like just *five* yards away."

"Sir, you're going to have to take me and all my men out, because we're not leaving," Harden said after letting his hearing return somewhat to normal. "Unless you want to be responsible for wounding or killing fellow Americans, I urge you to follow my orders and surrender."

There was a long pause on the line; then, in a sincere fatherly voice, Luger said: "I really admire you, Lieutenant. We were being honest when we said you made it farther than the other SEAL unit. They surrendered the first time we hit them with the microwave emitter, and they even told us your identity when we captured them—that's how we knew who you were. You guys did good. I know you didn't mean to kill Staff Sergeant Henry. He was the NCO piloting the CID."

"Thank you, sir, and no, I didn't mean to kill anyone, sir," Harden said. "We'd been briefed on that microwave weapon your robots carry and we knew we had to knock it out."

"We developed the microwave disruptor grenade because we were afraid the CID technology had fallen into Russian hands," Luger said. "I didn't think it'd be used *by* our own *against* our own."

"I'm sorry, sir, and I'll take responsibility of personally informing his next of kin." He had to keep him talking as long as he could. The main occupying force, a Marine security company from Camp Pendleton, was due to arrive in less than thirty minutes, and if this guy Luger had second thoughts about attacking more Marines, maybe he'd hold off long enough for the others to arrive. "Should I go back and help the staff sergeant?"

"No, Lieutenant. We'll handle that."

"Yes, sir. Can you explain how—?"

"There's no time for explanations, Lieutenant."

"Yes, sir." Time was running out. "Listen, sir, no one wants this. Your best bet is to stop fighting, get a lawyer, and do this the right way. There don't have to be any more attacks. This is not who we are supposed to be battling. Let's stop all this right now. You're the unit commander here. You're in charge. Give the order, have your people lay down their weapons, and let us come in. We won't hurt anyone. We're all Americans, sir. We're on the same side. Please, sir, stop this."

There was another long pause. Harden truly believed that Luger was going to back down. All this was *insane,* he thought. Have some guts and stop this, Luger! he thought. Don't be a hero. Stop this or . . .

Then he heard a whirring sound overhead—the little trash-can robots returning—and then Luger said: "The pain will be more intense this time, but it won't last very long. Good day, Lieutenant."

Harden leaped to his feet and yelled, "All squads, fire grenades for effect and make for the fence, *go, go, go!*" He raised his MP5, loaded a disruptor grenade into the launcher breech, racked it home, and raised the weapon to . . .

. . . and it felt as if his entire body had instantly burst into flame. He screamed . . . and then everything quickly, thankfully went dark.

THE WHITE HOUSE CABINET ROOM, WASHINGTON, D.C.

LATER THAT MORNING

"I can't believe this . . . I fucking can't believe this!" President Joseph Gardner moaned. He and a handful of Senate and congressional leaders were being briefed by Secretary of Defense Miller Turner on their efforts to detain the members of the Air Battle Force and secure their weapons, and the information was not good. "They knocked out and captured *two* SEAL teams in Dreamland? I don't believe it! What about the other locations?"

"The SEAL team sent to Battle Mountain encountered light resistance and managed to capture one of their manned robots, but the robot had apparently either malfunctioned or was damaged and was abandoned," Turner said. "The aircraft and most of the personnel were gone; the SEALs captured about a hundred personnel without resistance. The FAA couldn't track any of the aircraft because of heavy jamming or netruding and so we don't know where they went."

" 'Netruding'? What in hell is that?"

"Apparently the next-generation aircraft based out of Dreamland and Battle Mountain don't simply jam enemy radar, but they actually use the radars and their associated digital electronic systems to insert things like viruses, false or contrary commands, false targets, and even programming code changes into the radar's electronics," National Security Adviser Conrad Carlyle responded. "They call it 'netruding'—network intruding."

"Why wasn't I briefed about this?"

"It was first put into use on McLanahan's planes deployed to the Middle East," Carlyle said. "He disabled a Russian fighter by commanding it to shut itself down. Most digital radar systems in use these days, especially civilian sets, don't have any way to block these intrusions. He can do it with all sorts of systems such as communications, the Internet, wireless networks, even weather radar. Plus, since a lot of the civilian networks are tied into the military's systems, they can insert malicious code into the military network without even directly attacking a military system."

"I thought he shot a missile at the fighter!"

"The Russians claimed he shot a missile, but he used this new 'netrusion' system to force the MiG to turn itself off," Carlyle explained. "McLanahan had his heart thing before he could explain what happened, and we took the Russians' word on the incident after that."

"How can he send a virus through radar?"

"Radar is simply reflected radio energy timed, decoded, digitized, and displayed on a screen," Carlyle said. "Once the frequency of the radio energy is known, any kind of signal can be sent to the receiver, including a signal containing digital code. Nowadays the radio energy is mostly digitally displayed and disseminated, so the digital code enters the system and is treated like any other computer instruction—it can be processed, stored, replicated, sent out over the network, whatever."

"Jee-sus . . ." Gardner breathed. "You mean, they could already have infected our communications and tracking systems?"

"As soon as McLanahan decided to embark on this conflict, he could have ordered the attacks," Miller said. "Every piece of digital electronic equipment in use that receives data from the airwaves, or is networked into another system that is, could have been infected almost instantly."

"*That's every electronic system I know of!*" the President exclaimed. "Hell, my daughter's handheld game machine is tied into the Internet! How could this have happened?"

"Because we *ordered* him to find a way to do it, sir," chairman of the Joint Chiefs of Staff General Taylor Bain replied. "It's an incredible force multiplier, which was important when almost every long-range attack aircraft in our arsenal was destroyed. Every satellite and every aircraft—including his unmanned aircraft and Armstrong Space Station—is capable of electronic netrusion. He can infect computers in Russia from space or simply from a drone flying within range of a Russian radar site. He can prevent a war from happening because the enemy would either never know he was coming or would be powerless to respond."

"The problem is, he can do it to *us* now too!" the President exclaimed. "You need to find a way to shield our systems from this kind of attack."

"It's in the works, Mr. President," Carlyle said. "Firewalls and anti-virus software can protect computers that already have it, but we're developing ways to plug the security gaps in systems that aren't normally considered vulnerable to network attacks, such as radar, electronic surveillance such as electro-optical cameras, or passive electronic sensors."

"The other problem," Bain added, "is that being the unit that developed and is designing the netrusion systems, the High-Technology Aerospace Weapons Center has been in the forefront of developing countermeasures to it."

"So the guys who are employing the thing are the ones who know how to defeat it," the President said disgustedly. "Swell. That helps." He shook his head in exasperation as he tried to think. Finally he turned to the two congressmen in the Oval Office. "Senator, Representative, I asked you in here because this has become a very serious problem, and I need the advice and support of the leadership. Most of us in this room think McLanahan is unhinged. Senator, you seem to feel differently."

"I do, Mr. President," Senator Stacy Anne Barbeau said. "Let me try talking with him. He knows I support his space program, and I support *him*."

"It's too dangerous, Senator," the President said. "One man has died, and several more have been injured by McLanahan and his weapons."

"A frontal assault with armed troops won't work unless you're going to attempt a D-Day invasion, Mr. President," Barbeau said, "and we can't pen him up inside Dreamland when he's got spaceplanes, unmanned aerial vehicles, and bombers roaming around inside a thousand square miles of desert, patrolled by gadgets no one's ever heard of before. He won't be expecting me. Besides, I think I might have some folks on the inside who will help. They're just as concerned as I about the general's welfare."

There were no other comments made—no one had any other suggestions, and certainly no one else was going to volunteer to stick their heads in the tiger's jaws like the Navy SEALs had. "Then it's decided," the President said. "Thank you for this undertaking, Senator. I assure all of you, we'll do everything possible to see to your safety. I'd like to speak to the senator in private for a moment. Thank you all." The White House chief of staff escorted them all out of the Cabinet Room, and Gardner and Barbeau moved to the President's private office adjacent to the Oval Office.

No sooner had the door closed than Gardner's arms were around her waist and he was snuggling her neck. "You macho hot bitch," he said. "What kind of crazy idea is this? Why do you want to go to Dreamland? And who is this guy you say you've got on the inside?"

"You'll find out soon enough, Joe," Barbeau said. "You sent in the SEALs and they didn't get it done—the *last* thing you want to do is start a war out there. Your poll numbers will go down even farther. Let me try it my way first."

"All right, sugar, you got it," Gardner said. He let her turn in his arms, then began to run his hands over her breasts. "But if you're successful—and I have no doubt you will be—what is it you want in return?"

"We have a good deal going already, Mr. President," Barbeau said, pressing his hands even tighter around her nipples. "But I'm interested in one thing Carlyle was talking about: the netrusion thing."

"What about it?"

"I want it," Barbeau said. "Barksdale gets the network warfare mission—not the Navy, not STRATCOM."

"You understand all that stuff?"

"Not all of it, but I will, in very short order," Barbeau said confidently. "But I do know that Furness at Battle Mountain has all the bombers and unmanned combat aircraft that use netrusion technology—I want them at Barksdale, along with *all* the network warfare stuff. All of it. Downsize or even eliminate the B-52s if you want, but Barksdale runs network warfare for anything that flies—drones, B-2s, satellites, the space-based radar, everything."

The fingers on Barbeau's nipples tensed. "You're not talking about keeping the space station?" Gardner asked. "That's five billion I want to go to two aircraft carriers."

"The space station can fry for all I care—I want the technology behind it, especially the space-based radar," Barbeau said. "The space station is dead anyway—folks consider it McLanahan's orbiting graveyard, and I don't want to be associated with it. But the nuts and bolts behind the station are what I want. I know STRATCOM, and Air Force Space Command will want netrusion aboard their reconnaissance, airborne command posts, and spacecraft, but you have to agree to fight that. I want the Eighth Air Force at Barksdale to control netrusion."

The President's hands began their ministrations once again, and she knew she had him. "Whatever you say, Stacy," Gardner said distractedly. "It's a lot of hocus-pocus gobbledygook to me—what bad guys around the world understand is a fucking aircraft carrier battle group parked off their coastline, in their *faces,* not network attacks and computer magic. If you want this computer-fucking virus thing, you're welcome to it. Just get Congress to agree to stop funding the space station and give me my two aircraft carriers, minimum, and you can have your cyberwar shit."

She turned toward him, letting her breasts slide tightly across his chest. "Thank you, baby," she said, kissing him deeply. She placed a hand on his crotch, feeling him jump at her touch. "I'd seal our deal in the usual manner, but I have a plane to catch to Vegas. I'll have McLanahan in prison by tomorrow evening . . . or I'll expose him as a raving lunatic so severely that the American people will be clamoring for you to take him down."

"I'd love to give you a big going-away present too, honey," Gardner said, giving Barbeau a playful pat on her behind, then taking a seat at his desk and lighting up a cigar, "but Zevitin's going to call in a few minutes, and I've got to explain to him that I'm still in control of this McLanahan mess."

"Screw Zevitin," Barbeau said. "I suspect that everything McLanahan said about the Russians putting a super-laser in Iran and firing on the spaceplane is true, Joe. McLanahan might be going off the deep end by ignoring your orders, attacking without authorization, and then battling the SEALs, but Zevitin's up to something here. McLanahan doesn't just fly off the handle."

"Don't worry about a thing, Stacy," Gardner said. "We've got good communications open with Moscow. All they want are assurances that we're not trying to bottle them up. McLanahan is making the whole world, not just the Russians, nervous, and that's bad for business."

"But it's good for getting votes in Congress for new aircraft carrier battle groups, honey."

"Not if we have a rogue general on our hands, Stacy. Take McLanahan down, but do it *quietly*. He could ruin everything for us."

"Don't worry about a thing, Mr. President," Barbeau said, giving him a wink and a toss of her hair. "He's going down . . . one way or another."

Barbeau met up with her chief of staff Colleen Morna outside the executive suites, and they walked quickly to her waiting car. "The trip's all set, Senator," Morna said after they were on their way back to her office on Capitol Hill. "I have the billing codes for the whole trip from the White House, and they even gave us authorization for a C-37—a Gulfstream Five. That means we can take eight guests with us to Vegas."

"Perfect. I got a verbal agreement from Gardner about relocating and centralizing all of the DoD network warfare units to Barksdale. Find out which contractors and lobbyists we need to organize to get that done and invite them along with us to Vegas. That should water their eyes."

"You got that right, Senator."

"Good. Now, what about that hard-body boyfriend of yours, Hunter Noble? He's the key to this Las Vegas trip as long as McLanahan is up in that space station. What did you dig up on him?"

"You had him pegged from day one, Senator," Colleen said. "Our Captain Noble seems to be stuck in junior high school. For starters: he got a woman six years older than him pregnant in high school—the school nurse, I think."

"Happens every year where I'm from, sugar. The only virgin in my hometown was an ugly twelve-year-old."

"He was expelled, but it didn't matter because he already had enough credits to graduate two years early from high school and start engineering school," Colleen went on. "Seems his way of celebrating graduation is getting some woman pregnant, because he did it again in both college and grad school. He married the third one, but the marriage was annulled when yet another affair was uncovered."

"McLanahan he definitely *isn't*," Barbeau said.

"He's an outstanding pilot and engineer, but apparently has a real problem with authority," Morna went on. "He gets high marks on his effectiveness reports for job performance but terrible marks for leadership skills and military bearing."

"That's no help—now he sounds like McLanahan again," Barbeau said dejectedly. "What about the juicy stuff?"

"Plenty of that," Morna said. "Lives in bachelor officers' quarters at Nellis Air Force Base—barely six hundred square feet of living space—and has been written up many times by base security for loud parties and visitors coming and going at all times of the day and night. He's a regular in the Officers' Club at Nellis and piles up a pretty hefty bar tab. Rides a Harley Night Rod motorcycle and has received numerous speeding and exhibitionist driving citations. License just recently returned after a three-month suspension for unsafe driving—apparently decided to race an Air Force T-6A training aircraft down the runway."

"That's good, but I need the *real* juicy stuff, baby."

"I saved the best for last, Senator. The list of female visitors admitted for on-base visits is as long as my arm. A few are wives of married men, a couple known bisexual women, a few prostitutes—and one was the wife of an Air Force general officer. However, visits on-base seemed to have subsided a bit in the last year . . . mostly because he has signature credit authority with three very large casinos in Vegas for a total of one hundred thousand dollars."

"What?"

"Senator, the man hasn't paid for a hotel room in Vegas in over two years—he's on a first-name basis with managers, doormen, and concierges all over town, and uses comped rooms and meals almost every week," Colleen said. "He likes blackjack and poker and is invited backstage a lot to hang out with showgirls, boxers, and headliners. Usually has at least one and many times two or three ladies in tow."

"One hundred grand!" Barbeau remarked. "He beats out every Nevada legislator I know!"

"Bottom line, Senator: He works hard and plays hard," Colleen summarized. "He maintains a low profile but has made some fairly high-profile transgressions that have apparently been swept under the rug because of the work he does for the government. He's contacted regularly by defense contractors who want to hire him, some offering incredible salaries, so that probably makes him cocky and contributes to his attitude that he doesn't have to play the Air Force's games."

"Sounds like a guy living on the edge—and that's exactly where I like 'em," Barbeau said. "I think it's time to go pay Captain Noble a little visit—in his native habitat."

CHAPTER TEN

The deed is everything, the glory nothing.

—JOHANN WOLFGANG VON GOETHE

MASHHAD, ISLAMIC REPUBLIC OF IRAN

THAT NIGHT

The city of Mashhad—"City of Martyrs" in English—in northeast-ern Iran was the second-largest city in Iran and, as the location of the shrine of the eighth imam, Reza, it was the second-largest Shiite holy city in the world and second only to Qom in importance. Over twenty million pilgrims visited the Imam Reza shrine every year, making it as noteworthy and spiritual as the Haji, the pilgrimage to Mecca. Located in a valley between the Kuh-e-Ma'juni and Azhdar-Kuh mountain ranges, the area had brutally cold winters but was pleasant most of the rest of the year.

Located in the hinterlands of Iran, Mashhad held relatively little military or strategic importance until the rise of the Taliban regime in Afghanistan in the 1980s. Fearing that the Taliban would try to export its brand of Islam westward, Mashhad was turned into a counterinsurgency stronghold, with the Iranian Revolutionary

Guards Corps operating several strike teams, intelligence units, counterinsurgency fighter-bomber and helicopter assault and attack units from Imam Reza International Airport.

When Hesarak Buzhazi's military coup hit, Mashhad's importance quickly grew even stronger. The remnants of the Revolutionary Guards Corps was chased all the way from Tehran to Mashhad. However, Buzhazi barely had the resources to maintain his tenuous hold on the capital, so he had no choice but to let the survivors flee without mounting a determined effort to root out the commanders. With the surviving Revolutionary Guards Corps commanders freely moving about the city, and with a very large influx of Shiite pilgrims that continued almost unabated even during the growing violence, the Pasdaran had lots of recruits to choose from in Mashhad. From mosques, the marketplaces and malls, and from every street corner, the call to *jihad* against Buzhazi and the Qagev pretenders went far and wide and quickly spread.

Spurred on by the powerful spiritual aura of the city and the entrenched power of the Revolutionary Guards Corps, acting Iranian president, chief of the Council of Guardians, and senior member of the Assembly of Experts Ayatollah Hassan Mohtaz was emboldened to return from exile in Turkmenistan, where he had been living under the protection of the Russian government. At first there was talk of all of the eastern provinces of Iran splitting from the rest of the country, with Mashhad as the new capital, but the instability of the coup and the failure of Buzhazi and the Qagevs to form a government postponed such discussions. Perhaps all Mohtaz had to do was encourage the faithful to *jihad,* continue to raise money to fund his insurgency, and wait—Tehran might drop right back into his hands soon enough all by itself.

Three full divisions of the Revolutionary Guards Corps, over one hundred thousand strong, were based in and around Mashhad, nearly the entire surviving complement of frontline elite troops. Most of the Pasdaran forces, two divisions, were infantry, including two mechanized infantry brigades. There was one aviation brigade with counterinsurgency aircraft, attack and assault helicopters, transports, and air defense battalions; one armored brigade with light tanks, artillery, and mortar battalions; and one special operations and intelligence brigade that conducted demolition, assassination, espionage, surveillance, interrogation, and specialized communications missions such as propaganda broadcasts. In addition, another thirty thousand al-Quds paramilitary forces were deployed within the city itself, acting as spies and informers for the Pasdaran and theocratic government-in-exile.

The Revolutionary Guards Corps' headquarters and strategic center of gravity was Imam Reza International Airport, situated just five miles south of the Imam Reza shrine. However, all of the tactical military units at the airport were relocated to make room for a new arrival: an S-300OMU1 *Favorit* air defense regiment from the Russian Federation.

The S-300 strategic air defense system was considered one of the finest in the world, equal to the American PAC-3 Patriot missile system. An S-300 battery consisted of a long-range three-dimensional scanning acquisition radar, a target engagement and missile guidance radar, and twelve trailers each loaded with four missiles, along with maintenance, crew support, and security vehicles. One such battery was set up at the airport, with another northwest and a third positioned west of the city. The S-300 missile was effective against targets flying as low as thirty feet aboveground, as high as one hundred thousand feet, as fast as Mach 3, as far out as one hundred and twenty miles, and deadly against even low-flying cruise missiles and theater ballistic missiles.

The S-300s were augmented by the Tor-M1 air defense system, which were tracked armored vehicles that fired eight high-speed, short-range radar-guided anti-aircraft missiles from vertical launch tubes. The Tor-M1 was designed to protect mobile headquarters vehicles, vehicle marshaling areas, refueling areas, and ammunition dumps from attack helicopters, unmanned aerial vehicles, and low-flying subsonic tactical bombers. Although the Tor-M1 had a crew of three, it was designed to be a "set and forget" system, allowing for fully autonomous engagements, or it could be tied into the S-300's fire control system to form an integrated air defense system. Together they formed an almost impenetrable shield around Mashhad.

That day, Mashhad was one of the most heavily defended cities on planet Earth . . . and it was about to be put to the test.

About two hours before dawn, the first alert was issued from the long-range air defense radar at S-300 battery number two, located thirty miles northwest of Mashhad: "Alarm, alarm, alarm, this is *Syeveer* battery, high-speed low-altitude target inbound, bearing two-eight-zero, range one-fifty, velocity nine-six-five, altitude nine-zero."

"*Syeveer,* this is *Tsentr,* acknowledged," the tactical action officer, Captain Sokolov, responded. His tactical display showed three high-speed, low-altitude targets heading toward Mashhad. "Contact, sir," he reported to the regimental commander. "Looks like a terrain-following bomb run, right where you thought they'd be."

"Completely predictable," Colonel Kundrin, the air defense regimental commander, said confidently. As if sensing that something might happen that morning, he had been dressed and at his post in the regimental air defense command center on the top floor of the administration building at Reza International hours earlier. "The planes may change over the years, but the tactics remain the same. We placed that battery in perfect position—the bomber is trying to terrain-mask down the valley, but the mountains funnel right down to where we placed that battery. A fatal flaw in their mission planning. He can't continue straight ahead, and if he pops up over the ridges he'll be exposing himself even more."

"Too fast and too low for a B-2 stealth bomber—this must be a B-1 bomber," Sokolov surmised. "And they haven't launched their hypersonic cruise missiles either."

"I don't think they have any stealth bombers left after President Gryzlov and General Darzov expertly pounded their bases and caught the fools flat-footed on the ground," Kundrin said. "Besides,

this is not the American air force we're up against—it's just McLanahan, the general that went crazy up in space. He's probably fired all
his missiles already. Tell *Syeveer* to engage at optimal range, and be
sure to watch for a trailing aircraft. If he's got more than one bomber,
he'll either be in close trail or attacking from a different axis. I don't
want anyone to slip inside."

Sokolov relayed the order. "Order to engage confirmed, sir,
fifteen seconds to go . . . wait one! Sir, *Zapat* battery reports new
hostile target inbound, bearing two-five-zero, range one hundred, altitude one hundred, speed eight-seventy and increasing!"
Zapat was the westernmost battery, situated fifty miles west of
Mashhad.

"I knew it! Predictable, all too predictable," Kundrin said happily. "Looks like we placed that number three battery in a perfect
place too—covering the Binalud ridgeline west of the city. If I were
to plan an attack on the airport, I'd hug the ground along the ridge,
then pop around the end of the ridge and launch missiles right at
rollout. That's exactly what McLanahan did—and we were in exactly the right spot to nail him! He'll have his bomb doors open and
his radar signature will be massive! Tell *Zapat* to engage when
ready!"

Each battery had three missile trailers, separated by several miles
but linked to each other via microwave datalink, each carrying four
48N6 vertical-launch interceptor missiles which were already raised
to launch position. Once the order to attack was given and the
proper attack mode set—launch at optimal range—the engagement
was virtually automatic. As soon as the target came within range, a
nitrogen gas catapult pushed the missile out of the launch tube to a
height of about thirty feet and the rocket motor ignited, accelerating
the missile to greater-than-a-mile-per-second velocity in less than
twelve seconds. Three seconds later, a second missile automatically
fired to assure a kill. The S-300's missiles climbed to an altitude of
only twenty thousand feet, guided to a predicted intercept point.

"Status?" the regimental commander asked.

"Batteries engaging targets, four missiles in the air," Sokolov reported. "Targets making only minimal evasive maneuvers and little jamming. Solid lock-on."

"The last act of overconfidence," Kundrin said. "They have no room to maneuver in any case. Too bad they're unmanned aircraft, eh, Captain?"

"Yes, sir. I'm concerned about those T-waves, or whatever they hit our fighter with."

"We'll see in a moment, won't we?"

"Missiles tracking perfectly . . . targets making slightly more aggressive maneuvers . . . channel-hop away from jamming, still locked on . . . three . . . two . . . one . . . now."

There were no other reports from the tactical action officer, which confused the regimental commander. "TAO, report!"

"Sir . . . sir, both missiles reporting ground contact!" Sokolov said in a low, confused voice. "Negative warhead detonation. Complete miss!"

"Release batteries and launch again!" Kundrin shouted. "Target range and bearing?"

"Second volley processing . . . missile three launched . . . missile four launched," Sokolov said. "Target range nine-zero, bearing steady at two-eight-zero."

"What of battery three? Status?"

"Battery three engagement . . ." And then his voice cut off with a sharp intake of breath.

Kundrin flew out of his seat and stared at the display. It was unbelievable . . . "They *missed*?" he exclaimed. "Another ground impact?"

"Battery three re-engaging . . . missile three launch . . . missile four . . ."

"Say range and bearing on battery three's target?"

"Range eight-zero, bearing steady at two-five-zero."

"That . . . that doesn't make sense," Kundrin said. "Both target bearings did not change even though they fell under attack? Something's not—"

"Sir, batteries two and three second-engagement missiles show ground impact as well!" Sokolov said. "All engagements missed! Battery two re-engaging. Battery three—"

"Negative! All batteries tight!" Kundrin shouted. "Inhibit auto engage!"

"Repeat that last, sir?"

"I said, *all batteries tight, inhibit auto engagement*!" Kundrin shouted. "We're being meaconed!"

"Meaconed? You mean, jammed, sir?"

"They're broadcasting false targets on our displays and making us fire at ghosts," Kundrin said.

"But we have full countermeasures and anti-jam algorithms in place, sir," Sokolov said. "Our systems are in perfect working order."

"We're not being jammed, dammit," Kundrin said. "Something's *inside* our system. Our computers believe they are processing actual targets."

The command network phone rang; only the regimental commander could answer it. *"Tsentr."*

"This is *Rayetka*." It was General Andrei Darzov himself, calling from Moscow. "We copied your notification of an attack response, but now we see you have canceled all engagements. Why?"

"Sir, I think we're being meaconed—we're reacting to false targets generated by our own sensors," Kundrin said. "I've inhibited automatic responses until . . ."

"Sir, battery two S-300 and Tor units receiving automatic engagement commands and are preparing to launch!" Sokolov shouted.

"I *gave no such orders*!" Kundrin shouted. "Countermand those orders! All batteries tight!"

"Tsentr, are you positive those are false targets?" Darzov asked.

"Every missile launched so far has hit the ground," Kundrin said. "Not one of our units has reported visual, optronic, or noise contact even though the targets are at very low altitude."

"S-300 battery two launching against new multiple inbound

high-speed targets!" Sokolov reported. He ran over and pushed the communications officer out of the way, slapping on his headset. "*Syeveer* and *Zapat* batteries, this is *Tsentr* TAO, batteries tight, repeat, batteries tight! Ignore the computer's indications!" He hurriedly made out a date-time code for authentication—but as he did so, he watched as still more S-300 and Tor-M1 units launched missiles. "All units, this is *Tsentr* TAO, stop launch! Repeat, stop launch!"

"Stop those damned units from launching, Captain, *now*!" Kundrin shouted. There were now more targets appearing on the display—flying in exactly the same tracks, speed, altitude, and bearing as the first sets of targets! Soon battery one, the S-300 company at Reza International Airport, was beginning to launch missiles. "*Rayetka,* this is *Tsentr,* we're picking up more inbound hostile targets, but they're flying the exact same speed, altitude, and track as the first hostiles! Recommend we stop all responses and go to standby on all sensors. We're being spoofed, I'm positive."

There was a long pause, with the command net crackling and popping from the shifting encryption decoding routines; then: "*Tsentr,* this is *Rayetka,* deploy *Fanar.* Repeat, deploy *Fanar.* Stand by for engagement authentication."

"Repeat that last, *Rayetka?*" Kundrin asked. For God's sake, the regimental commander cried to himself, I just recommended to the guy that we shut *everything* down—now Darzo wants to roll out the biggest gun and the biggest sensor they had! "Repeat, *Rayetka?*"

"I said, deploy *Fanar* and stand by for engagement authentication," the order came back. It was followed by an authentication code.

"I copy, *Rayetka,* moving *Fanar* to firing position, standing by for engagement authentication." Darzov must be getting desperate, Kundrin thought. *Fanar,* the anti-spacecraft laser, was probably their last chance. The anti-aircraft artillery units scattered around Mashhad had no chance against fast, low-flying bombers. He picked up his regiment's command network phone: "Security, this is *Tsentr,* move *Fanar* to firing position and notify the crew to prepare to engage enemy aircraft." He gave the security commander an authentication code to move the trucks.

"Sir, we managed to get all units to respond to a weapons-tight order," Sokolov said. "We're down to twenty percent primary rounds available."

"Twenty percent!" Shit, they wasted *eighty percent* of their missiles on *ghosts*! "They had better be reloading, dammit!"

"We're in the process of reloading now, sir," Sokolov went on. "The Tor-M1 units will be done within fifteen minutes, and the S-300 units will be done before the hour."

"Get on it. The real attack may be happening at any moment. And make sure they *do not* respond to any more targets unless they have optronic verification!" Kundrin rushed to the exit, down the corridor, out the emergency exit, and up to the roof of the administration building. From there, using night-vision binoculars, he could see the progress of the security units.

The four *Fanar* trucks were just emerging from their hiding places. They had been hidden in a tunnel that ran under the runways which allowed vehicles to go from one side of the airport to another without going all the way around the runways. They were headed for a firefighting training pad on the north side of the runways, which had some old fuel tanks arranged to look like an airliner which could be filled with waste jet fuel and ignited to simulate a crashed airliner. The command vehicle was just now unfolding the huge electronically scanned radar antenna and datalink mast, which would allow the radar to tie into the S-300 fire control network.

Kundrin's secure portable radio crackled to life: *"Tsentr,* this is *Rayetka,"* Darzov spoke. "Status."

"Fanar deployment under way, sir," Kundrin replied.

"Tsentr, this is the TAO," Sokolov radioed.

"Stand by, TAO," Kundrin said. "I'm talking to *Rayetka.*"

"They are setting up on the southeast pad as directed?" Darzov asked.

Southeast pad? There was a fighter alert pad on the southeast side, but it was still in use by Revolutionary Guards Corps tactical attack helicopters and also as secure parking for the Russian transports. They had never briefed using it to employ the anti-spacecraft laser. "Negative, sir, we're using the north firefighting training pad, as briefed."

"Acknowledged," Darzov said. "Proceed."

Moments later, the TAO burst through the door to the roof observation post. "Stop, sir!" he shouted.

"What in hell is going on, Sokolov? What are you doing up here?"

"The authentication from *Rayetka—it was not valid!*" Sokolov said. "The order to deploy *Fanar* was not valid!"

"*What?*" A dull chill ran through Kundrin's head. He had *assumed* that because the person on the radio used the proper code name and was on the proper encrypted frequency that he was who he said he was and gave a valid order—he didn't wait to see if the authentication code checked . . .

. . . and he realized that he had just told whoever it was on the other end of that channel *exactly where* Fanar *was located!*"

He frantically raised his radio to his lips: "Security, this is *Tsentr,* cancel deployment, get those trucks back in hiding!" he shouted. "Repeat, get them into—!"

But at that exact moment there was a flash of light, and milliseconds later an impossibly thunderous explosion, followed by several more in quick succession. Kundrin and Sokolov were blown off their feet by the first concussion, and they frantically crawled away as crashing waves of raw heat roiled over them. They could do nothing but curl up into protective balls and cover their ears as the explosions continued one after the other.

It seemed to last an entire hour, but it was actually over in less than twenty seconds. Kundrin and Sokolov, their ears ringing from the deafening noise, crawled over to the shattered front of the administration building and peered out across the runways. The entire area north of the runways was on fire, centered on the firefighting training pad. The fire on the pad itself—obviously the burning chemicals used by the laser—seemed so hot and intense that it was radioactive. The alert aircraft parking area to the southeast had been hit too—every helicopter and transport was on fire.

Then they heard them, and in the brilliant reflection of the fires they soon saw them too, as plainly as if in daytime: a pair of American B-1 bombers, flying right down the runway. They obviously knew that all of the air defense units had been ordered to shut down their systems and not open fire. The first one wagged its wings as it passed by the administration building, and the second *actually did an aileron roll,* flying less than two hundred feet aboveground. When they finished their little airshow spectacle, they ignited afterburners, sped off into the night sky, and were soon out of sight.

Las Vegas, Nevada

That same time

Stacy Anne Barbeau loved casinos, and she spent quite a bit of time in them on the Mississippi River in Louisiana and on the Gulf Coast in neighboring Mississippi. But this was the first time in many years that she had been in a big Las Vegas casino, and she was impressed. They were much more than gambling halls now—they were spectacular destinations, a sensory bombardment not only of lights, colors, and sounds, but of scenery, landscaping, architecture, and art that was truly amazing. The last time she was here, the decorations seemed cheesy and campy, almost Disneyesque. Not anymore. It was definitely Las Vegas elegant—bright, a little gaudy, loud, and extravagant, but it *was* elegant nonetheless.

"You know what I love the most about these places, darlin'—you can be completely anonymous so easily, even dressed like this," Barbeau said to her assistant Colleen Morna as they strode from the hotel elevators through the wide, sweeping hallway and across the rich red carpeting of a very large Italian-themed casino on the Strip in Las Vegas. She was wearing a silvery cocktail dress, diamond earrings and necklace, and carrying a mink stole, but except for the frequent and appreciative glances, she felt as if she was just another part of the scenery. "So where is 'Playgirl'?"

"Private poker room in the back," Morna said. She produced what appeared to be a thick ruby-encrusted brooch and pinned it to Barbeau's dress. "This is all you need to get in."

"It's ugly. Do I have to wear it?"

"Yes. It's an identification and tracking transponder—an RFID, or radio-frequency identification tag," Morna said. "They've been tracking us ever since I picked it up a half hour ago while you were getting dressed. They track all your movements; it sends information to all the cashiers, croupiers, maître d's, security, hotel staff, and even to the slot machines about who you are, what you play or do, and—more importantly to them, I'm sure—how much is left in your account. The security staff watches you with their cameras and automatically compares your description to their database to keep an eye on you while you're on the property. I think if you took more than one or two wrong turns anywhere around this place, they'd send a couple hospitality guys after you to steer you in the right direction."

"I like the sound of that—'hospitality guys,'" Barbeau cooed. "I don't much like the idea of being tagged like a brown bear in the woods, though."

"Well, keep it with you, because it's your room key, access to your line of credit, your charge card, and your admission pass to all the shows and VIP rooms—again, you don't need to know a thing because these guys will escort you everywhere you want to go. *Anywhere.*"

"But they don't know who I am, do they?"

"I would assume they know *exactly* who you are, Senator," Morna said, "but this is Vegas—here, you are whoever you *want* to be. Tonight you're Robin Gilliam from Montgomery, telecommunications and oil money, married but here alone."

"Oh, do I have to be from Alabama?" she deadpanned. Morna rolled her eyes. "Never mind. So how did I get into this private poker room if I'm not who I say I am?"

"A fifty thousand dollar line of credit is the best way to start," Morna said.

"You used the billing codes from the White House for this trip for a line of credit in the casino? Smart girl."

"It's just to get us in the door, Senator—don't actually *use* any of it, or the sergeant at arms will crucify you," Morna said.

"Oh, pish on him—he's an old fuddy-duddy," Barbeau said.

Morna rolled her eyes, silently hoping she was kidding. Washington careers were ended by a lot less. "Everything is all set. The management is as attentive as they are discreet. They'll take good care of you. I'll be in the room next door to yours if you need me, and I've got a casino employee bought and paid for that will tell me exactly where you are at all times."

"Thanks, but I don't think I'll need a wingman tonight, darlin',"

Barbeau said in her best man-slaying voice. "Captain Hunter 'Boomer' Noble will go down as easy as catching catfish in a barrel."

"What do you plan to do, Senator?"

"I plan to show Captain Noble the best way to get ahead in the United States Air Force, which is very simple: Don't cross a United States senator," she said confidently. She stuck out her chest and moved the mink aside. "I'll show him a couple advantages of pleasing me instead of opposing me. You're sure he's here?"

"He checked in last night and has been playing poker all day long," Morna said. "He's doing pretty well too—he's up a little."

"Oh, I'll make sure he's *up,* all right," Barbeau said. "Trust me."

"I know where his suite is—it's right down the hall from ours—and if he takes you there my guy will tell me," Morna went on.

"Any other ladies with him?"

"Just a few that have stopped by briefly at the table—he hasn't invited any of them to his room."

"We'll see about that, won't we?" Barbeau said. "Don't wait up, sugar."

Exactly as Colleen said, the casino staff knew she was coming without a word being spoken. As Barbeau left the main casino floor and began walking toward the ornate gold entryway of the private poker room, a man in a tuxedo with a communications earpiece in one ear smiled, nodded, and said, "Welcome, Miss Gilliam," as she passed by.

As she approached the doors she was met by a tall, good-looking man in a tuxedo and a woman in a tuxedo suit and skirt, carrying a beverage tray. "Welcome, Miss Gilliam," the man said. "My name is Martin, and this is Jesse, who will be your attendant for the rest of the evening."

"Why thank you, Martin," Barbeau said in her best Southern accent. "I'm quite taken by this extraordinary level of attention."

"Our goal is to assist you in any way possible to have the best evening while a guest at the hotel," Martin said. "Our motto is 'Anything at All,' and I will be here to be sure all your desires are met tonight." The waitress handed her the glass. "Southern Comfort and lime, I believe?"

"Exactly right, Martin. Thank you, Jesse."

"My job is to make you comfortable, get any dinner or show reservations you may like, get you a seat at any gaming table you'd
prefer, and make any introductions while you're in the private hall.
If there's anything at all you'd like—*anything* at all—please do not
hesitate to tell Jesse or myself."

"Thank you, Martin," Barbeau said, "but I think I'd like to
just . . . you know, prowl around a little bit to get comfortable. That's
all right, isn't it?"

"Of course. Whenever you need anything, just motion to us. You
don't have to look for us—we'll be looking out for *you*."

It was a very secure feeling, Barbeau thought, to know that she
was being watched every second. She took her drink and began to
stroll around the room. It was plush and ornate without being too
ostentatious; there was just a hint of cigar smoke, not too bad, almost
pleasant and reassuring. A room in the back had several sports
games on huge wide-screen flat-panel monitors, with women who
definitely didn't look like spouses hanging onto the shoulders of the
spectators—male and female alike.

What happens in this place, Stacy thought as she took a sip of her
drink, *definitely* stays in this place.

After a short hunt she finally found him, at a card table in the
back: Hunter Noble, dressed in a T-shirt and jeans, with a single
thick-link gold chain around his neck, an old-style metal POW
bracelet on one wrist, and a black nylon Velcro watchband on the
other wrist with its protective watch flap closed. He had an impressive stack of chips in front of him, and only two players and the
dealer at the table with him—and the other players definitely looked
perturbed, their chip stacks much lower than his, as if they were
frustrated at being beat by this young punk. One of the other players
had a cigarette in an ashtray beside him; Noble had an ashtray beside him too, but it was clean and empty.

Now that she saw him in his "native habitat," she liked what she saw.
He was the perfect cross between lean and muscular—a naturally
toned body without having to do a lot of weight lifting, not like McLanahan's chunky muscularity. His hair was short and naturally teased,

without having to mousse it, which had to be the most unmanly thing Stacy had ever seen in her life. His movements were slow and easy, although she noticed his quick eyes when cards and chips started flying across the table in front of him. He certainly didn't miss much . . .

. . . and at that moment his eyes rested on *her* . . . and he didn't miss anything there, either. He smiled that mischievous naughty-boy smile, and his quick eyes danced, and she instantly felt herself being visually undressed once more—then, just as quickly, his attention was back to his game.

It was not too long afterward that Barbeau saw Martin supervising the dealer counting up Noble's winnings. He saw him ask Martin a question, the host responded, and soon he sauntered over to her table with a drink and a cigarette in his hand. "Pardon me, Miss Gilliam," he said, speaking very formally but with that same mischievous smile, "but I took the liberty of asking Martin who you were, and I thought I'd introduce myself. My name is Hunter Noble. I hope I'm not intruding."

Barbeau sipped her drink but eyed him over the rim of the glass, making him wait while she surveyed him. He simply stood before her patiently with that playful boyish smile on his face, standing casually but provocatively as well, as if he had no doubt that she would invite him to sit down. Well, *shit,* she thought, the guy flies hypersonic spaceplanes for a living—a mere *woman* isn't going to rattle him. "Of course not, Mr. Noble. Would you care to sit down?" Barbeau responded just as formally, enjoying playing the game of being strangers.

"Thank you, I would." He took a chair beside her, set his drink down, then leaned toward her. "Senator Barbeau? Is that you?"

"Captain Hunter 'Boomer' Noble," she said in response. "Fancy meeting you here, sir."

"Fancy nothing, Senator. Did you track me down here?"

"I don't know whatever you mean, Captain," Barbeau said. "The assistant hotel manager here happens to be a friend of mine, and he invited me to this wonderful VIP room when I came to town." She looked him over once again. "Where's your RFID tag, Captain?"

"I don't wear those things—I like tipping in cash and I can unlock my own room door without Big Brother doing it for me."

"I think it's fun, being surveilled all the time. Makes me feel very secure."

"You'll get tired of it," he said moodily. "You're here to shut down Dreamland, aren't you, Senator?"

"I'm here to talk with the SEALs who tried to assault the place, speak with General Luger about his actions, and report to the President," she replied.

"Then why are you *here*? Are you spying on me?"

"Why, Captain Noble, you sound like a man with something to hide," Barbeau said. "But I am surprised, quite frankly, to find a young Air Force captain who makes less than seventy thousand dollars a year before taxes here in a VIP gambling room, where the price of admission is usually a fifty-thousand-dollar line of credit with the casino, with such a large stack of chips in front of him."

"Playing poker for money is not against Air Force regulations, Senator. Neither is spending a good deal of my bachelor take-home pay on playing cards. Do you investigate guys who spend that much on cars or cameras?"

"I don't know of anyone who's been blackmailed by bookies or loan sharks because they buy camera gear," Barbeau said. "Being a habitual gambler certainly does look . . . how shall I say it, unseemly? For someone in such a highly critical job as yours, being such a gambling devotee—or perhaps even a gambling addict?—might look very suspicious to some."

"I'm not addicted to gambling," Boomer said defensively. The senator's eyes twinkled—she knew she had hit a nerve. "But why this charade, Senator? Why this campaign to destroy the program? You're opposed to the Black Stallion and the space station—fine. Why take the political opposition so personally?"

"I'm not an opponent of the XR-A9 project, Captain," Barbeau said, sipping her drink. "I think it's a remarkable piece of technology. But the space station has many very powerful opponents."

"Like Gardner."

"*Many* opponents," Barbeau repeated. "But some of the technology you use is of great interest to me, including the Black Stallion."

"Not to mention scoring some points with folks in the White House and dozens of defense contractors, too."

"Don't try to play politics with me, Captain—my family invented the game, and I learned from the best," Barbeau said.

"I see that. You're more than willing to destroy military careers for your own political gain." .

"You mean General McLanahan? Perfect example of a smart, dedicated guy wading into political waters that were way over his head," she said dimissively, taking another sip. She was finally starting to feel relaxed, immersed in an atmosphere in which she was very comfortable . . . no, not just comfortable: one in which she was *in control*. McLanahan had destroyed himself, and because Hunter Noble cared about him, he was going to *go down* next.

Captain Hunter Noble was pretty, and obviously smart and talented, but this was business, and he would become just another one of her victims . . . after she had a little fun with him!

"He'll come out okay—as long as he backs off and lets me tell the White House what is best for the Air Force," Barbeau went on casually. "McLanahan's a war hero, for God's sake—everybody knows that. Very few people know what happened in Dreamland and Turkey." She snapped her fingers with a wave of her wrist. "It can be swept under the rug like *that*. With my help and with his maximum cooperation, he'll get off with a general court-martial and loss of his pension. But then he can get on with his life."

"Otherwise, you'll let him rot in prison."

Stacy Anne Barbeau leaned forward, giving him a good look at her bosom underneath her silvery low-cut neckline. "I'm not here to make *anyone* miserable, Captain—least of all you," she said. "The truth is, I would like your help."

"My help?"

"Next to McLanahan, you're the most influential person attached to the space project," she said. "The general is done for if what he's

done in Dreamland and in Turkey gets leaked out. I don't think
he'll cooperate with me. That leaves you."

"What is this, a threat? You're going to try to destroy me too?"

"I don't want to attack you, Captain," she said in a low voice. She
looked him straight in the eye. "To be honest, I'm quite taken by you."
She saw the look of surprise in his face and knew she had him by the
balls. "I've been attracted to you since I first saw you in the Oval
Office, and when I saw you here, looking at me like you were—"

"I wasn't looking at you," he said defensively, not too convinc-
ingly.

"Oh yes you were, Hunter. I felt it. You did too." He swallowed
but said nothing. "What I'm trying to say, Hunter, is that I can take
your career in a whole new direction if you'd let me. All you need to
do is let me show you what I can do for you."

"My career is just fine."

"In the Air Force? That's fine for eggheads and Neanderthals,
but not for you. You're smart, but you're savvy and in control. Those
are special qualities. They will get suppressed in the military under
layers upon layers of old-school bullshit and endless, faceless
bureaucracy—not to mention the possibility of dying in combat or
up in space, flying a jet built by the lowest bidder.

"I'm offering you a step out of that hellish cattle-call existence,
Hunter," Barbeau went on in a low voice, pumping as much sincerity
into it as she could. "How do you think other men and women rise
above corporate Pentagon mediocrity and advance their futures?"

"The general did it by being dedicated to the mission and his fellow crewmembers."

"McLanahan did it by being Kevin Martindale's whipping boy,"
Barbeau said firmly. "If he died in any of those missions he sent
him on, Martindale would have just found another mindless robot
to activate. Is that what you want? Do you just want to be McLanahan's sacrificial lamb?" Again, Boomer didn't reply—she could see
the wheels of doubt churning in his head. "So who's looking out for
you, Hunter? McLanahan won't be in a position to do it. Even if he

doesn't go to prison, he'll have a federal conviction and a less-than-honorable discharge on his record. You'll wither away too out there if you blindly follow idealistic men like McLanahan."

He didn't say it, but she knew what he was asking himself: How do I get out of this? He was putty in her hands, ready for the next step. "Come with me, Hunter," she said. "I'll show you how to rise above the swamp that McLanahan has stuck you in. I'll show you the *real* world, the one outside of spaceplanes and shadowy missions. With my help, you can *dominate* the real world. Just let me show you the way."

"And what do I need to do?"

She looked deeply in his eyes, took a deep breath, then gently placed a hand on his left thigh. "Just trust me," she said. "Place yourself in my hands. Do what I tell you, and I'll take you to places, introduce you to the most influential people who really want to hear what you have to say, and take you through the *real* corridors of power. That's what you want, isn't it?" She could feel those rock-hard thighs jump at her touch, and couldn't wait for those long legs to straddle her. He was practically gasping for air like a marathoner at the end of a race. "Let's go."

He stood, and she smiled and took his hand as he helped her to her feet. He's mine, she thought . . . *mine.*

She felt a little dizzy as she got to her feet—one glass of whiskey, after a half day of skipping meals preparing for this trip, was doing her in. After she dealt with Hunter Noble, she vowed to treat herself and Colleen to a late-night supper in the suite and toast her success. First Gardner, then McLanahan, and now this studly hard-body military astronaut.

"May I help you in any way, Miss Gilliam?" her waitress Jesse asked, appearing as if out of nowhere. She reached out as if to help steady her.

"No thank you, Jesse, I'm fine," Barbeau said. She watched as Martin came over and looked as if he was going to physically restrain Noble, who was discreetly following her, but she raised a hand. "Mr. Noble and I are going to take a walk together," she said. "Thank you, Martin."

"If you need anything, Miss Gilliam, just pick up a phone or give a signal—we'll be right there," Martin said.

"Thank you so much. I'm having a wonderful time," Barbeau said gaily. She tipped him fifty dollars, then headed for the door. Hunter opened the door for her; Martin took the door from him, and she noticed him giving Noble a stern warning glare . . . and he didn't tip him either. Well, she thought, maybe "Playgirl's" reputation was wearing a bit thin in here. That would be another weakness of his to explore if he didn't cooperate.

They walked together without talking until reaching the elevator, and then she took him by his slender waist, pulled him closer, and kissed him deeply. "I've wanted to do this ever since I first saw you," she said, pressing herself tightly against him. He whispered something in return, but the music in the elevator seemed a little loud, and she couldn't hear him.

At their floor they were met by a floor attendant. "Welcome, Mr. Noble, Miss Gilliam," she said brightly, obviously notified by the ever-present hotel security system of their arrival. "Is there anything I can do for you tonight? Anything at all?"

"No, I've got this one all taken care of myself," Barbeau heard herself say, reaching down between his legs and stroking him. "But if you'd care to join us a little later, sugar, that'd be fine, just fine." And then she heard herself giggle. Did she just *giggle*? That Southern Comfort was hitting her harder than she thought. Never party on an empty stomach, she reminded herself.

As she passed Colleen's room she pretended like she stumbled a bit and banged into her door just to give her a warning that she was back, and then they were at the door to the suite. "You just relax and let me do the drivin' for now, big boy," she said, starting to untuck his shirt from his pants even before he had the door open. "I'll show you how we like to party down on the bayou."

President's private retreat, Boltino, Russia

Several hours later

"Why haven't you answered my calls, Gardner?" President Leonid Zevitin thundered. "I've been trying for hours."

"I've got my own problems, Leonid," President Joseph Gardner said. "As if you hadn't noticed, I've got to deal with a little mutiny over here."

"Gardner, McLanahan has bombed Mashhad, Iran!" Zevitin cried. "He's destroyed several Russian transports and killed hundreds of men and women! You said he would be forced under control! Why haven't you dealt with him yet?"

"I've been briefed about the attack," Gardner said. "I've also been briefed about the target—an anti-spacecraft laser that was supposedly used to shoot down one of our spaceplanes. Wouldn't happen to know anything about that, would you, Leonid? What were all those Russian personnel and transports doing in Mashhad?"

"Don't change the subject!" Zevitin shouted. "The Duma is going to meet soon, and they're going to recommend a permanent change in military posture, including a call-up of ready reserves, mobilization of the army and strategic air forces, and dispersal of mobile ballistic missiles and submarine forces. Was this your plan all along, Gardner—have McLanahan act crazy, attacking targets all over the planet, and forcing us to respond as if we are going to fight a world war? Because this is exactly what it looks like!"

"You think I'm *conspiring* with McLanahan? The guy is *nuts*! He's completely out of control! He's attacked American military forces, taken over a top secret military base, and stolen several highly classified aircraft and weapons. No one has any contact with him for almost half a day—we think he might have committed suicide on the space station."

Well, Zevitin thought, that was the best news he's heard in a *long* time. "No one will believe any of this," he told Gardner. "You have got to give me something to tell my Cabinet and the leaders in the Duma, Joe, or this thing could spin out of control. How did he do that attack on Mashhad, Joe?"

"It's a thing they call 'netrusion,' Leonid," Gardner said. Zevitin's eyes widened in surprise—the American President was actually going to *tell* him! "Some of McLanahan's aircraft and spacecraft have a system where they can not only jam radar and communications, but actually insert bogus code and signals into an enemy system. They can reprogram, crash, or control computers, invade networks, inject viruses, all that egghead shit."

"This is astounding!" Zevitin exclaimed. Yes—astounding that you're *telling* me all this! "That's how the bombers made it over Mashhad?"

"They made the air defenses around the city react to false targets," Gardner said. "The air defense guys apparently shut down their missile systems so they wouldn't shoot at stuff that wasn't there, and that let the bombers slip in. McLanahan also hacked into their encrypted radio transmissions and gave them false orders, which allowed the bombers to locate and attack the laser site."

"If all this is true, Joe, then we must put a deal in place to share this technology," Zevitin said, "or at least pledge not to use it except in time of declared war. Can you imagine if this technology got into the wrong hands? It could devastate our economies! We could be thrown back into the Stone Age in a flash!"

"It's all McLanahan's geeks at Dreamland coming up with this stuff," Gardner said. "I'm going to shut Dreamland down and have that bastard McLanahan shot. I think he's left the space station and is back at Dreamland. He's ignored my orders and done what he pleases for too long. I've got a friend, a powerful senator, who's going to try to bring McLanahan out in the open, and when she does I'll nail his ass to my wall."

"Who is the senator, Joe?"

"I'm not ready to divulge the name."

"It will lend credibility to my arguments before the Duma, Joe."

There was a bit of a pause; then: "Senator Stacy Anne Barbeau, the majority leader. She went to Dreamland to try to meet with McLanahan or Luger to try to defuse this situation."

He's got the Senate majority leader spying for him? This couldn't be better. Zevitin's mind was racing ahead. Dare he suggest it . . . ? "You don't want to do that, Joe," he said carefully. "You don't want to expose yourself or Barbeau any further. McLanahan is a very popular man in your country, is he not?"

"Yes, unfortunately he is."

"Then let me propose this idea, Joe: as over the Black Sea and over Iran, let us do the deed for you."

"What?"

"You told us where those bombers would be and when, and we took care of them for you; you told us about the spaceplane and put them in a position where we could strike—"

"What? You did what with the spaceplane . . . ?"

"Bring McLanahan out into the open," Zevitin went on, almost breathlessly. "Have Senator Barbeau tell us where he is. I'll send a team in to sanction him."

"You mean, a *Russian hit team?*"

"You don't want McLanahan's blood on your hands, Joe," Zevitin said. "You want him out of the way because he's much more than an embarrassment to you—he's a danger to the entire world. He's got to be stopped. If you have a person on the inside, have him or her contact us. Tell us where he is. We'll do the rest, and you don't have to know anything about it."

"I don't know if I can do that . . ."

"If you were seriously considering dispatching him yourself, then you are serious about the danger he poses not just to world peace, but to the safety and very *existence* of the United States of America. The man is a menace, pure and simple. He is a wild dog that needs to be put down."

"That's exactly what I said, Leonid!" Gardner said. "McLanahan has not just crossed the line, but I think he's become completely unhinged! He's brainwashed his men to attack American troops . . . or maybe he's used that 'netrusion' shit to brainwash them. He's got to be stopped before he takes down the entire country!"

"Then we are of one mind, Joe," Zevitin said. "I'll give you a number to call, a safe and secure blind drop, or you can code a message through the 'hot line.' You need not do anything except tell us where he is. You need not know a thing. This will be completely deniable."

There was a long pause on the line; then: "All right, Leonid. Convince your people that America doesn't want war and has no designs on Russia, and we'll work together to stop McLanahan." And he hung up.

This was too good to be true! Zevitin exclaimed to himself. Two of the top politicians in the United States were going to help him assassinate Patrick McLanahan! But who to trust with this project? Not his own intelligence bureau—there were too many shaky alliances, too many unknowns for this type of job. The only person he could trust was Alexandra Hedrov. Her ministry certainly had agents who could do this job.

He went into his bedroom adjacent to his executive office. Alexandra was sitting alone in bed in the darkness. The speakerphone was on; he had hoped she would listen in and be ready to give him advice. She was a valuable adviser and the person he trusted more than anyone in the entire Kremlin. "So, my love," Zevitin said, "what do you think? Gardner and Barbeau are going to tell us where McLanahan is! I need you to assemble a team, get them into Nevada, and be ready to strike." She was silent. Her knees were drawn up to her chest, her head down, touching her knees, her arms wrapped around her legs. "I know, love, this is ugly business. But this is an opportunity we can't miss! Don't you agree?" She remained still. "Darling . . . ?" Zevitin flipped on the light switch . . . and saw that she was unconscious! "Alexandra! What's happened? Are you all right?"

"I can help you there, Mr. President." Zevitin turned . . . and standing in his closet, concealed by the darkness, was a figure in a dark gray uniform, a combination of a flight suit and body armor . . . a Tin Man battle armor system, he realized. He carried a large weapon, a combination sniper rifle and cannon, in his arms. "Raise your hands."

He did as he was told. "Who are you?" Zevitin asked. He took a step backward . . . toward the light switch, which if he could flip it off and back on quickly would send an emergency signal to his security team. "You're one of McLanahan's Tin Men, aren't you?"

"Yes," the man said in an electronically synthesized voice.

"McLanahan sent you to kill me?"

"No," Zevitin heard a voice say. He turned . . . and there, wearing another Tin Man battle armor suit but with the helmet removed, was Patrick McLanahan himself. "I thought I'd do that myself, Mr. President."

Zevitin whirled, pushed McLanahan, lunged for the light switch, and managed to flip it off, then on again. McLanahan impassively watched as Zevitin furiously moved the switch up and down. "Very impressive feat, sneaking past my guards, into my private residence, and into my bedroom," Zevitin said. "But now you'll have to fight your way past a hundred trained commandos. You'll never make it."

McLanahan's armored left hand snapped out, closed around Zevitin's wrist, and squeezed. Zevitin thought his hand had popped completely off his arm, and he sunk to his knees in pain, screaming in agony. "It was about sixty-two guards, and we took care of them all on the way in," McLanahan said. "We also bypassed your security system's link to the army base at Zagorsk—they'll think everything is normal."

"'Netrusion,' I believe you call it?"

"Yes."

"Ingenious. The whole world will know about it by tomorrow, and soon we'll unleash it on the rest of the world when we reverse-engineer the technology."

McLanahan's right hand whipped out and closed around Zevitin's neck. His face was purely impassive, emotionless. "I don't think so, Mr. President," he said.

"So. You've become an assassin now? The great air general Patrick Shane McLanahan has become a common killer. Betraying your oath and disobeying your commander-in-chief weren't enough for you, eh? Now you're going to commit the ultimate mortal sin and destroy a life for no other reason than a personal vendetta?"

McLanahan just stood there, no expression on his face, looking directly into Zevitin's sneering face; then he nodded and replied simply: "Yes, Mr. President," and he effortlessly squeezed his fingers together and clenched them until the body in his grasp went completely limp and lifeless. The two Americans stood there for a minute, watching the blood pour onto the polished wood floor and the body make a few twitches, until finally McLanahan let the body fall from his grasp.

"Didn't think you'd do it for a second there, boss," Major Wayne Macomber said in his electronic voice.

Patrick went into the closet and retrieved his helmet and electromagnetic rail gun. "I've been thinking about nothing else for a long time, Whack," he said. He put on his helmet and hefted his rail gun. "Let's go home."

Main Lodge, Naval Support Facility
Thurmont (Camp David), Maryland

That same time

This is all going to shit, President Joseph Gardner said to himself. But it's not *my* damned fault. McLanahan needs to be gone, *soonest*. If he had to make a deal with the devil to do it, so be it.

He went from his private office back into the bedroom suite of the Camp David presidential retreat, where he found his houseguest—the staff sergeant he'd had aboard Air Force One—standing at the wet bar on the far side of the room, wearing nothing but an almost transparent negligee, open all the way down, her hands enticingly behind her. Damn, he thought, that was one hot future Air Force officer! "Hey, honey, sorry to take so long, but it couldn't wait. Fix us a drink, will you?"

"Fix it yourself, you fucking sleazeball," he heard, "then go shove it up your ass." Gardner whirled around . . .

. . . and found none other than Senator Stacy Anne Barbeau standing before him! *"Stacy!"* he blurted. "How in hell did you get in here?"

"Compliments of General McLanahan," he heard. He turned the other way and saw a figure in some sort of futuristic body armor and helmet standing by the wall. He heard a sound behind him and saw yet another figure in head-to-toe body armor and helmet, carrying a huge rifle, step into the suite.

"Who are you?" the President exclaimed. "How did you get in here?" He finally recognized who they were. "You're McLanahan's Tin Men! *He* sent you to kill me?"

"Never mind them, Joe!" Barbeau cried. "What was all that about? You made a deal with Zevitin to have McLanahan assassinated by Russian agents?"

"It's starting to look like a damn good idea, Stacy, don't you think?"

Gardner asked. "This is exactly what I was afraid of—McLanahan is going to assassinate all his enemies and take over the government!"

"So to plan a strategy to deal with the crisis you bring a bimbo to Camp David, screw around with *her* awhile, then make a deal with the president of Russia to have an American general assassinated?"

Gardner whirled around. "Help! Help me!" he screamed. "I'm in the suite and there are armed men in here! *Get in here! Help!*"

One of the armored figures strode over to Gardner, put a hand behind his neck, and squeezed. Gardner's vision exploded into a cloud of stars from the sudden intense pain. All of his strength immediately left his body, and he collapsed to his knees. "They're all out for now, Mr. President," the armored figure said. "No one can hear you."

"Get away from me!" Gardner sobbed. "Don't kill me!"

"I should kill you myself, you piece of shit!" Barbeau shouted. "I wanted McLanahan out of the way, maybe embarrass or disgrace him if he didn't cooperate, but I wasn't going to *kill* him, you stupid idiot! And I certainly wasn't going to make a deal with the *Russians* to do it!"

"It's McLanahan's fault," Gardner said. "He's crazy. I had to do it."

The figure grasping Gardner's neck released him. Gardner collapsed to the floor, and the armored figure stood over him. "Listen to me carefully, Mr. President," the figure said in a weird computerized voice. "We've got you on tape admitting to conspiring with the Russians to shoot down American bombers and the Black Stallion spaceplane, and conspiring with the president of Russia to have Russian agents enter the country to assassinate an American general."

"You can't kill me!" Gardner cried. "I am the President of the United States!"

The figure slammed an armored fist right beside the President's head, then two inches down through the resawn maple floor and concrete foundation in the bedroom suite. Gardner screamed again and tried to scurry away, but the figure grasped him by the throat, putting his helmeted face right up to the President's. "I can kill you easily, Mr. President," the figure said. "We stopped the Navy SEALs, we stopped the Secret Service, and we stopped the Russian air force—we can certainly stop *you*. But we're not going to kill you."

"What do you want then?"

"Amnesty," the figure said. "Full and complete freedom from prosecution or investigation for everyone involved in actions against the United States or its allies from Dreamland, Battle Mountain, Batman, Tehran, and Constanţa. Full retirements and honorable discharges for everyone who doesn't want to serve under you as their commander-in-chief."

"What else?"

"That's all," the other figure said. "But to ensure that you'll do as we say, the Tin Men and CID units will disappear. If you cross us, or if anything happens to any of us, we'll come back and finish the job."

"You can't stop us," the first Tin Man said. "We'll find you no matter where you try to hide. You won't be able to track or detect us, because we can manipulate your sensors, computer networks, and communications any way we choose. We'll monitor all your conversations, your e-mails, your movements. If you betray us, we'll find you, and you'll simply disappear. Do you understand, Mr. President?" He looked at the two women in the room. "That goes for you two as well. We don't exist—but we'll be watching you. All of you."

EPILOGUE

He that falls by himself never cries.

— TURKISH PROVERB

LAKE MOJAVE, NEVADA

SEVERAL WEEKS LATER

The young boy cast a fishing line into Lake Mojave from his spot at the tip of a rocky point beside the long, wide boat-launching ramp. Lake Mojave was not really a lake, just a wide spot of the Colorado River south of Las Vegas. It was a popular winter venue for seasonal residents, but they could begin to feel the onset of summer heat even now in early spring, and you could sense the stirring in the place that people were itching to leave. Not far behind the boy was his father, in shorts, sunglasses, nylon running sandals, and Tommy Bahama embroidered shirt, typing on a laptop computer in the shade of a covered picnic area. Behind him in the RV park, the "snowbirds" were packing up their campground and preparing to take their trailers, campers, and RVs to gentler climes. Soon only the most die-hard desert-lovers would stay to brave southern Nevada's brutally hot summer.

Amidst the bustle of the campground the man heard the sound of a heavier-than-normal car. Without turning or appearing to notice, he escaped out of his current program and called up another. With a push of a key, a remote wireless network camera on a telephone pole activated and began automatically tracking the newcomer. The camera zeroed in on the vehicle's license plate, and in a few seconds it had captured the letters and numbers and identified the vehicle's owner. At the same instant, a wireless RFID sensor co-located with the camera read a coded identification beacon broadcast from the vehicle, confirming its identity.

The vehicle, a dark H3 Hummer with tinted windows all the way around except for the windshield, parked in the white gravel parking lot between the marina restaurant and the launching ramp, and three men alighted. All wore jeans, sunglasses, and boots. One man in a safari-style tan vest stayed by the vehicle and started scanning the area. The second man wore an untucked white business shirt with the collar open and the sleeves rolled up, while the third also wore an open safari-style tan vest.

The man at the picnic table received a tiny *beepbeepbeep* in his Bluetooth wireless headset, telling him that a tiny millimeter-wave sensor set up in the park had detected that one of the men was carrying a large metallic object—and it wasn't a tackle box, either. The second man in the vest stopped about a dozen paces from the picnic area beside the ramp to the boat-launching ramp next to a garbage can and began scanning the area like the first. The third man walked up to the man at the picnic table. "Hot enough out here for you?" he asked.

"This is nothing," the man at the picnic table said. He set his laptop down, got to his feet, turned to the newcomer, and removed his sunglasses. "They say it'll get above a hundred by May and stay above a hundred and ten for all of June, July, and August."

"Swell," the newcomer said. "Cuts down on visitors, eh?" He looked past the man and to the boy fishing beside the boat ramp. "Cripes, can't believe how tall Bradley's getting."

"He'll be taller than the old man any day now."

"No doubt." The newcomer extended a hand. "How the hell are you, Patrick?"

"Just fine, Mr. President," Patrick McLanahan said. "You?"

"Fine. Bored. No, bored out of my *skull*," former President of the United States Kevin Martindale replied. He looked around. "Kind of a bleak place you got here, Muck. It's not San Diego. It's not even Vegas."

"The desert grows on you, especially if you come here in late winter and experience the gradual change in the temperature," Patrick said.

"You planning on staying?"

"I don't know, sir," Patrick said. "I bought a homesite and a hangar at the airpark in Searchlight. Don't know if I'm ready to build yet. The place is growing. I'm homeschooling Bradley now, but the schools here are getting better, they say, as more and more folks move to the area."

"And Jon Masters is just a little ways up Highway 95."

"Yeah, and he bugs me just about every day to come work for him, but I'm not sure," Patrick admitted.

"That hotshot astronaut Hunter Noble signed up with him. I heard he's a vice president already. But I'm sure they'll make a place for you if you want it."

"Been there, done that."

"There's another thing that we've both done before, Patrick," Martindale said.

"I figured you'd be showing up sooner or later about that."

"You have the Tin Men and the CIDs, don't you?"

"The what?"

"You're a horrible liar," Martindale said with a laugh.

"Is there any use trying to lie? I'm sure your intelligence network is good . . ."

"As good as the one you've reportedly built? I doubt it. I doubt it very much," the former President said. "Listen, my friend, you're still needed. The country needs you. *I* need you. Besides, the stuff you have stashed away is government property. You can't keep it."

Patrick gave him a direct glance—just a fleeting one, but the meaning was loud and clear. "Okay, you probably *can* keep it, but you *shouldn't* just squirrel it away. You can do an awful lot of good with it." Patrick said nothing. Martindale took off his sunglasses and wiped them with a shirttail. "Heard the latest about Persia?"

"About the new president being assassinated?"

"When that hits the news the entire Middle East will go bonkers again, and Mohtaz will re-emerge from whatever rock he crawled under when the Russians left and claim the presidency again. The people want Queen Azar to take control of the government until new elections can be held, but she insists the prime minister, Noshahr, take charge."

"She's right."

"Noshahr's a bureaucrat, a bean counter. He can't run the country. Azar or Buzhazi should take charge under emergency authority until elections are held."

"He'll be fine, sir. If he's not, Azar will go to Parliament and recommend someone else. Buzhazi flat out won't do it."

"You think she'll ask Saqqez, the deputy prime minister?"

"I hope not. He's taken too many trips to Moscow to suit me."

Martindale nodded knowingly. "I knew you were keeping tabs on this stuff," he said. "Speaking of Moscow—what do you think about that replacement for Zevitin, Igor Truznyev, the former FSB chief?"

"He's a bloodthirsty goon," Patrick said. "He's doing a quiet little purge out there. The word is Hedrov will be next to be 'reassigned' to Siberia."

Martindale smiled and nodded. "Even I haven't heard that one yet, Patrick!" he said excitedly. "Thanks for the tip. I owe you one."

"Don't mention it, sir."

"Too bad about Zevitin, huh?" Martindale commented. "Unfortunate skiing accident, they said. That tree jumped out from nowhere and nearly took his head off, I hear. Poor bastard. Have you heard anything else about that?" Patrick had no comment. "Funny about that happening right around the same time Buzhazi attacks

Mashhad and you come back from Armstrong all of a sudden. I guess strange things do happen in threes, huh?"

"Yes, sir."

"Yeah. Sure they do." Martindale put an arm around Patrick's shoulders. "You see, my friend, you can't leave the biz behind," he said. "It's in your blood. I can name a couple hundred hot spots in the world and you'll tell me something interesting about each one."

"Sir, I'm not interested in—"

"Mongolia," Martindale interjected. He smiled when he saw Patrick's eyes light up. "Aha, you know something. What is it?"

"I heard General Dorjiyn will be replaced as chief of staff because he's too chummy with the United States," Patrick said.

"So now he can run for president, right?"

"No, because he was born in Inner Mongolia—China—and proclaimed his allegiance to Beijing as a young officer," Patrick said. "But his son will run."

Martindale slapped his hands together. "Damn, I forgot about Myren Dorjiyn . . . !"

"Muren."

"Muren. Right. He graduated from Berkeley two years ago with a master's degree, right?"

"Double doctorate. Economics and government."

Martindale nodded, pleased that Patrick passed the two little tests he had given him. "See? I knew you were keeping up on this stuff!" Martindale exclaimed happily. "Come on back, Patrick. Let's join forces again. We'll set this world on fire."

Patrick smiled, then looked out at his son fishing and said, "I'll see you around, Mr. President," and walked out to join his son in the warm spring morning.

ACKNOWLEDGMENTS

Thanks to fellow author Debbie Macomber and her husband, Wayne, for their generosity.

AUTHOR'S NOTE

Your comments are welcome! E-mail me at readermail@airbattleforce.com or visit www.AirBattleForce.com to read my essays and commentary and get the latest updates on new projects, tour schedules, and more!